African Heartbeats

A Novel
Revised Edition

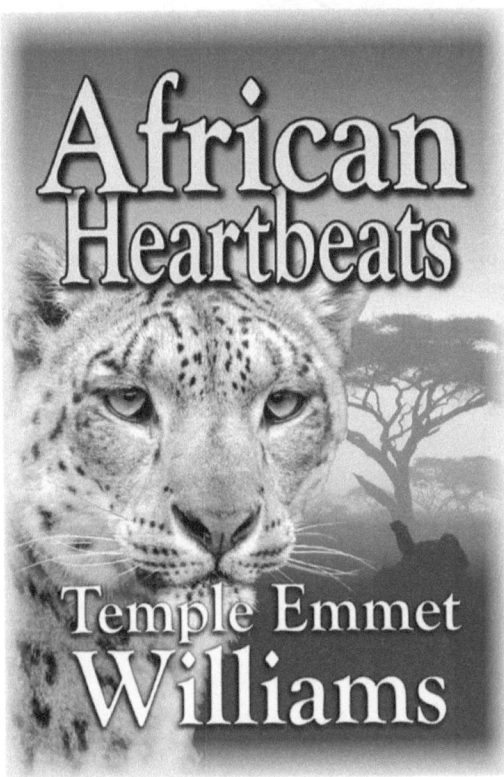

Published by Templeworks Properties LLC
3755 Mykonos Court, Boca Raton, Florida 33487
Text: (561) 251-6187 Fax: (561) 241-6358 (office)
http://www.africanheartbeats.com
http://www.templeworks.biz
E-mail: temple@templeworks.biz

Williams, Temple Emmet
African Heartbeats: A Novel
1. Thriller-Terrorism 2. Mystery-General 3. Action 4. Homeland Security

ISBN-13: 978-0-9991977-1-4

Library of Congress Control Number: 2016905002

Books by Temple Emmet Williams

Fiction: Wrinkled Heartbeats
Poison Heartbeats
African Heartbeats

Non-Fiction: Warrior Patient
Warrior Patient Heartbeats

Most Americans don't care about Africa. They should. It will become one of the most powerful continents in the world, dominated by China and terrorism.

Chapter 1

Her pet monkey saves Sharonda Nelson's life. It chases a lizard into a newly-built safe room in her home in Tanzania, East Africa. Her husband, Samuel, an ex-cop from Boca Raton, Florida, finished building it a week and a half earlier.

It's a tiny closet in the bathroom wall with simple plumbing, and it's an almost undetectable, armored part of a much larger toilet area that contains a shower, a bidet, and a toilet. It all leads to a French drain dug behind the house with the help of police recruits from the southern highlands.

Only Sharonda and Samuel know about the safe room and why it exists.

At a ribbon-cutting ceremony, Samuel told Sharonda's students and his police trainees in the Mbeya Region of Tanzania: "We will save East Africa one toilet at a time."

Most people laughed politely at a joke that they did not understand. Unfortunately, others who did comprehend the ex-cop from Boca Raton, Florida, failed to appreciate his arrogance – another ugly American.

Sharonda and her husband, Samuel, have come to the southern highlands of Tanzania, disguised as Peace Corps volunteers. They have also returned to their ancestral roots.

They replace Shadrach and Sookie Ringer in the town of Chimala. The local people do not know their real intentions, accepting them as teachers and instructors. The locals do not understand their role as anti-terrorism warriors from Homeland Security in America.

Some of the locals wonder why Shadrach and Sookie Ringer, also members of the Peace Corps, never returned from their vacation in Lesotho several years earlier. Neither Sharonda nor her husband explains why, although they know the Ringers well. They will work with them to defeat terrorism in Africa, as they did once in America, in Virginia.

Sharonda sees Sophia, their baby baboon, hopping around the bathroom.

The monkey plays with a gecko in the left-hand corner of the new glass-enclosed shower, letting it go, recapturing it, and eventually chasing it into the open "safe" room next to a shelf of towels and toiletries.

"You're not going to come out, are you, Sophia?"

Sharonda steps into the safe room and hears a loud bang that makes the house shake. At first, she thinks the late afternoon wind sweeping through her new home has slammed a door shut hard.

Then she realizes that no draft is possible because she has closed the front and back door and locked the small ventilation outlet high up on the safe room wall.

Sophia jumps into Sharonda's arms and starts to chitter. Sharonda cradles and silences Sophia as the sounds of gunfire erupt in the schoolyard.

The small baboon clings to Sharonda, safe in what she considers her mother's arms.

Sharonda slowly secures the safe room door from the inside. It fits perfectly into the wall, with no visible entry, and then she opens the small air vent to the outside.

The gunfire lasts for almost five minutes, single shots and rapid-fire from assault weapons, bursts of death. Two explosions occur, probably grenades. Silence does not return because an occasional pop signals the murder of another hiding teacher or student.

Sharonda understands that terrorists are killing her students to whom she has been teaching English. She told them that she and Samuel were returning to their roots in Tanzania in her first class.

"What are roots?" one student asked.

"Our beginnings. Our heritage."

Sharonda remembers the classroom of blank stares.

"Three hundred years ago, my family lived here," she explained to her students.

"In Chimala?"

"No, in Tanzania, in the southern highlands, near here, we don't know exactly where. My ancestors were from the Nyakyusa tribe, although my husband was Ndali."

She buys two dozen copies of *Roots: The Saga of an American Family* by Alex Haley.

The *Reader's Digest* published the book after its editors helped turn it into an easy-to-read international bestseller almost half a century earlier.

"It is a good way to learn English," she tells her uniformed students. Their ages range from eight to 11.

"Is that how you learned to speak English so well, even though you are one of us?"

In Swahili, she explains that she was born speaking English in America, in a place called Florida, and now she must learn to speak Swahili.

"You will help me do this, and in return, I will teach you English."

From the start, the students like her because of this. They have made a bargain of equality. She gets a copy of the TV mini-series of "Roots" and shows portions of it to her students each week.

"Were you a slave?"

"No," she tells her students. "But my great-great-grandfather was."

Now she hides in a safe room. She opens the door carefully and releases the monkey. Sophia disappears quickly into the peach, plum, and pear trees behind the house.

There is also a large guava tree there, about which her neighbors have warned her. When her pet monkey grows up, it will get drunk on its over-ripe fruit and do crazy things.

Sharonda, hidden in the safe room, hears voices, but they are not Swahili or English. It is Arabic.

Anger and sadness bring tears to her eyes as sporadic gunfire, heard through the vent, continues to slaughter her students and fellow teachers. It sounds like popcorn, turning her hands into tight fists. The grown-ups have become family friends, and the children represent the ones she and her husband, Samuel, never had and never will.

She remains in the closet, sitting on a small chair, wishing that she had stored her assault weapon here, not under the bed at the other end of the house.

ISIS terrorists have arrived in Chimala.

Sharonda waits for the sounds and odor of burning, expecting them to set her brick hut with its sheet metal roof on fire with gasoline. She smells nothing. She thinks to herself, "The terrorists are probably going to use my home for one of their leaders." It's the best house in the area.

She hears more gunfire, further away, across the Chimala River, probably at the Mission Hospital. Sharonda also works there. In America, she is a Nurse Practitioner with a master's degree and a DNP (doctor in nursing practice), similar to a doctor, but without serving a residency. Her colleagues at the Chimala Mission Hospital call her Super Nurse. She knows more about diagnostic tests, infectious disease prevention, specialty care, and diagnosing illnesses than the doctors at the Mission.

One more day and none of this would have happened. Now she is trapped in a safe room.

She hears someone enter and use the toilet. After the ISIS fighter leaves, she is reasonably sure that he suffers from dysentery. She hopes Sophia has escaped.

heartbeats

Director Mac McKlane from Homeland Security, aided by US intelligence services, including the CIA and the FBI, defines the Chimala Mission Hospital as a likely "soft" terrorist target. The Homeland Security team Countering Weapons of Mass Destruction (CWMD) trains to protect it and two other possible ISIS objectives on the freighter that brings them from New York City to Cape Town, South Africa. The trip takes 28 training days.

Once they reach Africa, the CWMD team travels north through the Karoo desert by railroad. Sookie Ringer falls in love on the train with a tiny bush baby with huge eyes. The furry creature, the pet of a fellow passenger, snuggles into one of her hands.

"They have perfect little fingers," Sookie laughs as it crawls up her arm and inspects her ears, eyes, and mouth. "Why are their hands so sticky?"

"They can climb better that way," the pet owner says.

"It's adorable," Sookie says.

"Their hands are clammy because they tinkle on them to get a better grip on things," he says.

Shadrach and the rest of the anti-terrorist team laugh as Sookie falls out of love with the tiny bush baby with big eyes and sticky fingers.

"You're so fickle," Shadrach tells his wife.

Sharonda, with a baby baboon on her shoulder, says, "You need to find a monkey with better manners."

Shadrach and Sookie Ringer get off in Johannesburg and drive to a 10-acre farm in Witkoppen, near that city. Bootie van Zale owns the farm.

He saved their lives from terrorists when they were on vacation in Lesotho a few years earlier at the Royal Peacock Resort and Lodge.

At the time, they had been Peace Corps volunteers in Chimala, Tanzania. Through them, Samuel and Sharonda have first-hand knowledge of the city bordering the Buhoro Flats before they ever see it.

Shadrach and Sookie Ringer's new assignment focuses on Pelindaba, the main research center of the South African Nuclear Energy Corporation.

Bootie van Zale spends a lot of time fishing for giant carp called "Harties" with Shadrach in the Hartbeespoort Dam, which lies in the shadow of the nuclear power plant's steaming water towers.

The rest of McKlane's anti-terrorist team travel to Zimbabwe, Malawi, and finally into East Africa.

Charlton and Ernestine Tremwallis remain in Zimbabwe, once called Rhodesia, where they both work for the Bulawayo24 News station in the Harare office. From there, they keep their eyes and ears on Kariba, a town on the border of Zambia known for its crocodile farms, the Kariba Dam, and some worn-out but well-used casinos.

Kariba sprawls in the Zambezi Valley. Its population of 27,000 swelters in 90-degree heat all year long. The dam has been in place long enough to produce hydroelectric power steadily. The level of Lake Kariba drops through evaporation and a complete lack of rainfall stretching from June to September. The rainy season replenishes it.

Lake Kariba sports a new cruise ship for European guests, the *Blue Nile Dreamship*.

The Minister of State for Provincial Affairs heralds the ship's launch as "proof that Zimbabwe is open for business." American Intelligence and Homeland Security recognize the boat and the dam as a perfect soft terrorist target.

The CWMD team practices defending each of the three destinations – Chimala, Pelindaba, and Kariba – during their 28-day voyage aboard the 24,800-ton freighter, the *S.S. Nomad*.

The most likely initial anti-terrorist operation remains the Chimala Mission Hospital, with five members of the team and almost two dozen Army Rangers, Navy SEALs, and Marine Raiders secretly assigned to guard it.

The Tanzanian authorities do not know that they do this. The Americans all become Peace Corps volunteers in the Mbeya region, whose population has grown to more than two and a half million.

Some of Mac's team work on tea plantations in the mountains, trying to reclaim them from years of neglect.

And some of Mac's warriors are "fake" patients at the Chimala Mission hospital.

The Christian clinic in Chimala started as a one-room mud hut in the late-1950s.

It teetered on the verge of being tossed out of the country by the anti-colonial activist Tanzania's first President Julius Kambarage Nyerere, who considered "missionary" and "colonial" synonymous terms.

Captain George McKlane, the patriarch of his family and the grandfather of General George 'Mac' McKlane III, entered the clinic on his first and last visit to the Southern Highlands of Tanzania in 1963.

A medic named Jean-Claude Joubert treated him for life-threatening malaria with massive doses of Levaquin. After four days, Captain George McKlane walked out alive, shakey, and 20 pounds lighter.

The one-room clinic had no real doctor, only the medic, Joubert, a former French Foreign Legionnaire. He prevented the local tribal leader from draining blood by slicing deeply into both sides of McKlane's forehead to relieve the bad blood of his blinding headaches.

"I will teach you a great piece of magic if you don't do that," Joubert told the tribal doctor.

The man understood the importance of magic, and he agreed, provided he thought the magic was worth it.

"Sit down at the table," Joubert asked as Captain George McKlane groaned on a hospital bed in the background. "This Magic was taught to me by the Consul General of Sweden in Salisbury, Rhodesia, a man name Leif Shallen. He always performed the trick in a white, linen suit, which was a bit shabby and spotted from his excessive drinking habits." Many years later, in 1982, Salisbury was renamed Harare, becoming the capital of Zimbabwe.

"The trick," the tribal leader said.

"You must imagine me in a white, linen suit," Jean Claude Joubert said, briefly checking on McKlane and increasing the Levaquin drip.

"The trick," the tribal doctor said.

Jean Claude sat down and took a shiny shilling in the palm of his left hand. He rubbed it on his right elbow after slapping it from hand to hand.

"I will make this shilling disappear," he said.

He rubbed the coin very hard. The shilling fell away from his elbow and onto the table.

"That is not a very good trick," the tribal doctor said. "I will get my knives."

"Wait."

He slapped the shilling from palm to palm again, then rubbed it, furiously, into his right elbow. Slowly, very slowly, he let the hand holding the shilling drop on the table palm up. The shilling was gone.

The tribal doctor grabbed Joubert's arm, feeling for the coin. "Where is it?"

"It has disappeared. It is gone. I cannot always find it afterward. Wait. I feel it. I, uh, look under Captain George McKlane's head. But gently. I will help you."

They lifted the patient's head, and there it was.

"But how?"

"You must promise not to slice the patient's head."

"I promise. This is great magic."

And so Jean-Claude Joubert taught the local tribal doctor how to slap the coin from palm to palm, then keeping it in his right hand and dropping it down his collar as he furiously rubbed his elbow.

"Everyone always watches the elbow, not the coin. But you must remember to drop the coin by mistake first. It will disarm your audience."

"But how did you get it under his head?"

"I did that before I started the trick."

"Ah," said the local tribal doctor.

"The Consul General of Sweden always performed this trick in bars, and he would have the owner place coins under different bottles. The owner sold more drinks, and the Swedish Consul had an endless supply of free liquor with which he could stain his white linen suits."

Two days after leaving the clinic, the Tanzanian police arrested Captain McKlane as a foreign spy in Mbeya, 35 miles southeast of Chimala, where he recovered from his battle with malaria while drinking scotch with the proprietor of the Mbeya Guest House, Nessie Whapshot.

The Tanzanian police also charged Captain George McKlane with the theft of valuable Tanzanian artifacts, most notably the Tree of Life Sculpture that he bought and sent back to the United States several weeks earlier.

The Golden Tree of Life became a centerpiece in George McKlane's six million dollar Boca Raton home.

The Head of African Affairs in Washington, Congresswoman Frances Payne Bolton, intervened for Captain McKlane. President Nyerere released the Korean War veteran, looking the other way as he disappeared into Malawi.

The Chimala Mission Hospital also got a reprieve.

A Tanzanian surgeon trained in Russia joined the medic and prevented the clinic from dying.

The clinic developed into a 200-room model hospital in the next 57 years. One of its best-known patients was a local tribal doctor who died of liver cirrhosis after many magical years.

heartbeats

In 24 hours, the city of Chimala, population 30,000, will have the protection of men and women of war under the command of Mac McKlane, the son of Marine Major General John McKlane II, and the grandson of the original Captain George McKlane, a Medal of Honor recipient during the Korean War.

Sharonda had cared for Captain McKlane, and he had told her stories of the village of Chimala, where he almost died, many years earlier. It represents an ironic circle of history, one day late.

A lifetime in bullets, Sharonda thinks.

She knows that her husband, Samuel, remains at a ceremony in the original capital of Tanzania, Dar es Salaam, the "Bay of Peace." That coastal city is 477 miles away by road, although much less by helicopter.

Samuel Nelson, a decorated Marine and an ex-cop from Boca Raton, Florida, would probably put his life on the line in a losing battle in Chimala.

Holly Smolkes McKlane, Mac McKlane, Samuel, and a dozen Marine Raiders, Navy SEALs, and Army Rangers attend the presentation of the Tree of Life to the family of its original creator Johannes Sebastian Massamungu. He lived in Chimala in the early Sixties.

Johannes originally sold the gold-plated sculpture for 8,000 shillings to Captain George McKlane.

"I know you are okay in Dar es Salaam, Samuel," Sharonda whispers to herself in the safe room. "Stay there. Stay alive. I hope we see each other before I die."

She is not brave. She is angry and trapped in a secure closet.

After two hours of silence, Sharonda Nelson creeps out of the bathroom. She sees the monkey in the darkness on the back porch, and Sophia makes some noise. That's what Sharonda wants her pet to do.

She tiptoes through the four-room brick hut, hoping to get the assault rifle from under the bed.

It's gone, along with her cellphone, and now a man is snoring loudly in her bed.

Suddenly she wants the monkey to be quiet.

She takes a backpack hidden in a kitchen cupboard, a large hunting knife in its sheath that she attaches to her belt, and then she sneaks back into the safe room.

Sophia is gone.

It starts to rain hard, much later than usual.

The nurses working with her at the Chimala Mission Hospital often tell Sharonda, "You could set your watch using the rainy season 20 years ago. The rain always began at four o'clock in the afternoon, every day, for months. It lasted for about three hours. Then the stars came out."

"Climate change," Sharonda tells them.

Horizontal rain and strong winds come as darkness sweeps across the grassland veld of the Buhoro flats, howling up the mountains behind the city of Chimala.

Sharonda looks forward to the sounds and safety of Africa's night.

But she worries about Sophia.

She will move into the bedroom.

The monkey will wake the terrorist sleeping there.

It's a bad storm, with lightning flashes and crashing thunder that might conceal gunfire. The house doors, now open, swing back and forth, finally slamming shut.

The snoring in the bedroom stops.

heartbeats

Over a year and a half earlier, a Medal of Honor winner who fought in Korea and the family patriarch died peacefully in his bed in Boca Raton, Florida, slumped sideways towards a painting of his late wife, Agnes.

They shared lives for 52 years.

"She was reaching for Captain George," Sharonda says, "and him for her."

She finds peace in thinking that love wrapped the heart of the war hero's final moments.

He often spoke openly to Agnes towards the end, even calling Sharonda by his wife's name occasionally, despite Sharonda's dark skin.

The emptiness of his death fills the beautiful home.

Sharonda had taken care of George McKlane for years. She also cared for his wife, Agnes, who died several years before her husband, "Captain George."

Sharonda and Samuel, a Marine officer in the Military Police and then a police sergeant of the color guard in Boca Raton, live in a separate house attached to Captain George's home on an ocean-access canal in The Royal Coconut Yacht & Country Club.

The area is arguably some of the most expensive real estate in Palm Beach County.

Sharonda and Samuel have shared laughter and bullets with George McKlane, saving his life more than once. Their loyalty has made them wealthy, although this was never a consideration in their actions.

George's death creates a multi-million dollar annuity for Sharonda and Samuel Nelson.

One of its conditions requires repatriation of the Tree of Life Sculpture to its creator in Tanzania, Johannes Sebastian Massamungu, or his family.

The gold-plated statue is a focal point of George McKlane's mansion, where a sweeping staircase surrounds it under a spotlight in the multi-storied vaulted ceiling of the living area. Sharonda remembers a man who told her he hated it because he detested all things African.

He was a white nationalist, and Sharonda, black, was showing him around the house.

She never forgave the man. However, she did get even with him, and so did the mafia boss for whom he worked.

Sharonda and Samuel Nelson join the Peace Corps without ever going through any of its training programs.

Their paperwork occurs so quietly that only the Acting Director of the Peace Corps knows that they have joined its ranks, along with many other American military men and women who work in the Southern Highlands of Tanzania focussed on the town of Chimala, 35 miles from Mbeya.

Sharonda and Samuel study and quickly become fluent in Swahili, which they speak to one another when alone. They start with conversations punctuated by silence. Their promise not to use English quickly leads to conversations that last more than five minutes. One night, they make love speaking only Swahili.

"I think I have discovered our past," Sheronda says afterwords.

"You discovered my root," Samuel laughs.

They say this in Swahili, and they laugh. Then, in English, Sharonda tells her husband that you are on the way to fluency when you can joke in another language.

"I find that very satisfying," Samuel says in Swahili, and they laugh some more.

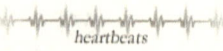

George McKlane, the Medal of Honor winner, wants no ceremony at his funeral.

His son, at the time a one-star Marine Brigadier General working in the Pentagon, tries to make sure that his father's burial follows those wishes, but it's hard not to celebrate the life of "Captain George.".

On a cloudless Sunday in February, Holly Smolkes powers her fishing yacht, *The Wholly Mackeral*, through the Boynton Beach inlet and heads due east.

She has buried many men at sea, several of them previous husbands, one of them alive as he drowned.

Holly Smolkes performed wet work for the mob for well over a decade.

Then she fell in love with Captain George's grandson, George 'Mac' McKlane III, a director at Homeland Security and a full-bird colonel in the Marine Raiders.

She married his grandson after saving him in Virginia and nursing him back to health at Walter Reed.

"Captain George" is the first person she buries at sea, whom she admires. Mac McKlane, Sharonda, and her husband, Samuel Nelson, Charlton Tremwallis, and his girlfriend, Ernestine Johnston, Sookie and Shadrach Ringer, and the carefully-wrapped body of Captain George McKlane are aboard Holly's boat, *The Wholly Mackeral*.

On the outside of his wrappings, George's son carefully pins the Medal of Honor.

The codicil of his final will does not prohibit or even mention the nation's top military award, which the captain has hidden in a large walk-in closet for many years. He calls it his War Room.

Photographs of the men who died under his command in Korea line one wall.

A small armada follows *The Wholly Mackeral* through the Boynton Beach inlet. It includes the Commandant of the Marine Corps.

They travel three miles beyond the United States' territorial limits and then power down on a calm ocean. Several small boats filled with Marine Raiders, and the Commandant, stand and salute the Korean War hero as a single bugler plays Taps. The notes drift across the water for less than a minute.

There is no 21-gun salute. Captain McKlane's codicil specifically requests its absence, stating and underscoring: "I have heard enough gunfire in my life."

A bell rings eight times, the end of Captain McKlane's watch, and then his wrapped, weighted body tips upward and slips beneath the waves with almost no splash.

Men and women, many in uniform, turn the image of this event into a mental photograph, not soon forgotten.

In Tanzania, almost two years later, Sharonda slips back out of the bathroom closet around midnight as the storm rages outside. She opens the back door, and Sophia rushes back into the supposed safety of the house. The monkey is no longer quiet.

Sharonda carries her backpack and checks her hunting knife in its sheath.

Her scruffy dog, Fubar, appears out of the tall grass behind the hut, soaking wet, but he does not bark. He has never barked. He has always feared the night, this one more than most. So he stays in the grass, and Sheronda thinks she knows why he does not follow Sophia into their brick home.

Sharonda looks north, past a city darkened by an electrical failure. Lightning gives her stuttered glimpses across the swollen Chimala River and up a large hill to the 200-room Mission Hospital.

The water is higher than the bridge. There are no lights, even though Sharonda knows the Mission Hospital has four backup generators.

Perhaps closed shutters conceal light from the windows. The rain slants toward Sharonda. She should be able to hear the generators. Instead, she only hears the wind, the river, and the deluge.

She carefully slips back into the four-room brick hut. Fubar still does not follow. The scruffy dog disappears into the tall sawgrass bordering the cement porch at the back of the house. It continues to rain.

The monkey jumps on furniture and starts to make some noise. Sharonda hears a man snoring again in the bedroom. Then he snorts and says something. She backs against the wall separating the sleeping quarters from the main room, glad to be black.

The man comes into the living area and fires a shot at the sound of the monkey, missing it in the darkness. His weapon has a suppressor. His gun pops two more bullets, one in the wall, one in the roof, before he passes out in the unbreakable stranglehold Sharonda has thrown around his neck. She maintains her grip until he goes limp. She does not use her knife to slit his throat.

She has trained most of her life to "Do No Harm," but in battle, at this moment, it does not enter her mind.

She lowers one hand to his neck, feeling a faint pulse.

She tightens her lock on him and slowly counts to 60 before releasing his dead body.

She crawls into the bedroom, slowly, with the terrorist's gun cradled in her arms like a soldier going under barbed wire in a training maneuver.

She keeps one finger on the trigger until she knows that the man is alone. She confirms that the assault weapon she had under the bed is not there. Her cellphone is gone. She checks the body of the dead man, but he does not have it.

She finds a large pot in the kitchen area in the darkness and places it under the new leak in the metal roof.

At first, the water slowly pings into the pan.

It turns into a plunking sound after 15 minutes.

She knows the bullet hole is small from the weapon because it uses a .222 caliber round.

She understands that as it pierces the ceiling, it pushes the metal up and out, leaving a hole of extended aluminum, minimizing the leakage.

Although Sharonda recognizes the size of the bullets, the weapon seems very old.

It is not the one under her bed but rather a relic from the German Army, a Sturmgewehr assault rifle the Nazis developed in 1938 and still a terrorist weapon in parts of the Middle East, mainly in The Lebanon.

Sharonda empties the bullets from the two magazines, taped together and easily reversed in battle.

The unused magazine holds 30 cartridges, the other just 12, plus one chambered round.

Sharonda counts the bullets twice, hoping they will somehow multiply and knowing that they won't.

She reloads her arsenal.

She practices swapping the magazine in the gun, in the dark, until it becomes a smooth and natural act. Finally, she opens the back door, and Fubar enters, shaking his shaggy coat, showering water everywhere.

She settles with her back to the wall, one round chambered, hoping the storm cloaks the death of the terrorist.

The monkey, Sophia, moves around the house, frozen in lightning flashes through the windows, at times trying to catch the drops falling from the hole in the roof. However, she does not go near the dead man.

Fubar presses against Sharonda, silent, never lowering his head. He stands up several times and looks at the intruder's body. He makes no move towards it.

Sharonda waits for dawn as the storm rages outside. On and off, she sleeps sitting up in the corner.

"I have 43 shots at sunrise," she tells the darkness.

Most freighters out of Brooklyn, New York, heading for Africa, have Filipino and Guatemalan crews. The 24,800-ton *S.S. Nomad* includes two Guatemalans, three Filipinos, and four followers of Islam, but like the rest, they are all Navy SEALs, Army Rangers, or Marine Raiders.

The *S.S. Nomad* is a large freighter that has been ready for McKlane and his anti-terrorist team for over a year. The sudden release of hundreds, perhaps thousands of ISIS fighters as Turkey bombs the front lines of the Kurds in the Middle East brings the ship from the backburner to the forefront of America's defense against Islam's forces and intentions in Africa.

The death of Abu Bakr al-Baghdadi underscores the importance of sub-Saharan Africa as America's battleground for democracy.

Before boarding the freighter for Cape Town, Mac McKlane tells his new bride, Holly Smolkes: "The Mbeya highlands of Tanzania overlook the Buhoro Flats. It's a great place for a honeymoon. Grandpa told me about it. You won't believe the wildlife."

"It's a great place for a fight," she answers. She knows what's happening.

She looks at the freighter rusting in an unused and broken-down dock. Everything suffers from old age.

"I know a much faster way to get there, Mac."

"We'll be training on the boat for the entire trip to Africa," he says. "It takes about 28 days."

His wounds from their last battle against terrorism in Virginia heal after almost two years of rehab at the Walter Reed National Military Medical Center in Washington, D.C.

"Time to go back to work," he says.

The Captain of the broken-down *S.S. Nomad* is a naval officer, a full colonel named Maria Montoya. She does not wear her uniform. One more successful mission and she will become a rear admiral. She greets each CWMD member personally. No salutes, just handshakes.

Nobody gets piped aboard.

Everyone gets a surprise.

Mac McKlane is the first person up the gangplank.

"Welcome aboard, General Mac McKlane," Captain Montoya says.

"I'm just an 0-6 like you," Mac says, "a full colonel." He gives the military equivalent of his rank as a director at Homeland Security. Montoya hands him an envelope with two separate silver stars in it and a meritorious promotion.

"As I said, welcome aboard, General McKlane." She smiles. "Just remember that I'm the boss on this ship."

"Yes, sir," Mac says, "Ma'am.".

Montoya turns to the woman behind him.

You must be First Lieutenant Holly Smolkes McKlane," she says, handing Mac's wife an envelope with silver bars, a promotion. "You have my permission to fraternize with your superior officer. That's an order."

They laugh and promise that they will strictly follow her commands.

"This is our honeymoon," Holly says.

"Your stateroom is ready, and we sail in a little over an hour," the Captain says. "It will be an unusual honeymoon."

Sharonda and Samuel Nelson greet Captain Montoya next. "Welcome aboard, Commander Nelson," Montoya says to Sharonda, handing her a package with her new metal grade insignias. "Would your monkey be more comfortable if you had rank boards on your shoulders?"

The captain watches as a baby baboon perches on Sharonda and grooms her hair.

"This is Sophia," Sharonda says. "I have all the export papers required to ....."

"I've seen them," Montoya says. "Congratulations on becoming a commander, and I guess the monkey is also returning to her roots."

She turns and greets Sharonda's husband. "Welcome aboard, Major Samuel Nelson."

Samuel holds up the palms of his hands in a wait-a-second, not-so-fast manner.

"I'm just a cop from Boca Raton, Florida," he says.

Montoya smiles. "Well, at the request of the Department of Defense, you have re-enlisted."

Samuel tightens his lips in protest as Montoya hands him his metal insignia and a letter calling him back to duty. The ship's captain puts a hand on his right arm.

"Look at it this way, major, you get top pay, over 90 grand a year, and, uh, you're only one pay grade below your wife, the commander."

Both women laugh, and Samuel joins in when Montoya repeats her joke about fraternizing with a superior officer being an absolute necessity aboard the *S.S. Nomad.*

"Also," the captain says, "when this is all over, I'll cashier you out personally, Major Nelson. I promise."

"And I promise I'll accept," Samuel says.

"With a much better retirement package, too," Sharonda says, although neither one of them needs money.

"You bet, commander," he says, giving his wife a careless salute and a sloppy kiss that has her pushing him away and saying, "Down, Major. That's an order."

They all laugh.

Shadrach and Sookie Ringer walk up the gangplank five minutes later.

"Thank you for your service in Africa at the Royal Peacock Resort and Lodge in Lesotho," Montoya says.

"Wow, how did you know about that?" Sookie asks.

"I know a lot about both of you, Major Sookie Ringer," the captain answers.

"I retired as an Army captain," Sookie says.

Montoya hands her a service recall letter from the Department of Defense along with her promotion papers and a major's insignia, adding, "Not anymore."

Sookie looks at Shadrach.

So does the captain.

"You are a problem," the captain says.

"You're telling me," his wife, Sookie, replies, bringing an unexpected laugh from the captain.

Shadrach says nothing, deadpan. He knows he's probably in trouble.

"You're a retired non-com in the Marines, and I can't recall you to service."

"No, ma'am, you can't."

"You could always volunteer," his wife says.

Her husband stares at her.

"You're Army. I'm just a Marine grunt," he says. "We never volunteer." With a smile, he adds: " Hell, we don't even know how to read."

"What if I made you a warrant officer?" Captain Montoya says, smiling.

She shuffles through a folder that contains a variety of enforcement letters.

"What kind of warrant officer?" Shadrach asks. "I mean, I was thinking about a master gunnery sergeant or a sergeant major, an E-9."

He looks at his wife. "Then you could call me 'Gunney,' honey."

They both laugh.

"I can make you Chief Warrant Officer Ringer," the captain says. "It's a much better pay package, W-5."

Shadrach looks at the papers she hands to him.

"Don't I have to go to school for this?"

"Not on my watch," the captain says.

She knows that she is meeting unusual characters.

She has read about all of them in official, secret, and highly classified documents.

She knows they will be very good at what they do. This team knows how to fight and win against ISIS.

Shadrach sticks his thumb at Sookie.

"Does she have to call me 'Chief'?"

The captain laughs.

"I'll let you two figure that one out," she says.

Before they step aboard the *S.S. Nomad*, Commander Maria Montoya tells them: "By the way, you'll be meeting an old friend when we finally arrive in Cape Town four weeks from now."

The Ringers both raise their eyebrows and say, in unison: "Who's that?"

"Major Bootie van Zale," the captain says. "He was a captain in the South African Army when he debriefed you at the Royal Peacock Resort and Lodge. He still talks about how far you threw your Motorola Encrypted phone, Chief."

Shadrach established a firing perimeter with a record toss of his rubber-encased cell phone down a mountainside in Lesotho, the Switzerland of Africa. It saved his and Sookie's life. Shadrach has the arm of a major league baseball outfielder.

"Is Bootie part of the group?" Sookie asks.

"He is."

Once again, in unison, they say: "Good."

The final CWMD Homeland Security members up the gangplank are Charlton and Ernestine Tremwallis.

"Congratulations on becoming a Marine Raider," the captain says to Charlton as he steps off the gangplank. "I understand you graduated with perfect marks on the rifle range." Charlton nods

"I know Sergeant Squirrel, who you fought with on the Jackson River in Virginia, and he says you can shoot the whiskers off a fairy diddle, a chipmunk, at 100 yards."

"Dang, you know Squirrel?" Charlton asks, "Sir?"

Captain Montoya surprises the young couple by saying, with a perfect Virginia mountain accent: "Why I grew up just a hoot an' a holler down the road from that man. Known him since I was a little girl out and about in Warm Springs."

"Dang," Charlton says again. "Can you tell us how that man is doin'?"

The captain slips back into her trained New England accent, with a hint of Boston and Harvard at its edges.

It is a voice that commands.

"He's doing fine. He spends most of his time fishing on the Jackson River."

"Must be hard for him," Ernestine says.

Charlton says, "We lost some good men on that river, especially Fishbait."

It is the nickname of one of his best friends who dies in combat on the Jackson River, a few miles above Lake Moomaw in Bath County, Virginia.

Fishbait is a young Marine disguised as a fisherman during a terrorist attack. He takes a point position on the Jackson River. He hooks a big brown trout, and he can't get his rifle out of his waders fast enough when terrorists appear on the banks of the river. He dies.

"Yes," the captain says, "I met Fishbait often at the Cascades Trout Club. He taught me how to fly fish. You must always remember you saved thousands of lives on that day on the Jackson River. You kept America safe."

"Yes, ma'am. But I sure do miss Fishbait all the same," Charlton says.

His wife nods. So does the captain.

Montoya hands an envelope to Charlton, containing the silver bars of a first lieutenant, an unexpected promotion from being a shavetail, a second lieutenant.

"Welcome aboard, lieutenants," she says, emphasizing the plural.

She hands another envelope to Ernestine containing a second lieutenant's bars.

"Those are on loan, Lieutenant Ernestine Tremwallis," the captain says. "After this mission is complete, you can go to Quantico to make your position permanent."

For the third time, the captain talks about relaxing the rules about fraternizing with superior officers.

Nobody laughs at the joke this time. Memories of Fishbait fail to push the remark beyond a polite smile.

Sharonda, with a baby baboon on her shoulder, surprises the Lieutenants Tremwallises. They think she and her husband, Samuel, already live in Tanzania.

That morning in bed, Charlton had told Ernestine: "You remember Samuel and Sharonda Nelson? They worked for Director Mac's grandfather in Boca Raton, Florida. They have a pet monkey in the southern highlands of Tanzania. Let's go visit them over there."

"You talk too much when we're making love, Charlton. Stop monkeying around." They laugh, "Yes. Yes. There. Harder. Oh, God. Oh, sweet Jesus. Yes."

Then she starts to giggle, and Charlton feels her tighten around him as she does this. He explodes. It is the giggling that excites him. Even when she makes the sound in public, he gets excited., and she knows it.

On the boat, they learn that Sharonda's monkey comes from America, not Africa.

"She's called Sophia," Sharonda says as the baby baboon grooms what she considers her mother's hair. "She's returning to her roots along with us. Both Samuel and I have ancestors in Tanzania, according to our DNA records."

Sophia hops on Ernestine's shoulder and starts to groom her blonde hair.

Ernestine giggles, smiling after she does, with a sideways glance at Charlton.

Charlton turns away from them.

"The baboon's full name is Sophia Loren," Samuel Nelson says. "And you, Charlton, are now a monkey's uncle. Are you all right? You're bending over a bit."

Charlton's wife laughs and shakes Samuel's hand. They have not met, although she knows his name well.

"I'm Auntie Ernestine. Charlton's getting his sea legs."

"You have a very a firm handshake," Samuel says.

Giggle? Sophia Loren? Firm handshake?

Charlton is about to crouch down and start crawling when Captain Maria Montoya's voice calls the team together over the intercom. As they crowd around her, she says: "Stow your gear, and then we meet in the dining hall at 17:30. All of you must remain in your cabins until then. I don't want to see any of you on the deck waving goodbye to the Statue of Liberty. Do it now. God willing, we will all see her again."

Charlton grabs his wife and takes her quickly to their suite. She starts to giggle as soon as she sees his problem. "You're the horniest man alive," she laughs.

"Prove it," he says as he takes off his clothes.

The *S.S. Nomad* passes under the Verrazano bridge 45 minutes later when Charlton finally calms down, although his wife calls him an animal as she giggles.

Some crew members finish lashing down containers on the deck, although most seem to be sleeping.

It seems odd that two Coast Guard cutters, rather than tugboats, accompany the freighter.

They break off when the armada reaches three nautical miles beyond the coastline.

The tanker chugs along at quarter speed, deep in the water, a sloppy ship proving to any onlooker that it hardly deserves to fly the tattered American flag on its rusty stern.

The interior of the vessel is quite different.

Captain Montoya invites them below deck after the team enjoys a five-course meal in a two-floor, surprisingly luxurious dining hall that could seat 200 people.

They enter the hold of the 28,400-ton *S.S. Nomad.*

The hatch closes behind them.

Total darkness blinds every one of Mac's anti-terrorism team. They stand on a platform beyond the top floor of the dining hall, below the bridge at the ship's stern.

At the bow, well over five football fields away, sparks shower from a welding operation.

The ocean slaps faintly against the double-reinforced ship's hull, but nobody hangs onto anything for balance because the vessel remains stable.

Several of them hold their hands up to their faces. They cannot see them.

"The stability of this vessel makes it feel like an ocean liner, not a small freighter," Montoya's voice says. "We take on maximum ballast, and computerized piping shifts the seawater from starboard to port and from bow to stern, tens of thousands of gallons in a matter of seconds. It's like an icebreaker, only we program it for open seas rather than sheets of ice."

At the bow of the ship, the welding stops.

The captain shouts into the darkness.

"Light it up."

Chapter 2

Faint sunbeams lift Sharonda's eyelids from a restless night. Fubar has gone sound asleep next to her. The dog has lowered his head in the safety of sunrise over Tanzania's Buhoro Flats.

Sophia sleeps in Sharonda's lap, bouncing awake as Sharonda slowly moves and looks out the window into the schoolyard. The woman holds a finger to her lips, and Sophia remains quiet.

Sharonda trains her to do this.

Fubar sleeps, exhausted from being awake all night.

Several dozen terrorists dressed in black drag dead children and teachers into a heap on the far side of the playground's soccer field, over 150 yards away.

Red five-gallon gasoline drums lay to the left of the growing pile of schoolyard victims, stacked in rows like a log cabin. Some seem to be still alive but severely wounded. These are primarily young girls beaten and bleeding from apparent rape.

Several terrorists split apart from the group and move in the direction of Sharonda's brick home. They both carry assault weapons.

She has 43 bullets.

She knows she will not use more than half of them before her death.

She moves to the rear door.

It is less than fifteen feet to the tall sawgrass that grows every rainy season in a mile-thick blanket reaching the mountain beyond. A single baobab tree grows in its middle.

Sharonda takes a bag of rice from the kitchen, almost tripping over the filled pot of water from the storm. At the rear door, she looks left and right, seeing nobody. She crouches low and moves into the sawgrass with Sophia hanging onto her backpack and Fubar trailing grudgingly behind.

The sawgrass closes behind them, leaving no break, although foot and pawprints in the mud remain visible.

After about five minutes, Sharonda hears distant shouting behind her. She shifts direction, knowing what is about to happen, moving diagonally to her right. She hears the Chimala River roaring out of the Southern Highlands., but its sound disappears into gunfire, ripping through the sawgrass to her left.

"Down," she says, and Fubar hugs the ground while Sophia moves between her knees. Sharonda now realizes that she has probably left a trail of footprints before entering the sawgrass.

She needs to get to the Chimala River to conceal her escape. Huge boulders offer protection. Raging water will erase their trail.

She knows the river because Samuel, Sophia, Fubar, and herself have climbed up the gorge, which cuts in a series of waterfalls and crystal clear pools down the mountainside for many miles. They never made it to the flatlands at the top, but they came close on their eight-day hike.

It is the last day of her life.

Instinct tells her this.

She slowly, almost painfully, moves out of the forest towards a single baobab tree in the middle of the sawgrass.

It has always been her favorite tree, perhaps because she has mated and whelped so often there, or probably because she was a lazy hunter in the rainy season, waiting in its branches to fall on unsuspecting prey.

The leopard is old, near the end of a solitary life, which she only shares when she mates or raises her young. She once weighed almost 125 pounds, but her chronic liver disease has now cut that in half.

She has not eaten for days, unable to catch even the small animals of the forest.

She comes close to catching one of three river otters playing in a deep pool of the Chimala River. They were all about five feet long, but the one she almost caught wiggles free from her broken claws.

She watches all of them slip from pool to pool until they are out of sight.

She laps muddy water from the swollen river, quenching her constant thirst.

Finally, the leopard reaches the bottom of the mountain and enters the sawgrass. The emaciated animal moves quietly to the base of the lone baobab tree. The leopard tries twice to climb into its branches, falling back to the ground each time, finally settling at the tree's base, panting, waiting for death.

She hears the crackling of gunfire whistling through the sawgrass, lifts her head, but then drops it back down, tired, no longer interested in living. Her audible range remains exceptional, however. Her ears twitch as an animal moves toward her. She struggles to her feet, moving back from the tree. She crouches. She suddenly feels younger than her years.

A two-leg appears. The man has a shooting stick that he slings over his shoulder as he starts to climb the baobab tree. He can spot the person who has left footprints behind the home where someone murdered his terrorist leader from its branches.

He does not see the leopard.

Further away, at the edge of the sawgrass, men wait for their man to appear in the baobab tree and point to where they should direct their bullets.

He does not appear.

They hear screaming and a roar.

"It is a lion," one man says, stumbling back towards the schoolyard from which the group has come. They direct their fire at the baobab tree.

They hear another roar, even louder, triumphant in its rage, followed by yet another human scream, not as loud as the first one.

The leopard pulls the man to the ground, and the broad trunk of the baobab tree protects her from bullets buzzing through the sawgrass.

The man remains alive, his shoulder locked in the jaws of the leopard. The cat draws up its rear legs and rips them down the man's front, gutting him. The man screams and dies, but not right away. The bullets eventually stop, and the starving leopard slowly starts to eat its final prey. It doesn't taste good, but it's food.

After a few hours, giant vultures begin to circle high above the baobab tree.

Although the fire in the schoolyard keeps them aloft until close to sunset, they will eventually pick the man's bones, reluctantly sharing him with hyenas.

They will also discover the gaunt leopard stretching along the lowest of the tree branches. The African leopard has died licking its paws clean after its final kill.

heartbeats

In Dar es Salaam, the presentation of the Tree of Life to the family of its creator goes well.

"My grandfather," Mac McKlane tells a crowd of over 50 distinguished guests, including the President of Tanzania, "had a final wish before he died. He wanted this magnificent sculpture returned to its original creator in the country where its great artist first imagined the Tree of Life."

Mac pulls off the white silk covering from the six-foot-tall, golden sculpture, the Tree of Life cradling the moon.

It drifts to the floor as people applaud.

A young man stands up and joins Mac McKlane, who steps back after introducing the great-grandson of the original sculptor, Johannes Sebastian Massamungu.

His name is Amadeus Massamungu.

His voice sounds like a song, unusual for a man wearing the uniform of a lieutenant in the Tanzania People's Defence Force.

Amadeus Massamungu flies one of two helicopters in the Air Command, an old UH-60A/L Black Hawk. It spends more time under repair than aloft.

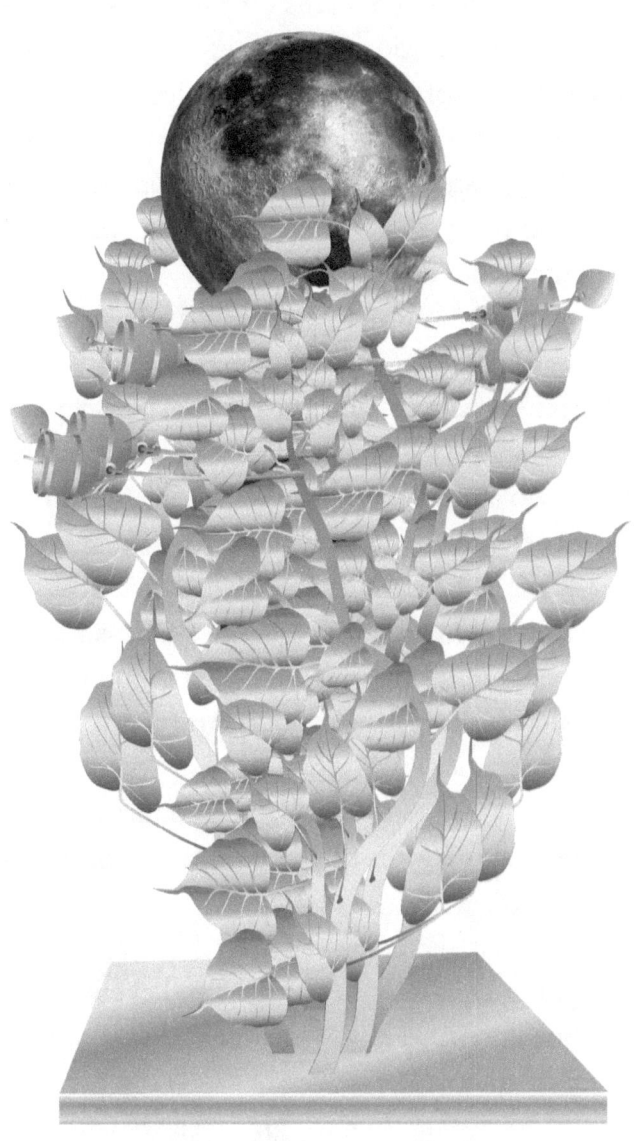

Lieutenant Amadeus Massamungu strokes the gold-plated statue that once stood in the 6-million dollar Boca Raton home of Mac's grandfather, Captain George McKlane.

"In the beginning, there is only mud and a single tree," the lieutenant says, closing his eyes, leaning into the microphone with a soft, almost poetic voice.

"And the tree is a god in a barren world where there are no men." He speaks Swahili, and he opens his eyes and translates what he says into perfect English, with an Oxford accent and the same melodic rhythm.

Women hum and sway, several warbling quietly with their tongues as the lieutenant continues.

"There is the tree, and there is one woman, the great goddess, Ma. She does not go near the tree because it will capture and violate her. She flies above it, into the heavens, turning her back on its tangled, hungry branches."

He lowers his voice, seeming to growl. "But the tree's roots gather up mud and throw it at the goddess Ma."

Women, dressed in evening clothes, stop warbling.

"When the huge ball of mud strikes Ma, the moon is born," the lieutenant says.

The humming now stops. "The goddess Ma falls back to earth, into the branches of the tree, the Tree of Life. And there she is raped."

The room is silent.

"And the children of this earth and every tribe on this earth are born," Amadeus Massamungu says with a loud, steady voice of triumph.

The room bursts into applause as the lieutenant translates the beginning of humankind into English.

The President of Tanzania stands up and claims the sculpture of The Tree of Life, created by Johannes Sebastian Massamungu, for all East Africans to enjoy and revere.

He shakes the hand of the young lieutenant, salutes him with a broad smile, and then reaches for Mac McKlane. He pulls him close and whispers in his ear.

Mac steps away from the crowd of onlookers surrounding the statue. He puts his arm around Holly Smolkes' waist and squeezes her.

She brushes him off.

She says: "Rape? That's how these assholes think the world began? The MeToo movement is not going to buy one word of this shit."

She says this loud enough for people to hear.

"Mythology." Mac smiles. "The ancient folklore of ignorance. We all know that the moon is made of cheese."

"What did the President of Tanzania whisper in your ear?" she asks. "Did he tell you a dirty joke?"

"He said my grandfather was a thief but a man of principle. I told him that was why grandpa won the Medal of Honor in Korea. I don't think he likes us being here."

"Well, I don't particularly like being here either, but I love you, General Mac McKlane," Holly says. "Cheese, huh?"

"Love is all that counts," he says.

"And a good Brie from Ile de France," Holly says. "Or even a Camembert from Normandy." They both laugh."

Amadeus Massamungu pulls Mac and Holly aside.

"We have a problem," he says.

Mac looks in his eyes and says, "Shit," before hearing what the problem is.

"Chimala is under attack, General McKlane. How many of your warriors can you fit into a Black Hawk?" Lieutenant Amadeus Massamungu asks.

Samuel Nelson has joined them and hears this.

"Why the hell did we bring so many of them here?" Mac asks nobody.

He knows, too late, that he should have left more Marine Raiders, Navy SEALs, and Army Rangers at the Chimala Mission Hospital.

"Perfect 20/20, Mac, but after the fact," Holly says.

Only three Marine Raiders and three Navy SEALs stayed behind in the Chimala Mission, fake patients with assault weapons under their hospital sheets.

"My wife, Sharonda," Samuel Nelson says to himself. "Damn it."

"What model Black Hawk?" Mac asks the Tanzanian lieutenant as he squeezes Samuel's shoulder.

"UH 60A/L," Massamungu says.

"You have a co-pilot?"

"Not a good one."

"You do now. Me."

Mac's father spends much of his career in a Marine Corps Air Wing before his assignment to the Pentagon. Mac learns more about Black Hawks than most helicopter mechanics do, and he flies them in both combat and peace.

"Do you have a crew chief?" Mac asks.

"Not a good ...."

"You do now," Samuel Nelson says.

He has never been a crew chief in his life, but Mac says, "Best crew chief I ever met."

"Don't forget me," Holly says.

"You can squeeze 15 fully-equipped combat troops in a UH-60A/L," Mac tells Massamungu, wondering why the young lieutenant does not already know this. "That includes 11 fully-armed warriors with all their toys, a pilot, you, a co-pilot, me, and two crew chiefs."

He nods at Holly.

"We can be in the air in twenty minutes," the Tanzanian pilot says.

On their way out, Mac grabs the President of Tanzania, exciting his bodyguards. They fall back at their leader's raised hand.

Mac says: "It's been a fun party. We're off."

"Chimala" is the only word the president says.

General Mac McKlane understands that the president might know about this, but he wonders whose side he is on.

The Chimala trip continues to be a secret, although numerous leaks always seem possible. Still, Mac thinks the president might not support the Americans. Africa changes once the terrorists start fleeing down the continent, licking their wounds from the Middle East, buying safe havens.

Mac McKlane needs to watch Lieutenant Massamungu closely. He pulls aside Holly and Samuel.

"The Black Hawk has armored pilot and co-pilot seats," he says. "If Lieutenant Amadeus Massamungu tries anything funny, Holly, you must take him out. You sit in the first crew chief jumpseat behind him."

Mac McKlane formulates his action plan. "If I ask you for some mushroom tea, Holly, you eliminate Massamungu, but you must reach around and shoot him from the front, in the heart, pointing into his seat. That will make sure you don't blow a hole in the helicopter."

Holly repeats his orders word for word.

"I'll maintain control of the helicopter," Mac says.

"How will you know he's screwing us?" Samuel asks.

"I'll know. Massamungu will do something stupid."

"They always do," Holly adds. "Trust Mac's radar."

Sharonda reaches the swollen Chimala River and crouches into the forest that sprawls up the Southern Highlands.

She hears faint gunfire, barely a whisper, as she stands next to the raging river. The storm the previous night floods the flatlands far above, where the river has its headwaters.

She climbs a mountain with a river spilling water over its edges. It's not easy.

At one point, she looks through the trees and sees the Mission Hospital in the distance, far below. She sits on a bolder and watches.

"Stop it," she says to Sophia, who is tugging at Fubar. The baboon pays no attention to her, lifting the dog's ear like a rag and playing with it.

Then Sophia starts to groom the dog's back with careful picking, constantly raising her fingers to her mouth and biting the ticks and bugs, often imaginary, that she finds. Fubar is sound asleep, exhausted by the previous night's watchdog duties.

"You're the only hound I know that never sleeps at night," Sharonda tells Fubar.

She remembers the eight-day hike up and down the mountain with Samuel.

He throws Fubar in a dead man's carry around his shoulders for hours as they climb, and the dog falls asleep in that position.

"You have the right name," she tells the scruffy hound with the acronym of FUBAR. Fouled Up Beyond All Recognition slumbers quietly at her feet.

The dog has a habit that can save them, too, a valuable one. Fubar senses danger long before people do, and when he does, he lays down flat on the ground and makes a ruffling noise through his mouth.

It sounds like "*fluuf-fluuf-fluuf.*"

Fubar does it with fear, but it remains an excellent early warning device.

Twice during their initial climb, they avoid dangerous animals in the forest because of *"fluuf-fluuf-fluuf."*

Sharonda sees no movement at the Mission Hospital. Patients, nurses, and soldiers do not appear in the gardens. She sees none of the Rangers, Raiders, or SEALs disguised as patients, all of whom she has met.

She does see smoke from a funeral pyre in the schoolyard. She wishes her assault weapon had a scope on it. Perhaps she could pick off a few of the men in black still throwing bodies on the fire, but she knows it would be revealing, angry, and stupid.

She will need her 43 bullets to fight the terrorists who will eventually come after her.

They know the killer of their leader is climbing up the mountain behind Chimala.

They are not stupid.

Another storm starts to brew over the Buhoro Flats, whispering thunder in the distance. She must find some sort of shelter before the rains come.

Late in the afternoon, she discovers a cave near the river, in a rocky crevice well above the water.

She does not know it belongs to the leopard that saves her life earlier at the baobab tree in the sawgrass.

The shallow fissure with a roof of broken rocks is where she gives birth to four of the eight litters in her lifetime. The rest were born at the thick base of the baobab tree in the field of sawgrass.

Sharonda squeezes into the back of the small cave and opens her backpack, pulling out the bag of rice she grabbed in the kitchen.

She has a small metal meal kit to cook it in, but she can not build an open fire in the cave. It might become a beacon for the terrorists.

She finds a rock and starts to dig a hole in the back of the cave, where she can set a container of Sterno below ground level and cook one of the cans of beans.

She does not use her knife because it must remain sharp. She might need that. She decides she can serve rice and beans on shallow stones.

She is almost done with the nine-inch deep fire pit when Sophia shows up with dinner, fruit that she has picked from the forest, including a ripe mango.

"Where did you find that?" Sharonda asks.

She steps out of the cave and, in the fading light, spots the mango tree filled with fruit.

As the storm starts to dump water on the Highlands, Fubar, Sophia, and Sharonda feast on ripe mangoes in the whelping cave of the leopard.

Fubar does not particularly like the fruit, but he eats it when Sharonda adds some rice to the mix. Their shelter is not waterproof, and the can of Sterno, never lit, goes back into Sharonda backpack.

She pulls out thick, pleated tinfoil from her pack, wrapping it around her. It's a survival sheet.

"This beats standing in the rain," Sharonda tells her soaking menagerie.

Sophia climbs into her lap, under the foil, and goes to sleep immediately. Fubar pushes next to her, but she knows he will not sleep. Sharonda does doze on and off, propped up in the back of the cave. Her assault rifle points at the entrance. She reluctantly welcomes the protection of bad weather. She awakens many times as lightning outlines the cavern's entrance.

At one point, she sees something at the cave's mouth, but it disappears when she raises her assault weapon. It makes no sound, merely vanishing, perhaps a dream. She remembers no "*fluuf-fluuf-fluuf*" coming from Fubar.

As sunrise flickers through the forest, Sharonda wakes up to a soft growl.

"Be quiet, Fubar," she says. The dog has never made such a sound. "Hush."

It is not Fubar that makes the noise, however.

heartbeats

Lieutenant Massamungu's Black Hawk lifts off from Mikumi Airport on the outskirts of Dar es Salaam and banks into the sunset, heading due west.

Mac McKlane waits for the pilot to turn south towards Chimala. He taps the fuel gauge, and it is full. Through his headset, he says "Chimala" to the pilot.

"Yes, of course," Lieutenant Massamungu says through the intercom. "First, we must go to Ngerengere Air Force Base. The president has personally requested that our Air Force Commander replace me as the pilot. Of course, as a senior military man yourself, you know that I have no choice in this matter. I'm sure you realize this, General McKlane."

It sounds like a very long-winded lie.

"I told you to call me Mac."

"Mac," the pilot says.

Ngerengere Air Force Base is 75 miles west of Dar es Salaam and has 3,500 people who make up the Tanzania Air Force Command.

Ngerengere Air Force Base was built by the Chinese under their Belt and Highway Program, like much of Africa's newest infrastructure.

"We need to get to Chimala right away," Mac tells the pilot. "Can the commander of the Tanzanian Air Force Command fly this Black Hawk?"

"Oh, yes, of course," Lieutenant Massamungo says. "He has often flown our president in the Bell 206L-1 Long Ranger II helicopter at Ngerengere Air Force Base."

Apples and oranges, Mac thinks. "Okay," the general says to the pilot. "I understand."

Mac McKlane and Holly both note that Maasamungu is sweating profusely.

Mac turns to Holly, and then he appears to relax. "Maybe I'll doze off for a few minutes."

After about 60 seconds, he turns to Holly in the jumpseat. "Did you bring me that thermos of mushroom tea, sweetheart? Co-pilots should never sleep."

"You bet," Holly says.

The helicopter lurches slightly to its left when she steps forward between General Mac McKlane and Amadeus Massamungo, shooting the lieutenant.

Fingering his neck, she says, "Won't be much blood. Right through the heart."

As the sun sets, a body is thrown from the Black Hawk shortly after it changes course to the south, heading for Chimala in the Mbeya Region of the Southern Highlands.

"We'll land on the flatlands above Chimala," Mac tells Samuel, who sits in the co-pilot's chair, baffled by dials.

Some bloody rags separate them, the result of cleaning up the pilot's seat. Holly bags them and asks a Navy SEAL to toss it out, too.

"Sharonda and I climbed up and down most of the Chimala River," Samuel says. "Well, almost. We never made it up to the flatlands, although people told us about it."

"What's there?" Mac asks.

"I think some tea plantations, but there should be some villages up there as well."

"It's going to be a bumpy ride," Mac says as the storm begins to appear on the horizon, framed with lightning in billowing black clouds.

It's slightly less than 400 miles from Dar es Salaam to their destination.

They have spent some fuel heading towards the Ngerengere Air Force Base.

"We're probably going to be running on empty when we get to the flatlands above Chimala," Mac tells his warriors over the intercom. "We might have to go on foot the last ten miles or so. We'll land wherever we land in about two and a half hours. Try to get some sleep. Make sure you check your night vision gear first."

The Black Hawk starts to bounce around in the weather closing in on them.

The storm is massive, a cyclone in a part of the world that has never witnessed such an event.

Not many people can sleep in a helicopter that acts like a Mexican jumping bean, but most men and women fall asleep immediately. It's part of their training and, in some cases, a reaction to their fear.

It is a leopard growling at Sharonda's cave entrance, and it appears to be relatively young.

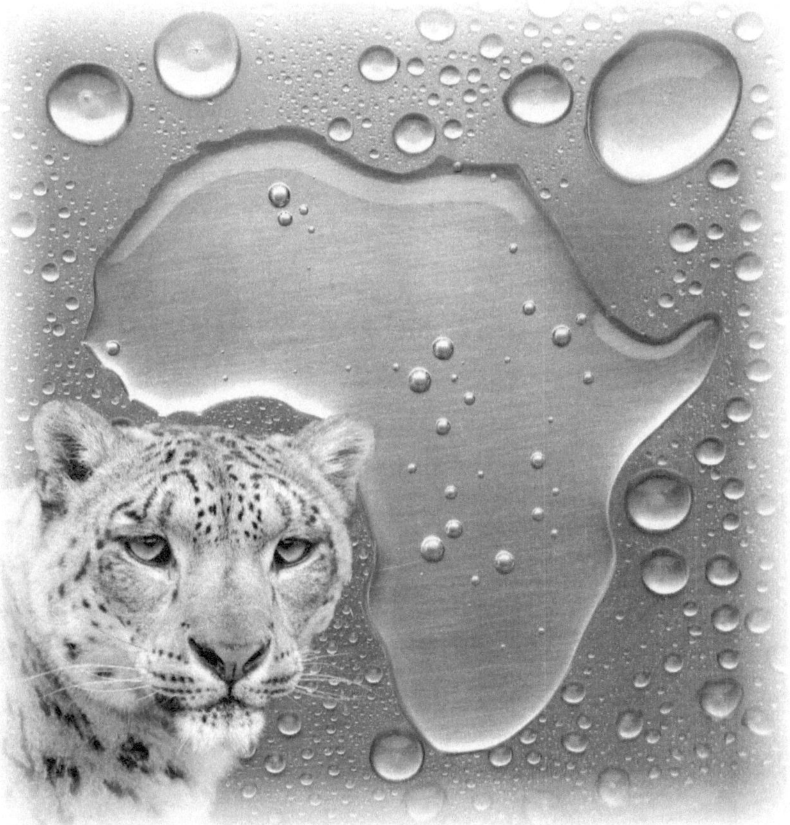

Sharonda does not want to shoot it, giving away her position, but she may have no choice.

"If this is your home, we can leave peacefully," Sharonda says, rustling the tinfoil survival blanket and her metal meal kit into her rucksack without removing the aim of her weapon from the young leopard, preventing their escape.

Sophia is on her backpack, silent.

Very slowly, Sharonda shoulders the backpack, one arm at a time. The monkey does not let go of its grip as she does this.

Fubar "*fluuf-fluuf-fluufs*" with his head flat on the floor of the cave.

"It's a bit late for that," Sharonda says without taking her eyes off the leopard or her finger off the trigger.

The young leopard turns sideways, backs up, and pees on a bush near the entrance.

"You're pregnant," Sharonda says, looking at the cat's very swollen stomach. "You're about to give birth."

Sharonda moves slowly to the front of the cave, and the leopard backs away about twenty feet.

Sophia dashes out and into the Mango tree, making a lot of screeching noises.

The young leopard never takes her eyes off the crouching woman. As Sharonda moves out of the cave, the leopard backs off further, lifting her haunches on a bush and then moving back. She swishes her tail against a large tree. She steps up to it and claws down its trunk several times, leaving yellow lines in the bark.

Sharonda has Fubar by the scruff of the neck, dragging him with her, pointing her weapon at the leopard.

She releases Fubar, saying, "Go." She is ready to shoot the leopard if it tries to kill her or the dog.

The leopard stops clawing the tree trunk, still swishing its tail, and never taking her eyes off Sharonda.

Fubar gallops up the river, not making a sound, as Sharonda backs away from the entrance to the cat's cave. She moves slowly up the mountain, backward, almost tripping twice. She goes over thirty yards before she sees the pregnant leopard slowly enter her lair.

Sharonda continues up the mountainside, moving from pool to pool, with Fubar at her side. It's a challenging climb. The river crests its banks. She guesses that they're nowhere near a quarter of the way up to the flatlands. She looks down at Fubar, flat on the ground but not asleep.

"I can't carry you," she tells the dog.

After half an hour, she sits down a safe distance from a swollen waterfall. Sophia jumps on her shoulder.

Fubar, reluctantly following, pushes hard against Sharonda's body. The dog immediately falls asleep.

"Not a bad idea," Sharonda says, dozing off in the speckled sunlight that reaches through an umbrella of trees to the floor of the forest.

Her assault weapon always points downstream.

"We can land in the Buhoro Flats or on the flatlands above Chimala," Mac tells Holly and Samuel in the cockpit. "It's going to depend on this weather."

The helicopter bounces a lot.

They are flying on instruments, and they are picking up pings coming in from the north.

"Do we know what kind of planes the Tanzania Air Force Command has?" Samuel Nelson asks, looking at the dots on their radar sweep.

"I do," Holly says. "They used to have a bunch of Shenyang F-7s, sort of like MiG21s, but made in China. I seriously doubt if any of them are airworthy." She tries to remember the data she has read.

"I think they say they operate 14 fighters and 11 fixed-wing attack aircraft, but that information is one or two years old. As I recall, the last action anyone has seen from them is the crash of a Chinese jet trainer in the Indian Ocean. Both of the pilots died."

"Those pings are real," Mac says, tapping the radar. "And they're moving a lot faster than we are."

Nobody says anything as they watch the dots creeping towards them.

"They will close the gap within 45 minutes, probably less", Samuel says.

"They all came out of Morogoro," Mac says.

"That's the Ngerengere Air Force Base," Holly says.

"At least they won't enjoy this weather any more than we do," Samuel says. "I guess we can't cloak the Black Hawk, can we?"

"Only if we shut it down," Mac says.

They all watch the pings closing in on them.

"We land on the flatlands above Chimala," Mac says over the intercom. "We won't have much protection there, but it's always better to take the high ground."

As they start to run low on fuel, they see the dots on their radar screen suddenly turn and head back to Morogoro.

"I guess their pilots suck," Holly says. She does not realize that two of the four planes have experienced Chinese pilots in the cockpit of fully-armed and completely airworthy Shenyang F-7s. Tanzanian airmen fly the other two planes.

Perhaps more important, the crew of the Black Hawk does not realize that the retreat is because of a massive cyclone growing in the Indian Ocean, threatening Tanzania for the first time in modern recorded history.

It's a climate event that has no precedent.

The cyclone will move ashore south of Dar es Salaam in a matter of hours as a Category Four storm.

A month earlier, the deadly cyclone, Idai, shreds and soaks Mozambique, a nation bordering Tanzania to the south. That storm leaves over 1,300 people dead and perhaps four times as many missing. It turns Mozambique into a lake.

The estimated cost of Cyclone Idai is $2.2 billion U.S. dollars, making it the costliest tropical storm ever in the South-West Indian Ocean basin.

Cyclone Idai tears apart Mozambique's infrastructure. Over 6,000 homes disappear in its floodwaters, with another 16,000 homes affected.

The storm destroys eight hospitals, flattening as well as flooding them.

Over 420,000 acres of crops disappear, covered with mud and, often, ocean saltwater.

More than three million people experience the direct effects of Cyclone Idai in four different countries: Madagascar, Malawi, Zimbabwe, and Mozambique.

Now a new cyclone, Kenneth, is crossing the eastern coast of Africa.

It approaches with 145 mile-an-hour winds and torrential rain. According to the World Meteorological Organization, the cyclone targets an area never hit by such a tropical storm. Tanzanians go to higher ground to seek shelter.

Mac McKlane and his crew hear none of these warnings, although the hard buffeting of the Black Hawk wakes up everyone sleeping in its passenger seats.

Mac turns on the Black Hawk's powerful searchlights. They must be flying well above the ground because they can not see it.

Suddenly he pulls up, narrowly missing the jagged edges at the start of the flatlands.

"We are forty miles from Chimala," General Mac McKlane says over the intercom, "but we're landing now, here, fast, and probably hard."

A Navy chief petty officer in the body of the Black Hawk says: "Good idea." He looks at a portable military laptop that shows that Cyclone Kenneth is well past the coast of Tanzania.

In the cockpit, Mac sees the same thing.

General McKlane turns the Black Hawk into the wind and angles it to the ground.

It lands surprisingly softly, an indication of his superior flying skills.

"Everyone out," he says over the intercom. "Anchor the ship and move away from it. Take all of our gear with you. Leave nothing aboard. And start digging foxholes at least six feet deep. Some serious wind will hit us within an hour."

The rain comes first, and it is cold.

Within minutes, all the warriors are up to their necks in holes filled with mud.

Lightning reveals the helicopter straining at its double tethering. Suddenly it lifts in the wind and disappears over the edge of the flatlands' jagged cliff.

It does not seem to make any noise, no crashing sounds, or bending of metal. It almost seems to have taken off, blades whirling.

"It's going to be a long night," Holly says, sharing a foxhole with Mac.

"You wanna fool around?" he asks.

"Cut it out, Mac."

"You got a headache, sweetheart? For God's sake, we just got married."

"You need to work on your honeymoon destinations," Holly says, shivering in the mud. Then, as Mac pushes slowly into her, she tells him he has to build a bigger foxhole next time. She needs to put her legs over his shoulders. The rain does not feel warmer.

"You're quivering," Mac says. "I can't hold back if you're ...."

"I'm not quivering, Mac. I'm shivering. So calm down. Take your time. Show a little discipline, General." She is whispering in his ear, and her breath is warm.

After less than a minute, she says, "NOW I'm quivering, Mac. Even my toes are quivering."

Mac loses himself shouting into the wind.

A Marine Ranger in another foxhole says, "Hey, keep it down. The walls in this landing zone are thin."

People laugh.

They need to laugh.

Some of them decide to follow their leader.

A young Marine Raider sergeant points out to the Army Ranger who climbs into his foxhole that they are enjoying the coldest, most miserable orgy in history.

"Be quiet," she says, biting his lower lip harder than he likes and pressing into him. "We're bonding."

Chapter 3

When the captain of the *S.S. Nomad* shouts, "Light it up," everyone on the platform under the bridge shades their eyes and utters their version of "Wow," except for Mac and Maria Montoya. They know how it looks.

Banks of floodlights reveal the freighter's hold.

Sookie elbows her husband, Shadrach Ringer. "Don't say 'Holy Shit,' Chief." She remains a devout Presbyterian.

"You just did," he says.

Sookie elbows him again, and then she holds his hand.

Before them, they see a city, three cities, including something that looks like a lake with a boat floating on it far away, where the welding sparks had died in the bow before Commander Maria Montoya yelled, "Light it up."

Four stories below them, most of the crew of the *S.S. Nomad* stands at parade rest in combat uniforms: Navy SEALs, Army Rangers, Marine Raiders.

Battle cries of "Oorah," "Hooah," and "Hooyah" combine as the troops click their heels together, commanded to attention by General Mac McKlane.

The combat troops, 100 men and 45 women, represent the best of their respective military branches, although none of the SEALs are women.

All of the troops have seen warfare in Iraq and Afghanistan. Quite a few have led or been part of covert operations in Africa. A number of them are medics who have saved many lives. Almost all of them are qualified snipers.

A gunnery sergeant with many hashtags, each indicating four years in the service, survived the 1993 Battle of Mogadishu in Somalia. A book titled "Battle of Mogadishu" by Mark Bowden in 1999 made it famous. It led to the movie adaption of the book, directed by Ridley Scott in 2001, called "Black Hawk Down."

All these men and women are volunteers, chosen by a team of Homeland Security experts for their abilities and professional anti-terrorism records.

"At ease," General Mac McKlane shouts. "Fall out."

The troops disperse into the three "cities" built in the hold of the ship.

The CWMD Homeland Security members step onto a platform. It takes them down the four stories to a flat surface leading to the cities, all at or below sea level. They start to move through what Mac calls their "training ground."

The first has a large sign that says, "Chimala, population 30,000, Mission Hospital, Target One." An aerial view of the city appears below this message.

"American Intel says this is the first and most likely target of ISIS because it's the easiest one to attack, and we have intercepts that say they consider Chimala a trial run into sub-Saharan Africa," Mac tells them. "They're going to practice on a hospital that has 200 rooms for patients."

He points to it with a baton.

"Some of those beds will be armed with Marine Raiders, Army Rangers, and Navy SEALs."

He moves his baton to the top of the city.

"And this is where Sharonda and Samuel Nelson will live. It's at the edge of a schoolyard on the other side of the Chimala River. We've almost finished your monkey's new brick home with an all-weather tin roof, Sharonda."

"Almost?"

"It's missing a safe room with a toilet."

She looks at Samuel. "That's your job, superstud."

"So right away, I start my new life in the shithouse," Samuel says. They laugh.

"It's important that you gain the trust and respect of your neighbors with a shovel in your hands," Mac says.

"I know how to build a toilet and a French drain," Samuel says. "I built one on my grandfather's farm in North Carolina. That's how I gained his trust and respect."

They laugh again.

"Welcome to Chimala," Mac says, moving beyond the sign to an abbreviated mockup of a street in the city.

Most of the homes are brick with either tin or thatched roofs. Some use mud walls with thatched roofs, like the Pombe Shop, the local pub.

After that, they come to a facade of the Chimala Mission Hospital.

"My grandfather almost died of malaria, but this hospital saved him," Mac says. "Although it has hundreds of beds today, back then, it was just a one-room Christian clinic with a medic who was a former Foreign Legionnaire. He was an interesting man. For a start, few men ever leave the French Foreign Legion. You enlist until you die."

Mac tells the story of Jean-Claude Joubert, a man his grandfather credited with saving his life.

"Grandpa always said Jean-Claude's coffin was too small for him. The size of it surprised him at the funeral. He always thought Jean-Claude was over six feet tall. He was five inches shorter than that. My grandfather, Captain George, said he acted seven feet tall."

Jean-Claude Jobert was buried in his hometown, near Avignon, next to his brother, Renau.

"Grandpa flew to France for the funeral. He always stayed in touch with the men who saved him, and there were quite a few of them. Jean-Claude was one of his favorites. His sister called my grandfather the day he died. She was a nun at a convent near Avignon."

Both Jean-Claude and Renau Joubert, his brother, served in the French Foreign Legion. Renau Joubert died in Algeria, outside a town called El Bayadh.

"They were in the *Guerre d'Algérie*, the Algerian War of Independence." As he tells the story, the CWMD Homeland Security members lean closer to General McKlane. They know that this tale will probably teach them something.

"Terrorists, Freedom Fighters, they are all the same, depending on which side you choose. French Algerians, loyalists, fought against the Muslim National Liberation Front. When the French President, Charles de Gaulle, decided to pull out of Algeria, the legionnaires abandoned their blockhouses and forts and returned home. The Algerian freedom fighters captured both Jean-Claude and Renau Joubert as they retreated."

Mac looks at the members of his team.

"Torture is a common theme in every war we fight," he says. "It makes us uncomfortable, but it always occurs – in

World War I and II, in Korea, in Vietnam, Afghanistan, and especially in the battle against ISIS and other Muslim terrorist groups. But the French Foreign Legion has always been famous for their torture techniques, and when the Algerians captured Jean-Claude and Renau, they paid a terrible price."

The Muslim insurgents identified both men as members of the OAS, the *Organisation de l'armée secrète*.

They staked them in the desert sands of Algeria, standing up, bound tight, facing one another, and 10 feet apart. The terrorists played a game with stones in the sand, finally pointing at Renau.

They stripped and disemboweled him. It took over an hour for him to bleed to death.

"When Jean-Claude tried to look away, the Muslim terrorists pointed his face at his brother. When he tried to close his eyes, they held them open," Mac says.

After his brother died, the terrorists released Jean-Claude, driving him back to his withdrawing fellow legionnaires, dumping him a mile in front of the dust of their retreating column.

"That's where they found him," Mac says. "Beaten, bleeding, disoriented, crazy, crying uncontrollably."

Everyone is silent.

"Here's the lesson of this story," Mac says. 'Two years later, he's a medic in Tanzania, on his way to becoming a doctor, and he saves my grandfather. He moves from hatred and darkness to saving people. The shadows of life do not capture him."

Shadrach coughs. He's heard a little more of this story.

Mac looks at him and says, "What?"

"How did he die? Is he still alive?"

"Well," Mac says. He's not sure he wants to get into this part of the story. Everyone looks at the General, and nobody says anything. He tells the story.

"Jean-Claude Joubert did an unthinkable thing for a Frenchman in the Sixties. He married his mistress."

Holly crosses her arms. The Tremwallises look at the general with no comprehension.

"They got married in Mbeya, at the Guest House run by Nessie Whapshot. The wedding happened a few months after my Grandpa returned from Tanzania to America. There was a stupid, chauvinistic rule in France in those days. You never married your mistress."

"A very dumb rule," Holly says, keeping her arms crossed and staring hard at General George McKlane, her fourth husband.

"Yes," Mac says. "A lot has changed in the last half-century. But in those days, the stupidity existed."

Mac wants to end the story here, so he says: "Jean-Claude shot himself, committed suicide."

"Because he married his mistress?" Sookie asks.

"Are you joking?" Ernestine asks.

"Some stories just don't end well," Mac says. Nobody moves, and now he suddenly realizes *why* he must continue.

"After the wedding at the Guest House in Mbeya, they flew from Tanzania to France for their honeymoon. Jean-Claude's wife knew his parents."

Mac pauses, then adds: "She knew his father. She knew him very well. He introduced his son to her."

A few of the listeners say, "Oh." Samuel says, "Shit."

"Everything came out in the open in a huge family fight," Mac says. "His wife had never told Jean-Claude that she had been his father's mistress."

Holly unfolds her arms and shakes her head.

"Jean-Claude and his mother stormed out, according to Sister Rebecca, his sibling, the nun."

Sister Rebecca told Mac that Jean-Claude returned to his family's home about an hour later.

"He found his father holding his almost naked wife. They were in the honeymoon suite, but they were not making love there."

"Were they fucking?" Holly asks to make sure that "making love" was not a contact sport for the father.

Mac McKlane remains silent for a while. Then he finally says, "Yes." Jean-Claude went to his father's study and returned to the bedroom with a pistol. His new wife was hysterical, on her knees, begging for her life."

"Did he kill her?" Charlton asks, holding his wife close to him, trying to protect her somehow from this terrible story.

"No," Mac says. "He didn't. I think the horrors of Algeria flooded his mind, the loss of his brother. No one will ever know. I think Jean-Claude suffered a flashback to Algeria. He shot his father in the crotch and then stood there as the man he loved and always respected started to bleed to death. His sister, the nun, was in the room at that point. Both women were on their knees, one praying to the Lord and the other begging for her life. They watched Jean-Claude shoot his father in the head, ending his agony, and then he sat down on a chair and shot himself through the heart."

After a while, Mac says, "That's the end of the story."

"The redemption of him becoming a medic at the Chimala Mission sort of gets tarnished by his post-traumatic disorder, or anger, or whatever possessed him," Holly says.

"Yes," General McKlane says. He did not plan to tell them the entire story of how Jean-Claude Joubert died. Once again, he remembers his grandfather telling him how small his coffin seemed at the funeral.

General McKlane sighs and says: "We have all taken an oath to speak the truth to one another. I admit I did not want to tell all of this story. So I think three lessons come from Jean-Claude Joubert. First, he saves my grandfather in Tanzania after witnessing unthinkable horrors that end his brother's life in Algeria."

The general pauses, and then he says: "All of us have learned lessons in wartime that we did not want to discover in our lives, and we will continue to do so."

Many men and women nod in solemn agreement.

"Second, redemption can be very complicated in life. We often must pay, unexpectedly, for positive outcomes."

Ernestine Tremwallis says, "Perhaps that's the price of freedom, the reason it's never free."

Mac nods at this cliché, then he continues.

"And the third thing? I learned, again, that I must share the truth with you, not just a convenient portion of the truth. Prime Minister Wilson of the UK supposedly said that the first casualty of every war *was* the truth before America entered World War II. He paraphrased the line from Samuel Johnson, who wrote about it hundreds of years earlier in the mid-1700s. But it originated with the founder of tragedy, Aeschylus from Greece, more than 2,500 years ago."

General Mac McKlane looks at each member of the Homeland Security CWMD team and says: "We must never let the truth stand between us."

"What happened to Jean-Claude Joubert's wife?" Holly asks her husband.

"Complicated redemption, perhaps," Mac says. "She became a nun. I have no idea if she's still alive."

He opens the door of the Chimala Mission's facade, and they enter a hospital ward with four rooms and a lot of medical equipment in the corridor, all of which are real, all of which function.

"Consider this the ship's medical center," he says, "but it's also a replica of the Chimala Mission. Half a dozen of our men and women will be patients in this area."

"Geez," Shadrach says, "the walls are even a sickly hospital green."

Nobody has recovered sufficiently from Jean-Claude Joubert's story to laugh or even smile.

They move past the patients' rooms and medical equipment and come to an oversized boxing ring three times larger than usual.

The roped-in ring butts up to a workout area where crew members lift weights, use one of two rowing machines, and utilize the latest muscle-making gear on the market, from Stairmasters to stationary bikes, pull-up bars to bench presses.

Mac says: "You all have a free membership to this club, and you will use it often. That's an order, not a gift."

"The oversized boxing ring?" Sharonda asks.

"That's where you will either discover or hone your survival skills," Captain Maria Montoya says.

'Whew," Sharonda says. "I thought maybe we would have to box giants."

"That, too," Captain Montoya says.

"You know I'm a Nurse Practitioner," Sharonda says. "The only difference between a doctor and me is that I did not have to go through a residency."

"What does that mean?" Captain Montoya asks.

"It means I took an oath to do no harm."

"And is that why you killed fake cops protecting Captain McKlane, Mac's grandfather?" the captain asks.

"Wow," Sharonda says. "You do know a lot about us, Captain Montoya, maybe too much."

Her husband, Samuel, says, "No secrets."

After some silence, Sharonda says, "Truth."

Cyclone Kenneth dumps over 22 inches of rain as it slowly dies in Tanzania's Southern Highlands.

The electronic equipment used by the CWMD team stays shut down, sending out no signals, as they climb out of their foxholes after being battered by wind and rain for almost 36 hours.

No one has died or drowned. Some people have lacerations on their faces.

"Look at your hands," Holly says to Mac.

"They look like prunes," he says.

"That's the longest mudbath I've ever taken, and it's a day and a half ahead of second-place," Holly says.

The sun rises in an almost cloudless sky.

As the team surrounds Mac, he says: "Women, you dry out beyond those scrub bushes way over there, and men, we move to the edge of the flatlands to get naked."

Everyone starts to wring out their clothes and check their gear. Other than dampness, little damage occurs. The women marvel at the smoothness of their skin. Despite wrinkled fingers, mudbaths work. Everyone washes off in pools of water left in the wake of Cyclone Kenneth.

At the edge of the mountain range, the men search for their helicopter, finally spotting the mangled skeleton of the Black Hawk around four miles away, in the Buhoro Flats.

They see it sticking out of the sawgrass not far from Hell's Run.

"I think we should turn on the portable laptop for a minute or two," the Navy chief petty officer who first spotted the approaching cyclone says. "We need to see if anyone is approaching our virtually defenseless position. Although I think we could climb into the rocks below the flatlands and effectively disappear."

"I left most of the electronic gear on after we tethered the Black Hawk," Mac says.

"Smart," says the SEAL.

"Plus, we have very nice muddy holes to jump into."

They both look at the broken Black Hawk far below them, almost hidden in the blanket of sawgrass bordering the Buhoro Flats. Herds of buffalo and antelope graze nearby.

"Let's hope it keeps on ticking so they can pick it up on their radar," the Navy chief petty officer says. The Navy SEAL turns on his military laptop, which is waterproof and almost bulletproof.

The screen shows the Black Hawk but no approaching dots. "Turn it off," Mac says. "Check it every ten minutes. Let me know if you see anything."

"Roger that, General."

"Mac," General McKlane says.

"Mac," the Navy SEAL repeats. "You know we have six FIM-92 Stinger Surface-to-Air missiles with us. They're all in waterproof packaging. They can take out aircraft anywhere below 15,000 feet, they fly at over Mach Two speed, and they have a range of over three miles."

"We're probably going to have to use all the Stingers," Mac says. "How many flags do we have?"

He's talking about large black flags, six feet by 10 feet on the end of 12-foot poles, with ISIS Arabic slogans on them. They brought them in the cargo hold.

"The same number," the Navy SEAL answers.

"If they take out the Black Hawk, we'll need to get their attention by waving the flags."

"They'll have to be a little stupid to fall for that," the Navy SEAL says. "And they're not dumb."

"True," Mac says. "But they might do a fly-by first. Sort of a final goodbye."

"Their last goodbye," the Navy SEAL repeats.

He likes working for this general.

"We can also turn on all our cellphones, and that will attract them, too," the SEAL says.

Mac raises his voice and says: "Work on your suntans, people. Be ready to suit up, fast."

Quite a few of the team suit up right away. This group laughs, and so does Mac.

A dozen black American men and women don't have to work on their tans, and the mid-morning sun has already dried out their clothes.

An hour later, the military laptop picks up four beeps coming straight at them.

"They're moving fast, and it looks like they originated in Morogoro," the Navy SEAL says.

"I want six men dressed in black like Al-Qaeda warriors," Mac says, "but stay in the rocks until I give the order to wave your ISIS banners. Let's see what the Tanzanian Air Force has to offer us first."

The Navy SEAL says, "They should be here in about 30 minutes, maybe less."

Mac says, "Everyone get your clothes on and find a hiding place over the edge in the rocks. I want our six Stinger SAMs just below our flag bearers. Only fire four of them if they make a flyby when they see us. And no groundfire. Everyone got that?"

General Mac McKlane's orders pass down the line. Everyone gets it.

Six huge black flags unfurl on the ground. Four FIM-92 Stingers wait in the rocks just over the edge of the flatlands' cliff, with two more nearby.

The beeps close in.

"Turn it off," Mac says.

He does not know if he and his men will survive. They might find themselves trapped in a suicide mission.

Several bursts of gunfire further down the river awakens Sharonda. They are coming after her, but probably not many of them. She thinks perhaps the gunfire results from the terrorists crossing paths with the pregnant leopard.

She signals for Sophia to be quiet while Fubar lowers his head: *"fluuf-fluuf-fluuf."*

Sharonda moves up into the rocks, waiting.

After 20 minutes, she sees four terrorists picking their way up the mountain, slipping in the swollen river's mud.

Two of them have their weapons shouldered. Sharonda aims first at the men carrying their assault rifles in front of them, ready to shoot.

Two shots, two dead, but she knows now that the old assault rifle she's using pulls to the left.

She aimed for their hearts and tore apart their shoulders and right ribcages, still fatal shots. She has had no target practice with this weapon. She must point slightly more to the left.

She shoots the third terrorist straight through the head before he can shoulder his assault rifle, but the fourth one disappears behind a large boulder.

Sharonda waits.

She sees a leopard crouching on a second boulder above the bodies and the hiding terrorist. The animal moves very slowly in a surreal version of cat and mouse.

Sharonda sees that the leopard is sleek with no belly, and she thinks that the pregnant mother is probably dead. She imagines this cat as its mate or brother.

The leopard crouches.

Sharonda sees its muscles tighten.

It springs effortlessly at the out-of-sight terrorist.

The man screams and fires his gun, probably into the air as the leopard guts him.

Then Sharonda sees the 120-pound cat jump back onto the boulder afterward, apparently unhurt.

The leopard roars, looking up at Sharonda forty feet away. She stabilizes her weapon against a tree.

"Don't smile," she says to herself. "That will suggest you are baring your teeth, wanting a fight. Back up, slowly."

Before she shoots, the leopard looks away with a roar, dropping back behind the boulder. She watches it start to drag one of the men away, effortlessly placing him in the large branches of a tree. He does the same with all four men, seemingly decorating four different trees with bodies.

Sharonda sees Fubar over a hundred yards above her, standing. So that area is safe, no "*fluuf-fluuf-fluuf.*" She sees Sophia jumping around in a tree next to Fubar.

She joins them, continuing the climb towards the flatlands. She thinks she can reach the top in two more days, but the weather quickly changes her mind.

The sky goes black. Wind howls. The rain makes progress impossible.

She moves away from the river as it grows into a raging cascade that uproots anything in its path. She struggles to the highest ground, where a broken sausage tree has wedged its large trunk between two boulders, and that's where she hides from the storm with Fubar and Sophia.

The monkey knows that the trees are no longer safe to climb in. But Sophia likes the fruit of the sausage tree that has fallen between the rocks.

She huddles with Sharonda, picking at the food that gives the tree its name.

"This will pass," Sharonda tells her pets. They squeeze together, sharing some bitter sausage fruit, each one of which weighs over eight pounds.

The storm does not pass easily or quickly.

They eat four cans of spam, three cans of beans, and all of the wet rice.

The wind howls for almost two days, and the river comes within two feet of flooding their sanctuary. Sophia hangs on to the branches of the sausage tree, continually chattering, shaking in fear, and from the cold. She has no interest in the two-inch pieces of hail, which briefly bounce off the mountainside and quickly melt.

Fubar joins Sharonda under the emergency tinfoil blanket, never sleeping.

Everyone shivers in the cold, torrential rain.

Then, as suddenly as it begins, it ends.

The destruction is everywhere, with fallen trees, torn earth, and a river still swelling well over its banks. Sharonda has finally fallen asleep.

She wakes to the song of a bird and the sun shining on a cloudless day.

Sharonda, Fubar, and Sophia all go back to sleep, exhausted. Early in the afternoon, with no rain in sight, they continue their journey up to the flatlands. They have very little food left, just three energy bars.

That will have to last two days.

Sharonda does throw some of the dense sausage fruit into her backpack.

Sophia seems to like it. Sharonda and Fubar can't stomach it because of its bitterness.

Four Shenyang F-7s jets come in low over the Buhoro Flats, well below the flatlands of the Southern Highlands. General Mac McKlane sees them long before he hears them.

"I think the Black Hawk electronics have kept identifying the ship's position," he says as the MiG21 lookalikes start to close in on the wreckage four miles down the mountainside. "Get your videos going."

Two of the Tanzanian jets drop napalm and fire their air-to-ground missiles at the Black Hawk wreckage.

The attack sends herds of wildlife racing across the Buhoro Flats.

"No way those are Tanzanian pilots," Holly says. "Not unless there's been a major upgrade in their training."

"They're probably Chinese pilots," the Navy chief petty officer says.

"I think that is a very unfriendly gesture that the Tanzanians are making," General Mac McKlane says. "That's not how you treat a friend who just returned the Tree of Life to a grateful nation. Let's get all our ISIS flags waving."

Suddenly, at the top of the flatlands, terrorist banners unfurl as the Four Shenyang F-7s rise and move away from the mountain in an almost perfect formation.

They are far out of range of the FIM-92 Stinger Surface-to-Air missiles.

They do not turn towards Mac's position.

"Those pilots know how to fly," Holly says. They remain in a tight formation.

"I sure hope they look in their rearview mirrors," the Navy chief petty officer says.

"I think they just did," Mac says after about five seconds. Two of the Chinese MiGs roll right, and two left., joining up in a formation headed directly at General McKlane's position.

"I guess this is when we find out if we're on our final mission," Holly says, ducking as Mac crouches and turns his back on the Shenyang F-7s jets. He's holding one of the Stinger Surface-to-Air missiles, guessing at the future trajectory of the plane furthest left.

"They're not going to napalm the side of a mountain," Mac says. "They've probably dropped their full load already, and they're doing a flyover."

He hopes.

Holly keeps staring at the jets. She sees the Shenyang F-7s widen their formation as they approach the updrafts of the mountain. "Maybe they *are* dumb pilots," she says, ducking as the launch tube of the 6.5 foot Stinger held by Mac passes over her.

"*Allahu Akbar,*" General McKlane says as the jets roar overhead. He immediately launches one of four Stingers Three others launch at the same time.

Each one trails a different aircraft, quickly reaching Mach 2 speed and honing in on the Shenyang F-7s heat source before they escape the missiles' range of 3.2 miles.

The planes explode almost simultaneously. None of them even throw out flares to disguise their heat source.

The team watches for parachutes. None appear.

In Morogoro, the President of Tanzania looks at a radar screen on which his blips disappear all at once. He shouts: *"Nini kuzimu tu kilichotokea?"*

"What the hell just happened?"

heartbeats

When the terrorists who chase her fail to return to Chimala, Sharonda thinks they will send more men up the river after her. No rain has fallen for two days, and the runoff from the flatlands has almost turned back into its usual rush of water.

The highest river pools are practically clear.

Sharonda, Fubar, and Sophia are close to reaching the flatlands. Only the monkey has eaten the fruit of the sausage tree in the past 24 hours.

As they reach the final pools of the river, just below the flatlands, most trees have been broken in half. Many of them have no branches.

Near the top of the mountain, the cyclone unleashes its most brutal wind speeds.

"This looks like a War Zone," Sharonda tells Fubar and Sophia.

She thinks back to Hurricane Andrew that laid waste to Homestead, Florida, many years earlier, leaving leafless trees pointing at a clear, blue sky. She remembers the story of a mother having two children ripped from her hands as a tornado spawned by Hurricane Andrew reaches into the safety of her closet.

No one ever found the children. The mother survived.

Both Sharonda and Fubar suffer from hunger pains as they watch Sophia gnaw and pick at her remaining sausage fruit. Sharonda reaches for it, but the baboon scampers off, thinking it's a game.

Through the broken trees, Sharonda believes she sees the top of the mountain.

The river falls into two clear pools, separated by a fifteen-foot waterfall.

In the top pool, she sees three river otters slipping and sliding around each other, playing. She watches one catch a small fish, swallowing it whole. She does not want to shoot the animal because that will echo down the mountain, possibly attracting unwanted attention.

Like the leopard that helped kill the terrorist a few days earlier, Sharonda perches on a bolder above the pool. Her knife slowly slides out of its sheath. The otters have not seen her. They watch Sophia playing with sausage fruit on the river bank. Fubar is lying flat, out of sight, probably either doing his "*fluuf-fluuf-fluuf*" or sound asleep.

Sharonda leaps into the air.

She falls into the pool and grabs the tail of one of the river otters. They are much bigger than she realizes, and she drops her knife as she tries to hold onto the five-foot-long animal. It rolls on its back and stares at her, baring its teeth and fluttering its whiskers. It may try to bite her.

She does not know what to do, and she is about to release it when the animal's head bursts in blood-red water.

Sharonda looks up, still hanging on to the otter with both hands.

She thinks she is about to die.

On a boulder overlooking the pool, a fearsome warrior with a suppressor on his weapon looks down at her. His face is covered.

He drops the handkerchief and bares his teeth.

"What the hell are you doing, Sharonda?" Samuel asks.

Chapter 4

"I'm not sure how much of Chimala is still there," General Mac McKlane says as they gather at the top of the flatlands where the Chimala River spills over its edge.

"You're lucky you made it," Samuel says to Sharonda, holding her close.

"You're telling me," she says. "First, I had to hide in your safe room with Sophia, and then I killed a terrorist leader that borrowed our bedroom with the chokehold I learned on the ship to Cape Town. Here's his weapon."

She holds it out with her trigger finger on the housing and the safety switched on. One of the Army Rangers identifies it as a Sturmgewehr assault rifle, saying: "I have one just like it in my collection back home. Developed by the Nazis in the late 1930s. Pretty good weapon, still used in the Middle East."

"Still used on the Chimala River, too," Sharonda says. "I think I killed three out of four terrorists chasing me."

Some of McKlane's team drop down to one knee and start to examine the shattered trees below them.

"The fourth one is dead, too," Sharonda says. "A leopard killed him."

McKlane's men keep examining the landscape below for leopards rather than terrorists.

"Don't shoot any leopards. They're all Americans."

Mac's men and women don't lower their assault rifles, but some of them smile at the thought of leopard allies. Sharonda does not know that she has been saved twice by different leopards, nor will she ever.

"I think we have to climb down to Chimala and see how much of it is left," Mac says.

"What's left? What happened?" Sharonda asks.

"Cyclone Kenneth tore apart the border between Tanzania and Mozambique," the Navy chief petty officer tells her. "It must have dumped 30 or more inches of rain on the flatlands. Chimala probably got flooded out."

Sharonda tells them about the raped children and teachers being slaughtered and turned into a funeral pyre in the schoolyard as she makes her escape up the Chimala River with Fubar and Sophia.

The schoolyard was on high ground.

"Well," General McKlane says, "let's hope that's still there. It's a war crime, and we can document it, together with your first-hand knowledge, Sharonda."

"If it's gone, you still have my first-hand knowledge," she says.

General Mac McKlane adds: "We already have a video clip of the Tanzanian Air Command bombing the Black Hawk that brought us to the Southern Highlands."

He encrypts and messages this to Roberta Macumber, his assistant director at Homeland Security in the Washington office, with a short note saying:

"This is how the Tanzanian Air Force defines friendly fire. We destroyed all four of their planes. They looked like old Russian MiGs."

It takes less time going down the Chimala River than it does climbing up it. Sharonda shows where she had a gunfight with four terrorists. They see bullet marks in the boulders but no trace of the leopard that saved Sharonda from the fourth terrorist.

The ISIS warriors that the leopard dragged into the trees are gone, along with much of the forest.

"The flood probably sent them all into the Buhoro Flats," the Navy chief petty officer says. "It must have been a flash flood."

Sharonda checks the cave of the pregnant leopard further downhill, finding nothing but mud.

After they reach an area where Chimala becomes visible, the devastation suggests that hundreds of Tanzanians living in Chimala died with the terrorists trying to kill Sharonda.

The Chimala Mission Hospital still exists, with half of its metal roof torn off and replaced by a blue tarp tied to its fractured structure.

The funeral pyre in the schoolyard remains, although no smoke comes from it.

They see men with assault weapons near the hospital. They are all ISIS warriors, not the American men and women left to guard the area by General Mac McKlane. He thinks that his anti-terrorist warriors did not make it.

Fubar lays flat, head down: "*fluuf-fluuf-fluuf.*"

Sharonda has told everyone about this early warning system, and all of Mac's men and women crouch and take cover. They see movement in the forest. The glint of metal shines through broken trees and fallen branches.

A month and a half earlier, in the hold of the *S.S. Nomad,* the CWMD team moves past the workout area beyond the oversized boxing ring.

They enter a mock-up of a nuclear substation with a sign saying "Pelindaba East, Y-Plant, South Africa."

Radioactivity signs appear on every surface. A row of protective gear hangs on a series of pegs, looking like slumping spacesuits. Some of the team moves towards them while others take a few steps back.

"Don't worry," Captain Maria Montoya says, "there's no radioactivity here. But you're going to learn how to battle terrorists wearing those suits. It's not easy being an effective fighting machine when you look like a cross between a marshmallow and the Michelin Man."

Most of the team laugh, but Shadrach and Sookie Ringer only smile.

They know the safety of the South African Nuclear Energy Corporation's research center at Pelindaba will become their job, joined by their friend, Major Bootie van Zale, on whose small farm they will live.

"You will also learn how to disarm a dirty bomb," Captain Montoya tells the CWMD team.

They walk through a well-equipped laboratory where crew members in radioactive protective gear carry suitcases that everyone imagines are dirty bombs.

The middle of the lab is a room encased in clear, five-inch thick plastic sheeting with a waterproof metal entry and a sealed exit hatch on its top.

Seawater floods the 20x20x20-foot room. It comes through a series of punch holes in the hull of the *S.S. Nomad*. Each hole is one inch in diameter. A button on the bulkhead can seal them. When open, large pressure cylinders pump air into the 8000 cubic-foot chamber, maintaining the water level.

"All of you will have a chance to work on dirty bombs in what my chief engineer likes to call his Houdini Room," Captain Maria Montoya says. "Nobody has drowned in there, at least not yet, although some of the Navy SEALs have enjoyed close calls."

She smiles at General Mac McKlane's team of warriors, adding, "I'm not joking."

She leads the group around the thick, clear chamber. Some of the team knock hard on it as they pass. It hurts their knuckles, but it makes no sound

They continue picking their way through more laboratory equipment and finally come to a shallow lake in the hold of the *S.S. Nomad*.

So far, Mac's team has walked the distance of four football fields.

"Welcome to Kariba and the *Blue Nile Dreamship*," Captain Maria Montoya says. A boat floats on the shallow surface of the lake. Several members of the team reach down to touch the water expecting it to feel rubbery. It is pure water, with no salty taste.

"Most of you know that Zimbabwe used to be called Rhodesia," the captain continues, "named after Cecil John Rhodes, a British businessman, mining magnate, a politician in southern Africa, and a girl's best friend."

The group looks confused at the final three words.

"He was the founder of the De Beers diamond mines," Captain Montoya explains. She repeats the slogan, "Diamonds are a girl's best friend." Then she adds: "Rhodes was also a white supremacist and a British imperialist in a nation where most people were black. To his death, and even in his last will, he continued to maintain that the Anglo-Saxon race was the first race in the world."

"I guess that didn't work out so well in Africa," Samuel Nelson says.

"No, it did not," Captain Montoya says. She is a woman of color herself, born and raised in Puerto Rico before attending the Naval Academy, and she enjoys both history and science. She says, "Paleoanthropologists have found fossilized bones and stone tools dating back millions of years. The skeletons and rocks prove that the Olduvai Gorge in the great rift valley in Tanzania was the true cradle of civilization. It was not Britain, not Rome, Greece, Persia, and most certainly not White."

Captain Montoya explains that after the fall of Rhodesia and its rebirth as Zimbabwe, the nation once called "the Ireland of southern Africa" became one of the most impoverished and ruthless tribal societies on the continent.

"For 30 years, Robert Gabriel Mugabe ran Zimbabwe as a black nationalist, a Marxist, and a brutal dictator," the captain says. "The corruption he left behind is a magnet, a land of opportunity for the violence of ISIS."

General Mac McKlane tells the team that Zimbabwe is famous for the Victoria Falls and fishing for freshwater sharks in the Zambezi river. However, American intelligence sources have identified the Blue Nile Dreamship on Lake Kariba as a likely soft target for a terrorist attack. Once captured and under the control of ISIS, they will try to blow up the Kariba Dam, drowning much of Southern Africa.

heartbeats

There are men with weapons in the forest above Chimala, and General McKlane's team does not know who they are. He nods to Samuel Nelson, who points at the glint of metal behind a thick tree in the forest.

Samuel says, quietly and distinctly:

"Advance and be recognized."

He prepares for gunfire, as does the entire team crouched behind boulders and broken trees for protection.

A voice says: "Joseph Escott, Navy SEAL, serial number 3028458. There are three of us, one seriously wounded, four others killed fighting the terrorists at the Mission hospital. They did not drown in the flash flood. The terrorists murdered them along with every other patient in the hospital. We fought our way out before the deluge."

"Welcome home, Escott,' General Mac McKlane says, still crouching for protection and signaling his team to do the same. The man called Joseph Escott could easily be a terrorist speaking excellent English and reading numbers off of the dog tags of a dead Navy SEAL.

Four men step into sight, one of them in a dead man's carry on the shoulders of a Marine Raider. Mac's team steps forward and helps the wounded man to the ground. Sharonda examines him, ripping off his camo teeshirt and chest armor. The Marine Raider's wound is on the side of the chest, and he has lost a lot of blood. She rolls him over and sees the exit wound in his back, larger than the bullet's entry hole.

"How am I doing, Doc?" he asks with a weak voice. He knows Sharonda. He has met her at the Chimala Mission Hospital previously. He knows she is part of their operation.

"We're getting you back to the hospital," she says.

Mac McKlane looks at her and says, "That might be a fight worth having."

After listening to Mac and Samuel and Holly, they slowly spread out in the forest above Chimala, a force of 21 men and women, one seriously wounded, representing the best warriors in America.

The terrorists are easy to spot out in the open. They do not know how many of them are hidden in houses or inside the Chimala Clinic. Mac raises one finger, pointing right and left along his battle line at the edge of the forest. The finger signal passes down the line.

Because their weapons have suppressors, no sound other than a "pop" is heard from each sniper at the farthest edges of the antiterrorist warriors watching their ISIS targets. But the song of the bullet at its objective is loud as it breaks the sound barrier in its flight. It is a long shot. One man misses. A woman, shooting on the left, hits her mark, and a terrorist stumbles backward, dead before he hits the ground.

The man who misses quickly calibrates his scope and fires again. His target drops dead.

He pulls a twenty-dollar bill out of his pocket, and it passes along the jagged line in the forest until it reaches the woman who did not miss on her first shot. She takes it without smiling. Now, they are all busy shooting.

"They're like ants," Holly says as the ISIS fighters swarm around fallen comrades. They, too, die as a rain of death comes out of the forest. Their weapons' suppressors are far enough away to remain undetectable as their gunfire explodes through Chimala.

Some terrorists start shooting at the baobab tree, where the old leopard died after killing one of their leaders. It does not take their rapidly diminishing forces long to jump into trucks and head southeast, out of Chimala, escaping from the hail of extraordinarily accurate gunfire.

A white Toyota with a 50-caliber machine gun welded in its truckbed suddenly fills with a crowd of ISIS soldiers fleeing from the Chimala Mission.

One straggler left behind quickly dies as the truck races for the bridge crossing the river, firing wildly at nothing. A withering crossfire focuses on the truck as the flood-ravaged bridge collapses.

Terrorists try to swim in the river, but they quickly start floating.

Sharonda looks at her Navy SEAL patient, Joseph Escott. "What's your blood type," she asks.

'0-Positive, Ma'am." Nobody is wearing dog tags.

As soon as they get to the hospital, a dozen men and women are lined up, ready to donate their blood to Joseph Escott. Sharonda cleans his wounds and closes up his torn chest. Then she walks through the clinic.

All the patients are dead.

The cruelty of the hospital slaughter is videotaped, encrypted, and sent back to Roberta Macumber in the states. Several Navy SEALs cross the river to videotape the funeral pyre next to the schoolyard. The torrential rains have not washed away the bodies recognizable as children. The grownups in the stack of burnt bodies are probably teachers who Sharonda knows.

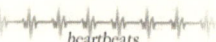

The Tanzanian Ambassador to the United Nations demands to show America's aggression to the Security Council. They have photographs of the culprits, prominent among them George McKlane III, a director at America's Homeland Security.

McKlane's picture dominates the chamber's video system screen, together with Samuel Nelson and several military men and women behind him. It's a still shot, apparently taken at the ceremony returning the Tree of Life to Tanzania, although the sculpture does not appear in the photo on the screen.

The Tanzanian Ambassador tells his United Nations colleagues: "This war criminal is a Colonel in the United States Marine Corps, the leader of a marauding band of mercenaries killing innocent villagers in the Southern Highlands of Tanzania. They are all professional soldiers. They wish to overthrow my country and trample upon the sovereignty and dignity of our great nation." He puts as much anger into his words as possible, sitting back into his chair with a scowl.

The American Ambassador to the UN leans into her microphone and says, without anger or malice: "Actually, he's a Brigadier General, Ambassador Kumangi, and I want to thank you for setting up all of the audio-video equipment for your unimpressive show of dishonesty."

"I will not listen to your false lies and fabrications," the UN Ambassador to Tanzania says. His English is perfect. He graduated from Yale University.

"Then, perhaps others will listen to the truth," the American Ambassador to the UN says.

Roberta Macumber, sitting behind the American ambassador, hands her a flash drive. An assistant plugs it into the computer equipment currently showing a smiling General George McKlane III, usually called Mac by people who know him at Homeland Security.

General McKlane is shaking the hand of a sullen Tanzanian president.

"This first video shows what the General calls 'friendly fire' from the Tanazinian Air Command, which bombed his Black Hawk helicopter on the ground when it landed in the Buhoro Flats in Tanzania's Southern Highlands."

At first, the screen shows a wide-angle shot of Tanzania's Buhoro Flats, and then it focuses on four Shenyang F-7 jets coming in low and dropping napalm on a Black Hawk. They also fire rockets that stampede wildlife.

"We believe that Chinese pilots flew at least two of the MiG-21 lookalikes. The jets are called Shenyang F-7s. A year ago, they were virtually grounded and useless."

The Chinese Ambassador stares at her, deadpan and unwilling to enter into the discussion.

The American Ambassador shows a lineup of Shenyang F-7s in a photograph used by the Tanzanian Air Command to show its state of readiness.

"According to our intelligence and first-hand accounts, not a single one of these planes, all made in China, were airworthy a year ago," the Ambassador says, smiling at the Chinese ambassador.

He does not smile back.

"General McKlane and his men were not in the Black Hawk when the pilots dropped napalm on it," the American Ambassador says, continuing the attack video.

The Shenyang F-7s turn over the Buhoro Flats and then fly back towards the camera. The photographer goes to slow motion on the Motorola Encrypted phone video at this point, killing the sound as the Tanzanian planes approach in a widening pattern.

The Chinese MiG-21s slowly soar over the edge of the flatlands above the Buhoro Flats.

Four smoke trails follow them to their destruction.

The Tanzanian Ambassador is on his feet, shouting: "This is an act of WAR, a blatant and obvious act of WAR." He keeps screaming this and shaking his fist until he hears a collective gasp from the chambers. He takes his eyes off the American delegation and looks at the screen.

He sees a pile of badly burned bodies, a few men and women, but for the most part, children. Someone has stacked the bodies like wood in a funeral pyre on what looks like a soccer field. Red five-gallon gasoline cans sit a safe distance away from the humans stacked like cords of wood.

The American Ambassador says: "These are the people that General McLane and his troops were trying to save from slaughter by ISIS terrorists in the Southern Highlands of Tanzania, in the city of Chimala."

Without saying anything, she shows the battle of Chimala, cutting to the hospital filled with murdered patients, and then back to the fleeing ISIS troops in trucks heading south from the city. The black-robed men shoot randomly at civilians during their retreat, killing many, including children. A pickup truck filled with terrorists collapses off the bridge over the Chimala River, and a smattering of applause, short and faint, occurs in the chambers of the United Nations.

"If the honorable ambassador of Tanzania would like copies of these videos to verify their authenticity, we will make them available immediately."

The American ambassador talks to an empty chair.

Everyone watches as the Tanzanian ambassador and his entourage exit the chambers.

The Chinese Ambassador remains in his seat, staring at the American Ambassador.

heartbeats

"You gotta hit a lot harder than that," Samuel says, sending Sharonda sprawling on the canvas of the oversized boxing ring on the *S.S. Nomad* as it travels towards South Africa.

They both have heavily padded pugil sticks used to hone their face-to-face combat capabilities.

Samuel has never hit Sharonda before in her life.

She shakes off the shock of what just happened to her. She reaches down and picks up her pugil stick, slowly circling a smiling Samuel.

"You bastard," she says.

"I'm saving your life, sweetheart. You might not ...."

She starts to thrust the pugil stick at his chest, quickly draws it back, and then she swivels 360 degrees, extending the stick as far as possible. She hits a home run on the side of his head. He falls, seemingly out cold.

Outside the boxing ring's ropes, Mac McKlane says: "I told him to wear protective headgear."

Sharonda is on her knees, cradling Samuel's head. He opens his eyes.

"Oh, thank God," she says, "I thought I killed ...."

Suddenly Samuel Nelson has her in a chokehold. She flails her arms, tries to bite him, reaches for his crotch to hurt him badly, managing a gentle squeeze that makes Samuel laugh. She is infuriated, trying to rip his hair out, treating him more gently than Sophia, their monkey, picking at imaginary bugs. Sharonda can't do anything.

She relaxes, hoping he thinks she's passing out, but he increases the pressure, unfooled.

She sags into unconsciousness.

Very quickly, an Army Ranger is at her side with oxygen. A Navy SEAL and a Marine Raider, a woman, hold her down as she recovers.

Samuel stands in a neutral corner.

Mac McKlane enters the ring next to Samuel.

"In a competitive fight, I would raise Samuel's hand and declare him the winner, but this is not a contest."

Sharonda, sitting up, looks like she wants to fight Samuel again immediately.

She wobbles to her feet, reaching for her pugil stick. The female Marine Raider kicks it out of her reach.

Sharonda is angry.

"This is life or death," McKlane says. "You are here to learn how to survive." He looks at Sharonda. "Calm down," he says. "Your husband has taught you something."

"He's a lot bigger than I am," she says.

"What did you think of the chokehold?" he asks her.

"He's a lot bigger than I am," she repeats.

"Size does not matter," Mac tells her.

"It does when you're as big as him." She spits out her mouthguard in the direction of Samuel.

"Okay, you're done for today, Sharonda. Tomorrow, you will put a chokehold on Samuel. I promise that you'll bring him down to size."

"I can't wait," Sharonda says, glaring at the loving husband who almost kills her.

"So, do we go after the bastards?" Holly asks Mac as she looks at the devastation of the city of Chimala. The clinic and the school remain because they're on high ground, but the Chimala River has scooped out the middle of the city, sending its broken pieces into the Buhoro Flats.

They hear a distant gunshot echo from the Buhoro Flats. They almost don't notice it.

"I guess we go out into the flats first," Mac says.

Vultures and hyenas have already started to work on the flood's aftermath.

Mac tells one of the Army Rangers sergeants to take a squad of men and women to go out there to see who's shooting what in the Buhoro Flats.

"It could be someone just protecting themselves," he says. "And it might also be some of the ISIS terrorists who know how to swim. If it's the latter, treat them with extreme prejudice. We don't have the time, the desire, or the resources to drag around a bunch of prisoners."

An hour passes, during which they remove the dead patients from the Chimala Mission and replace them with live ones hurt either by the storm or the shooting exit of the ISIS terrorists in the town.

Many people are thrown into the Chimala River, not by the American forces, but by neighbors who consider this the most efficient and quickest way to bury the dead. The cemetery and two funeral homes in Chimala are part of the debris washed out into the Buhoro Flats.

The Americans hear a series of shots from where the Army Ranger's squad went to investigate. They return with a very wrinkled, muddy man carrying an old M-1 carbine on his shoulder as if he's in a parade.

"He was in a tree, pretty much surrounded by three lions when we got out there," the Ranger says. "I think he was down to his last bullet. That's an old M-1 he's using."

Samuel Nelson speaks to him in Swahili for a while, then he turns to Mac and says: "He fought against the Germans in East Africa during the Second World War. The British let him keep his rifle. He says he won a lot of medals, but they're gone, along with his wife and children and home."

Sharonda says, "He looks like someone we know."

General McKlane salutes the old, mud-covered soldier.

The wrinkled man snaps to attention and salutes him in return, not shadowing his eyes like an American but showing his palm, a perfect British soldier acknowledging an officer. They take him to the hospital.

Fubar follows behind him, and he reaches down and pats the dog several times. They are old friends, and suddenly Sharonda realizes who the man is.

"You're the gentleman who gave us Fubar when we came to Chimala," Sharonda says as they enter the hospital. "I'll be damned. You own the land where we live. It's hard to recognize you all caked with mud."

She speaks to him in Swahili.

His name is Kibwe Khamisi.

"You were born on a Thursday," Sharonda says, which is the meaning of his last name. He smiles at her with perfect teeth, all of which are his own.

The old soldier says that life and the flood have erased his first name from his life.

Sharonda knows that Kibwe means "blessed." She puts a hand on his shoulder.

He speaks of his being alone, with no reason left to live. Sharonda tells him she wants him to take the dog back. He smiles at her, but just a little, and he agrees.

"And you're going to live in the home which we built on your land," she says, "because I'm leaving, and I want you to take care of it for my husband and me."

The soldier's chin quivers at this generosity.

"But who will teach the schoolchildren to speak English," he asks in Swahili.

"There are no schoolchildren left," she says.

They are silent for a while, looking at the floor of the hospital. "Children will be born," the old man finally says in perfect English. Then, speaking almost as if he was British, he adds: "I will teach them your language, and I will do it well. You must leave your schoolbooks with me."

"I will," Sharonda says, surprised at his confidence that he can become a good teacher and shocked at the ease with which he speaks British English.

"There a bullet hole in the roof of your new home, and you have to fix that," Sharonda says.

The man nods. "Bullets do that to metal roofs."

"You have a brand new bathroom, too," Samuel says. "I just built it and a safe room closet."

Samuel looks at Fubar, asleep at Khamisi's feet. "How about the monkey?" he asks Sharonda.

"The monkey stays with us," she says as the old warrior smiles, leaving the hospital for his new home and life.

The scruffy dog, which never barks, trails after him, turning once to look at Sharonda and Samuel before trotting after his original master.

"Sophia stays with us," Sharonda repeats. The baby baboon considers Sharonda as her mother. Sharonda thinks Sophia is her child. Samuel knows this and wonders why he would ask her such a stupid question.

The monkey may grow out of the relationship.

Sharonda will not.

Mac McKlane walks into the hospital. "How many nurses are left?" he asks.

"Three," Sharonda says. "And they're all good."

"So, you will come with us," Mac says.

"Yes, of course. We planned on it, Mac. We already gave away our house to Kibwe Khamisi, the old soldier your men saved. I have the feeling that you're going to need a fully qualified doctor with your team, and I'm the only person who fits that description, although you have lots of medics."

They call it "Hell's Run." It is a name that sticks long after the dirt and gravel road turns into a smooth, paved connection between Dar es Salaam on the eastern coast of Tanzania and

Lusaka, the capital of land-locked Zambia, a city with a population of over 2.5 million people.

For many years in the mid-1960s, Hell's Run becomes the only way Zambia can survive.

Huge trucks carry thick, rubber bladders of petrol off-loaded in Dar es Salaam, racing down the rutted, dirt road to Lusaka, over 1,200 miles away. They transport payment in copper on the return trip back to Dar es Salaam.

Rhodesia does not permit any fuel to reach Zambia by rail through the ports of South Africa.

The prime minister of Rhodesia, Ian Smith, is forced to ally his country with his southern neighbor, a nation in the white nationalist grip of apartheid.

Ian Smith issues a UDI, a Unilateral Declaration of Independence for Rhodesia, which has governed itself as a British territory since 1923.

Rhodesia's UDI made it a sovereign state on November 11, 1965.

Ian Smith and the white population of Rhodesia feel betrayed by the colonial government of the United Kingdom and its policies of decolonization, made famous by British Prime Minister Harold MacMillan's speech about "The Winds of Change" blowing across the continent of Africa. With a white population of only five percent, the principle of "No Independence Before Majority Rule" dooms Rhodesia.

The UK, the Commonwealth, and the United Nations all declare Rhodesia to be an illegal state.

The United Nations imposed its first sanctions ever on the breakaway colony. Smith's regime has no choice but to fall into the arms of South Africa, even though many white

Rhodesians disagree with the white nationalism and cruelty of apartheid.

Zambia, landlocked, suddenly has no fuel to run its industries, an unintended and immediate result of the United Nations' embargo. The Zambian economy, growing at 7.7 percent, suddenly plunges to almost zero.

Hell's Run is born, a dusty and exceedingly dangerous traffic jam of petrol lorries that try to keep Zambia alive.

The drivers get paid for each delivery of petrol bladders on flatbeds into Zambia. They're paid by the trip, not hourly, so they push themselves to the limit. Many fall asleep. Dozens of burned-out trucks border Hell's Run.

In some cases, vehicles explode when tracer rounds streak into the petrol bladders.

Rhodesian special operatives want Zambia's industries to starve to death. They sneak across the borders of Malawi and Zambia into the Southern Highlands of Tanzania. Rhodesian snipers turn dozens of trucks into fireballs. The Bush Wars are born.

Over the next 12 years, guerilla warfare engulfs Rhodesia as its government fights two communist-backed black groups.

During that time, the Chinese start building a pipeline from Dar es Salaam to Ndola in Zambia. They also lay down tracks for the Tanzania-Zambia Railway.

Zambia owes a massive obligation to China, which amounts to almost 20 percent of its total public debt.

When Rhodesia dies and is reborn as Zimbabwe, Hell's Run is an all-weather tarmac highway with a new name, the Great North Road.

The burned-out trucks are long gone, replaced by herds of elephants, giraffes, wildebeest, antelope, and gawking tourists in air-conditioned buses.

But many people still call it by its original name.

"We take Hell's Run to Mbeya," Mac tells his team. "We should have a pretty good satellite shot of the area in about twenty minutes. It will be a live shot, so let's see if we can spot ISIS's movements and hiding places."

They move into an operating theater in the Mission Hospital, and a technician hooks their military computer into a large screen on the wall.

Mac sends an encrypted message to Roberta Macumber in Washington. "Online and waiting."

A Navy SEAL shouts into the hospital" "We got a bird coming in."

Suddenly, everyone hears the faint sound of a helicopter approaching.

On the large screen hanging on the hospital wall, America's satellite shows a massive amount of military hardware on Hell's Run, outside Morogoro and heading east-southeast for Iringa.

The bottom of the screen shows a message from Roberta Macumber. It says, "Get out of there, Mac. Do it immediately. Tanzania has declared War on the US, and our administration has not yet returned the favor."

"Back into the mountains," General McKlane tells his troops. "And do NOT shoot your weapon unless your life depends on it. Sharonda, show us the way."

The team of 21 Americans, one wounded but walking, fades into the forest beyond the sawgrass bordering Chimala.

Not a single shot occurs.

A Navy SEAL petty officer photographs the landing of the only other helicopter left in the Tanzanian Air Command, the Bell 206L-1 Long Ranger II helicopter based at the Ngerengere Air Force Base in Morogoro.

It lands in a cloud of dust in the center of the school's football field, 50 yards from the funeral pyre of men, women, and children.

Nobody in the helicopter gets out until local Tanzanian troop carriers from Mbeya safely surround it.

Several of the vehicles have machine guns bolted in their truck beds.

Then the pilot, the head of Tanzania's Air Command, walks down the steps, swivels, and stands at attention as the helicopter blades wind down. He salutes the president of Tanzania, who follows him with some difficulty because of his weight.

"It's an easy shot, Mac," a Marine Raider sniper next to General McKlane says.

"No shooting."

"Nobody will even hear it," the Raider says.

They have suppressors on all their weapons, although they still make a pretty good pop when fired.

They make a lot more noise when they break the sound barrier at their objective.

"No shooting, and that's an order," Mac says.

At the helicopter, a thousand yards away, an American flag is handed to the president.

Some soldiers quickly dig a hole near the burned bodies on the football field.

The senior officer of the air command takes the flag from the president and stands on it as his troops from Mbeya tip a large metal flagpole into the ground.

They fill the hole with concrete.

The senior officer takes his finger and writes "1959" in the soft cement. Then they run the American flag up the pole.

"That was the year the American Peace Corps opened this school," the head of Tanzania's Air Command says in the schoolyard.

"Very smart," the President says, and the Commander gives him a sharp salute.

From the mountains, they record a very clear close-up of what just happened.

Several Tanzanian military cameramen and some photojournalists take pictures that appear as front-page news throughout Tanzania that evening and the following day, with headlines of **"Wamarekani wachinja watoto wa Tanzania."**

"Americans Slaughter Tanzania's Children."

No mention of terrorism or ISIS appears in any of the news stories.

A rogue force from the United States, military mercenaries wandering throughout the Southern Highlands, caused the deaths.

Tanzanians throwing rocks and Molotov cocktails surround the American Embassy in Dar es Salaam at 686 Old Bagamoyo Road. They rattle its unguarded gates. They toss dozens of Molotov cocktails over the reinforced-cement wall around the embassy. The military staff backs off with strict orders not to shoot unless people come over the fence.

The Oysterbay Police Station and Barracks nearby orders Tanzanian snipers to its rooftop. Still, they have no clear vision over the tall walls of the U.S. Embassy, although American snipers on top of the embassy do have them in their crosshairs.

In the capital of Tanzania, Dodoma, 281 miles west of Dar es Salaam, the government officially declares war on America. However, it remains meaningless until a Formal Declaration Of War reaches the American Ambassador.

It is the second time in its history that Tanzania has used a Formal Declaration of War. The first was the Kagera War, more commonly known as the Uganda-Tanzania War, a nine-month battle that led to the fall of the Ugandan dictator, Idi Amin. In that war, 373 Tanzanians died. Idi Amin killed over 300,000 of his people during his eight years of tyranny.

At the United Nations in New York City, the Tanzanian Ambassador of that organization tries to present his nation's Formal Declaration of War to the American Ambassador to the United Nations. She holds up her hands in a sign of helplessness.

She tells the Tanzanian delegation that it must hand its Declaration of War to the American Ambassador, currently trapped in the Embassy compound in the coastal city of Dar es Salaam.

The Tanzanian delegation starts to chant the slogan of their nation, "*Uhuru na Umoja,*" which appears on the coat of arms of Tanzania. "Freedom and Unity." The entire delegation chants it with increasing passion.

The American Ambassador smiles at this. "Yes," she says, "*Uhuru na Umoja.*"

The Tanzanian delegation suddenly stops chanting and stares at her. She repeats herself. "*Uhuru na Umoja.*"

She leans into her microphone.

"I was born in Vermont, Ambassador Kumangi." the United States representative says. "We have the same, identical saying, Freedom and Unity, but in English. It became our state motto in 1778. I believe you stole it from us in 1961."

Confused, his delegation continues to chant "*Uhuru na Umoja*" for several minutes as an audio-video machine gets plugged into its socket in the center of the chamber.

Suddenly, Ambassador Kumangi shouts: "*Wamarekani wachinja watoto wa Tanzania.*" It takes a few seconds for the translation to reach everyone in the chambers.

"Americans Slaughter Tanzania's children."

"And this is the photo you showed yesterday," Ambassador Kumangi says. "Before your CIA photoshopped it." The funeral pyre of dead men, women, and children appear on the screen, with the translation of what he has just shouted as a title in bright red letters across the top of the screen: "Americans Slaughter Tanzania's Children." A large American Flag is frozen next to the carnage. Another shot shows the base of the flag with the date in cement.

"1959 was when the American Peace Corps built this school," the Tanzanian Ambassador says.

Once again, Roberta Macumber hands a flash drive to the American ambassador to the U.N.

The screen switches videos.

Everyone in the room watches a Bell helicopter land in the middle of the soccer field in Chimala.

They see the President of Tanzania stand among his troops as they dig a hole and plant the American flag next to the funeral pyre.

They see a man with his fingers in the cement poured into the hole that will support the flag.

He writes, "1959."

"*Uhuru na Umoja*," the American ambassador says. "I hope everyone here today dares to recognize the dishonesty of Ambassador Kumangi. And I hope we all have the courage, unity, and foresight to condemn and reject his nation's Declaration of War against the United States."

The lights in the chamber brighten.

Everyone watches the Tanzanian delegation deserting their seats and hurrying out of the UN chambers once again.

"Freedom and Unity," the American Ambassador says. "*Uhuru na Umoja.*"

heartbeats

In Chimala, several shots ring out, but not from Mac's troops climbing into the mountains. The sound comes from the north of the football field.

"That's an M-1," an Army Ranger says. "Best weapon we ever invented. If something goes wrong with it, you slap it on a tree, and it goes back to working perfectly."

The M-1 Carbine has a very distinctive sound.

"That's the guy we saved from the lions," a Navy SEAL says. "I guess he found some extra ammo."

"Kibwe Khamisi is shooting at the Tanzanian troops from our house," Sharonda says. "I think he somehow knows what's happening."

The firing stops after about 20 rounds.

From the mountainside, they watch the old warrior dragged out of Sharonda's brick home.

He shouts something into the house's open door, and suddenly, a dog, Fubar, streaks out and into the sawgrass.

"They're going to hang him on the tree in the back of the house," Sharonda says as she sees a man approaching the old soldier who is being kicked and rifle-butted on the ground. His executioner drags a long rope behind him.

He slowly creates a noose and puts it around the old soldier's head.

He tries to throw it over a high branch in the tree. It takes time before he finally throws it correctly.

Mac turns to the Marine Raider next to him and says: "Charlton Tremwallis says you're just as good as he is on the rifle range. Now you need to prove it."

"I'm not sure what you're saying," the woman says.

At the hanging tree, Tanzanian soldiers start to pull the Kibwe Khamisi to his feet as they are tugging on the rope around his neck.

It catches in the crook of the tree.

The terrorists loosen it and start all over again, with more people pulling.

"You've got one shot," the general says to the woman next to him. "I don't want to see that old man's feet jerking when they get him up in the air. I do not want to see him suffer for a single second."

She has already laid prone on the ground.

She takes an exaggerated deep breath.

She adjusts the scope.

She slowly squeezes the trigger.

The suppressor on her weapon goes "pop."

As the terrorists hoist the old soldier up, his body jerks, slumping from the impact of her bullet. The men trying to hang him drop the rope and scatter at the sharp sound of the shot, looking for cover.

The Marine Raider shooter, prone at Mac's feet, a woman of color, says, "Now he's dancing with angels."

"Yes," Mac replies. "Sharonda, I want you to send that man's name."

"Kibwe Khamisi."

"I want Roberta Macumber to find out everything about him. He won a bunch of medals fighting the Germans in the Second World War. They had to be British medals. Find out what they were and why."

"On it."

"Did we get video on his lynching?" Mac asks.

"Yes, sir," a Marine Raider says. "Three different Motorola Encrypted phones, including the latest model."

"Don't edit out the kill shot," Mac says, "and encrypt it to Macumber along with Sharonda's request."

The helicopter blades start to turn on the Bell 206L-1 Long Ranger II helicopter slowly in the schoolyard. News of the unexpected death of the old soldier spreads quickly. Men fire random shots into the mountainside, nowhere near the position of Mac McKlane's team.

Surrounded by his soldiers, the Tanzanian President and the senior officer of the air command rush up the helicopter steps, quickly closing the drop-down entry to the ship. The co-pilot bangs on the door as the blades whirl faster to liftoff speed. He cannot board the Bell 206L-1 Long Ranger II helicopter.

They are going to leave him behind.

In the cockpit, the senior officer shouts to the president of Tanzania as he slowly lifts off from the ground: "Surface-to-air missiles shot down the Shenyang F-7s, Mister President."

Outside the helicopter's left side bubble window, the pilot watches his co-pilot raising his hands in frustration. He throws a rock at the pilot. Why has he been left behind?

The senior officer of Tanzania's Air Command keeps the helicopter low, almost touching the gravel and tarmac of Hell's Run, swerving around a tourist bus and several cars. He remembers some of the burning trucks that gave the Great North Road its nickname when he was a young officer. He does not want to join them.

Sitting next to him, in the co-pilot's seat, he sees the white knuckles and sweating face of his Commander in Chief, the President of Tanzania, who cannot fly a helicopter.

"*Haraka,*" the Tanzanian President says. "*Haraka na haraka.*" "Faster and faster."

The pilot waits for the "beep-beep" warning of an incoming surface-to-air missile.

Chapter 5

During the *S.S. Nomad*'s third week at sea, everyone learns more about nuclear reactors than they want. It starts with a popular television series about Chernobyl, a reasonably accurate documentary.

It moves to the nuclear disaster at Three Mile Island, the most significant accident in America's commercial nuclear power plant history.

Scientists shut down one of Three Mile Island's two cooling towers after releasing radioactive coolant into the atmosphere.

It takes over fourteen years to clean it up at the cost of almost a billion dollars.

"Consider the utter devastation in August of 1945 at Hiroshima and Nagasaki," Captain Maria Montoya tells the assembled men and women seated next to what her chief engineer likes to call his Houdini Room.

Mac McKlane says, "Radiation has been scaring the people who own it since splitting atoms entered our vocabulary. One United States President was part of the radiation cleanup crew at the Chalk River nuclear facility in Ontario, Canada."

The group looks puzzled. Nobody can remember or even imagine a president who was a member of a nuclear radiation cleanup team. "He was a young lieutenant in our Navy, a nuclear engineer," Captain Montoya says.

Everyone's face remains blank.

"His name was Jimmy Carter, the 39th President of the United States."

"Is that for real?" one man asks.

"Yes, it is," Captain Montoya says. "Now, all of you are going to get a shot at walking in the footsteps of President Jimmy Carter."

"Damned," a Navy SEAL says. "I should have voted for him. I thought he was just a peanut farmer."

Captain Montoya smiles and opens a suitcase in front of her, similar to the ones that everyone saw being carried back and forth on the first day they visited the training sites in the *S.S. Nomad*'s hold.

Next to the suitcase is a glass of water.

The captain holds up a yellow pill, and because most people can't see it, she tells them: "When you take this pill, you have about five minutes before you pass out. The pill will not kill you, but it represents the number of minutes you have to disable a dirty nuclear bomb. Underwater. Which is where both you and it will probably be."

"What if it was a real dirty bomb?" a Marine Raider asks the captain.

"You would suffer from severe radiation poisoning if the bomb went off. You would never know it because you'd be dead from the explosion. And so would probably hundreds of thousands, perhaps millions of other people."

"So you're telling us that this is a suicide mission," an Army Ranger asks.

The captain scans the faces of all the men and women seated before her.

"Not if you disable the bomb."

"But it's a dirty bomb," the same man asks.

"They're quite beautiful," Captain Montoya says. She reaches into the suitcase and pulls out a large, gleaming, silver ball with a six-inch radius.

She lets it drop on the table with a thud. It slowly rolls to the edge and starts to fall. None of the men or women move except for the Army Ranger asking questions. He catches it with both hands just before it hits the deck. It's lighter than he thought.

"Nice catch," the captain says. "Most of you know it's not unstable like nitroglycerin. It's like C4 or any plastique explosive you carry into battle. You're all demolition experts. You understand this stuff. It needs a detonator."

She holds up what looks like a small TV remote.

"If I press this button, that dirty bomb explodes, and everyone within five miles of it eventually dies. The lucky ones meet their maker immediately."

She smiles at the Ranger.

She presses the button.

General Mac McKlane and his small army start to climb back up to the edge of the flatlands above Chimala. There's a lot of noise coming from the bushes at one point, and everyone crouches at the approaching sound.

"Hold your fire," Sharonda shouts.

Fubar races towards her, immediately collapsing at her feet. The dog wags its tail four times and drops his head.

The monkey on Sharonda's shoulder jumps down and starts to play with the dog's ears. Then Sophia begins to meticulously groom Fubar's back, finding both real and imaginary bugs.

"Uh, does that hound have narcolepsy?" a Navy SEAL asks. The dog has fallen into a deep sleep. "That's a very scruffy animal," he adds.

Samuel steps forward and picks up the dog like a sack of potatoes, throwing him around his shoulders.

"He never sleeps at night," Samuel says. "only during the day, unless he's escaping a threat."

"Fubar sleeps when he feels safe," Sharonda says.

"Fubar, good name," most of the Navy SEALs say. They all know what the acronym stands for.

"But he's not really 'fucked up beyond all recognition,'" Samuel says.

"He wakes up if there's any danger," Sharonda says. "He puts his head on the ground and says, '*fluuf, fluuf, fluuf* with flapping lips."

Very few of the Navy SEALs, Army Rangers, or Marine Raiders believe this.

"He saved my life twice that way," Sharonda says.

"Well, he has a perfect name," the Navy SEAL repeats. He will discover the value of Fubar later, but for now, he watches Samuel shoulder the dog in a fireman's carry, continuing the climb towards the flatlands.

The dog, he notices, is sound asleep. *That has to be narcolepsy*, he thinks.

Just before they reach the flatlands, two Shenyang F-7s roar overhead, flying low. Fubar awakes, jumps to the ground, lies flat, and starts his *"fluuf, fluuf, fluuf."*

None of the general's team notices this because they are watching the planes.

The jets cannot see Mac's small army because they fly too fast. Mac's men and women have not yet started to march on the Flatlands. The team hugs its craggy border. They are hard to spot in their camouflaged fighting gear.

On the general's orders, nobody has any electronic equipment working that might give away their position.

Mac asks the two men with the team's remaining Man-Portable Air Defense System surface-to-air missiles to join him, along with the Navy SEAL petty officer holding one of the team's combat flip-top computers.

"Give them a ten-second look at us," Mac says to the Navy SEAL. He boots the machine.

As the man counts out loud to ten, Mac's small army sees a group of black-clad terrorists about a mile east southeast, further out in the flatlands, waving large black flags at the jets.

ISIS warriors also climb up to the flatlands, perhaps anticipating the Americans' move, calling for air support in an expected battle.

The Shenyang F-7s drop no bombs on them, so they must communicate with the pilots.

Mac watches each of the two Shenyang F-7s separate in opposite directions.

They turn back towards Mac 20 seconds after the Navy SEAL turns off his military flip-top computer.

Mac says to the two men with the Stinger surface-to-air missiles: "Don't miss."

Two SAMs streak up toward the approaching Shenyang F-7s at Mach 2 speed, but they need to reverse course to find the planes' heat signature. They only have a range of 3.2 miles. At first, they seem to miss, stall, but then they spin and find their target.

Both planes explode in fireballs.

"Take cover," Mac shouts.

Even though the jets disintegrate over a mile away, their airspeed will send burning debris into the forest at the edge of the flatlands.

"The worst part is that ISIS now has a good idea of where we are," Samuel says as he stomps out a small fire. "And we have no surface-to-air missiles left."

Mac nods, but he does not think he has made a tactical mistake by eliminating the two Shenyang F-7s. He only counted 11 black-clad warriors signaling to the jets.

He says to Samuel: "I think the Tanzanians are running out of airplanes. And I'm willing to bet that our terrorist buddies have some useful weapons that we can borrow from their dead, cold hands."

Samuel nods but without smiling.

"Let's move halfway down the mountain," General McKlane tells his men. "And keep your eyes peeled for booby traps as well as bad guys. Remember that we operate with extreme prejudice. We take no prisoners."

An Army Ranger on point with Sharonda is about to cross a tripwire. He sees Fubar drop flat on the ground, "*fluuf, fluuf, fluuf.*" The Army Ranger almost continues because he believes he's witnessing narcolepsy, not a warning sign. Then he sees what looks like a thick black fishing line stretched a few inches above the ground. He holds up his fist, and every man and woman in the unit freezes.

A black shadow moves from behind a tree.

Three rifles go "phut."

The shadow drops to the forest floor, dead.

The Army Ranger traces the tripwire carefully to what looks like a Claymore mine; only the writing on it appears to be Chinese. He neutralizes the weapon, which could have killed at least six of his fellow soldiers and him.

"Good dog," he says to Sharonda. "Did you teach him that?" She shakes her head negatively.

"That's how he came to me from the old guy that gave him to us. It was the old warrior who fought for the British in World War II. I think he was a canine trainer."

"Dog's not that old," the Ranger says.

"No, but his trainer was. He's the old guy they hung in the tree behind my house."

Fubar has fallen sound asleep.

The Army Ranger picks up the dog gently in a fireman's carry, and they continue forward. Samuel says: "Thanks, sergeant."

The dead ISIS soldier, who looks like a teenager, contributes another .222 Sturmgewehr assault rifle to Mac's army, along with a few extra 30-round magazines taped together for battle.

However, none of their suppressors will fit the weapon, and it makes a lot of noise when fired.

"Might be a good decoy," Samuel says.

After moving quietly through the forest for ten more minutes, Mac has everyone halt. They have seen no other ISIS terrorists.

They will wait for darkness, an hour off. The team's night-vision equipment will tip any battle in their favor.

"But we have to watch for booby traps," Mac says. "You hear that, Fubar?" Many men and women smile and pat the dog, although he has fallen sound asleep at Sharonda's feet.

heartbeats

On Old Bagamoyo Road outside the American Embassy in Dar es Salaam, the police from the barracks across the street clear the way for Tanzanian government vehicles heading for the Embassy's locked gate.

The Tanzanian Ambassador to America has returned home to present the American Ambassador with an official Declaration of War.

He sits in one of two identical, bulletproof, black Mercedes. Nobody knows which one. On the roof of the American Embassy, a CIA sniper asks the person talking into his ear if he knows what the hell he's saying.

Suddenly, the Central Intelligence Agency head, whom the sniper has met several times in Washington D.C., talks in his ear with a gruff baritone voice.

The CIA sniper immediately recognizes him in an encrypted picture that fills a small square at the bottom of his cellphone's screen.

The orders are for real.

"Understood, sir," the sniper says. Both doors of the twin black vehicles open, and the Ambassador gets out of the second one.

The sniper puts the Tanzanian Ambassador in the crosshairs of his .22 long rifle.

The ambassador stands about 250 yards away. The sniper takes a deep breath, relaxes, and fires two shots in as many seconds.

His silenced rifle makes a pop-pop, and both of the men on his left and his right, each twenty paces away, hear it and react to what he has just done with puzzled faces. They are also in the CIA.

The Ambassador is dead before his knees hit the pavement. The sounds of the shots on the street are much louder than on the embassy's roof. It's because of the subsonic crack of the bullets. The Ambassador's tan, African tunic blossoms red.

The men protecting him are confident that the shots come from the rooftop of the American Embassy.

Still, suddenly people in the street start shouting that the Tanzanian soldiers have killed him. It is a coup d'état to overthrow the president who has murdered men, women, and children in Chimala.

Tanzanians are passing out photographs of the President smiling next to the funeral pyre on the schoolyard football field.

The Central Intelligence Agency's informants' fund supports the people making these accusations in the street, and most of them are longtime Central Intelligence Agency contacts. Several are agents themselves.

The sniper who killed the ambassador crawls over to the man on his left. Then he does the same to the one on his right. To each man, he plays a recording of the orders he received, captured on his cellphone.

They recognize the picture of the man on the screen. They, too, know the ill-tempered voice of the Director of the Central Intelligence Agency.

One sniper says: "Theirs not to make reply, Theirs not to reason why, Theirs but to do and die." The original sniper adds: "Into the valley of Death rode the six hundred."

Inspired by Alfred Lord Tennyson and disregarding the actual outcome of the Charge of the Light Brigade, the CIA snipers take a few shots at police officers and Tanzanians wearing military gear. It's not part of their orders, but they know what's happening on the street. They know the sounds of the gunshots reverberate beyond the embassy walls, not from their rooftop positions.

Suddenly, the police withdraw back into their barracks. The government vehicles race off after putting the dead ambassador in the black, bullet-proof Mercedes that drove him to his death.

As night falls, the streets remain clear. Nobody seems to know what is going on. The police stay in their barracks.

The truth finds an ignorant and comfortable home in deception, bloodshed, and silence.

heartbeats

The spaceman comes from nowhere. He lands a few miles inside of the fourth largest national park in Tanzania, near the village of Mikumi. He falls into a group of baobab trees, pinned in their broken, topmost branches.

A local guide is thrilled at showing the pride of over a dozen female lions in the baobab trees to a bunch of tourists from Minneapolis, Minnesota.

"You see," the guide tells the safari vacationers, "we have a much better chance of showing you lions in the wild than people who visit the Serengeti."

A headline on their glossy brochures touts the lion-spotting adventures and wild animal discoveries possible at the Mikumi National Park.

One of the tourists says: "Do you always bait your trees with spacemen?"

Near the top of one of the baobab trees, something looks like an astronaut, wearing a helmet and a flight suit. It is being clawed at by a lioness that perches on the tree's highest branches. She can't quite get a grip on the human being.

The guide is on his intercom to the camp's headquarters, and within minutes the tree is surrounded by park vehicles. The rangers have chased off all the lions, but not before the spaceman tumbles to the ground. One of the lionesses tries to drag him away, but gunshots chase her off.

"This has got to be the best safari I have ever been on," a man from Minneapolis says, and he's the recognized safari expert in the group, having taken more than a dozen trips to Kenya, Uganda, and Tanzania in the past 15 years.

The tourists' bus moves quickly away, although they see military and police vehicles with flashing lights and sirens heading toward's the spaceman near the baobab thicket.

In Dodoma, the capital of Tanzania, the president receives a phone call from the head ranger at the Mikumi National Park.

He almost does not take the call because he's busy with the debacle at the American Embassy in Dar es Salaam. The name "Massamungu" brings him to the phone.

With the device in his hand, he looks at his Chief of Defence Forces (CDF) and says: "I thought that Lieutenant Amadeus Massamungu was a spy for the Americans."

"He was not?" the CDF general asks. The president hands the phone to his CDF General, who talks to the head ranger and hangs up after about one minute.

"They found a pride of lions playing with his body and eating it in the Mikumi National Park," the president says.

The CDF general nods, but he says nothing.

"Lieutenant Amadeus Massamungu appears to have been thrown, like garbage, from the helicopter that General McKlane stole from us," the president says. He turns his attention to the head of Tanzania's Air Command.

"Do you have any news for me?"

"We have lost two more Shenyang F-7s, both piloted by the Chinese, Mr. President."

"How many do we have remaining?"

"None, sir, although we are working on consolidating the parts of four remaining planes."

"Then how many will we have?

"One, sir," he says.

The president hits him across the face with a leather baton. The man winces, almost falls, but steadies himself, saluting the president as blood trickles from his nose and a welt appears on his cheek.

He looks back at the CDF general, who also prepares himself for a lashing from the President.

"I want the body of Amadeus Massamungu brought to Dodoma," he says. "He will be awarded the Tanzania People's Defence Force Staybrite cap badge. We will parade his bravery before the entire world, and it will be at the expense of the Americans."

"Excellent, Mr. President," the CDF general says.

"I want an open casket in the center of Jamhuri Stadium, in Dodoma, not Morogoro, and I want every single one of its 10,000 seats filled."

"The lions may have made an open casket less than desirable," the CDF General says.

The president slaps his leather baton against his uniform. "But, I am sure we can restore his features to an acceptable level of bravery," the CDF General says.

The general has no idea if this is possible.

"Good," says the president. "Next to his open casket, on a royal blue pedestal, we will place the Golden Tree of Life created by his grandfather."

"Excellent, Mr. President," the head of Tanzania's Air Command says, still bleeding from his nose.

"Get to work on my jet," the president tells him. "We cannot defeat the Americans with propaganda. We need to kill them. We need to kill them all."

He looks at the CDF general.

"How many men do we have chasing these cowards in the southern highlands?"

"We have an infantry brigade, an armored brigade, and one mortar batallion either in the area or heading towards it."

"I want you to send another infantry brigade to the border we share with Malawi. That is where these cowards will try to escape."

"And Mozambique?" the head of Tanzania's Air Command asks.

The president looks as if he will belt the major general of the air command one more time. Instead, he scowls and says: "Mozambique is still underwater from Cyclone Idai. I do not think the Americans will try to swim to safety. Get to work on my air force, general."

heartbeats

Roberta Macumber puts out classified feelers for a World War II Tanzanian veteran named Kibwe Khamisi. She does not expect much, but three hours later, a senior CIA operative who is black and very large is sitting in front of her. His name is Colin Rafiki.

"What do you currently know about Kibwe Khamisi?" he asks.

He has a slight accent, but she cannot place it.

"Nothing," Roberta answers.

"That's good to hear," the man says, getting up to leave her office.

"He's dead," Roberta Macumber says.

The CIA agent sits back down.

"How?"

"He died fighting ISIS terrorists in a town called Chimala in the southern highlands of Tanzania."

"That was his home. That was where he lived for most of his extraordinary life."

"He fought them off with an old M-1 carbine until he ran out of bullets. He had been saved before that by my boss, Brigadier General John McKlane III, whom we call Mac. The flooding Chimala River washed Mr. Khamisi out into the Bahuutto flats along with most of the town. Mr. Khamisi was up in a tree fighting off lions."

"The Buhoro Flats," the CIA agent corrects her.

"Yes," she says. "I've never been there."

"What do you want to know about Kibwe Khamisi?"

"Well, anything you can tell us. We know, from Khamisi, that he fought against the Germans in East Africa in the Second World War."

"That's true. Kibwe also fought them in Italy."

"He told Mac's team that he'd won a lot of medals, but they and his home were all washed out in the river flood caused by Cyclone Kenneth."

"That's true, about the medals. I don't know much about that cyclone, although I do understand the devastation in Mozambique from the previous one, Idai."

Roberta Macumber asks Agent Colin Rafiki: "Did Kibwe Khamisi work for the CIA?"

The large black man with a faint, mysterious accent says: "Give me a few minutes. I have to make a phone call."

Colin Rafiki steps outside of her office and starts talking on his cellphone. Roberta turns on her decrypting device to watch the words of his conversation on her computer screen and perhaps even detect to whom he is speaking. All she sees is a bunch of bunny rabbits hopping around in a field of grass, eating carrots, and chasing small golden retriever puppies.

The man hangs up his phone, re-enters her office, and sits back down in front of her desk.

"Like the cute little bunny rabbits and golden puppies?" Colin Rafiki asks.

"You people scare the crap out of me."

"Yeah, I know. Sometimes we scare the crap out of ourselves, Assistant Director Macumber." He smiles. "Let's talk a little bit about Kibwe Khamisi. I know a lot about him for two reasons. Number one, I married his daughter. Number two, he saved my life once, long before I married his daughter."

"You have an accent, barely discernable," Macumber says, seeing if she can put him off guard.

"Yes, good ear. I grew up in Kenya. My first language, like Kibwe's, is Swahili." Colin Rafiki pauses.

"I think his English was better than mine because he graduated from Sandhurst in England."

"He was a British officer?"

"And very much a gentleman," the CIA agent says. "He won the Victoria Cross fighting with the Fifth Royal Gurka Rifles in Monte San Bartolo, in Italy, in 1944. I don't think any of his troops thought he was an African; they just thought his skin was a bit darker than theirs. He spoke the Nepali language perfectly, as well as Hindu, and, of course, Swahili and the King's English."

"We had no idea who we saved from the lions in the Buhoro Flats."

"No, you didn't."

"General McKlane would like to know more about him. He watched Kibwe Khamisi as ISIS terrorists dragged him out of his home and lynched him on a tree in the back of it. We had two operatives living in his home."

The CIA man nods.

"What will you tell his daughter, your wife?"

The man lifts one hand off the chair he's sitting in with a cavalier movement, which Macumber finds both cold and unexpected.

"I guess I'll tell her to say 'hello' to him. She died a long time ago."

Roberta sees his eyes dampen, and she feels terrible about misreading his offhand reaction.

Just as quickly, she realizes that the man is analyzing her emotions correctly, almost like a doctor of psychiatry.

"So," he says, "we have some valuable assets in Tanzania, Mozambique, and Malawi that can help you and General McKlane.

They both stare at one another.

Then Colin says: "I need to know what you are doing there. From the looks of it so far, you have almost managed to get Tanzania to declare war on us, which is fine by me. I'm from Kenya. But you need to fill me in on some of the other details of your operation."

"How did Kibwe Khamisi save your life?"

"Ah. Do you know what Cane Rats are?"

"Not really. Are the rats old? Do they use canes?"

Colin Rafiki laughs. Roberta thinks the sound is lovely, rich in its depth.

"No, they are enormous rats that forage on sugar cane, and they are delicious to eat, and they're as big as groundhogs. But they're rats, and the local tribes in Uganda, where I worked many years ago, won't eat them. So when the locals beat the sugar stalks and club the cane rats as they try to escape into the river, the local leader will ask his men to cut off some of their rat tails. Tribe members lay the cane rats out in rows, and the chief walks down the line with an ivory cane.

He says, 'rat, rat, no rat, no rat, rat, no rat.' The tribe can eat the ones with no tails.

"The first time I saw this, I also saw a boy swimming in the river. I jumped in to save him. As I'm dragging him back to shore, Kibwe Khamisi starts shooting at me. I'm just trying to save the kid. My first thought was that this guy was a horrible shot.

"Then suddenly, I realize he's not shooting at me. All the Cane Rats with tails are suddenly getting hurled into the water downstream from us.

"Kibwe Khamisi is shooting at the hungry Nile crocodiles that think me and the kid are lunch. One of them was shot twice in its open jaws just before it clamped the life out of the kid and me.

"Kibwe never stopped shooting until we dragged ourselves ashore. The chief grabs the boy, wrapping his arms around him. It was his son that I saved. And Kibwe Khamisi saved me."

"That's an amazing story."

"And true," Colin Rafiki says. "I was drunk in that village for three days on a somewhat undrinkable alcoholic beverage at the request of the chief. So, please fill me in on the details of your mission."

"I can't do that," Roberta Macumber says. "You know I can't. Just as you can't tell me how the Tanzanian Ambassador died just outside our embassy in Dar es Salaam when he tried to deliver his nation's Declaration of War."

The CIA man laughs again, and it's a beautiful sound, perhaps genuine, perhaps acting.

"I'm glad we're on the same side," he says.

"Me, too."

"Your unit in Chimala has destroyed the entire Tanzanian Air Force, except for a helicopter used by the president and four dead-on-the-airfield Shenyang F-7s."

Macumber nods.

"General McKlane does not know this. So tell him."

"Thank you," Roberta says. "I will."

"They are currently trying to patch together another Shenyang F-7 out of the four unserviceable ones they have in Morogoro, and they've almost finished the job."

"I'll pass that along," Macumber says. She decides that she likes Colin Rafiki.

"That plane will never get off the ground."

He smiles at Roberta Macumber, and then they are silent for a while.

Colin Rafiki says: "Abu Bakr al-Baghdadi is finally dead, but that makes ISIS more dangerous, not less."

"I agree," Macumber says.

"One of Abu Bakr al Baghdadi's fellow leaders is Tarad Muhammed al-Jarba, also known as Abu Muhammed al-Shimali. I guess he doesn't know if he comes from Jarba or Shimali, but it doesn't make much difference. He supposedly died in the al-Baghdadi raid, but it's not true. He's the ISIS African expert. He's the reason they're pushing into sub-Saharan regions. And we believe he's working with a lot of brilliant people."

"Thank you," Roberta says.

"The terrorists General McKlane fights against are a splinter group of ISIS, like all of them. You know they work bottom-up, not top-down. ISIS is entirely decentralized, just like a bunch of legitimate, successful corporations in America. But right now, none of them have money, and they're running out of weapons.

"The oil fields in northeast Syria are no longer under their control, and that was their primary cash crop. Your team needs to know that the terrorists you want to eliminate have no mortars, maybe a few grenade launchers, and no drones, not even simple ones. They have a lot of ancient assault rifles."

Macumber looks down at a note on her desk and says: "Sturmgewehr .222 assault rifles, made by the Nazis in the 1930s, and nowadays used mostly in The Lebanon."

The CIA agent seems impressed by this, but Macumber thinks it's probably an act.

"Here's what you must realize," the agent says. "If, after he eliminates the Chimala nest of ISIS terrorists, General McKlane tries to get out of Tanzania through Malawi, he's going to come up against a reasonably well-armed Tanzanian Infantry Brigade."

Macumber knows that the Tanzanians use the British structure, indicating as many as 5,000 armed combatants against Mac's tiny army. General McKlane and his men would never make it.

"Most of the brigade are untested transcripts, " Colin Rafiki says. "Tanzania still has a draft system, but you need to understand that its officers can make them shoot in the right direction. The officer corps is pretty good. They have seen action in the M23 Rebellion of 2013 and against the ADF in Uganda and the Congo. These wars are still going on. Many Muslim radicals work for the African Development Fund, and they have a typical decentralized connection to ISIS. They may even be making some deals to end their differences with the Sunnis and consolidate forces."

"Thank you," Macumber says.

The entire transcript is on her screen, with no bunny rabbits or labrador puppies.

'So why are you in Chimala?" the agent asks.

"Because our Homeland Securities Countering Weapons of Mass Destruction Division identified the Chimala Mission Hospital, one of the largest medical facilities in East Africa, as a practice run for several other sub-Saharan targets for ISIS. We intend to protect such targets in Africa, and General McKlane is my director at the CWMD section of Homeland Security."

"I wish I could have warned my stepfather, Kibwe, about Chimala being an ISIS target, but I don't think it would have made any difference. He just would have stocked up on more ammunition. He was 96 years old, and he could still run five miles, a truly amazing human being. How much damage did ISIS do in Chimala?"

She shows him the pictures of the funeral pyre of teachers and children and then the dead bodies of patients in the 200-room Chimala Mission Hospital.

Colin Rafiki has already seen the burned stack of children in African newspapers and secret American videotapes revealing the United Nation's closed sessions.

Macumber adds that Cyclone Kenneth did more damage to Chimala than the terrorists, probably with a much higher death toll.

Colin Rafiki sighs. "Do you have pictures of my stepfather's death?"

Macumber shows it to him, unedited, saying that a sniper in Mac's team shot Kibwe before they hanged him.

"Why the hell didn't you shoot the terrorists?"

Colin Rafiki appears angry.

"We were very far away. We took our best shot to make certain that your stepfather did not suffer."

She can tell that Colin does not accept this, and she feels his resentment.

She tells the CIA agent that they have a minimal force in Chimala.

"How many men have you lost so far?" he asks.

"We had a few military patients in the hospital killed by ISIS before they could get their weapons out from under the sheets of their beds. Three of them died. One should still be in the hospital, but he's gone up the mountainside with Mac's team. We now control the hospital. ISIS took off for Mbeya. Most of Mac's forces survived."

"How many troops on the ground?" His face shows anger, concealing nothing.

"The current count in the Southern Highlands is 21."

The number surprises the CIA agent, both because of its small size and its significant accomplishments.

He's no longer angry at the sniper who kills his stepfather.

He now understands the reason for it.

"Our total force in Africa is now 142 men and women, all either Navy SEALs, Marine Raiders, or Army Rangers."

"But McKlane's force in Chimala was only 21?"

"We have other objectives to protect."

"Can you share them with me?"

"Probably not."

"Is one of them the DeBeers diamond mine complex in Botswana?"

"No."

He stares at her.

"I will not lie to you, Colin Rafiki," Macumber says. "I did not have to show you the unedited version of Kibwe Khamisi's death. I did so because I think that you deserve that truth. DeBeers is not something we plan to protect. That would not be a critical sub-Saharan target in Homeland Security's opinion."

"Good," the agent says. "Because we will defend it with every tactical weapon we have, from eyes on the ground to bunker busters and UCAVs, combat drones, including the Reaper. The DeBeers diamond mines are where the terrorists think they can find a new source of money now that the Syrian oilfields are off-limits. If we have to bury the DeBeers complex, we will."

"I'm glad you're there."

"Buy some diamonds. Their price will probably go a lot higher pretty soon."

Roberta Macumber smiles and absently fiddles with the one-carat wedding ring she wears even though her husband died ten years earlier,

"You still don't want to share any of your other targets with me?"

"I can't without first talking to General McKlane," she says. "You know that, and the general is pretty busy getting his team out of Tanzania right now."

Agent Colin Rafiki types something on his cellphone, and an encrypted phone number appears on Roberta Macumber's screen. "Please give that number to the general along with whatever else you send him, and keep it for yourself," Agent Rafiki says. "The CIA has a lot of resources in southern and central Africa. Not as much as the Chinese, who distribute Pterodactyl drones everywhere they go. Those are very good for surveillance, by the way, as well as for airstrikes. We've reverse-engineered them, and they're almost as good as our Reapers. Anyway, a lot of our material and knowledge can help your team out of tight spots. Also, the Tanzanians have no Pterodactyl drones at the moment. They have no military drones other than a few four-propeller units which can drop a small bomb or do surveillance work. They're weaponized toys, not overly dangerous."

"Thank you, Colin," Roberta Macumber says, and the agent smiles at her use of just his first name.

They will work together, and they both know this. Colin and Roberta also realize they might have a hard time not liking one another personally and professionally.

Chapter 6

Night slips across the Southern Highlands as General McKlane's team moves through the forest halfway up the mountain. They have killed four ISIS terrorists and recovered three assault rifles and one grenade launcher, as well as the original Chinese Claymore mine that Fubar prevented one of the Army Rangers from detonating.

"We can't use the grenade launcher against planes like the Shenyang F-7s, but it's a powerful weapon against ground troops," Samuel says.

Mac stops and holds up a fist.

Everyone halts with him. Several men and women surround and protect him after he says, "Message coming in from Washington, from Macumber."

He huddles over the black screen with white type and reads Macumber's meeting transcript with a CIA agent named Colin Rafiki.

Then he reads Roberta Macumber's notes, finally telling the group, "We've done a good job."

He points out that they have virtually destroyed the Tanzanian Air Command.

"They might be able to build a single Shenyang F-7 from the four remaining plane carcasses in Morogoro, but it will take the Tanzanians time to do that, and according to the CIA agent, someone named Colin Rafiki, it will never get off the ground. Even if Rafiki is wrong, we'll be gone before they get their final MiG-21 lookalike in the air," Mac says.

"In Swahili," Sheronds says, "Rafiki means 'friend.' We need some of those."

"Especially right now," Mac says. "A State of War almost exists between Tanzania and America."

"Almost?" asks a Marine Raider.

"It has yet to be officially declared because a mob killed the Ambassador to Tanzania in Dar es Salaam before he ever had a chance to deliver his country's official Declaration of War to the American Ambassador."

He tells everyone that Macumber says the Tanzanian people initiated a coup d'etat to kill their ambassador because of the mass murder in Chimala.

Holly says, "So I guess the President of Tanzania has surrounded himself with a bodyguard of faithful warriors."

Mac nods. "He needs his Praetorian Guard because of the video clips we took in Chimala. They have gone viral around the world, with millions of views. It makes it hard for anyone to believe the Tanzanian newspaper headlines accusing us of killing children and teachers in Chimala."

He looks at all his men and women. "However, unless I give the order, we don't kill any Tanzanians. We're not at war yet. Stick to taking out ISIS terrorists."

Macumber wrote Mac that there's a possibility it was not the mob that killed the Tanzanian Ambassador, but rather CIA snipers on the roof of the American Embassy. Mac thinks that this may or may not be accurate since it appears to be Macumber's interpretation of her conversation with the CIA agent.

"CIA agents don't always tell the truth," Mac thinks.

Then he repeats, "Don't kill Tanzanians until I say it's okay to do so. Or if they try to use deadly force against you."

Mac also tells his team about the old warrior the terrorists hanged behind Sharonda and Samuel Nelson's home in Chimala.

"Kibwe Khamisi was a British officer who won the Victoria Cross in Italy during the Second World War," he says. "That's our equivalent of the Medal of Honor. He was 96 years old. He lived a full, eventful life. He was an officer who graduated from the Royal Military Academy near Sandhurst in Berkshire. I've given presentations at that military academy, which I equate to West Point in America. I am glad he did not suffer when he died."

Mac nods to the female Marine Raider, who shot Kibwe Khamisi just before his feet came off the ground as his ISIS executioners tried to hang him.

"We're also changing our exit strategy from Tanzania, Mac says. "The existing government, assuming it's still in control, has sent an entire brigade to the border with Malawi. That's about 5,000 combatants. We should see them driving down Hell's Run sometime tomorrow. Fighting them would be foolish. So our exit will be through Mozambique, a nation still underwater from the first cyclone that hit it over a month ago." He smiles. "Macumber says she hopes we brought our water wings." A few people laugh, but not many.

"How big is the ISIS force we're fighting right now?" a Navy SEAL asks.

"Pretty small," Mac says. "They might have another grenade launcher, but they have no mortars and no eyes in the sky, no drones. And we already know they have no night vision gear, at least not the ones we've killed so far."

"So why don't we take a couple of their old assault rifles, tie them to trees, and form a circular firing squad? Maybe we can flush them out." Samuel says. He holds up about twenty yards of wire from the Claymore mine from which Fubar saved them.

One of the Army Rangers, a woman, pulls out four hundred yards of 20-pound filament.

"I like fishing," she says.

Others have ropes.

They set up the Chinese Claymore mine in the dark and tie five Sturmgewehr assault rifles to trees. It takes them almost an hour.

The weapons have full magazines, and they all point a few feet above the Claymore Mine in the center of the circular firing squad, which has a radius of about 20 yards.

Mac's troops creep up the mountain, well above and out of the firing range.

One of the Sturmgewehr assault rifles empties its 30-bullet magazine into the forest at one o'clock in the morning.

Nothing happens, but Mac's team does see shapes moving in the direction of the action.

Another Sturmgewehr unloads 30 bullets into the forest, then another, and suddenly war starts with Mac and his team safely watching it from higher ground. A dozen terrorists start shooting, mostly one shot at a time. Then the Chinese Claymore mine goes off, sending a shower of metal through the forest at the speed of bullets. Now everyone is shooting, including Mac's team, using their night scopes.

Not a single American dies, but the ISIS soldiers are all dead in the forest below them.

"We'll clean up in the morning," Mac says. "I want 30-minute alternating watches, left, right, above us and below us. Everyone else try to get some sleep."

Sharonda feels Fubar push against her, awake and unable to sleep. Sophia is inside her uniform, alert at first, but then the monkey relaxes into the warmth of her body and dozes off. "You're getting heavy," she says, falling asleep

Sharonda wakes up when Fubar starts to "*fluuf, fluuf, fluuf*" at her side. Sharonda is right next to one of the watchmen. She pulls her night vision equipment down to her eyes, and she immediately passes the word, whispering, which spreads through the team:

"Stay very still. Do NOT shoot the leopards."

Three leopards pass within 40 yards of the team's perimeter, headed downhill. One of them is a cub carried in the mouth of its mother.

They make no noise as they move through the forest. The group watches as the leopards reach some of the dead ISIS soldiers 80 yards down the mountain, almost beyond thermal vision sight.

The mother leopard keeps walking with its cub, but the male cat scratches dirt and tree leaves on some terrorists and marks them.

He drags one of the ISIS soldiers into the branches of a tree, seemingly effortlessly, then another. He rejoins the mother and her cub, walking clear of the thermal vision of Mac's team.

"What was that about?" Samuel asks Sharonda.

"I think the mother saved one of her cubs from the flood. And the larger leopard probably dragged those men into the trees to save them as a future source of food."

"Why didn't they attack us?"

"Because we never threatened them. The leopards don't like human beings."

"Well, they seemed to like the ISIS fighters that the big one dragged into the tree branches."

"I guess they taste a lot better when they're dead," Sharonda says. She realizes she has turned into a tough person as her husband laughs. She also knows it might save her life.

In Morogoro, technicians surround the remaining four Shenyang F-7s. They strip them down and then use the spare parts to build a single plane most likely to fly.

The Chinese decide to add flaring devices to the functionality of the jet so it can shower the air with fireworks before any surface-to-air missiles from the Americans can knock it out of the sky.

The American SAMs will miss the plane because the showering sparks thrown away from the fuselage alter its heat signature enough to send the surface-to-air missiles into a tailspin. The plane bristles with both napalm and ground strike missiles just unpacked from China.

Xiao Zheng, a pilot and the grandson of a four-star Chinese general in the Korean War, General of the Army Xiao Jinguang, is the primary Chinese air force consultant working with the Tanzanians. He does not call it the Korean War, but rather the Fatherland Liberation War of 1950.

"In the next 24 hours, or less, you must complete all of this work," Zheng says to the General of the Air Command, who has no clue what this means. He covers his mouth to prevent himself from laughing at the Swahili coming out of Xiao Zheng's mouth.

It sounds as if he wants to have sex with all the disassembled parts spread across the hangar's floor.

"I will oversee the work myself," Xiao Zheng says to the relief of the general, who salutes smartly and walks away, still managing to control his laughter.

At 3:30 in the morning, under a bank of spotlights, a gleaming new Shenyang F-7 rolls out of the hangar. Pushback tugs point it down the airfield.

It rolls to the end of the longest runway under its own power, turns 180 degrees, and the pilot lets its engine roar with full brakes on. He wakes everyone in the village next door to the airbase, beyond the wire fences topped with razor barbed wire.

In the cockpit, Xiao Zheng releases the brakes, and the plane quickly gains airspeed. Zheng experiences the part of flying that makes his heart soar. He is alone in an almost cloudless night, pointing the small pitot tube on the nose of the Shenyang F-7 at the moon, high in the sky, thrusting himself towards it.

He takes the jet well past Mach 1, the speed of sound, enjoying the total silence in the cockpit once it breaks that barrier. The thunder that ripples along the ground wakes up the people in many rural villages.

After a while, he backs off, still well above Mach 1, and points the jet back to earth. He notices bright lights coming from a stadium over in Dodoma. The young Lieutenant Massamungu, who Zheng himself was training to fly the Shenyang F-7, will be honored in this stadium in front of 10,000 people.

The stadium is empty but brightly lit in the middle of the night, and he sees men pushing a casket to the center of its soccer field in preparation for the memorial.

He rolls the plane and does a flyby 200 feet above the top of the stadium, over Mach 1 at about 815 miles an hour. "You would have been a great pilot, Amadeus."

As Zheng climbs back into the sky, he laughs at the men scattering like ants away from the casket as the lightning-strike repercussion of breaking the sound barrier engulfs them. He turns back to Morogoro, landing perfectly on its primary runway at 04:15.

"All systems are good to go," he tells the general of the Tanzanian Air Command, who has been awaiting his return. "I will fly the plane myself to the Southern Highlands, but first, I need some sleep. Make sure you put the Tanzanian flag on the F-7's fuselage."

The general is covering his mouth again, hiding a smile at Zheng's Swahili. He understands that the Tanzanian flag is needed, but he doubts if the pilot will have a consensual relationship with the plane in the Southern Highlands.

In English, Xiao Zheng tells him that he has honored the pilot, Amadeus Massamungu, with a sound-breaking flyover at Jamhuri Stadium, in Dodoma as six people rolled his casket to the center of the field.

Zheng's English is much better than his Swahili. The General snaps his heels together and salutes him. He will tell the president about the great honor Xiao Zheng has accorded Lieutenant Amadeus Massamungu.

Zheng says, "the casket bearers scattered like mice during the Shenyang F-7's low-level pass at Mach 1." They both laugh at this.

"I will perform the flyover again tomorrow after returning from the Southern Highlands," the Chinese pilot says, "breaking the sound barrier again. Remind the general to wear earplugs. Now, I must sleep."

An immense pushback tug hooks onto the plane and moves it back into the hanger at the Ngerengere Air Force Base in Morogoro. Technicians, primarily Chinese, swarm over and under the aircraft, checking, fueling, and arming it. A Tanzanian pilot sits in the cockpit and pretends he is piloting it. The Chinese techs smile at this childlike behavior.

Two hours earlier, as the Shenyang F-7 takes off under the control of Xiao Zheng, the pilot now playing in the cockpit receives an encrypted message from Colin Rafiki, the CIA agent.

"Make sure it crashes," the note reads, and it suggests several ways to rig the Shenyang F-7's control column to guarantee flight failure during takeoff.

What the Chinese interpret as a Tanzanian's childish behavior in the cockpit is sabotage.

At 10:30, the presidential limousine pulls up to the hanger, and both Xiao Zheng and the President step out. The General of the Tanzania Air Command has been waiting for them for an hour and a half.

They all watch the Shenyang F-7 rolled out from the onlookers at the back of the hangar.

The pushback tug unhooks from the sleek, polished plane, and Xiao Zheng salutes the Tanzanian President and the general.

Zheng climbs into the cockpit, slapping the Tanzanian flag just installed on the fuselage.

The turbines spin slowly, and the pilot throws a switch that kicks in the engine. He pulls the lock-up on the throttle until he sees adequate fuel flow.

The Shenyang F-7 begins to move.

Xiao Zheng gives a thumbs up to the small group of Chinese and Tanzanian spectators.

Then he takes the F-7 to its starting point at the end of the longest runway.

He feels a slight stickiness in the control column, but he thinks this will vanish once he's airborne.

He rotates the jet 90 degrees to face its takeoff trajectory. The tackiness in the control column is still there, and he briefly considers canceling the flight.

It will take care of itself once he's off the ground, he decides. Xiao Zheng chooses to live in this single moment of greatness, knowing that his dead grandfather, four-star Chinese General of the Army, Xiao Jinguang, would admire and approve his actions.

The jet roars down the runway

Xiao Zheng pulls slightly on the control column as soon as he reaches flight speed.

He waits for the plane to lift off. Xiao Zheng remains on the ground.

He yanks back the control column as hard as he can, and the plane starts to lift. Then it rolls very slowly with the left wing less than forty feet off the ground.

"He's showing off," the President of Tanzania says, expecting an entire roll of the plane as it darts higher into the clear blue sky.

They know differently in the control tower, where a stream of Chinese fills the headphones of the Tanzanian Air Traffic controllers.

None of the Africans understand the words. The Chinese have all moved to tower windows to celebrate the jet's takeoff after reconstructing it 24 hours a day for the past three days.

The Shenyang F-7 punches a massive hole in the earth. On its nose, the small pitot tube hits the ground first, followed by a fireball and multiple explosions in the community just beyond the gates and wire fencing protecting the Ngerengere Air Force Base.

The explosions are powerful enough to crack but not break the windows of the control tower.

The President of Tanzania, flat on the ground outside the hangar, narrowly escapes death.

The General of Tanzania's Air Command, crouching with his mouth open next to the president, gratefully joins his leader's good fortune of survival. It lasts until his commander in chief pulls the pistol's trigger that he points at the General of the Tanzania Air Command's left ear.

General Mac McKlane receives an encrypted message from Roberta Macumber telling him he does not have to worry about any more attacks from Shenyang F-7s. They are all gone. She credits the CIA with the destruction of the final plane at the Ngerengere Air Force Base in Morogoro. In a reminder of his exit through Mozambique, she repeats: "Don't forget to wear your water wings." Mac laughs again, knowing that every team member has qualified swimming training while wearing a 50-pound backpack.

They continue through the forest without seeing any more ISIS warriors, reaching the tea plantations above the town of Mbeya before nightfall.

The cultivated areas are overgrown with weeds. No one has picked a tea leaf on the plantation for years. Nobody lives here, and his men carefully clear all the broken-down shacks.

As the team settles down for the night, with changing guards on every side, Mac McKlane tells the story of someone his grandfather, Captain George, called Bunny Brown.

"He was a British citizen who stopped traveling around the world the day the British government started telling people that you needed something called a passport to do so," Mac says. "I think that was when Bunny Brown was about 30 years old, maybe even younger."

"How old was he when Captain George met him?" Sharonda asks. Although she was the principal caretaker of Mac's grandfather for many years, she never heard him speak about Bunny Brown.

"My grandfather said that Bunny was over 100 years old when he met him," Mac says. "Bunny Brown hated bureaucracy. Although the British government started issuing a form of passport during Henry the Fifth's reign for their diplomats, it never stopped British citizens from wandering around the world without any documentation. Passports became necessary when Bunny was around 30 years old."

"That would have been in the 1800s," Holly says.

"Right. And Bunny told my grandfather that if he couldn't cross a border as a British citizen paper-free, he would stop traveling. He was in Tanzania when he made the decision, living here in the Southern Highlands. He died in Tanzania without ever crossing any borders, except when England fought the Germans. Then he dipped a toe and quite a few bullets into Kenya. He probably owned the tea plantation on which we're bivouacking."

The team looked around and agreed that the farm was left to rot, covered in vines and weeds.

"If this was his place, it was the best tea plantation in Tanzania when Bunny Brown was alive. And Bunny Brown was a great storyteller, too. He always spent his weekends playing gin rummy with Nessie Whapshot at the Mbeya Guesthouse, which no longer exists from what I see."

They could make out the lights from houses and multi-storied hotels in the town of Mbeya from their encampment on the rundown tea plantation. Nothing on their maps suggested a guest house.

"The Mbeya Guesthouse was where all the Peace Corps kids gathered back in the Sixties, and Bunny Brown loved to tell them stories. He'd talk about the great goldrushes in Tanganyika when prospectors pulled up to the bar with bottles of gold nuggets. This nation became Tanzania when it united with Zanzibar after the Night of the Chickens."

"What's the Night of the Chickens," a Navy SEAL asked General McKlane.

"That's when local Africans overthrew the Sultan of Zanzibar. They say the ocean surrounding the island turned red for days. Historians dispute the death toll of Arabs, but some say as many as 20,000 died in one night. The history of the Arabs as slave traders didn't help the Sultan's cause. The left-wing Umma Party slaughtered them like chickens, mostly using machetes to cut off their heads, and I guess that where the 'Night of the Chickens' comes from."

"This is a vicious country," an Army Ranger says.

"A vicious country with a lot of gold," Mac says. "Tanzania is the third-largest producer of gold in Africa, after South Africa and Ghana. Most of it is further north, but many miners tried to strike it rich out in the Buhoro Flats. According to Bunny Brown, they would buy two square meters of land and start digging for China. Some of them found nuggets, and old Bunny Brown told stories of men coming into the Mbeya Guest House with a bottle of them. They'd shake out a few for room and board and whiskey and then get drunk for days. People robbed them when they passed out."

"Who would buy two square meters of land?" a Marine Raider asks.

"Well, if the two square meters contained nuggets of gold, lots of people. If you walk around in the Buhoro Flats, according to my grandfather, you'll find these perfectly square holes from time to time, about six feet by six feet. They can go down twenty or thirty feet, sometimes more. Bunny Brown loved to tell the story of the man who struck nuggets at the bottom of his pit and started yelling about it: "Gold! I'm rich! I hit the motherlode!"

"The miners in nearby pits pulled up the ladder he had built to reach the bottom and demanded that he toss them a few nuggets before they'd replace it. He ran out of nuggets because he hadn't hit the imagined motherlode. Then his supposed buddies shoveled a lot of the dirt he'd hauled out back into the pit — not much honor among thieves."

"Any other happy stories from Bunny Brown?" Holly asks her husband.

"He had a favorite story he used to tell," Mac says. "Grandad said he talked old, with a croaking voice that you had to lean into to hear. It was like turning wrinkled pages in a history book. He loved the story about the Great White Hunter, who showed up in Mbeya because he wanted to kill an elephant."

Holly did not think she would like this story because she had always loved elephants.

Her adopted father, a CIA agent named Charles Smolkes, called "Red" because of his hair color, took her to a circus when she was nine years old.

She fell in love with a baby elephant that could barely walk because it had just been born.

"Bunny Brown hated people who killed animals they didn't eat," Mac says, and Holly relaxes.

"This guy shows up with a white tunic with cloth ammunition slots filled with .50 caliber bullets, and a huge elephant gun with a walnut carved stock with his name on it," Mac says. "He asked Bunny to be his guide, and Bunny asked him how he felt about ants."

"Ants? Like the creepy crawlies, not like my Aunt Mable in Sandusky, Ohio?" a Marine asks."

"The creepy crawling ones," Mac says. "The Great White Hunter doesn't know what his elephant guide is saying. He doesn't know what he means, so Bunny Brown explains that the best way to kill an elephant is to position yourself on the tallest anthill you can find and wait. You've all seen these anthills. They're mountains of dried, red mud, and some of them are 10 or 15 feet tall. You never see any ants crawling around them because the nests are on the inside, deep down where it's a lot cooler."

They've all seen the anthills, and most of them avoid the dried mud castles.

"So Bunny takes this guy out in his little Morris-Minor, which in those days looked like a golf cart low-rider with a miniature truck bed behind the driver cab. It sounds like a pack of motorcycles because Bunny has no baffles on the engine. When anyone hears that ruckus, they get off the road because Bunny was not a good driver."

The Great White Hunter told Bunny that the Morris-Minor made too damned much noise, scaring off the elephants. Bunny Brown assured the American that the elephants considered it a mating call.

The hunter believed him.

Some of Mac's men and women are already laughing.

"He got the Great White Hunter a ladder to climb a 15-foot anthill, the biggest one around, and then the fat guy squashed his sizeable butt into the top, waiting. Bunny Brown started driving his Morris Minor around the anthill in ever-widening circles."

"Did an elephant show up?" Samuel Nelson asks.

"Yes," Mac says, "but not before a lot of ants showed up first. The Great White Hunter slipped down the anthill, and he's swatting his dirt-stained white linen uniform as the ants start biting him, mostly in the ass but increasingly over his whole body. They have a hard bite."

"An elephant showed up?" Holly asks. "Did the bastard shoot it?"

"No. The Great White Hunter never took a shot because he had already dropped his monogrammed rifle," Mac says. "A giant bull elephant showed up, flapping its ears and charging him.

Bunny Brown kept yelling at the man and even tried to make a run towards him to save his badly-bitten ass."

The elephant kept charging.

"Bunny told my Grandad that he thinks the Great White Hunter never even saw the huge Bull Elephant that killed him."

Mac McKlane's grandfather says that Bunny Brown tells several versions of this story to people at the Mbeya Guesthouse, and all of them end with the ivory tusk of a giant bull elephant driven through the Great White Hunter. Sometimes the hunter sees the elephant charging, but usually, he's just hopping around trying to get rid of the ants covering his body. The bull elephant runs off with the Great White Hunter halfway up his left tusk.

"What happened to the elephant?" Holly asks.

"They never found him, according to Bunny Brown. It took the police two days to discover the remains of the Great White Hunter, chewed up by hyenas. They had to use what Bunny Brown called bird radar."

"What's bird radar?" several team members ask.

"Buzzards," Mac says, but most of them figured out the answer before he said it.

Chapter 7

Abu Muhammed al-Shimali hides in the 'Fairy Chimneys' of Turkey, located on the high plateau of central Anatolia. The chimneys are millions of years old, remnants of a more volcanic time in the Persian Empire.

Persia becomes Iran, but the mountains of Anatolia remain in Turkey.

Over eons of geologic time, volcanic ash hardens into a porous rock they call "tuff" with a layer of volcanic basalt on top of it.

Erosion washes away the softer deposits, creating pillars that stand as tall as 130 feet.

Almost all fairy chimneys have a protective, mushroom-shaped cap made of dark, finely-grained volcanic rock. It lets people use them as homes.

These chimneys are in Cappadocia, part of the Silk Road trading route made famous by Marco Polo.

A long list of empires invades the area: Europeans, The Hittites, the Persians, Alexander the Great, the Romans, the Byzantines, the Ottomans, and now, secretly, the leadership of ISIS.

Abu Muhammed moves from chimney to chimney, changing his headquarters daily, waiting for a significant victory somewhere in Africa where he can move to and establish himself in a new, Islamic state.

"I am disappointed at what has happened in Tanzania," he tells his two confidants. "How much longer can we call the Chinese our friends?"

"We need their money."

"The Russians and the Americans have stolen our oilfields in Syria," Abu Muhammed says. He spits on the dirt floor of his current "safe house" chimney. "They are cowards and thieves," he says.

"The only source of money we can claim is in southern Africa," one of his confidants says, "the diamond mines in Namibia, Botswana, and South Africa. We have many followers of Islam in those countries."

They discuss the De Beers diamond consortium in Botswana, the most accessible source of diamonds to attack. "We still have no friends there," Abu Muhammed says.

"But they are Muslims."

"They must fear us enough to fight for our cause to become our friends. They must be willing to die for us."

"This is true."

"We can force them to believe in us with bold action," Abu Muhammed says. "Especially if we finally become a nuclear power."

"We need money for that."

"We need control of Pelindaba for that. South Africans have been hiding our nuclear weapons from the world, yet they are the most accessible atomic bombs on earth. We need more military success than we have seen in Tanzania to remind them of this; we need a victory greater than flying a few planes into large buildings in New York City or the Pentagon in Washington. That created the hornets' nest that has almost destroyed us. That is what murdered Abu Bakr al-Baghdadi, *rahimah Allah aljana.*"

"*Rahimah Allah aljana,*" both confidants repeat. "May Allah take al-Bhagdadi into paradise."

"Our timing must be better."

"Yes, and most importantly, we must be ready to rule," Abu Muhammed says.

He talks about the explosion in Botswana in June of 2018, which produced a spectacular fireball and a series of loud detonations.

ISIS called it a test firing of its latest weapon.

Astronomers confirmed it was an asteroid between six and 25 feet in diameter.

The locals in the area were unsure who to believe, although the Muslims carrying guns appeared to have a strong argument.

"If ISIS had been ready at that time, we would own the DeBeers diamond complex today," Abu Muhammed says. "We can no longer afford cowards like the fighters defeated in Tanzania. And we must not stoop down to stealing schoolgirls for pleasure."

He refers to the hundreds of Nigerian girls kidnapped by Boko Haram militants in the Islamic State in West Africa. Although he considers this group a stain on ISIS, they remain the most successful terrorist organization on the continent.

"It is time to move to a new safe house, Abu Muhammed," one of his confidants suggests. The ISIS leader has little to take with him other than an assault rifle, a small bag of clothing, a prayer blanket, and the Koran. He wears an explosive vest, even when he sleeps.

Abu Muhammed looks at his two confidants: "We need a victory, bagfuls of diamonds, and a mighty atomic weapon. Only then will the American Devil and the rest of the world believe that it must deal with us as equals."

As they enter their new safe house, Abu Muhammed says, "America has given us a great victory with the assassination of Iran's military commander, Qasem Soleimani. I spit on that general's grave. But perhaps we can now fight America together, despite our differences with the Sunni."

For decades, Soleimani tracked down and killed the leaders and followers of ISIS. He probably eliminated more terrorists than the United States, but his death brings Sunni and Shiite Muslims together, at least briefly. Now, thanks to a well-publicized assassination by the Trump administration, ISIS can fight for lasting power in Sub-Saharan Africa.

As they prepare to leave the run-down tea plantation initially owned by Bunny Brown, Mac's 21-person team watches an entire brigade of Tanzanian soldiers marching through the city of Mbeya towards the border with Malawi.

Mac thinks they must have far more intelligence about his American warriors in Tanzania.

Surely they will position forces at the boundary of Mozambique and Malawi, even if no formal Declaration of War exists.

"Expect to fight at every border crossing," he says.

They are about to move towards Mozambique when war suddenly breaks out beyond Mbeya.

'Here comes some more planes," Samuel Ringer says as silver jets fly low over the Southern Highlands.

"Those are drones," Sharonda says as her monkey, Sophia, hops into the trees and shrieks back at their subsonic roar. Fubar flattens out on the ground, *"fluuf-fluuf-fluuf."*

General Mac McKlane says, "They're going too fast for American Predators."

"Almost twice as fast," one of the Navy SEALs says. "Those are Reapers or Chinese Pterodactyl drones." The Pterodactyl drones are no faster than the Reapers, although they can stay airborne longer.

The drones pass over the city, and its civilians remain safe. At first, it looks as if the drones might attack the brigade, but they pass over them as well and fall far beyond the Tanzanian forces.

"That looks like a warning shot across Tanzania's bow," a Navy SEAL commander says.

The drones look like small jets with no cockpit, probably dropped from bombers far overhead. They see contrails barely discernible high above the horizon. None of the drones have identified markings on them, although one of Mac's men says he saw Chinese lettering on the first one. It exploded at least ten miles beyond the brigade. Three other drones hit even further away, clearly missing on purpose and exploding in unpopulated areas.

"Good time to hightail it out of here," Mac tells the team. Fubar is already on a Raider's back, sleeping. Sophia drops out of the trees and hangs on to Sharonda's backpack.

They climb into the mountains southeast of the tea plantation, much higher than the flatlands overlooking the

Buhoro Flats. They never see any Tanzanian soldiers as they head towards Mozambique.

The following day, Lake Nyasa sparkles in the distance. It is the fourth largest freshwater lake globally, also called Lake Malawi, which creates its shoreline on the western edge of that nation.

McKlane's forces move south towards Mozambique, running into the Ruhuhu River in southern Tanzania, the most significant inflow into Malawi's 11,400 square mile body of water. They see a ferryboat going slowly back and forth across the river using pulley ropes, carrying people as well as an occasional car or truck.

Samuel adjusts the sight of his assault rifle.

"Looks like he's using a cellphone," Mac says. "Don't see a lot of electricity around here."

"Let me go talk to him," Samuel says.

"Don't kill him," Sharonda says.

"I just want to see who he's talking to," Samuel says.

The team huddles in the bushes and watches as Samuel, carrying an assault rifle on his back and wearing a sweaty teeshirt as well as camo pants and boots, walks up to the ferryboat. He shouts to him in Swahili and immediately jumps on the ferry when the man starts fumbling with the pulley ropes.

Samuel's assault rifle persuades the ferryboat pilot to stop and carefully surrender his cellphone. Samuel starts shouting into it. Ten seconds later, the man on the far side of the river voluntarily throws his cell phone as far as he can into the Ruhuhu River. Suddenly, 20 well-armed Americans appear on the road with a scruffy dog and a monkey.

The man on the far side of the river starts to break for an old, sun-scorched Citroen that still shows a few streaks of its original red color. Four shots ring out from one of the Navy SEALs, shattering the car's front window and flattening two of its tires.

The last gunshot kicks up the dirt a few feet to the right of the man. He freezes with his hands in the air.

The Navy SEAL, who blew out the car's front window and flattened its tires, takes each of the man's hands and lowers them, one at a time, once they cross the river.

The man has not moved in 10 minutes, although his fingers shake.

Mac gives the ferryboat captain and his terrified dockman three hundred dollars each, plus another four hundred dollars for car repairs and another two hundred dollars for a new cellphone for the one thrown in the river.

After neutralizing it, Samuel hands the pilot's cellphone back to him by removing its battery, but not the SIM card.

Everyone seems happy with this outcome, and the pilot suggests that if they come back this way, he would be delighted to give them another ride across the Ruhuhu.

He has made more money in the last hour than he will make in the coming year. His dockman is also happy.

The Navy SEAL, who took the shot that freezes the man in place, pats him on the shoulder and says, "You'll get over it."

Samuel tells him, in Swahili, that the Navy SEAL "could hit a dik-dik from three hundred yards, maybe more, so count yourself lucky."

As they walk away, the SEAL looks at Samuel and says: "I heard you say dick-dick to him. Did you suggest I could have made him a world-famous falsetto?"

Samuel laughs. "No, I said you could hit the smallest antelope in the world, which is called a dik-dik, from three hundred yards. I think they're around 15 inches tall, and they weigh about ten pounds. They whistle through their noses when they run. Other animals use it as a warning sound. They can zig-zag at over 20 miles an hour."

"I'm not shooting any dik-diks," the Navy SEAL says. "Look at what happened to that trophy hunter who tried to shoot an elephant."

They both laugh.

heartbeats

The objective of Mac's team is now Lake Kariba and the *Blue Nile Dreamship.*

Mac's youngest officers, Lieutenants Charlton and Ernestine Tremwallis, work for the Bulawayo24 News station out of Zimbabwe's Harare office.

Lake Kariba is not as well-known as Victoria Falls, considered one of the Seven Natural Wonders of the world, which flows into the western side of Lake Kariba between Zambia and Zimbabwe.

Over 132 million gallons of water roar over the edges of Victoria Falls every minute during the rainy season, and the flow rate has increased three years in a row.

It creates a curtain of spray that people can see up to 30 miles away.

Charlton and Ernestine are assigned to watch Kariba, a town on the Zimbabwe side of the lake.

It's near the Zambian border but a long way from Victoria Falls, which spills over granite rocks beyond the eastern side of the lake.

The town of Kariba is known for its crocodile farms, the Kariba Dam, and two reconditioned well-used casinos.

The *Blue Nile Dreamship* is a paddlewheel boat that circles the world's largest human-made lake every week. According to The Minister of State for Provincial Affairs of Zimbabwe, it's a great success. She often publicizes the ship as "proof that our great nation is open for business."

The *Blue Nile Dreamship* captain happily points out, "I need to buy a large 'NoVacancy' sign to hang on the bow." Every stateroom is full.

The only accommodation left on Lake Kariba is the dozens of houseboats that speckle the lake's edges.

The *Blue Nile Dreamship* captain is an expatriate Englishman from Liverpool who is an alcoholic and a compulsive gambler. He does not pay much attention to his passengers, but he's surprised that all of them are American men and women who refuse to use the boat's staff to clean their rooms.

The captain increases his profit margin by putting most of his cleaning employees on temporary, unpaid leave, not knowing that each stateroom houses well-armed American Rangers, Raiders, and SEALs.

The captain rents the cramped cabins of his laid-off workforce to accommodate other Americans who clamor to join the cruises.

He's never made so much money in his life.

"I intend to upgrade my drinking habits to a very expensive single malt scotch," he tells one of three bartenders who have kept their jobs on his boat.

The bartender says: "It's the only way you'll stay sober with so many passengers."

The bartender laughs and pours him some 21-year old Glenfiddich after dusting off the bottle.

"Ah, that's a rich and spicy malt raised in the glens of Scotland," the captain says. "But, oh, how I miss my regular trips to the casino at the Caribbea Bay Resort."

He swivels to a passenger on the barstool next to him and says, "I'm a card-counter, you know, lad, they can't beat me in blackjack. They don't have a chance."

"I used to be a riverboat captain on a boat like this on the Mississippi River," the passenger says. "It would be an honor and privilege to take the helm in the wheelhouse for a bit, with your permission, sir."

The captain's eyes twinkle.

Lightbulbs go off in his head.

For several days, the riverboat captain guides the *Blue Nile Dreamship* around the edges of Lake Kariba.

"My good fellow," the captain says, "would you consider assuming this position on a more permanent basis?"

"I would love it," the American riverboat captain says.

"Done, old man," the captain says to the Navy SEAL half his age. "All you have to do is check with me once a week. The office in Kariba is right next to the casino. You can work on a percentage basis, plus a generous salary."

"That sounds great, captain."

"Please, call me Roger."

He gives the American riverboat captain his contact address across the street from the Caribbea Bay Resort casino, where he spends most of his time.

The American passengers remain very interested in shoreline wildlife on the world's largest human-made lake.

The ship's guests continuously scan the water's edge with their powerful binoculars, looking through the stands of dead trees lining the borders of Lake Kariba.

They see a lot of crocodiles and hippos, but very few big game animals.

They do notice a lot of houseboats.

Everyone gives the captain a wild sendoff as he turns the boat over to one of their fellow SEALs.

They have to help the captain of the *Blue Nile Dreamship* ashore.

He demands to be taken directly to the casino rather than to his office and home located nearby.

Some Americans join in with him on shore, and they form agreements with the casino owners to make sure that the captain wins.

"Keep him drunk and keep him playing," a lieutenant commander tells the owner of the casino.

He gives him a wad of hundred-dollar bills.

"There's more if you need it."

A week later, the Msampa Fishing Village receives several tons of armor plating that a Bahamian company keeps in a warehouse in Livingston, Zambia.

Welders work on the inside of the *Blue Nile Dreamship,* making it as close to bulletproof as possible. The ship rides low and slow in the water. Under its name, someone paints *Old Ironsides*.

Meanwhile, the Captain continues on his pre-arranged winning streak in the casino. He has no interest in visiting his boat, and the riverboat captain assures him that everything is working very profitably a couple of times a week.

The *Blue Nile Dreamship* passengers become interested in the houseboats on Lake Kariba. Locals living in Bulawayo rent out the houseboats on the lake, especially since the *Blue Nile Dreamship* is always full of Americans.

"I would like to rent your home," a man carrying an assault weapon says.

"It's not for rent," the owner says.

"Yes, it is," the prospective renter says, sliding the bolt on his rifle.

"Uh, well, okay. Harriet!" the man shouts.

The prospective renter thinks he's calling his wife.

It's a signal to his fellow houseboat owner that they have an unwanted and possibly dangerous intruder.

His partner walks around the corner holding an old Glock pistol, but he has no chance to shoot it.

Both men die in a single burst of bullets that echo across the water.

It becomes the first warning shot in the Battle for Lake Kariba.

The houseboat next to them is quickly vacated by the owners, with no gunfire.

The people who rent the houseboats come from the Middle East.

They board the floating homes with assault rifles rather than fishing rods.

Within three days, all the houseboats fly small, black ISIS flags on their bows. "A naval battle is brewing on Lake Kariba," Charlton messages Macumber in Washington. "The dam itself may be in danger. Where's Mac?"

It would be a disaster if someone destroyed the Kariba Dam, flash-flooding the fourth largest river in Africa, the Zambezi, which pours into the Indian Ocean.

Although dozens of smaller dams exist, none of the towns and cities below the dam have levies or runoff streams for protection.

They would all wash away in a flood of mud if the Dam burst.

They move the *Blue Nile Dreamship* to the middle of the dam. They hear nothing back from Macumber for the next two days. By then, Lake Kariba echoes with gunfire.

At first, Roberta Macumber thinks it's a joke, some sort of office prank. It takes her a while to realize that the thin-lipped, unsmiling young man in front of her is serious.

"I am running three important CWMD operations for Brigadier General George McKlane III right now, young man, and I suggest that you get the hell out of my office and let me do my job.?" she says.

The man says, "You have 30 minutes to clean out your desk. You will leave any classified or unclassified materials in this room, together with any communication devices you might have, and any property of Homeland Security."

Macumber starts to type something on her computer, but one of the two men accompanying the person who says she is no longer an assistant director at Homeland Security takes her laptop.

She hits "send" as he does so. He disconnects her computer, then snaps it shut, hard.

"Who the hell are you?"Macumber shouts, attracting the attention of the staff outside her office.

The man does not raise his voice.

"You are running no operations at Homeland Security, and you have no office, Roberta Macumber. Right now, you have two choices. You can leave this office immediately, or you can get dragged out in handcuffs. I have officially canceled any cleanout period. We will send any of your personal effects to your home."

"On whose orders are you doing this, young man?" Roberta asks, trying to regain some form of control.

"The new Acting Director of Homeland Security."

"*Acting* Director?"

"You're about ten seconds away from handcuffs, Roberta Macumber."

"What happened to the real, Senate-appointed Director of Homeland Security?"

"The same thing that is happening to you right now." A smile flickers on the young man's face.

"Are you crazy? Do you have any idea how many of our assets you are putting in danger?"

The young man nods to one of the men standing behind him. The big man pulls plastic restraint cuffs from behind his back and approaches Roberta Macumber with absolutely no expression on his face.

"Screw you, screw every one of you," Roberta says, holding out her wrists. The man slips the restraint cuffs on but not overly tight.

He tries to cover them with her jacket on the back of her chair, but she angrily tosses the coat to the floor.

They lead her to the elevator and take her through the lobby wearing plastic restraint cuffs. Several building guards approach them, but Roberta tells them to back down.

One of the men accompanying Macumber unholsters his gun and holds it to his side. They release her on the street. The man rips her identity badge off of her shirt. She almost shouts, "Rape!" just for the hell of it.

Her torn shirt exposes her black bra. The man smiles and cuts off her restraints. He says: "Have a nice day."

Roberta Macumber bursts out laughing at the man's comment uncontrollably, and then she moves to a sidewalk bench and starts to sob, equally without control.

She wonders if what she managed to write on her laptop ever got through to General Mac McKlane.

In Mozambique, just as the general's team starts to turn toward Lake Kariba after sneaking across another military post at midnight, he gets a message from his assistant, Roberta Macumber.

It says: "I've just been fired and don't know who or why I am ...."

That's all it says.

Mac McKlane thumbs back through his previous emails and finds the number Roberta gave him. It's Colin Rafiki's private phone. He calls it.

"Hello?"

"Roberta Macumber gave me this number."

"Who is this?"

"General Mac McKlane."

"Where are you?"

"Near the bottom of Lake Kariba. Listen, Colin, and I assume I can call you Colin, call me Mac. I got a message from Roberta that ...."

"She's fired," Colin says. "So is the Director of Homeland Security, which now has an Acting Director whose only qualification is his political loyalty."

"I don't understand."

"Yes, you do. It's politics."

"Politics? I'm about to go into battle on Lake Kariba against a bunch of ISIS militants."

"A lot of people who don't know what we do for a living think that they know how to do it a lot better than us. You want my advice?"

"Yes," Mac says immediately.

"Don't answer your phone, especially if it's a call from Roberta Macumber. It won't be her. And don't use this phone number again. If you see it on your phone, it's not going to be me. And Mac?"

"Yes."

"Kill every damned terrorist that you can find before they shut us down."

"Roger that," he says.

He calls the team together and tells everyone what's happened. He does not understand it, nor do they, but they have trained for what they are doing, and nobody wants out.

"Welcome to Lake Kariba," Samuel says. They are 500 feet from the bottom of the dam.

"I always wanted to see Victoria Falls," Sharonda says to Sophia, riding on her shoulder. The monkey is getting heavy and growing fast.

"Let's go kill ISIS before the politicians in Washington kill us," a Navy SEAL says. Everyone agrees with that.

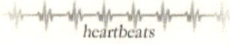

Two months earlier, aboard the *S.S. Nomad,* they all train for the Battle of Kariba. They practice with a mock-up of the *Blue Nile Dreamship* in the bow of the freighter.

"The good news," Captain Montoya says, "is that the captain of the *Blue Nile Dreamship* is a British drunk who would rather spend his time at a blackjack table than at his ship's helm. So we need to use his somewhat notorious weaknesses to take over the boat and armor it on the inside as if it was 'Old Ironsides' in the United States Civil War. ISIS forces will openly attack the ship once they know many dumb American tourists are aboard it.

You are all going to be stupid Americans."

She asks how many people know how to weld metal plates to a ship's existing iron frame. One man and a woman raise their hands. A week later, well over two dozen men and women can raise their hands.

"The *Blue Nile Dreamship* will become a naval destroyer on Lake Kariba," Captain Montoya says, "but the ship may not be enough. They might see it as a hoax, a deception because we think ISIS is dumb."

"They're not dumb," a Navy SEAL says. He served three tours in Afghanistan.

"That's true," Samuel Nelson says, 'but we can fool them. We did it in Virginia."

"We cannot rely on ISIS being dumb or foolish," General Mac McKlane says.

"And that brings me to the real problem, the dam itself," Captain Montoya says aboard the *S.S. Nomad*. "If ISIS figures out a way to blow a hole in the Kariba Dam, the destruction it causes will be far greater than the September 11 attack that killed 2,996 people in America." It's a death toll that most men and women have often heard about, which angers them.

"That number includes the 19 not-so-stupid plane hijackers," the captain adds.

She goes over the dimensions of the Kariba Dam. She hands out the construction blueprints from the Italian company that built it.

The Kariba Dam sits in a gorge on the Zambezi River.

It's 420 feet tall and stretches 1,900 feet across the valley, and it's the largest human-made reservoir in the world by volume, although more towering dam walls exist.

"Where's the weakness?" Charlton asks. "How can they blow up such a massive chunk of concrete?"

"The biggest danger will occur in the underground tunnels that lead to the turbines. It would take a massive amount of explosives to destroy the dam. They might try, and that's where they would do it, but they will settle for turning off the lights by shutting down the six transformers that generate electricity."

"How the hell do we protect the tunnels?" a Marine Raider asks.

"We become tunnel rats," General Mac McKlane says.

"There's another problem we need to think about," the captain of the *S.S. Nomad* says. "If they can turn off the lights long enough, they could create a nuclear meltdown at Pelindaba and Pelindaba East, the main research center of the South African Nuclear Energy Corporation."

"South Africa relies on energy from the Kariba Dam?" Mac McKlane asks.

"They do. The plan of the Third India-Africa Summit in New Delhi defines peace and security in some hazardous ways. Delegates made a lot of backroom deals, and many nations, including America, want Zimbabwe to flourish now that Mugabe is dead."

South Africa thought it might help if it relied on a lot of electricity produced by the Kariba Dam.

heartbeats

A flotilla of houseboats begins to gather at the top of the Kariba Dam.

They surround the *Blue Nile Dreamship,* which tries to break out on the right side of the ISIS fleet and starts to sink houseboats.

Suddenly, ISIS warriors stretch across the road on top of the dam. Charlton Tremwallis and Ernestine are firing accurately and with deadly results when Charlton sees the grenade launchers.

Charlton rolls off the ship's roof, taking Ernestine with him, falling over 25 feet into the water.

They both have their assault weapons, and they swim underwater as long as possible. The concussion of the grenade almost makes them blackout. They surface gasping for air and shooting as more explosions rock the *Blue Nile Dreamship.*

Weighted down with protective armor plating, the ship sinks quickly, but the men inside it have all well-developed lung capacities from their Navy SEAL, Army Ranger, and Marine Raiders' training.

They also surface shooting, quickly focusing their fire on the ISIS warriors strung along the road on top of the dam with minimal means of protection.

The ISIS warriors have no more grenade launchers, and only a few of them have ammunition left to fire their assault weapons at the Americans in the water.

Charlton knows a lot of his platoon's men and women have died. He can see them floating in the water. He and Ernestine swim to the southern shoreline, about 100 yards away. They climb out, crouching low.

They look down the road on the top of the dam.

"Frigging scope is foggy," Charlton says. He still shoots three ISIS warriors hiding below the roadside.

"I don't think they're the biggest problem," Ernestine says. "Look down below."

General Mac McKlane is popular. He gets dozens of phone calls from America on his cellphone, mostly from Roberta Macumber but some from the Director of Homeland Security with no name, just the designation. He has a call from the Marine Corps Commandant and the Secretary of the Navy. He gets several calls from the White House but none from the president.

He answers none of the calls.

"Who the hell are you?" one of the Navy SEALs says into his cellphone.

He quickly hangs up when General McKlane slashes his index finger across his own throat.

"We talk to nobody," the General says. "Not until we complete our missions."

The Navy SEAL's phone rings again. He turns it off, as does everyone else.

The SEAL looks at his best friend and says, "I think I just asked the Vice President of the United States who the hell he thought he was, and then I hung up on him."

"Would you want him in the foxhole next to you?"

"Right now? Only if he was dead."

"I thought you were a Republican?"

"I am."

Chapter 8

At the bottom of the Kariba Dam, dozens of ISIS terrorists have commandeered trucks and flatbeds, and they are loading them with explosives.

"If they get that material in the tunnel, they stand a good chance of blowing up the Kariba Dam," Ernestine says.

"Do we know what kind of explosives they use?" Charlton asks his remaining men and women as they climb out of the water above the dam.

"In Afghanistan and Iraq, their IEDs, the Improvised Explosive Devices, contained everything from artillery shells to toxic incendiary chemicals to gasoline cans, Claymore mines, cans filled with nails and gunpowder, pipe bombs, and hand grenades. In rare cases, they used plastique like C-4. The only commonality was that they all required a detonating mechanism, either timed, pushed, or cranked."

"Those big boxes they're forklifting onto the trucks could be just about anything. It looks like they're pretty close to getting everything loaded up, too."

Charlton Tremwallis lies flat and scopes the lead truck. He shoots the driver 450 yards away just as the terrorist tries to turn on the ignition. Another man tries to take his place but dies before he can remove the dead driver.

"What can't move, can't hurt us," Charlton says as other Marine Raiders, Navy SEALs, and Army Rangers lie prone and start shooting whatever moves. A jeep swerves around the truck that blockades the tunnel entry, but it never makes it, running headfirst into the Zambezi River.

A lot of ISIS military moves into the bush. Anyone who breaks for the cave dies.

An Army Ranger has loaded his rifle with nothing but tracer rounds taken from the bullet clips of his comrades. He starts to shoot the incendiary bullets into the truck loads.

ISIS terrorists have figured out where the Americans are, and they begin to barrage the area.

They hit two Marines and one Army Ranger. All three die instantly.

Their entry wounds are minor, but the exit wounds are enormous.

"They're cutting X-marks into the bullet heads," a Navy SEAL says. The "X" cuts down on accuracy, but if the bullet strikes anywhere essential, it opens up and shatters everything in its path. It's a common violation of the Geneva Convention, impossible to stamp out.

Suddenly, one of the biggest trucks blows up in a fireball that spreads to the other vehicles. The Army Ranger's tracer rounds have found their mark, acting like an explosive detonating mechanism.

Four Americans stand up and shake their weapons at the billowing smoke below. Two of them die instantly.

The man who dismissed Roberta Macumber rings her townhome doorbell in Georgetown.

She looks at the screen monitoring her front door. She goes back to reading the legal binders on her desk.

He rings six times before he walks away. She sees him talking on his cellphone and then watches him as he walks up to the cross street and waits with folded arms, looking north.

So it will be a forced entry, she tells herself. She grabs an always-ready overnight bag and quickly moves down to the basement. She's glad she has no pets. Her overweight, old black cat, called "Nightingale," died three months earlier.

She opens an almost invisible door in the basement wall and takes a short tunnel to the road behind her home. She sees several large black Chevy Suburbans at the bottom of the street, presumably driving to where she imagines the man ringing her doorbell is waiting.

As she gets into a safe car that she always keeps nearby, she hears loud voices and wood splintering. The United States Government has come to visit.

"Home Sweet Home," she says out loud, turning the key in a car that has a fake license plate as well as false vehicle registration. The engine starts immediately.

"And, thank YOU, Mac."

It is all his idea, including the tunnel, and she thinks it's pretty funny when he initially proposes it. She opens her overnight bag and looks at a phone number and address in Baltimore. She smiles at the title on the piece of paper: "Bureaucrats Underground Railroad."

A black SUV pulls up next to her and honks its horn. She slowly takes her hands off the steering wheel of the old Volvo in which she's about to escape. A Glock taps on her window. The black Suburban turns inward in front of her.

"Hello, Roberta Macumber. Please shut off the engine and accompany me back to your townhome. We can take the shortcut through the tunnel if you'd like."

General Mac McKlane hears the battle of Lake Kariba about five minutes before he sees it. He and his warriors come in fast from the northeast, below the dam. They watch as several trucks explode in a rain of tracer rounds in front of the tunnels leading into the Kariba Dam's turbines.

He looks across the river and sees ISIS terrorists climbing up the side of the mountain. He watches them shoot some of the American soldiers celebrating the detonation of the trucks.

Mac's men start picking off the ISIS warriors on the mountainside. They suddenly disappear as the six water chutes on the face of the dam open full blast, spewing out thousands of gallons of water a minute, flooding the Zambezi below the dam.

From above, Charlton Tremwallis and his men and women continue shooting the ISIS warriors climbing the mountainside. Now they know where they are.

"I guess we're going to be tunnel rats," Mac tells his men at the rapidly swelling river. Although the tunnels become flooded with the rising level of the Zambezi, his men can still float into them, helped by the current of rising, muddy waters.

The Tremwallises see Mac's troops at the bottom of the gorge. They try to call them, receiving an order to shut off all their electronic equipment and make no further calls. They must not answer any calls or messages, even if the caller ID is someone they know. "Do not take a call even if it says it's from the Director of Homeland Security."

Mac realizes that ISIS has managed to work its way into the dam's interior, far enough to open the chutes. They will have explosives with them. The turbines and transformers will be their targets.

Suddenly pieces of sunken houseboats start coming out of the chutes, chewed apart by the turbines. Then one of the six chutes falters, its stream cut in half. Suddenly the *Blue Nile Dreamship* tumbles out in pieces, but the chute never recovers its full flow because the welded protective plates tear apart its turbine.

Inside the tunnels, Mac and his men are wearing their night vision gear.

They are now above the rising water. In the distance, Mac's men and women see some ISIS fighters approaching the turbines. They send withering fire towards the terrorists. Bullets might damage some of the turbines, but they won't destroy them. They have plenty of welders to fix them, thanks to their training aboard the *S.S. Nomad*.

As they approach the turbines, they see a series of large metal wheels. It takes two people to close each one, but the water discharging from each chute turns into a trickle as they do this.

"You would have thought this would all be mechanized," an Army Ranger says.

"It probably is," Mac says. "They just turned off the electricity. We need to check the turbines and generators."

They find explosive devices next to every generator, and they are all active, flashing red numbers that will reach zero within an hour and a half. The Blue Nile Dreamship has already disabled one of the turbines.

"We're all demolition experts," one man says.

"It's going to be a lot easier just to carry them out of the tunnel," Mac says.

Three people cautiously carry each ticking charge, and within thirty minutes, the explosives are all out of the tunnel and slowly sinking several hundred yards downstream.

Mac and his men join the Tremwallises at the top of the dam. As the sun sets, the simultaneous explosion of all the devices lights up the gorge several miles downstream.

heartbeats

"What do you mean, Macumber refuses to come to the office?" the Acting Director of Homeland Security asks. "I want every senior member of this organization in the conference room in thirty minutes. Make it happen. Now."

Thirty minutes later, 16 people sit around a table, 14 of them looking at a leadership they have never met before.

Roberta Macumber is not there. Her excuse is that they fired her.

The man at the head of the table stands up. He looks likes he spends more time in fast-food restaurants than in an exercise gym. He is surprisingly young. His belt disappears beneath his paunch.

"I am the new Acting Director of Homeland Security," the man says. "My name is Joseph Menges. The man on my left is the Assistant Director, Jonathan Rose. We will now ....”

A hand shoots up at the far end of the table.

Joseph Menges continues. “We will not have any interruptions as I speak.”

At the end of the table, the raised hand remains straight up in the air.

“I’m sorry,” the Acting Director says, “do you need to be excused to take a tinkle, madam?”

Assistant Director Jonathan Rose thinks that this is very clever and funny, laughing out loud. Nobody else at the table even smiles.

At the far end of the conference table, the woman still holding her hand up asks: “Can you please tell us what happened to the real Director and Assistant Director of Homeland Security?”

“What is your name, madam?”

“Felicity Montrose,” the woman answers.

“And please enlighten me as to exactly what your political affiliation is, Missus Felicity Montrose?”

“That would be none of your damned business, Acting Director Menges.”

The Acting Director of Homeland Security flushes, pacing behind the oversized leather chair. Someone installed it that morning at the head of the table because he could fit into it comfortably.

He stops and stares straight at the questioner.

“I assume that you are a radical leftist, Missus Montrose, like most of the deep state people sitting around this table.”

"You're joking," she says. Quite a few people at the table laugh at the fat man, although others seem deadly serious and quite angry.

"I suggest you get your resumé in order, Montrose."

"Oh, I will," she says. "And just so you know who you are firing, Acting Director Menges, I have been a Republican for over 30 years."

She takes a few seconds to let this sink in.

"When I was a kid in Chatam, on Cape Cod," she says, "I went fishing with the Nixon family. My grandparents and parents were friends of Prescott Bush, the father of two American Presidents. I have many Republican, Independent, and Democratic friends in the Senate and the House of Representatives to attest to my political affiliation. I will also point out to you that politics has *never* played a role at Homeland Security."

Another person at the table says, "We are here to defend the Consitution of the United States against all enemies, foreign or *domestic*. Every one of us has taken a solemn oath to that effect. It's less than 50 words long, and we take its obligation freely, without any mental reservation."

The woman who initially held up her hand leans towards the new Homeland Security boss.

"I assume you and your sidekick have made the same promise. Please forgive our interruption and continue with your lecture to all of us professional Homeland employees."

The acting assistant director of Homeland Security passes a note to his boss.

The acting director glances at it and then announces that the meeting is over.

"We will resume this conference tomorrow," the Assistant Director says.

"I expect everyone to be here in their seats at 2 p.m. sharp," the Acting Director of Homeland Security says.

"You mean 14:00," someone at the table says.

"We use military time here, Acting Director Menges," another Homeland Security agent says.

"Two p.m. sharp," Menges repeats. "I was never in the military. Two p.m. sharp, understood?"

The meeting breaks up, and every person there understands perfectly.

heartbeats

Abu Muhammed al-Shimali learns of the failure of his ISIS terrorists at the Kariba Dam even before they are aware of it at the headquarters of the Department of Homeland Security's CWMD unit.

Homeland Security knows nothing because of the blanket of electronic silence from General Mac McKlane and his men and women.

The CIA is the first government organization to pick up the ISIS internet traffic of America's success on Lake Kariba and the minor damage to its dam.

They pass news of the American victory to the George Bush Center for Intelligence in McLean, Virginia.

In Turkey, Abu Muhammed scowls and shouts at his subordinates. "Where can we find victory rather than defeat?"

"We need to find money *and* power," ISIS's senior aide says to Abu Muhammed.

"Of course. That much a fool can understand. What choices do we have left?"

"The DeBeers diamond complex will give us the money we need to fight the Devil."

The final word is a synonym for the United States of America, the Devil.

"The Pelindaba facility in South Africa will give us atomic bombs," another senior aide says.

"Then our choices remain clear," Abu Muhammed says. "But do not focus on one. I want both of these objectives to become our primary goals. I want this done now. I am tired of struggling down this weak and unfocused road to success."

His aide says, "I was certain that a nation as corrupt as Zimbabwe would become a perfect home for us. It is the most unstable nation in Africa."

"We do not need a home," Abu Muhammed says. "We need a victory."

heartbeats

In America, the Acting Director of the Central Intelligence agency talks to the Acting Director of Homeland Security on a secure phone line.

He fills him in on the great victories that General George McKlane III has had in Tanzania and on Lake Kariba below the Victoria Falls.

"Tanzania has decided not to declare war on America," the CIA Acting Director says.

"That sounds like a good decision."

Both acting directors watched the fireworks between the Tanzanian and American ambassadors at the United Nations on TV.

"And the Kariba Dam has not been badly damaged."

The Acting Director of the Department of Homeland Security, Joseph Menges, does not know the location of the Kariba Dam. Even if he did, his knowledge of Zimbabwe goes no further than a general feeling that they had a bad leader who killed many local people.

It's a shithole country.

He says into the secure phone, "That sounds great."

Silence follows this, and then Director Joseph Menges asks: "Do you know anything about a Homeland Security Assistant Director named Roberta Macumber?"

The Acting CIA Director reveals that Roberta Macumber is one of General Mac McKlane's most trusted people. He calls her a great patriot.

The Acting Director of the Department of Homeland Security says nothing. The silence becomes uncomfortable, and both men say thanks and end the call.

Joseph Menges looks at his assistant, Jonathan Rose. He says: "I think we should consider telling the White House that our military forces in southern Africa have gone rogue, despite their apparent military successes."

Rose, who has listened to the call and who has known Joseph Menges for over twenty years, says: "Joe, I think we need to be very careful right now. I think we're way over our heads. My advice is to cancel tomorrow's 2 p.m. meeting and spends some time talking to the leaders of every division here at Homeland Security."

"What are you saying?" Joe Menges asks.

"I think we should listen before we fire," Jonathan Rose says to his acting boss.

"What the hell does *that* mean?" Joe Menges asks.

"It means that we should start by having me go to Montrose, the woman who raised her hand in the meeting, a woman who knows the father of two Republican presidents and Richard Nixon's family, and apologize and listen to her."

"Apologize to her for what?"

"I think you insulted her with your 'tinkling' comment, although I found it very funny at the time."

"It *was* funny."

"Yes, and clever, and also sexist. It's the sort of comment we might see in a federal or state lawsuit. We need to start over, or every department here at Homeland Security will stonewall us, and some of them may sue us."

"You don't think we can push around this den of deep state bureaucrats?" Director Joseph Menges asks.

"Oh, I think we can, Joe, but not by being stupid or stubborn." He pauses, wondering how much he can butter up to his boss.

"We have to be smart, like you," Rose says, hoping he hasn't gone over the top with false flattery.

The Acting Director of the Department of Homeland Security, Joseph Menges, thinks about this for a while.

He does not like the invasive nature of federal or state lawsuits, civil or criminal, especially if his name appears among the defendants.

Finally, he says: 'I'm not apologizing to that bitch. You do it for me."

"Done," Jonathan Rose says.

"And cancel tomorrow's 2 p.m. meeting and set up two appointments a day for us with the 14 people who were in that boardroom this afternoon."

"Good idea," Jonathan Rose says.

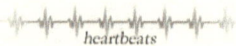

Several months earlier, during everyone's second week of training aboard the *S.S. Nomad,* Captain Maria Montoya introduces them to dirty nuclear bombs.

An Army Ranger catches a gleaming, 24-inch silver sphere that rolls off the table as the captain drops it.

She holds up something that looks like a TV remote and says: "If I press this button, that dirty bomb explodes, and everyone within five miles of it eventually dies. The lucky ones meet their maker immediately."

Then she pressed the button.

The sphere cracks open like an egg.

It's filled with jelly beans.

"They're not radioactive," the captain says. "Enjoy them. You have not survived your first nuclear attack. We're all dead. Now we start training for the second one."

They put on the protective gear that hangs on a series of pegs, looking like slumping spacesuits.

"As I said earlier," Captain Maria Montoya tells them, "you're going to battle terrorists wearing those suits. It's not easy being an effective fighting machine when you look like a cross between a marshmallow and the Michelin Man, especially when you're underwater."

They all stand next to what Captain Montoya and her chief engineer call the "Houdini Room."

It's an oversized aquarium encased in clear, five-inch thick plastic sheeting with a waterproof metal entry and exit hatch on the top.

The floor of the 20x20x20-foot enclosed room is flooded about 12 feet for training. A series of easily-closed punch holes let in seawater through the *S.S. Nomad*'s hull.

Pressure cylinders pump air into the 8000 cubic-foot chamber, raising and lowering its seawater level.

The team practices, fully suited in radioactive gear, on benches near the Houdini Room. They disarm an array of potential dirty bombs.

The wiring is different colors, and the detonator to the atomic device varies from bomb to bomb. The team climbs into their nuclear suits outside the Houdini Room for two days, popping multiple devices open. They produce an abundance of jelly beans.

Every time a sphere cracks open, a trainer says: "You're dead. Welcome to jelly bean heaven."

All of the men and women involved are demolition experts, and by the end of the fourth day, every dirty bomb is disabled without producing any jelly beans.

"Now you're ready for the Houdini Room," Captain Montoya says. "You're going to be wearing 30-pound weight belts with a timed release of five minutes. That is the amount of time you have to disarm the nuclear weapon. Two things will happen if you go beyond five minutes. First, this pill I am holding, which each of you will swallow at the start, will knock you out cold in 300 seconds. I've never seen anyone go beyond 350 seconds. At that point, your weight belt has released you, and you'll bob up to the surface of the Houdini Room so we can fish you out and take you to sickbay to recover. You'll wake up with the worst headache you've ever had, but that will go away after about 15 minutes."

She looks at them. "Who wants to go first?"

They all raise their hand.

Mac McKlane steps forward and has a weighted belt clipped around his waist. Captain Montoya says: "The 'fish duty' team will give you your pill just before you drop in the water, General McKlane."

"Mac," he says. "You going to have to learn to call me 'Mac,' Maria."

The general climbs the stairs leading to the top of the Houdini Tank.

The fish duty team makes sure he takes his yellow pill.

"Stick out your tongue, Mac."

They watch McKlane drop four feet into the water, which briefly rises as they open the hatch.

McKlane sinks to the bottom, where he opens a suitcase and starts to defuse a nuclear device.

He checks the wiring and reaches for some wire cutters in his radioactive suit.

He drops them, reaches down, retrieves them, and starts to retrace the installation.

He clips the correct wire, and then he starts to remove the detonator. Everything feels more sluggish underwater. Slow-motion sneaks into his brain.

All he has to do is remove the thingamajig from the whatchamacallit. That's all he has to do. But why is he doing this? It would be so much easier to swim around for a while. And a lot more fun.

General McKlane wakes up in sickbay with a splitting headache. There are three other men and a woman in beds like his, all of them unconscious.

Shadrach is standing at the foot of the bed.

"You almost made it, Mac," he whispers.

"Stop shouting," Mac says. "Why are you here?"

"I did make it," he says.

"That's great, Shadrach. You have to leave me alone right now." Mac says. "Jesus, my head."

"I understand that, Mac. But I'm not here for you," Shadrach whispers. "I'm waiting for Sookie to wake up."

He points to his wife in the bed next to Mac.

"She came close to making it, too. She would have if she didn't drop her wirecutters. So we need to figure out some way to attach them to the radiation suits."

"Stop shouting at me. I hear you. You're right. Get to work on redesigning the blubber suits. And leave me alone."

Sookie begins to wake up.

"Your wife is about to have one helluva headache," Mac says, massaging his forehead. Shadrach gives him four Tylenol tablets.

He has four more for Sookie, who has never had a headache in her life.

She turns as she opens her eyes. "Oh, Jesus," she says, "why are the damned sheets so loud?"

The Navy SEAL, who initially tells the owner and captain of the *Blue Nile Dreamship* that he's a Mississippi riverboat captain, tries to reach the owner on the phone.

The owner does not answer, so the SEAL riverboat captain looks for him in the casino next to the *Blue Nile Dreamship* office. The office is vacant.

Even the brochure racks and shelves are empty in the *Blue Nile Dreamship* office, and the door is locked. All the counters show dust.

He finds the ship's owner at a blackjack table with a pile of chips in front of him.

At first, the owner does not recognize him, and then he suddenly brightens up.

"My good man," he says, "please meet your new employer." He points to a large black man from Zimbabwe sitting next to him, with a much smaller pile of chips.

"My new employer?" the Navy SEAL asks.

"This fine fellow has purchased the *Blue Nile Dreamship* this very morning." He turns to the man from Zimbabwe. "This is the Mississippi riverboat captain I told you about." He points to the Navy SEAL. "I threw you into the deal."

The Zimbabwean extends his hand: "Pfungwa Maherem," he says. "And your name is?"

"Lieutenant Commander Charles Sikes of the United States Navy. I am a Navy SEAL. Have you signed a contract for the *Blue Nile Dreamship*, Mister Maherem?"

"Why, yes, I have. Why are you a Navy SEAL?"

The owner of the *Blue Nile Dreamship* asks the same question, stumbling over the new owner's words.

"I am Lieutenant Commander Sikes," he repeats.

The dealer at the blackjack table asks Pfungwa Maherem if he wants another card.

Pfungwa taps the felt blackjack table, asking for one more card, and he hits 21. The dealer is showing a six, the worst possible card he could have. The dealer asks the former owner of the *Blue Nile Dreamship* if he wants another card. He holds at 15, refusing the offer.

The dealer flips over his undercard, a nine of spades, so he must draw another one with a count of 15. He lays down the 10 of spades and busts. Both the former and current owners of the Blue Nile Dreamship win their bets.

"Must be our lucky day," they say in unison.

"I don't think so,' the lieutenant commander says.

Shadrach Ringer hooks a huge carp in the Meerhof area of Hartbeespoort Dam. He and Bootie van Zale have found a 20-foot dropoff on the shoreline, and they know the irregular bottom will fill with Harties carp.

They are using nightcrawlers for bait, big fat worms they caught the previous night by walking through the lawn surrounding Bootie's house in their bare feet, with a flashlight. They can feel the giant worms slipping away under their feet.

They have to grab them quickly, and they slowly pull them out, throwing them in a pail of loose dirt. Bootie and Shadrach catch over 50 of them in an hour and a half. Most of them are about eight or nine inches long.

Early the following day, they leave for the dam. The Harties carp can't resist fat, juicy nightcrawlers.

"It's a monster," Shadrach says, his fishing rod an inverted "U" shape.

"Let him run," Bootie says, dropping his rod and getting the fishing net.

"He won't run," Shadrach says. "He's just sitting there like a rock."

"Straighten out your rod, point it right at him, then tug him up a bit."

Shadrach does this, managing to reel in about three feet of his 30-pound test line. It goes limp for just a second, and then the colossal carp makes a break for it. The plastic line sings off his reel.

He's wearing gloves because he's done this before, ending up with a massive blister on the end of his thumb that still has not entirely healed.

"I think I'm going to run out of line," Shadrach says as the huge carp breaks for deeper water.

His Motorola Encrypted phone rings. Only a handful of people have his and Bootie's and Sookie's number.

"Bad timing," Shadrach says. "You take it, Bootie."

Bootie snaps the Motorola Encrypted phone off Shadrach's belt and looks at the name. It's General Mac McKlane, and Bootie says, as a joke in Afrikaans: "*Goeiemôre, generaal, ek hoop dat u 'n wonderlike dag beleef.*" "Good morning, General. I hope you're having a wonderful day."

A man snaps back, "Who is this? Who the hell is this?" The voice does not belong to Mac McKlane.

Bootie looks at the phone as the person on the other end keeps shouting. He clicks the phone off just as the large carp snaps Shadrach's line, sending him flat on his butt in the shoreline mud.

"Goddammit," Shadrach says. "Who was that?"

Bootie takes the phone and throws it as far as he can into the Hartbeespoort Dam.

"What the hell?" Shadrach says. "That was brand new, the latest model."

"Hang on a minute," Bootie says, holding his hand up to Bootie. He uses his phone to call Sookie at his farm.

She picks up on the second ring. "Has anyone phoned you, Sookie?" he asks.

"No. What's wrong?"

"Do a hard shutdown on your cellphone. I'm not joking. And tell every one of our men and women down there to do the same thing. Immediately."

"What's going on?"

"I'll tell you when we get home. I want every cellphone invisible, every single one of them. Do it with a hammer if necessary."

Bootie looks at Shadrach, still sitting in the mud. He tosses his cellphone to him.

"Show me how far you can throw it, Shadrach."

The man with the arm of a major league baseball outfielder tosses Bootie's Motorola Encrypted phone over three times further than Shadrach's traveled.

"Shit," Shadrach says. "I forgot to turn it off. They're going to think you drowned, Bootie."

"Still, a nice toss," Bootie says. "You have quite an arm." They both smile at the memory of Shadrach's chuck down the mountainside of Lesotho when he established a firing perimeter for Bootie's attack helicopter at the Royal Peacock Resort and Lodge three years earlier. It saved his and Sookie's life in a slaughter by terrorists that killed every other guest at the Lodge.

"Now, you want to tell me what's going on?" Shadrach asks. "Your Motorola Encrypted phone was old, but mine was the latest model. It cost over a thousand bucks."

Bootie answers: "I think I just made the greatest mistake of my life."

"Good, so you're going to go swimming for my new Motorola Encrypted phone now, right?" Shadrach asks.

"Nope, that was not a mistake. You asked who phoned. Your caller ID said it was General McKlane, but it wasn't him. I answered in Afrikaans as a joke, but the guy on the other end went nuts. No way it was Mac. I think THAT was the greatest mistake of my life. And it was a good one."

"An even bigger mistake than that big fish I just lost?"

"I have the feeling you might have lost more than the fish," Bootie says.

In the car back to Witkoppen, where Bootie van Zale owns a small, 10-acre farm, he tells Shadrach something the American never knew.

"I'm a member of the NIA," Bootie says, "not just a Major in the South African Army."

"The National Intelligence Agency?" Shadrach says. "That explains your weekday trips to Pretoria. I think Sookie and I had that part figured out."

"I've been a member of the NIA since 1994, the first year we held multiracial elections in South Africa. They never knew I didn't support apartheid, although I was a member of the old South African Secret Service."

Bootie pauses, catching a memory.

"I spoke to Nelson Mandela when the government imprisoned him on Robben Island for 18 years. I told him we could get him out of there. He turned me down. He said he was more dangerous as a prisoner than as a fugitive. I think he was one of the smartest, bravest men I ever knew."

After a while, Shadrack asks, "Why did you throw away my brand new Motorola cellphone into the dam?"

"Because our intel suggests your government no longer supports you or General McKlane. They replaced the leadership of your Homeland Security with an acting director who has no experience in national protection, and they fired Roberta Macumber. That was NOT General McKlane calling you on your phone."

Shadrach says nothing.

"We are friends," Bootie says after five minutes of silence. "I want to give you, Sookie, and the 15 men and women staying in the outbuildings on my farm some time to think about what you're doing and where you go from here."

"We are friends," Shadrach says. "Thank you."

Shadrach Ringer is unwilling to discuss their operation with Bootie, who probably already knows what they're planning.

"How big do you think that fish was that I hooked?" he asks as they near Witkoppen.

Bootie laughs and shakes his head.

"It probably weighed more than 20 kilos," Bootie says, "almost 50 of your pounds. We would have to chop it up and soak it in salted water for three days to get the Hartbeespoort mud taste out of it. But it would have fed all your troops."

Six minutes later, they turn into the gravel drive leading to Bootie's 10-acre farm.

As they approach his three-car garage, they see Sookie and all the American men and women waiting for them, fully-armed, some crouched down. Most of them stand in military formation at parade rest as Shadrach Ringer and Bootie van Zale step out of the car.

Chapter 9

They hear the helicopters before they see them. All of the aircraft land on the Kariba Dam road. They seem empty except for their pilots and a machine gunner at each doorway. They are Denel Oryx helicopters built in South Africa, and they resemble American Black Hawks, with less firepower but more room for troops.

The markings on the side of each chopper identify them as part of the South African National Defence Force.

Shadrach and Sookie Ringer appear and step down from the lead helicopter, along with Bootie van Zale, as the blades wind down and eventually stop.

There are seven helicopters, and a huge black man steps out of the furthest one. He walks up to General McKlane and holds out his hand.

Only when McKlane returns the handshake do his warriors move their fingers from the triggers to the sides of their weapons' activation guards.

"Nice to meet you, General," the man says. "I'm Colin Rafiki." General McKlane smiles as he grips the man's large hand. It comes close to wrapping entirely around his own.

"I wonder if you could introduce me to the woman who shot Kibwe Khamisi before they hung him."

"How do you know it was a woman?" the general asks.

"Roberta Macumber told me, and she also showed me the video of his death."

A Marine Raider steps forward.

She says: "It was me, sir."

Colin Rafiki bear hugs her before she can move back. The large man moves quickly. She expects the embrace to be soft because he looks quite a bit overweight. She discovers that he is all muscle.

"Thank you," Colin Rafiki says, releasing her. "Kibwe Khamisi was my father-in-law."

"Oh, my God. I am so sorry."

"Don't be sorry," Colin tells the woman. "I think I would have done the same thing under the circumstances."

"Your poor wife," the Marine Raider says.

"No, now they are together. My wife died a long time ago." He turns to General McKlane. "The next time you see Roberta Macumber, get her to tell you the story about cane rats and how Kibwe Khamisi saved my life."

"I will," General McKlane says. "Can you tell me why you're here?"

"I want to borrow some of your men," Colin Rafiki says. "And, in return, my old friend Bootie van Zale will give you and the rest of your men a free ride to your next target, Pelindaba East, the Y-Plant. It's their Safari Nuclear reactor."

The general sends a piercing look at Shadrach and Sookie. "How did you know about Pelindaba?" he asks, without taking his eyes off of them. They both raise their hands in surprise at what Colin Rafiki has just said.

"Bootie van Zale and I have worked together for a very long time, haven't we, Bootie? We both know that Pelindaba and Pelindaba East are critical targets for ISIS, although the Y-Plant is not easy to break into."

"We have worked a long time together," Bootie says. "You're the only one who understood what my grandfather said after the bee stings."

"The bee stings?" Mac asks. "What does that mean?"

Bootie explains.

His grandfather was one of the founders of BOSS, the old Bureau of State Security in South Africa, which over the years, became the Foreign Branch of South Africa's State Security Agency, its equivalent of the CIA, the Secret Service, and the FBI combined.

"BOSS was associated with apartheid," Bootie explains, "but my grandfather disliked and feared the concept of black and white segregation, even though he was an Afrikaaner. I think the prime minister of South Africa, B.J. Vorster, found out about this.

"He and my grandfather went out on a honey-hunting trip outside Cape Town in 1967, just the two of them. My grandfather was stung by honeybees from head to toe. He was completely naked when we found him."

Prime Minister Vorster told Bootie his father had just run away, tearing off his clothes as the bees attacked him.

"I later found footprints and knee marks all around where my grandfather fell. I told this to my grandmother, and she swore me to secrecy."

Bootie explains that she said their lives depended on it.

"I was a child. I did not even talk about it with my mother or father. My grandfather never recovered. He never spoke again. He spent the last nine years of his life in a wheelchair. His caretaker was a young boy from Kenya named Colin Rafiki. They would spend 14 hours a day together, never saying a word, and Colin would then tell me what he said with his eyes."

"It was the way he blinked," Colin Rafiki says. "Not just 'two for yes' and 'one for no.' Half blinks, quarter blinks, triple blinks, different shades of blinking linked to his eye direction. It became something similar to hand gesturing. He spoke an entire language with his eyes and eyelids, perhaps over a thousand words before he died. It was always a unique and unbreakable code."

"And only Colin could understand it. He would talk to me and my grandmother about it at night," Bootie van Zale says. A few people see silent tears running down Colin Rafiki's face, quickly replaced by a laugh. It sounds very much like a double bass instrument in a one-person symphony.

"Bootie's grandfather, with the help of his grandmother, started underground movements with his eyes, activist publications," Colin Rafiki says. "He started the largest weekly newsmagazine in Africa, called *News/Check*, run by an anti-apartheid editor name Otto Krause. Bootie's grandfather's eye language was, truly, a secret language, an invisible threat to inequality, discrimination, and unfairness. A man stung almost to death by bees helped destroy apartheid, and nobody knew about it. He did not live long enough to see Nelson Mandela move off Robben Island in Table Bay and become the first Black President of South Africa. For that, I am sorry. But he is the reason I ended up in America, in the Central Intelligence Agency."

The story leaves everyone quiet for a moment, and some of the women have decided they could fall in love with a man like Colin Rafiki.

"Why do you need some of my highly-trained warriors," General McKlane finally asks.

"To protect the DeBeers Diamond Complex from being taken over by ISIS. It is their planned replacement for the oil fields they have lost in eastern Syria, and I know your section at Homeland Security does not consider it a sub-Saharan target they can defend."

Mac notes that several women have already raised their hands as potential volunteers for the mission.

"How many people do you need?"

"Maybe a dozen, more if you can spare them."

"How many of your CIA people can you count on?" Mac asks the large man.

"I'm not sure, General McKlane. I think I'm sort of in the same position you are right now. I don't answer my Motorola encrypted phone either. I don't trust whoever is on the other end, especially if it's the new Acting Director of the Central Intelligence Agency. The senate-approved director resigned three days ago."

"Colin Rafiki threw my brand new Motorola encrypted phone into the Hartbeespoort Dam," Shadrach says.

"Yes, Shadrach, but you threw mine three times further," Colin Rafiki says.

General Mac McKlane smiles and asks Bootie if any of his contacts in South Africa remain reliable.

Bootie says the best answer he can give him is "Maybe," which is better than "No."

"Can you find out if a freighter named the *S.S. Nomad* is still in Cape Town?" Mac asks.

"As of this morning, yes it is," Bootie says.

"So, you know about the *S.S. Nomad*?" Mac asks.

"From the inside out," Bootie answers. "It's a helluva training ship, General McKlane."

"Mac," he says. "Everyone calls me 'Mac.'"

Abu Muhammed al-Shimali says: "Atomic bombs were made by South Africa as far back as 1966. We need one or two of them to become a nuclear power."

"We have several people inside Pelindaba who can help us do this," one of his ISIS leaders says.

Pelindaba is South Africa's main nuclear research center near the Hartbeespoort Dam, where Bootie and Shadrach often go fishing for Hartie Carp along its embankments. Both of them tossed away their Motorola Encrypted phones there.

The word "Pelindaba" seems fitting.

It is Zulu for "end of story" or "the conclusion."

The nuclear research center is 22 miles from Pretoria, the original capital of South Africa, during the dark ages of apartheid and white nationalism.

After apartheid crumbles into several years of rioting and lawlessness, Pretoria becomes one of the three capitals of the Republic of South Africa.

Pretoria remains the home of the executive branch of South Africa's government.

Cape Town becomes the legislative capital, housing the National Assembly and the National Council of

Provinces, of which there are nine. Cape Town is the nation's second-largest city, following Johannesburg.

Cape Town is famous for Table Mountain and The Seven Sisters, a dry and mountainous area that produces some of the world's best wines.

It is also near the current port of the *S.S. Nomad.*

The third capital in the Republic of South Africa is a city in the center of the nation called Bloemfontein, densely populated by Afrikaners, descendants of 17th-century Dutch settlers. They fought a long and bloody war against the British from 1899 to 1902, called the Boer War, which they lost.

It was the first time that trench warfare entered into warfare's military lexicon.

Bloemfontein houses the second-highest court in the land, the Supreme Court of Appeals, although the Republic of South Africa's Constitutional Court, equivalent to America's Supreme Court, is in Johannesburg.

"Pelindaba," Abu Muhammed says, "is the only place that counts in the Republic of South Africa."

He knows the history of Pelindaba, and he appreciates that it means "end of story" in the African language of Zulu.

"Its first research reactor came from America, the SAFARI-1," Abu Muhammed says. "Tell me, why would the Americans use a Swahili word for a 10.5 million dollar reactor in a nation where no Swahili exists?"

In Swahili, the word "safari" means "a trip."

"The Americans do not understand Africa," one of his aides says.

"And this has always been our advantage on this continent," Abu Muhammed says.

Enriched uranium for the SAFARI-1 originally comes from the United States, subject to the International Atomic Energy Agency, which prohibits its use for any military purpose, especially nuclear weapons.

During Pelindaba's inauguration, future cooperation with France, not America, appears likely. Knowledgeable people say that South Africa could produce an atomic weapon in 1966. A French nuclear weapons test suggests an atomic bomb created in South Africa is responsible for elevated radiation levels in the Pacific Ocean.

In 1970, Prime Minister John Vorster, a staunch supporter of apartheid, revealed a pilot enrichment plant for uranium-235 at Valindaba, Pelindaba East, or the Y-Plant.

The word "Valindaba" means, "we don't talk about this at all" in the tongue-clicking language of Lesotho.

In 1975, Vorster ordered more shipments of weapons-grade uranium from the United States "for peaceful uses only." America agrees and sends the uranium to South Africa on the condition that any enriched, weapons-grade plutonium produced from its fission will return to America immediately.

Not an ounce of enriched plutonium ever leaves the Republic of South Africa.

South Africa decided to abandon its nuclear program in 1989. It calls itself the only nation on earth to build a nuclear weapons program and then unbuild it.

South Africa has seven atomic bombs and one under construction when they stop their bomb-building program. The South African government says the enriched uranium is extracted, melted down, and cast into ingots.

No verified, international proof of this exists.

Even if it is true, the survival of weapons-grade nuclear fuel means that South Africa can quickly become a nuclear state again.

One of the biggest concerns to the United States remains its belief that the atomic bombs at Pelindaba still exist, and they are the world's most vulnerable to theft from terrorists like ISIS.

The South African government rebuffs repeated demands from America to surrender their nuclear fuel. South African politicians call it "discrimination," a word that dismisses and often quiets any claims from the United States, but never its fears.

Another potential nuclear power makes a similar claim of prejudice: the state of Iran.

However, the Muslim politics of Iran never quell American intentions. They are willing to destroy Iran.

A silver vault in Pelindaba is said to hold almost 500 pounds of enriched uranium.

It resembles the "Houdini Room" aboard the *S.S.Nomad,* although it's not clear plastic.

America does not know if the highly-enriched uranium is ingots or "ready to go and blow" bombs in polished silver spheres.

But they do know where it is.

So does Abu Muhammed al-Shimali.

Mac McKlane and Bootie van Zale sit alone, away from the helicopters and Mac's warriors.

"I have a problem with you, Bootie."

"What's that?"

"You are South African."

"What don't you like about South Africans?"

"We're here to steal all of your weapons-grade plutonium and send it back to America."

"I know that."

"It doesn't bother you?"

"Not a bit. Can we include Colin Rafiki in this conversation? He knows me much better than you do, Mac."

The general asks Colin Rafiki to join them.

"What's up?" the large man says, "Other than me." He releases another deep laugh.

"General McKlane thinks I'll go bonkers if the Americans recover all of the atom bombs that we've stored at Valindaba at the Y-Plant.'"

"He won't be pissed off," Colin Rafiki tells Mac.

"Why not?"

Bootie answers.

"Because we promised America, over 50 years ago, that we would return every ounce of weapons-grade plutonium we produced to the United States. Prime Minister Vorster made and then broke that deal. And so has every leader of the South African Republic since then."

General McKlane looks at both men, then leans towards Bootie. "It has always given you a place at the leadership table."

Bootie nods.

"You don't care about that?" Mac asks.

"My grandfather did not care about that. Nor do I."

Colin nods.

Bootie points to his forehead. "My grandfather is still alive in here. He was the wisest man I ever knew, although I can't even remember the sound of his voice. He never thought that South Africa should be a nuclear power in terms of weaponry, although he thought it made sense for electricity production."

Colin says, "He blinked that all the time."

After a while, Mac says to Bootie: "You had an extraordinary childhood."

"Yes, I did."

"I hope we can honor your grandfather's wishes."

"Before ISIS does," Colin says.

They all agree on that.

"For your DeBeers operation," Mac says, "you can take a dozen of my best people, but not Holly, Shadrach, Sookie, Charlton, Ernestine, Sharonda, Samuel, or the monkey, Sophia."

"Damned," Colin says to both men. "The monkey was my first choice. How about that scruffy dog?"

They laugh.

"And, Colin," Mac McKlane says, "I don't want you to take only women, either. Take some Navy SEALs. No harems, even if most of the women already love you."

"Well, diamonds ARE a girl's best friend," Colin says.

"No harems."

"Deal. And thanks, Mac."

Before they can shake hands, the shooting starts.

When the seven South African helicopters enter the airspace of Zimbabwe and land on the dam of Lake Kariba, a Chinese People's Army military advisor working in Bulawayo sees it on the encrypted device he uses at home for discovery and tracking purposes. He immediately reports it to his superior officer in the Chinese Belt and Road Initiative. This program improves Zimbabwe's infrastructure and Chinese influence in Harare, the capital of Zimbabwe. The informant suggests that South Africa is attacking the Kariba Dam, and his superior officer hears reports of massive explosions in that area even before he hangs up.

He immediately phones President Emmerson Mnangagwa, who was appointed the president of Zimbabwe following a coup in November 2017.

The Zimbabwe Defence Forces tried to unify three revolutionary groups after the Rhodesian Bush Wars, which lasted from July 1964 to 1979, but unification never worked. The Zimbabwe National Army (ZNA), initially trained by British military personnel in 1980, quickly supports Robert Mugabe's terror and mass brutality reign. Mugabe achieves his liberation struggle in 1988.

With a total population of slightly over 14 million people, three million of them fit for service, the active-duty military personnel numbers 30,000.

The country's airpower shows they have more Trainer planes than Fighters, Attack Craft, and Transports combined.

They have a total of 28 helicopters, of which only six are attack aircraft.

They have 42 combat tanks, many of which are under constant repair. They have 300 armored fighting vehicles and

65 towed artillery pieces, most of which require well-paved roads on which to operate. Zimbabwe is a nation of rutted, poorly-managed dirt roads. The Chinese Belt and Road Initiative is trying to fix this, but it takes time and usurious loan agreements that send Zimbabwe deeper into debt traps from which the nation will never recover.

"President Emmerson Mnangagwa," the senior Chinese officer says, "we believe your nation is under attack by South African forces on Lake Kariba."

"We will beat them back," the president says, knowing that he has few resources with which to accomplish such a task. President Mnangagwa phones the Commander of the Zimbabwe Defence Forces. "We are under attack by South Africa at Lake Kariba," he says.

Commander Chimonyo of the Zimbabwe Defence Forces says: "I have a combat group of 35 men training in Matusadona National Park as well as a boat squadron at Nyami-Nyami on Lake Kariba itself."

The Zambezi River God inspires the naming of the Nyami-Nyami boat squadron. Tonga tribe members originally persuade God Nyaminyami to tame the great Zambezi River.

The god has the body of a snake and the head of a fish, and nobody knows how big he is. Although a Tonga Chief named Sampakaruma claims to have seen him twice before white men came to Lake Kariba, God Nyaminyami had never shown himself in full display.

Ironically, the boat squadron also does not show itself. All of its vessels remain in drydock, under repair. They do hear the explosions at the dam but make no move to discover the problem.

They assume the government is demolishing and deepening the riverbed above the dam to improve the water flow during the current drought.

The call from Commander Chimonyo surprises the boat squadron.

"We can have our boats in the water in two days," the commanding officer assures him. It takes him a while to realize he is talking to a dead phone.

The commander has better luck with the combat group in Matusadona National Park, which is already moving towards the dam and the sounds of explosives.

"There are six, no seven helicopters, commander," their senior officer reports, looking through high-power binoculars. "And, yes, they all have South African markings on them."

"Destroy them," the commander says. "Kill them all."

The senior officer immediately orders his men to fire at the enemy. He keeps his phone open so that his commander can hear them shooting.

They are well over a mile away from the helicopters.

heartbeats

"I don't want to start a war with Zimbabwe," Mac tells Colin Rafiki. "Everyone load up," he shouts. "Colin," he says more quietly, "I don't want any of your chopper surgeons, your door gunners, firing at anyone."

Colin nods and passes it along.

"The first three eggbeaters are yours," Mac says. "The last four are mine."

"Good luck in Valindaba. That's where the bombs are, Pelindaba-East, at the Y-Plant. They call it Valindaba."

"Good luck at DeBeers," Mac says. "It must be intuition," he says, looking past Colin's left shoulder."

Colin turns around.

Mostly women Marine Raiders and Army Rangers are jumping into the first three choppers.

Mac orders a dozen Navy SEALS to join Colin's group, replacing the same number of female warriors. No woman has made it through SEAL training, although one person had the chance to try in 2019, opting for the Army Rangers instead.

"You know," Colin says as the SEALS replace the women in his helicopters, "it's gotta be the diamonds. They ARE a girl's best friend."

Mac laughs, and then he ducks as a lucky shot from far away punches a hole in his helicopter.

"Get 'em outa here," he shouts as the Denel Oryx helicopters' blades come up to speed. He jumps into the fourth one with his team, and all the helicopters rise off the road.

The Zimbabwean commander is shouting into his phone. He has heard all the gunfire. Now he expects results.

"How many of the helicopters have you destroyed?" the commander asks.

"We have scared them all away," the senior officer of the combat group in the Matusadona National Park says. "They are all gone. They flee like hens."

"Hens?" the commander asks. "How many did you shoot down? How many people did you kill?"

"We were probably six kilometers away when you asked us to fire," the senior officer of the combat group says, exaggerating the distance enormously.

The commander is quiet, trying to control himself. Finally, he says: "You have a video of this South African invasion, correct?"

Now the senior officer is quiet. Then he says: "You did not ask us to shoot pictures, commander. You asked us to shoot bullets."

"And how many of the South African terrorists did you kill? How many are wounded?"

"We will call you with the number of dead South Africans when we get to the dam, commander."

"You better find bodies," the commander says, "a lot of them."

They find quite a few corpses an hour and a half later, but none of them are wearing South African uniforms. They all appear to be Muslim terrorists.

The senior officer of the combat group calls the commander.

"We have found more than three dozen dead men," he says.

"Take pictures of them," the commander says.

"They are all wearing black," the senior officer says. "They appear to be ISIS freedom fighters, commander, not South African terrorists."

The phone is silent.

"ISIS freedom fighters, commander," he repeats.

The phone is dead again.

After flying miles down the gorge, the leading three South African Denyl Oryx helicopters turn slightly southwest, heading through Zimbabwean airspace.

They fly toward the nation of Botswana and the DeBeers Diamond Complex.

The diamond company was founded in 1888 by Cecil Rhodes, who had the backing of a South African diamond magnate. He was the rich man who put Cecil Rhodes in touch with powerful bankers at N.M. Rothschild & Sons in the United Kingdom.

The remaining four helicopters continue going east, heading into Mozambique.

Then they will turn south, heading across the border into the Republic of South Africa in an hour.

All of the helicopters are refueled in the air as they fly towards their rendezvous with ISIS.

Initially, Bootie thought about fuel bladders stationed at bases along the route, but he eventually rejected the idea for security, secrecy, and logistical reasons.

His decision to refuel in the air almost kills him.

The South African National Defence Force was born in 1994, resulting from a long line of primarily White fighting organizations. Conscription was limited to White people until 1971, with a few exceptions for those who possessed mixed ancestry.

After 1971, the infantry included several Black battalions on a tribal basis, but always under the command of a White commissioned officer.

Armed White troops quelled minority rule complaints during apartheid, often supported by the South African Police. The South African Army also fought in the long-running Angolan and Mozambique wars, siding with the Portuguese colonists, not the freedom fighters in Frelimo or the National Freedom Front. The South African Army battled Cuban soldiers and tribal leaders from the north and south of Angola.

South African troops tried but failed to destroy Frelimo in the Portuguese colony of Mozambique, which dominated politics in that nation after 1962.

In South Africa, the first Black soldier became a commissioned officer in 1986, but only Black soldiers and non-commissioned officers were under him.

South Africa has almost 600,000 active and part-time soldiers. Bootie van Zale is a Major in the nation's supposedly disbanded Commando Forces, on the staff of two Black Lieutenant Generals who share duties as the Chiefs of Joint Operations. Bootie initially trained in the South African Air Force under Lieutenant General Jan Petrus Benjamin van Loggerenberg, Chief of the Air Force and a long-time friend of his grandfather.

Loggenberg gave the eulogy at Bootie's grandfather's funeral. He also shared many of his grandfather's beliefs, especially about apartheid.

Neither one of Bootie's current commanders knows where or how Major van Zale disappeared with seven Denel Oryx helicopters attached to the 16 Squadron at the air force base at Bloemspruit, near the capital city of Bloemfontein. The helicopters carry up to 20 fully-equipped troops, with a door-mounted machine gun and two pilots.

"Is he on a training mission?"

"That's what his flight sheet says, but there was nothing like that planned. His squadron commander says they were expecting a week for maintenance."

"You've tried to raise him?"

"Of course. Major van Zale has been on vacation on his small farm in Witkoppen. He does not answer his secure phone, although we can locate it several hundred yards offshore at the Hartbeespoort Dam."

"He loved to fish. Perhaps he's drowned."

"With seven of our Denel Oryx helicopters?"

"Sorry, Commander."

"Yes, you are."

The two South African lieutenant generals will not share their leadership.

However, the air force chief assumes tactical priority over the head of the army in this case. They are on the same team but competitive.

The older chief of the air force will enjoy making fun of the younger general behind his back with the story of drowning helicopters.

They decide to make some calls to see if they can unravel the mystery of Major Bootie van Zale.

A MiG-21 fighter scrambling out of Beira Air Base in Mozambique helps identify the major's whereabouts.

Bootie's helicopter is being refueled in the air when the MiG-21 makes its first pass. Between 1977 and 1989, the Russians supply Mozambique with military equipment. In 2014, a Romanian company named Aerostar contracted to upgrade Mozambique's eight remaining MiG-21s. As Bootie's helicopters skirt the border between Zimbabwe and Mozambique, *Força Aérea de Moçambique* sends one of its two operational MiG-21s up to take a look.

The Portuguese pilot identifies four fully-armed Denel Oryx helicopters flying in a tight formation.

He flies close enough to the attack helicopters to see their array of air-to-air missiles.

He watches as they move in and out of Mozambique's air space, apparently heading for South Africa.

The Portuguese pilot asks for orders.

"They have violated our sovereignty," an aide to the army chief, Major General Filipe Macaringue, says. He is young and eager to prove his value to the history of

Mozambique while his leader, the Major General, relaxes at a resort on the coast with his family.

"What do you see?" the aide asks the pilot.

"They are currently refueling one of the Denel Oryx helicopters," the MiG-21 pilot says as he makes his second pass over the group.

"Did you say they were attacking us?" the aide asks.

The Denel Oryx helicopters have now spread further apart, protecting both the refueling plane and the formation.

"No," the MiG-21 pilot says, "I said they were attack helicopters, very power ...."

"The refueling helicopter is weak. Shoot it down," the aide says.

"The Denel Oryx helicopters are not weak," the pilot says over his intercom.

"Shoot it down."

"On whose authority?" the pilot asks.

"On the orders of Major General Filipe Macaringue," the aide says. "Shoot it down."

All the Denyl Oryx pilots see the MiG-21 turn and lock on to Bootie van Zale's helicopter.

Bootie sees it as well and breaks away from the refueling craft.

The Mig-21 opens up with its machine guns as the helicopters dive, but the MiG-21 has no air-to-air missiles. The Denel Oryx helicopters fire their rockets. No bullets pierce any of the helicopters.

Bootie watches as the MiG-21 explodes, and he feels somewhat relieved when he sees a parachute open below and well behind its flight path.

Although he's confident that the pilot bailed before Bootie's helicopters fired their first rockets, he still can't resist saying, over the intercom:

"You should never bring bullets to a rocket fight."

He tasted metal in his mouth as the MiG-21 made its approach. That was often the sign of fear that he never showed. A MiG-21 armed with rockets would have destroyed all of them.

Bootie immediately realizes that he has made a monumental mistake. He has broken radio silence.

At the South African air force base at Bloemspruit, the leader of 16 Squadron does not appreciate the joke about bullets in a rocket fight, and he recognizes Bootie's voice.

"What sort of bloody nonsense is this?" he asks as he watches five aircraft move toward's South African territory.

One disappears from their scanning sweep shortly before Major van Zale breaks radio silence.

"Get in touch with these bleeding idiots," he says.

They try, but they only contact silence.

Four jet fighters take off from Air Force Base Makhado, South Africa's northernmost base near the border with Zimbabwe.

They are all Saab Gripens, delta-winged planes with a top speed of Mach 2, twice the speed of sound, powered by Volvo engines.

They quickly spot the Denel Oryx helicopters and slow their airspeed to carefully guide them back to Pretoria's Swartkop Airbase.

In Mozambique, the aide to Major General Filipe Macaringue sees his MiG-21 disappear, replaced by four new dots on the screen that suddenly come out of South Africa's northernmost airbase.

A young lieutenant working in Mozambique's Air Force reporting to Macaringue's aide asks, "Should we send up our other MiG 21 fighter, sir?"

The aide to Major General Filipe Macaringue, who sent up the first MiG, stares at him a long time and finally answers: "I don't know why YOU sent up the initial one."

Then the general's aide turns and, as he's walking out the door, says: "You are a moron, a complete idiot."

"Wait a sec... "

"Expect to be arrested for this," the general's aide shouts as he slams the screen door shut, looking for the military police.

On the border between Zimbabwe and South Africa, nobody on the helicopters makes an aggressive move. All the door gunners take their hands off their .50 caliber, armor-piercing machine guns and wave to their countrymen in the Saab Gripens flying past them."What are they saying?" the leader of 16 Squadron at Bloemspruit asks.

"Nothing," the wing commander says. "They're waving at us. Some of them are pointing at their helmets, indicating they can't hear, sir, and, uh ....""

"What?" the Squadron leader asks.

"I think a lot of them are Americans, sir. I mean, they have American flags on their helmets and camos, uh, I think one of them may be a general, sir."

"What the bloody hell is going on?"

"Not sure, sir. Jesus Christ, one of them has a monkey, sir. And there's a dog, too, a very scruffy dog. You know, it looks to me as if Major Bootie van Zale just saved a bunch of Yanks from something dangerous happening in either Zambia, Zimbabwe, Malawi, or Mozambique. I mean, they're all giving us a thumbs up, sir. It, uh, makes me feel proud, only I'm not sure what we should be proud of."

Bootie can hear everything the squadron leader says between the Saab Gripens and Bloemspruit.

He understands when the 16 Squadron leader says: "I want you to force them down in Swartkop."

It's an airbase outside Pretoria.

Bootie breaks radio silence once again, but this time on purpose. He says one word. "Witkoppen."

As the helicopters head east southeast, the wing commander of the Saab Gripens tells the leader of 16 Squadron, "They're turning towards Johannesburg, sir. I don't think we can get them to land at Swartkop unless we immediately shoot them down. *Kan hulle Johannesburg teiken?*" ("Could they target Johannesburg?")

"Witkoppen," the Squadron leader says. "They're going to land at Major Bootie van Zale's little farm in Witkoppen. I will be there within an hour."

"Witkoppen," the wing commander repeats. He sees a lot more thumbs up from the helicopters.

"Make sure you see them wind down before returning to Air Force Base Makhado. If they don't land in Witkoppen, blow them out of the sky. And always keep one of your Saab Gripens in the air within striking distance of Major van Zale's little farm. It's about to become an airbase."

"*Roger Dit,*" the Afrikaans wing commander says. Like the Squadron Commander, he has fought many African battles, from the border wars in Angola to Lesotho, the Congo, and Burundi. He has only recently returned from a tour in Sudan. He has never witnessed anything close to what he sees now.

Both the Squadron leader and the wing commander realize that anything can happen. The situation could quickly unfold into a ruthless and well-disguised attack on Johannesburg, less than 25 miles from Witkoppen.

Chapter 10

The Witkoppen Health and Welfare Center was born in the impoverished shadow of SOWETO, an acronym for the South West Township created by the white supremacy of apartheid. It supplies Johannesburg and its gold mines with Black workers and a dominant White population with houseboys and cooks, calling their employers "master."

Three public-spirited nurses establish the center, and after over 70 years, it has become a provider of high-quality healthcare to needy people regardless of nationality. They serve over 1.3 million people, including three dozen ISIS warriors who have recently settled in the area near the Orlando East mosque.

"They know we are here," one man says as the Saab jets and one attack helicopter fill the airspace above the city.

"We need to speak to Ginger," another man says. "I warned you about him."

Ginger works for the owner of a 10-acre farm just a few miles away. He is just a bit over 5 feet tall but a hardworking man and a recent convert to Islam.

He has stopped working for the farm owner because people suddenly show up at his employer's house carrying assault rifles.

Ginger has never been brave.

The ISIS terrorists find Ginger Mbeki, whose last name is the city he grew up in, in a bar just south of Bootie van Zale's 10-acre farm.

Ginger drinks millet beer, an opaque alcoholic beverage, and he's in the process of buying a wife.

"We have told you not to drink, Ginger," the ISIS leader they call Jalaluddin Shekau says as he and his men step into the bar.

Jalaluddin Shekau's cousin is the leader of the Boko Haram terrorists in Nigeria. The Muslim men block the doorway as most people slide off barstools and scrape back table chairs, exiting through the back door.

Ginger points to a young girl in the corner of the bar. "I am celebrating my new wife," he says, lifting a glass of milky fluid that most people still call Bantu beer.

The older man sitting next to him nods. He holds a fistful of 100 and 200 rand notes, called ZAR. He has just sold his granddaughter to Ginger for 6,000 ZAR, a little over $400. The currency is falling fast in an economy that suffers from severe inflation.

The grandfather had asked Ginger to throw a couple of goats into the deal, but Ginger owns no animals, only a tiny, broken-down hut on a barren plot of land a half a mile closer to Bootie van Zale's farm.

The marriage turns into a cash deal.

The granddaughter cries, tears running down her cheeks. The man she loves makes Ginger look like a wrinkled prune. Her boyfriend is 30 years younger than Ginger. He stands in the corner of the bar, waiting for Ginger to try to claim his bride.

A well-muscled freelance auto mechanic who lives from paycheck to paycheck, he's holding a thick, round, metal rebar as if it were a walking stick. The boyfriend is more than willing to bend it over Ginger's head.

The man moves towards Ginger's new wife but halts when he sees the men wearing keffiyehs, traditional Arab headdress, enter the bar.

He has many Muslim friends, but none go to bars, although he knows some drink in private.

"We need to speak," the ISIS leader says to Ginger, and his robe opens a bit, showing an assault weapon.

Drinkers who remain in the bar back up, although the granddaughter's boyfriend does not. He says: "*Salaam.*"

Jalaluddin Shekau glares at him.

The boyfriend says, in English, "I am here to protect my wife, who is NOT the property of the man you call Ginger. I do not drink. I follow the laws of Allah and the last prophet of Islam, the great Muhammad."

It's a lie since he's a Baptist from birth, but who cares?

Nobody moves or says a word, although the ISIS leader smiles. He looks down at Ginger and says: "We need to talk now, Ginger Mbeki."

"I must bring my new wife with me," Ginger says. Another terrorist blocks his way to the granddaughter. She is scared but no longer sobbing, looking at her boyfriend rather than the men wearing Arab headdresses.

"Leave the woman," Jalaluddin Shekau says. Two terrorists grab Ginger and pick him up quickly, moving him through the entrance of the bar.

"But my money," Ginger shouts.

"Leave the money," the Muslim leader says. The girl's grandfather has already stuffed it into his baggy trousers.

Jalaluddin Shekau stops in the doorway, looking at the black man holding a thick metal bar.

He says: "alsalam lak ya 'akhi."

The boyfriend bows slightly as the ISIS leader leaves.

The girlfriend is in his arms, sobbing again, but for a different reason.

The grandfather disappears through the back door.

"What did he say?" his girlfriend asks.

He said: "Peace to you, brother."

"Am I your wife?"

"I think so," the boyfriend answers.

Nobody at the bar ever sees Ginger Mbeki again.

The helicopters land at Bootie's 10-acre farm, and they open all their communication lines. Bootie, Shadrach, Sookie, and Mac all listen to the conversation between the wing commander and the Squadron leader.

They hear his threat to blow them out of the sky if they try to take off again. They have no intention of doing this, and all the helicopter blades wind down and freeze in place, although they do not lock them. Troops exit, stack their weapons, and sit on the ground.

"Squadron Leader, this is Major van Zale, and we will wait right here until you arrive."

A different voice comes on the line. Bootie recognizes the chief of the South African Air Force.

Bootie says, "shit" with his mouth but not his voice. "Brigadier General," he says out loud., "Sir."

"Neither you nor your American friends will make a move, Major van Zale. Remain in place until the squadron leader and I arrive."

"Yes, sir," Bootie says.

The line goes dead.

He looks at General McKlane, Holly, Shadrach, Sookie, Sharonda, Samuel, and the monkey, Sophia.

They shut off all their Motorola cellphones, knowing that whatever they say can be data preserved. Not a single word of their discussion reaches beyond themselves.

"We can't fool the chief of the air force with lies," Bootie says. "This guy has spent a lot of time in Tanzania, Angola, and Zimbabwe. After training in the USSR in the mid-1980s, he became a pilot in what people now call Kirghizstan. He knows more about helicopters than I do. He is the smartest communist I ever met."

"So we tell him the truth," General McKlane says.

"He will ask us where the other three helicopters are," Bootie says.

"And we will tell him the truth. A CIA agent who helped save us in Zimbabwe has taken them to the DeBeers complex in Botswana to protect the diamond mines from ISIS, at least that is what he told us."

They move into the home where Bootie lives to get their story straight.

The house is a series of rondavels that remind Sookie and Shadrach of the Royal Peacock Resort and Lodge in Lesotho, where they fought ISIS terrorism face-to-face and were saved and debriefed by Bootie van Zale three years earlier.

All the rooms in the house are perfectly round, some much larger than others, with straw roofs held up by umbrellas of thick, wooden beams. Between the round rooms, windowed hallways connect everything.

"He will know all about Tanzania and its Declaration of War on America. One of his original role models was the first president of Tanzania, Julius K. Nyerere," Bootie says.

"The war never happened," Sharonda says.

"I'm not so sure. The papers in South Africa said that American drones wiped out an entire brigade of Tanzanian infantry on the border with Malawi."

"We will listen to your chief of the air force, but we know that opinion is not valid," General McKlane says. "We saw the drones, and they all overshot the Tanzanian brigade southeast of Mbeya. We saw them explode. Perhaps some collateral damage occurred, but I doubt if any soldiers were even wounded, Bootie. Also, their ambassador died before he could deliver the Declaration of War against the United States."

Bootie says, "The commander might decide to imprison all of us anyway. He does not like Americans or anything about the United States."

"If your commander tries to put us in jail, we have a small army to threaten him with, and we won't even defer to the American Embassy before pulling the trigger. I'm not sure what we do about you, Bootie. Where will you find safety?"

Without even thinking, Bootie answers: "I will be safe in the memory of my grandfather."

"Your commander's bee stings might kill you."

"I know. We are all military people. We have all died many times. Do not worry about me, Mac, or any of you. Worry about your mission. I hope you succeed. Let me see if I can get Ginger to make us some iced tea."

He searches the house and then walks to his garage to look in the servant's quarters.

"I think it's Ginger's day off," Bootie tells the team as he returns. "I'll make the tea myself. The commander and squadron leader won't be here for another 25 minutes."

heartbeats

When the communications line goes dead between South Africa's air force commander and Bootie van Zale, both men assume that the other has hung up.

Although the commander feels angry about this, he has already moved to a Denel Rooivalk attack helicopter, commonly known as a "Red Falcon." The squadron leader sits in the co-pilot's seat.

The "Red Falcon" cannot carry any troops. Instead, it has lethal and powerful weapons operated by a two-person crew. The commander lifts the aircraft off the ground and heads for Witkoppen at top speed.

"Contact the Major," the commander says. He hands him the phone number to Bootie van Zale's encrypted Motorola cellphone.

In the Hartbeespoort Dam, someone has been dragging the bottom and finds Bootie's waterproof phone several hundred yards from shore, in shallow water. He cleans it off and then suddenly drops it into the bottom of the boat when it rings. He picks it up carefully and says, "Hello?"

"Give me the major," a voice says.

"Who's the major?"

"Don't get smart with me, soldier. I want to speak to Major Bootie van Zale immediately. Put him on. Do it now, and then I want your name and your *former* rank." He has switched his encrypted Motorola to speaker status so that the commander can hear the conversation, although their airspeed makes this problematic.

The commander grabs the phone and shouts, "This is a matter of national security. The major. NOW."

The man who dredged up the Motorola cellphone, who makes his living pickpocketing foreign visitors to the Hartbeespoort Dam, looks at it as if he is holding a poisonous snake. He wipes it clean, getting rid of his fingerprints, and drops it back over the side.

The commander and the squadron leader both hear a distinct "plunk," but nothing more.

"What the bloody hell is going on?" the commander says. "I want every one of those Saab Gripens back in the air and securing the airspace over Witkoppen. Do it now."

All but one of the Gripens land at Air Force Base Makhado near the border of Zimbabwe and immediately refuel. The remaining Saab Gripen, flying back and forth over Witkoppen, returns to its base, rocked by the Mach 2 passage of the rest of the wing on its way back to Witkoppen north of Johannesburg.

While this happens, Ginger suffers a brutal beating. The ISIS terrorists who have dragged him away from his nuptials punch him, breaking his cheekbones on both sides of the older man's face.

They ask him why he has revealed their location to the South African military. Ginger says he has done no such thing, but they hit him harder. One terrorist breaks Ginger's arm over the warrior's knee like a fragile twig. Ginger screams and admits that his boss is a Major in the South African air force. Immediately, the beatings stop. Ginger thinks perhaps he is safe now, but he realizes the gun suddenly pointed at him disagrees. He says, "my wife."

They are his last words.

"This piece of camel dung has betrayed us," the ISIS leader Jalaluddin Shekau says. They move outside their safe houses in Soweto, a suburb of Johannesburg with a population of almost 1.5 million, over 98 percent Black. They walk to the Orlando East mosque constructed in 2011. Few of the non-Muslim neighbors surrounding the mosque know what happens inside it. Nor do they want to.

Suddenly, the skies over Soweto roar with Saab Grippen jets. Jalaluddin Shekau says: "So, this is where we fight. Put on your vests."

He wraps his body with an explosives vest and then takes one of many surface-to-air missiles from the small room in the back of the mosque. He and his followers walk out of the mosque, some carrying several SAMs and grenade launchers. Civilians immediately hide in their homes.

Jalaluddin Shekau is the first to fire at one of the jets as soon as he exits the mosque, and it is a direct hit. The pilot does not even have a chance to throw out flares to protect his Gripen from destruction.

Then the ISIS terrorists jump in their brand-new Range Rovers and head for Witkoppen, where Ginger worked for a South African major.

It's about a fifteen-minute trip, and they destroy two more Saab Gripens before they get to the main road leading to Major Bootie van Zale's 10-acre farm.

They fire their rockets through the open sunroofs of their Range Rovers, burning the passenger seats.

They learn quickly to stand on the second-row passenger seats behind the driver, with their legs stabilized by fellow warriors, sending the backblasts over the rear of the expensive vehicles.

The pilots in the Saab Gripens do not immediately know the source of the missiles. They hear the beeping of an incoming rocket, try to flare, and then their planes explode in a fireball.

Only one pilot manages to parachute on the first hint of a "beep," and the explosion of his fighter badly burns him and shreds a bit of his cockpit parachute.

He lands hard and breaks some bones.

He's barely alive, and he dies surrounded by curious, black faces.

A single Saab Grippen remains in the area, piloted by the wing commander, and he is suddenly flying low and well south of Witkoppen.

"We have lost three Gripens," he tells the commander of the air force. "I only saw one parachute, commander. I assume my other pilots died in the attacks. The enemy is using surface-to-air missiles, and they seem to be coming from Soweto and just south of that township, sir."

"What the bloody hell is going on?" the commander asks. They are approaching Witkoppen from the northeast. They see a surface-to-air missile smoke trail rising towards the remaining Saab Gripen from somewhere south of Soweto, but not from Witkoppen. They see the massive explosion.

As their Denel Rooivalk attack helicopter drops quickly, flying only fifty feet off the ground, they look for a parachute. They see none.

The squadron leader in the Denel Rooivalk attack helicopter immediately contacts Air Force Base Makado. They are refueling the Saab Grippen that has recently landed from its crisscrossing flight pattern above Witkoppen.

"Keep it on the ground," the squadron leader says.

The squadron leader speaks into his encrypted Motorola phone and says: "Major Bootie van Zale, come in. COME IN NOW!"

A Marine Raider walks into Bootie's house and says: "You have a phone call, Major." She hands him her Motorola encrypted cellphone.

"Major Bootie van Zale here," he says.

He recognizes the voice of the brigadier general running the South African Defence Force, who is Black, and he notes that the commander's tone is at least an octave higher than usual.

"Major, what the hell is going on?"

Bootie says: "Ground your helicopter, General. We are under attack by the same ISIS forces from whom we saved our American allies, sir."

Mac McKlane holds out his hand for the phone.

"Good afternoon, General," he says, "I am Brigadier General George McKlane of the United States Marine Corps, and Major van Zale has saved us from an ISIS attack on the Kariba Dam. I believe similar ISIS forces have just shot down some of your delta-wing fighters. I think the major's advice to ground your helicopter is correct."

At Bootie's farm, they have seen some of the aerial explosions as they gathered outside in Witkoppen after hearing the first clap of thunder on a clear day. The only clouds in the blue sky are the remnants of the surface-to-air missiles' paths of destruction.

"We are touching down right now," the squadron leader says into his microphone.

They all see the Denel Rooivalk "Red Falcon" helicopter landing at Bootie's small farm.

"Our men are forming a protective perimeter around your helicopter," General Mac McKlane says, and over 100

Navy SEALs, Marine Raiders, and Army Rangers form a blockade of Bootie's small farm.

The commander is talking to the headquarters of the South African National Defence Force, created in 1994. It is 84 percent Black, Colored, or Asian, and only 16 percent of the troops are White.

Military people consider the South African army, navy, and air forces the most effective military power in sub-Saharan Africa.

ISIS warriors have eliminated close to half of its airborne military firepower in 30 minutes.

It eclipses one of the worst disasters to strike the nation since 13 South African soldiers died and 27 were wounded when Séléka rebels invaded Bangui, the capital of the Central African Republic, a decade earlier. What began as a United Nations Force Intervention quickly turned into an unexpected combat zone. The South African Air Force commander was in Bangui when the Séléka rebels tried to invade that city.

What has happened in the last 30 minutes puts every fiber of his body on alert. He calls the Sergeant Major of the Army, one of the most influential people in the nation's command structure. He immediately asks him to dispatch the Tshwane Regiment, a motorized infantry unit, to Major Bootie van Zale's 10-acre farm.

The South African soldiers stationed in Pretoria are thirty minutes away.

The head of the Defense Force and his squadron leader do not exit their helicopter, although they see American military men and women everywhere, many of them as black as he is. They are all pointing their assault rifles away from the helicopter, apparently protecting him.

Near where he has landed, next to a series of rondavals joined together by windowed passageways, he sees Major Bootie van Zale and a Marine General from the United States, both unarmed, walking towards his Denel Rooivalk attack helicopter. "Don't shoot them," the South African general says to his co-pilot and machine gunner, the squadron leader. "At least not yet."

He opens his cockpit door.

"Major van Zale."

'Welcome to my home, sir." Both he and Mac note that the helicopter's blades continue to whirl. Everyone has to raise their voice.

"Have you been enjoying your vacation?"

"No, sir."

The American General salutes the commander of South Africa's Army. He continues to hold his salute until the South African general finally salutes back. It takes a while.

"I am General George McKlane," Mac says. "I am also a director of America's Homeland Security."

"You are a long way from your homeland, General George McKlane."

"Yes, sir, I am. I work in the CWMD section, sir, which focuses on ISIS. CWMD is an acronym for Countering Weapons of Mass Destruction. I believe ISIS terrorists have shot down your Saab Gripen Delta Wing aircraft, sir."

The Commander of South Africa's Army stares at the American General and then disregards him.

He turns to Major Bootie van Zale.

"Your family has a long and distinguished reputation in South Africa, Major."

"Thank you, sir."

"Your grandfather is a legend among my people."

'Thank you, sir."

"I see four Denel Oryx helicopters on your property."

"Yes, sir."

"Are the other three in your garage, Major?'

"No, sir."

"Have they been destroyed like my Saab Gripen jets, Major van Zale?"

"No, sir, not to my knowledge."

"Not to your knowledge?"

Mac says, "Sir, if I may."

The South African General holds up his hand. "Your country and South Africa maintain bilateral relations, General George McKlane. In my opinion, I do not consider us allies, although I feel some comfort in knowing that your current executive branch admires the Russians who taught me how to fly. Perhaps you will even have a real ambassador in South Africa someday, rather than the currently appointed, South-African-born, American Fashion designer from the Palm Beaches. Kindly do not address me unless I ask you to."

Mac does not know what to say. He takes two steps backward, salutes the general, does an about-face, and returns to his well-armed men and women.

"You're missing three Oryx helicopters," the South African commander says to Bootie. "Where are they, Major?"

"I believe they are protecting the DeBeers diamond mines from an attack by ISIS terrorists in Botswana, sir."

"And who is commanding those three helicopters, Major van Zale?"

Bootie remains uncomfortable with Mac's truth approach. It will not work with South Africa's air force head, but he can't think of an alternative.

"They are commanded by Colin Rafiki, sir."

The general looks at his co-pilot and tells him to punch up the military profile of Colin Rafiki.

"He won't be there, sir," Bootie says.

"He's not South African?"

"No, sir."

"Is he another American General?

"No, sir. He was born in Kenya."

"Rafiki. It's Swahili, of course. It means *friend*."

The South African general lived in Tanzania for several years, long after his family escaped from South Africa's system of apartheid.

They initially sought exile in India.

When he returned to Africa, the South African general became a great admirer of Julius K. Nyerere, the socialist advocate and president of Tanzania, a nation bordering and south of Kenya.

"I never heard of Colin Rafiki," the general says.

"He was quite famous in Burundi," Bootie says.

"I never heard of him."

"No, sir."

"What exactly is this man famous for?"

"You would have to ask General McKlane, sir."

"Get him back here, Major van Zale."

Bootie goes back to his house to get Mac.

As he walks through the door, Mac grabs him and says: "Our radar says that we're about to be confronted by a motorized infantry unit coming out of Pretoria."

"The general wants to talk to you. He wants to know who Colin Rafiki is."

"We're the good guys, right?"

"I'm not sure the general agrees with that."

"OK. I'll talk to the general."

As he walks out of Bootie's home, he signals a Marine Raider and a Navy SEAL to accompany him.

As they move towards the Denel Rooivalk helicopter, Mac tells the Marine Raider to disable the "Red Falcon" by destroying the rear rotor blades.

He orders the Navy SEAL to get up close and personal with the machine gunner without exposing himself to the cannons on the bird.

"I understand you want to know who Colin Rafiki is?" Mac shouts.

Suddenly the "Red Falcon" shudders as the Marine Raider unloads 30 armor-piercing bullets into its rear rotor area in a matter of seconds. He flips the cartridge clip and fires another 30 rounds to confirm the helicopter's inability to take off and fly.

The Navy SEAL disables the helicopter's machine gun the same way, destroying its swivel firing mechanism beneath the cockpit with 30 armor-piercing rounds.

When he flips the cartridge clip for 30 more shots, he points his assault rifle directly at the pilot operating the destroyed machine gun and 700-round cannon. The pilot slowly holds up his hands as if he's under arrest.

"Wind it down, General, and please, come with me. If you want to bring your sidearm with you, I have no problem with that. We will outgun you even when your mechanized infantry unit gets here."

"This is an outrage," the South African general says.

"Yes, it certainly is," Mac says. "So, let's go have some tea or coffee, and please tell your squadron leader to lower his hands and join us. Oh, and Colin Rafiki is a member of America's Central Intelligence Agency, sir."

The general reluctantly gets out of the "Red Falcon." So does the squadron leader, but not before warning the mechanized infantry unit that Major Bootie van Zale's 10-acre farm is under the control of a sizeable and well-armed American military force.

"So be careful," he says. "They have just disabled our helicopter, and the commander of the South African air force and I appear to be their prisoners."

The squadron leader is surprised when the American soldier who blew apart the helicopter's machine gun does not disarm him.

He notices that the commander also continues to carry his standard-issue Vektor SP1 semi-automatic pistol, which holds 15 rounds of 19mm ammunition.

"Welcome to Major van Zale's home," the Navy SEAL says. "I am Lieutenant Junior Grade, Roger Simpson. Please follow me, sir."

The Navy SEAL is black.

Debswana is a diamond mining company located in Botswana, and it is the world's top producer of diamonds by value. It began as De Beers Botswana Mining Company in 1969, changing its name after the government of Botswana achieved its independence. Botswana increased its ownership to 50 percent in 1992.

The Debswana Diamond Company Ltd. operates four mines in Botswana.

Colin Rafiki and his men and women fly towards Botswana, and he briefs everyone over the intercom shared by all three helicopters.

The volume is turned up high enough to overcome the Denyl Oryx rotor blades.

"We're going to the capital, Gabarone. For many years, DeBeers has taken advantage of the people of Botswana. It's an interesting story."

Most of the men and women have already fallen asleep in the helicopters.

Years of combat have taught them to do this. Colin does not try to wake them up, but he nevertheless continues with the story.

"People have accused DeBeers of dirty tricks in their state-of-the-art complex in Gaborone. ISIS is trying to seize on this local anger as its entry card into taking over the entire company, saying they will share the wealth with the people."

Colin explains that the Muslim terrorists have increased their number in Botswana to more than 200 warriors over four years, all experienced militants.

"The number has doubled since they lost their oil fields in Syria. They need money, and that's why the De Beers operation is at the top of the hard target list of the Central Intelligence Agency."

He passes around a large, dirty, uncut diamond, which wakes up many combat sleepers. The same thing happens in the other two choppers using surrogates.

"For years, De Beers has stolen money from the people of Botswana using a straightforward trick," Colin continues. "They take that dirty diamond and use it to value their 50/50 partnership with Debswana. They give it an overnight salt bath, and that's why it's so dull."

Then Colin and his surrogates pass around a beautiful, gleaming, uncut diamond of about the same size as the dirty one. It sparkles.

Most of the women warriors are now paying attention. Colin points out that they hold a 24-carat uncut diamond in their hands.

"Debswana is a piggy bank for DeBeers," Colin says. "Because a small, diamond-cleaning operation exists in the Gaborone complex, solely owned by DeBeers., with no 50/50 deal with Botswana.

It lets the world's most famous diamond company conceal the actual value of the diamonds, with distinct tax advantages." Some of the men start to doze off.

Every day, DeBeers moves the rough diamonds from the Botswana Diamond Trading complex in Gaborone to a small De Beers operation nearby.

"Once there," Colin says, "scientists dip the very same diamonds in hydrochloric acid and then perchloric acid, a syrupy oxyacid of chlorine that contains a higher proportion of oxygen. I got one of the scientists drunk one night, and he kept telling me how they gassed the buggers in the trenches. He admitted that was how he persuaded his wife he was doing a dangerous, critical job."

The PR department at De Beers has always maintained that their partnership with Botswana demands that safety be as high a priority as value.

The "extremely" unsafe act of treating rough diamonds with hydrochloric acid and then perchloric acid prevents Debswanna from using a similar cleaning process at its gem cleaning plant.

"In reality, it's not that risky," Colin says. "But here's what it means."

As they pass around the dirty and gleaming 24-carat diamonds, Colin tells them that the dull, dirty one has a value of about $12,000.

"Or about $500 per carat," Colin says.

"What is this worth after getting gassed in the trenches," a wide-awake female Marine Raider asks, admiring the polished rock they've been passing around. She puts it on her wedding finger, trying to balance it.

"About $40,000, "Colin says. "At least three times as much. But that's only the beginning because they export them to Laos for over one hundred times their original, rough value. However, a large portion of that gain involves cutting, polishing, and, of course, various money-laundering schemes. That 14-carat rough polished diamond, when cut into multiple gems, would probably be worth well over half a million dollars." Some of the men start paying attention again.

"How does ISIS make money out of all this," a Navy SEAL asks.

Colin says, "They are preparing to take over the Debswana Diamond Company and wrestle profits away from the De Beers operations at gunpoint. ISIS now has five board members at the Botswana Diamond Trading Company in Gaborone, and they all plan to attend the next board meeting fully armed. The non-Muslim directors at the company will die. Other ISIS terrorists will attack the entire DeBeers Diamond Trading complex once they hear the starting gun in the corporate boardroom. Some of them are armed guards at the complex already. Others will go to their lockers, where

Muslim security guards have placed fully-loaded assault rifles."

"This will be the penultimate hostile takeover," says a Muslim Marine Raider who understands the world of finance.

Colin smiles but does not laugh.

The flight from the Kariba Dam to Gaborone by Colin Rafiki runs into the Botswana Defence Force as they fly over Francistown, the second-largest city in the nation, often described as the "Capital of the North."

The Botswana Air Force Presidential jet has done a flyover of the city after taking off earlier from the Gaborone Sir Seretse Khama International Airport, accompanied by half of their jet fighters, five single-seat Northrop F-5s.

They are "showing the flag" when three South African helicopters show up on their radar.

It is just dumb bad luck, but it puts Colin Rafiki and his men in harm's way.

Three of the four Northrop F-5s suddenly peel off from their guardian formation. The jets want to look at the troop-carrying Denel Oryx helicopters entering their airspace, presumably from South Africa.

Colin Rafiki's helicopters drop to within 100 feet of the relatively flat terrain, slowing down to what would be stall speed for a jet fighter. The F-5s flash past them at least 150 feet higher.

"No shooting," Colin Rafiki says.

The jets perform a complete turnaround.

Then they form up and come back towards the troop-carrying helicopters.

The F-5s are still 250 feet off the ground.

None of the planes fire a shot.

"I don't think those jets have any bullets," an Army Ranger says. And he's right.

The president of Botswana does not arm his jets because he does not trust the head of the air force, who he thinks wants his job.

"They're all show, no blow," a Marine Raider says, snapping a 60-round cartridge case into his assault rifle.

"No shooting," Colin Rafiki repeats.

He notices the presidential plane making a slow turnaround beyond Francistown, back towards the nation's capital.

The four Northrop jets rise to meet the presidential plane, but they fly well north of Colin Rafiki's helicopters to rejoin the president's new flight path.

"We can beat them back to Gaborone," Colin says.

"We'll be out of fuel when we do," the pilot says.

"Better empty than dead," Colin says. "There are some hiding places to the south of Gabarone, at the old dam on the Notwane River. I vanished there myself, years ago, in the bush, near what looks like a series of small mountains around a lake. I stayed there for days. Push it."

He watches the terrain whip past them. After a while, he says, "There." He points to a series of hills surrounding a lake south of Gaborone.

"Land anywhere."

They land on fumes.

"We can get plenty of fuel at the airport," Colin says. "But first, we have a job to do."

heartbeats

At Major Bootie van Zale's home in Witkoppen, the General of the South African Army clicks off his cellphone and says: "Your Colin Rafiki helicopters just attacked the Presidential plane in Botswana."

General McKlane looks at his senior Marine Raider and says: "Confirm that."

Even before the Marine Lieutenant Colonel hangs up, the South African general admits there was no attack and no damage done by the forces of Colin Rafiki.

"So here's how this is going to work, General," Mac says. "We are strangers. We do not know one another. We do not trust one another. We are going to tell the truth, or we are going to die."

"I'm not a big fan of dramatics, McKlane."

"Nor am I, General, and you can call me Mac or General McKlane, or General George McKlane III. You will not call me McKlane."

"And you will call me General."

"Fine, general."

"What are we going to talk about, *MAC?*"

He makes it sound like a bad word, and Mac smiles. He owns this guy.

"We're going to talk about saving the entire world, General, regardless of race, color, or creed. I understand you are a communist, or a radical socialist, or whatever you wish to call yourself."

"I am the General of the South African Air Force, *MAC.* I am not a politician."

"I wish my Russian was better since you might prefer to speak with me in that language, General. But my Russian is not good."

The General tests Mac's abilities to understand Russian by saying: "*YA rad eto slyshat.*" ("I am glad to hear that."

"I'm sure you are," Mac says, and he sees the General's eyes flicker in surprise."But we're going to stick to English. My Afrikaans is even worse than my Russian."

The South African General does not smile.

"Please stop the advance of your mechanized infantry unit while we discuss why Homeland Security has taken such an interest in your nation and Botswana."

"It may be too late for that," the General says, and within a few minutes, they hear explosions and gunfire.

"I told nobody to FIRE," Mac says to the Marine Raider lieutenant colonel standing next to him.

The entire group moves to the windows of Bootie's living room.

They see the Raiders, Rangers, and SEALs deployed around the farm.

None of them have fired at anything.

Beyond the trees, less than a mile away, they see smoke rising.

The head of the South African Forces is on the phone to Pretoria, and the central control patches him through to the commander of the mechanized force. They are under attack, having lost four armored fighting vehicles and one light tank.

South Africa started the day ranked 32 out of 137 nations on the global Military Power Index, but it has fallen below the halfway mark of 62 within less than 12 hours.

"Who is attacking you?" the South African General asks the commander of the mechanized unit.

"Arab terrorists, sir. They are well-armed. They have grenade launchers and missiles."

Mac shortens the answer by looking at the general and saying: "ISIS."

Explosions continue, and then the line to the commander of the mechanized infantry unit from Pretoria goes dead.

"I wish you had not destroyed my 'Red Falcon,' General McKlane."

"We have four other helicopters available, general, but I do not want you to commit suicide by using any of them."

"Clear the room," the South African General says. "General McKlane, Major van Zale, and my squadron leader will remain. Everyone else out."

The few American warriors in the room look at their commanding officer, Mac, and when he nods, they leave.

"Protect the perimeter," Mac tells them as they close the living room door.

The South African General pulls his Vektor SP1 semi-automatic pistol out of its holster. He drops the magazine clip out of the gun and unchambers the live round remaining in the weapon.

The general puts everything on the coffee table in front of him. He asks his squadron leader to do the same.

"And the chambered round," he says when the squadron leader conveniently forgets to do so. General McKlane and Bootie van Zale also place their weapons on the table, with separate magazine clips and no bullets chambered.

"So now we are all equal, friends or not, and I believe we are running out of time, General McKlane."

"I agree with every word you just said."

"What would you do if you were I?"

"I would take my ground troops and kill every ISIS terrorist I saw."

"My ground troops are under attack and do not seem to be doing very well at the moment."

"Then you should use your reserve troops," Mac says.

"And they are?"

"By my count, over 100 Marine Raiders, Navy SEALs, and Army Rangers."

"They are not under my command."

"No, they are not, nor will they be. The 100 warriors outside are under my command, and we are allies, general. Before this is over, we may even become friends."

"How will you deploy them?" the general asks.

"Quickly."

A slight smile creeps across the faces of both generals.

"Please do so," says the South African.

Mac stands up and asks the South Africans to reload their arms. Then he invites the South African general and his squadron leader to join him as he talks to his group's leaders, three men, and a woman.

"Execute," General McKlane says.

Suddenly 100 men and women are moving quickly beyond the trees and towards the battle with ISIS. They head towards where they saw the ISIS surface-to-air missiles launch, not towards the sound of fighting.

"That's very impressive," the head of the South African air force says.

"They are the best of our best," Mac says, "but without any false pride or ego. They will die for me, for you, for your squadron leader, for Bootie, for South Africa, and, of course, for the United States of America. They will die to stay alive and to defeat terrorism."

"That's very impressive," the head of the South African Defence Force repeats.

"Yes, they are. You do not want my people to be your enemy. We make a terrible enemy,"

"I'm sure you do."

"Please tell your mechanized infantry not to shoot any American troops. Tell them to fall back."

"Done," he says, placing an urgent call to Pretoria.

Chapter 11

Jalaluddin Shekau runners move to and from his group of terrorists and the impressive armory they have created over many years at the Orlando East Mosque on Mofutsanyane Street in Soweto.

Most of the arsenal comes from the middle east, smuggled into the country when the Turkish Cooperation and Coordination Agency decided to help construct another Mosque bombed by white supremacists and right-wing extremists in 2002.

The damaged Mosque was the first one ever built in Soweto, and its destruction offended many people. Winnie Mandela was the guest of honor at its original opening. The great Muhammed Ali, America's world-famous boxing champion, visited and prayed there.

The rebuilding of the badly damaged mosque takes longer than expected and involves a small amount of imported material from Turkey. According to the Turkish Cooperation and Coordination Agency leaders, most refurbishing and repair come from local suppliers.

A few wooden boxes here, a few there, all imported from Turkey, quickly clear customs. Nobody asks questions. After all, the Mosque regularly distributes food and aid during the Muslim holy month of Ramadan. The Mosque also partners with South African authorities to build and refurbish orphanages, especially for children born with HIV/AIDS.

None of the imported, heavy boxes labeled "Muslim Art" ever remain in the bombed and rebuilt section of the first mosque.

The wooden crates continue arriving in Soweto long after the bombed Mosque fully recovers. They all end up in a secret room in the back of the Orlando East Mosque on Mofutsanyane Street, creating an impressive armory of SAMs, grenade launchers, assault weapons, and ammunition covering Islamic art one wall from floor to ceiling.

Jalaluddin Shekau occasionally tells his followers that this room and these weapons will transform ISIS from freedom fighters into a nuclear powerhouse.

He knows that today, in Soweto, the trigger has fired too soon with the overflights of Saab Gripens, but that is Allah's will. Nobody should have ever revealed the armory to the prune-faced convert, Ginger Mbeki.

The fight continues with the South Africans, and the destructive power of the hidden arsenal rips into that nation's armed services with unexpected success. South Africa's military readiness has steadily declined for years. Now it has tipped over the edge.

The Delta Wing jets over Soweto and Witkoppen have never fired a shot.

The mechanized infantry is firing at ghosts as the ISIS warriors use hit and run tactics with grenade launchers.

They use SAMs, close up, to attack a light tank and four armored vehicles, destroying all of them.

Their assault weapons tear into the South African troops, who are primarily young conscripts and not hardened combat warriors.

Jalaluddin Shekau shouts: "Keep those runners going. We need more grenade launchers, more SAMs."

For two minutes, a lifetime in any battle, no runners from the armory in the Mosque return to the fight with new weapons. Jalaluddin Shekau knows that something is wrong.

"Back to the Mosque," he says, and his men quickly break off the engagement. Only two terrorists have died.

The South African infantry does not chase after them.

They remain in place, licking their wounds.

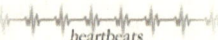

Colin Rafiki's small army lands its three helicopters in a small valley in Botswana, leading to the lake formed by an old dam on the Notwane River. They immediately go dark by shutting down everything, including their Motorola cell phones.

"We're going to operate as we did in the good old days," the CIA agent says. "Hand signals or voice only, preferably hands."

They all remember the hand signals drilled into them years earlier as recruits, their second language of fingers and fists and pointing that never dies.

Colin Rafiki calls together the top-ranked people among the Raiders, SEALs, and Rangers. He pulls a map from his armored vest pocket and shows them where they are. He then talks to them about diamonds.

One of the group leaders, an Army Ranger, says: "You mean the 2-carat wedding ring my husband bought ten years ago is not worth its appraised value?"

"Do you love your husband?" Colin asks her.

"Of course."

"Then it doesn't matter if you married a cheapskate."

She laughs.

"So we're going to destroy De Beers' ability to cheat?" another group leader asks.

"No. We're going to make sure that ISIS doesn't take over their operation in Botswana as an income replacement for the oil fields they no longer profit from in eastern Syria."

"So let's go make some blood diamonds," a Navy SEAL says, and some of them smile. A few people laugh.

"Our information says that at least 20 ISIS soldiers work in either the main office of the Diamond Trading Company of Botswana or in the small diamond cleaning operation there." Colin points to a part of the complex.

"Do you have people on the inside?" a Marine Raider captain asks.

"We think so, but we're not sure. We're relying on an ISIS turncoat, who might be playing us."

"So, how do we identify the bad guys?"

"Most of the men dress in thobes, the ankle-length shirts they wear. They're usually white, and some people call them a dishdasha or a kandourah. You know how they look. Only Muslims wear them. They're useful for concealing assault weapons, but it makes drawing and using any hidden firearm quite difficult."

"So they must keep their assault rifles somewhere a little more accessible."

"True," Colin says. "And some of them may be in plain sight. Some of the security men are armed Muslims, only wearing keffiyeh, a headscarf. They also call them ghutra or shemagh. Some may only wear a turban. If you see an armed guard wearing this sort of headgear, make sure your assault rifle is ready to rip."

"So we're walking into an area where people will immediately identify us, but we may not recognize them?"

"No, because you will all be invisible."

Some of the men and women suddenly think Colin Rafiki has lost his mind.

Others wait for the punchline.

"We'll be stopping at a house in Gaborone. You'll keep wearing your fatigues and bullet-proof vests, but you'll also have Muslim headgear. The turbans all have metal frames, military-grade helmets wrapped in cloth. There are also Kufis, close-fitting caps that come down to your ears. They don't offer as much protection, even though we make them with chain mail. Some of you will still have to wear traditional white thobes. We make the Hijabs and Chadors for the women with excellent chain mail. They're heavy. This stuff won't stop bullets, but it gives you some cover."

"And disguise," one woman says. She is a Muslim. "I'll show you how to wear them properly."

"And I'll help all the infidel men," a Marine Raider says. He is also Muslim. He laughs, and so do the men with whom he will fight.

Colin Rafiki hands out wads of Botswana currency to every person in his team, two, 10, 20, 50, and 100 Pulas.

He tells them, "Pula means 'rain' in Setswana, the official language of Botswana. Rain is very scarce in a nation that primarily consists of the Kalahari Desert. However, money is also in short supply."

"What's it worth in dollars?" an Army Ranger asks, holding about 1,000 Pulas like everyone else.

"That bundle of money in your hand is worth less than $100, and I know you're worth a lot more than that. Hang on to it. You will use it for bribery. So let's go," Colin says. "According to my information, we have about 24 hours before ISIS makes its move against Botswana's Diamond Trading Company in Gabarone."

The Muslim Marine Raider says, "*ana 'atahadath alearabiat bitalaqat 'iidha kan hdha 'ayu musaeadat.*" ("I speak Arabic fluently if that's any help.")

Colin Rafiki answers, "*kdhlk 'ana, wala ymkn 'an tudhia.*" ("So do I, and it cannot hurt.")

An Army Ranger slides the bolt on his weapon and says, keeping his finger off the trigger and his weapon on safety: "I don't know which one of you two guys to kill."

They all laugh harder than usual because they need to.

Information about the push against ISIS sub-Saharan targets in Africa by the Countering Weapons of Mass Destruction (CWMD) section of Homeland Security disappears. It happens three and a half hours after Roberta Macumber gets escorted out of Homeland Security's Nebraska Avenue Complex headquarters in Washington, D.C.

She drives to her townhouse in Georgetown and turns on an encrypted backup computer.

She does not try to contact Mac because she does not want to send out electronic warning flags. They have not yet blocked her access to sensitive information, probably because they do not know what they're doing or possibly because the people working with Roberta Macumber have stonewalled the political newcomers.

She spends the next three hours systematically scrubbing the Homeland Security mainframe computer, everything about George McKlane and his team's journey and objective aboard the *S.S. Nomad.*

She then goes into the backup of the mainframe and does the same. She searches Homeland Security's secure ".gov" cloud and finds nothing.

Then she permanently erases everything on the personal backup computer on which she has been working.

The entire mission disappears.

She installs the latest version of Windows on the cyberscrubbed drive of her home backup computer and puts a solitaire game on the screen. Macumber knows that she is leaving Mac in the dark, but he needs to find a way to complete his missions no matter who runs Homeland Security and the CWMD section. The following day, the expected knock comes on Macumber's front door.

"We have a warrant to search your house," says an agent Roberta has never seen before.

"Would you like some tea or coffee and cookies?" she asks. People in black suits wearing visible chest armor push her aside and ransack her home for over an hour.

"Do you think I would shoot a Federal agent?" she asks one young man.

"You never know," he says, pulling out a drawer in the kitchen and letting its contents tumble across the floor. The debris includes a fully-loaded Smith & Wesson, snub-nosed .38 handgun in a brown holster.

"You never know," he says, smiling and then bagging the gun.

"I have a carry permit for that weapon, young man."

"I'm sure you do," he says. "Georgetown is such a crime-ridden neighborhood."

They bag three guns during the search. All of the weapons are handguns, including a bulldog .45. Macumber has permits for every one of them.

They take the computer, but not before an agent sits down and asks why she did not move the black nine of clubs over to and under the red 10 of hearts in the Solitaire game that's on the screen.

"I didn't realize that was a crime," Roberta says.

The agent snaps the computer shut, hard, probably breaking its screen.

"Temper, temper," Roberta says as the agent dumps out every drawer on her desk.

They leave with everything of possible investigatory value, all of which fits into two large cardboard boxes.

They also take her cross shredder, which has turned all her paperwork into confetti.

"I guess someone in your department loves to waste time with crossword puzzles," she says.

After they leave, Roberta Macumber turns on her TV to watch the news, but her cable no longer works. Her phone line has a hollow dial tone, which it has never had before.

Later in the day, a single agent returns to her home and hands her a black bag containing her four guns.

"Where's my computer?" she asks.

"The screen broke," he says. "Buy a new one."

"Turn on my TV service."

"It will be back up in an hour or two."

"And stop tapping my phone."

"We don't do that sort of thing."

Macumber laughs and then asks, "No apology for the mess you all made in my home?"

"You can apologize if you want to," the agent says.

Roberta Macumber utters something she rarely says. "Fuck off."

"I'll be sure to put that suggestion in my report, ma'am. Have a nice day." Then he walks back to his black Chevy SUV and drives off, squealing his tires.

Roberta Macumber shakes her head.

In most respects, Roberta Macumber has made sure that the mission of General "Mac" McKlane has become a secret one. Still, it is lying in plain sight southeast of Cape Town, South Africa, in the port where the *S.S. Nomad* docks. The small freighter has six crew members, including the Captain, her chief, and four Marine Raiders who walk around in shorts and wear stained T-shirts. Nobody pays much attention to the old boat as men paint and re-paint rusty portions of it. Nobody ever uses its unstable-looking gangplank.

The U.S. Embassy in Pretoria knows nothing about the ship. The U.S. Consulate in CapeTown is separated from the docked freighter by the Muizenberg Mountains and the Silver Mine nature reserve. The U.S. Consulate General does occasionally see the ship after he plays golf at the Clovelly

Country Club. After an afternoon of golf, he likes to drive down to Fish Hoek and watch the sun drop behind the mountains and into the sea.

The rusted old freighter embarrasses the Consulate General with a tattered and faded American Flag on its stern. On one Sunday, after an exceptional round of golf in which he only cheated three times, he tries to brighten his day further by driving down to the ship docks and approaching the *S.S. Nomad* carrying a large, brown package.

He climbs the unsteady gangplank wishing he hadn't had that third drink. He meets a mean-looking man in a stained T-shirt who says: "Who the hell are you?"

"I am the American Consulate General in Cape Town, South Africa."

"Good for you," the man says, blocking his way.

"Permission to come aboard," the Consulate General says. He's an old Navy man who spent four years occasionally floating off Vietnam on a flattop where he worked in the kitchen as an assistant chef. After Vietnam, he struck it rich on Wall Street with some close friends who were all draft-dodgers who hid for a few years in Canada.

The man in the T-shirt backs away, revealing a woman, equally tough-looking, who says: "I am the captain of this ship, sir, and I will NOT grant you permission to board the *S.S. Nomad* unless you have a warrant to do so."

The Consulate General does not know what to do. He thrusts a package at the woman, which the large man in the T-shirt intercepts before it touches her.

"What is that?" Captain Maria Montoya, out of uniform, asks the Consulate General.

"That is a proper American flag for you to fly on your stern. Your torn and tattered flag is an embarrassment to our great nation."

"That's very kind of you," the captain says.

"May I come aboard?"

"No, sir, you may not."

"I was in the Navy," the Consulate General says. "I was a chief petty officer." It's a lie, but he's angry.

"I, too, was in the Navy," the captain says.

"And your rank?"

"Commander," she says. Now two other huge men have appeared behind her in stained T-shirts.

"Your name, Commander?"

"Captain."

That's all she says as they stare at one another. Behind her, men lower their arms, ready for a fight.

The Consulate General steps back and salutes the captain, then he does an about faces, grabbing the railing as he almost stumbles.

He's had too many drinks at the golf club, and he walks carefully back down the gangplank, almost tripping at the bottom. They watch him move slowly towards his large car with prominent diplomatic license plates.

"Crap," Montoya says. "Open the package and make a big show of replacing the flag on the stern."

Her men do this, and the Consulate General, leaning against his car, watches as proper stars and stripes flutter on the back of the *S.S. Nomad.*

Captain Montoya waves and salutes. The consulate general does not wave back.

"Crap," she says again. She goes to the Captain's suite and phones Roberta Macumber at Homeland Security. A voice she has never heard before answers.

"I need to talk to Roberta Macumber," the captain of the *S.S. Nomad* says.

"Macumber no longer works at Homeland Security."

"Since when?"

"Who is this," the person answering the captain's call asks again.

"Just a friend," Captain Montoya says.

"This is not a friendship phone number," the person at Homeland Security says. When he realizes that the connection is lost, he asks someone to trace the call.

"Not connected long enough for that," he's told.

In Cape Town, Captain Montoya addressed her chief engineer and crew.

"I think it's time we went on a cruise," she says.

Outside Witkoppen, Mac's troops approach Soweto. They see the white spire of the Mosque that has become the source of Radio Islam.

As they move through Soweto toward this Orlando East Mosque on Mofutsanyane Street, the citizens of Soweto form a curious crowd behind them. They do not know who the armed men are, but they recognize the American flags on their uniforms, and many of these soldiers, women, and men, are Black.

Some of the South Africans point towards the mosque. One man tells them: "Many guns in the back."

All the Rangers, Raiders, and SEALs have suppressors on their weapons, although they still make an audible popping sound when fired.

They watch a terrorist run into the back of the mosque and reappear, carrying several grenade launchers. Another goes in and comes back with surface-to-air missiles.

The American forces do not immediately kill these men. They wait until over a dozen weapons runners are en route to the battle on the outskirts of Soweto.

Then, with a few hand signals, they kill them all within a matter of ten minutes. The dead terrorists' weapons become their own.

The leader of the Muslim terrorists, Jalaluddin Shekau, sees one of his men drop several blocks away, carrying four SAMs and a backpack of ammunition.

He sees many armed men and women moving in towards the Mosque. He crouches and says something to his followers. Suddenly they all remove their Arab clothing, taking shirts and pants off the clothesline of their neighbors. They remove their headdresses and turbans and blend into the crowd.

Within minutes they become invisible.

"Half our force is gone," he tells an aide."But half our strength remains."

"With no weapons," the aide says. Their enemy will discover their armory.

"We have some enormous weapons twenty miles from here in Pelindaba and Pelindaba East, at the Y-Plant. And we have men in place there already."

He waves his hand dismissively.

"This was a battle, but it is not the war. The men we have lost are now in paradise."

They also still have the weapons they have been fighting with, although they're short on ammunition.

Ten Muslim warriors begin the trek from Soweto to the primary research center of the South African Nuclear Energy Corporation. It will take them more than 24 hours because of their need for concealment.

As they approach the dam a day later, they come across a bait and tackle shop.

"We have wonderful worms, and the Harties are biting," the owner of the store tells them. The two men at the counter and those milling about outside do not look like people interested in fishing. It's been a slow season.

"You have wonderful worms?" one man asks with a strange accent.

"The best."

He steps from behind the counter and moves over to a square bed of loose earth. The Muslim men notice that he is wearing a gun in a holster attached to what looks like a cowboy's belt around his waist.

The store owner reaches deep down in the soft earth, lifting a squirming bunch of large nightcrawlers in his hands. Some of them are almost a foot and a half long. The man who asked about the beautiful worms backs away, saying something in a foreign language.

The other man, the apparent leader of all these half-baked, dark-skinned men, asks: "You eat these worms?"

The store owner drops the nightcrawlers and starts to move towards his gun. These are not people going fishing. He has a lot of dirt on his hand, and before he can pull his Colt .38 out of its holster, he sees and feels the metal of a more powerful gun on his forehead.

The other man takes away his Colt .38, holds up a large nightcrawler, and says to the man, "Eat this."

"I'm no bloody fish."

"Eat it."

"No."

"Eat it."

"I'm not a bleeding Hartie, mate."

"No, you are a bleeding man," the man holding the gun to his head says.

The terrorist is surprised that the store owner shows no fear before he pulls the trigger.

The man is angry, then dead, sprawled on the floor.

"What is a Hartie?"

The leader points to an enormous fishhead mounted on the wall that says, "Biggest Hartie Ever Caught." It weighed 30.4 kilos, almost 67 pounds.

"It's a fish," the leader says.

They rob the bait and tackle shop, take all the store owner's money, and empty the fridge in the back. They leave the frozen fish in the freezer.

They scoop up all the energy bars and candy on the counter and then turn the sign on the door to "closed."

They each take a fishing rod, but they leave behind the bed of worms.

They drag the dead owner deep into the bushes behind his store, where wild animals will make him disappear without a trace.

There's an old hound in a doghouse behind the store, and it starts barking and then lies down, looking at the men with a cocked head, curious.

"Do not kill the dog," their leader says. "Just turn it loose." They unchain the dog.

It does not run away. It wags its tail and licks the hands of the men.

"Take all the frozen fish in the freezer and throw them out here for the dog. He will eat them when they thaw out."

They leave with their fishing poles over their shoulders, holding them like rifles in a parade, marching through the night towards Pelindaba East and the Y-Plant.

The dog follows them, but he turns and trots back towards his home after a while.

Very few cars pass the fishermen, and none of the passengers in the vehicles ever see them because the Muslim warriors drop into the road's deep ditches for concealment when they see oncoming headlights.

Early the following day, they make out the tall, well-lit outer fences surrounding the Y-Plant at Pelindaba East. All the men surround Jalaluddin Shekau.

"By this time tomorrow," he tells them, "we will be a nuclear power."

heartbeats

The American consulate general in Cape Town calls the American Embassy in Pretoria. Born in South Africa, the ambassador is currently on vacation at her home in Palm Beach, Florida.

"There's an American freighter in Cape Town," the consulate general tells the ambassador's foreign service officer, who remains miffed that he did not become ambassador when the previous one left. "They refused permission for me to board their ship, called the *S.S. Nomad.* Do you know anything about the ship?"

"Let me check," he says.

He comes back on the line in less than a minute and says, "Nothing here."

The American consulate general in Cape Town says that the ship's captain is a former commander in the Navy, one grade below an admiral. "And a woman," he says.

He detects some frustration in the sigh of the foreign service officer.

"Can you check on former commanders with our Navy?" the consulate general asks. "And I need you to get me a warrant to search the ship as well."

The foreign service officer says nothing.

"This may involve a threat to the national security of the United States," the consulate general adds. "If necessary, I will call the American Ambassador at her home in Palm Beach. She's a neighbor of the president."

He knows how to bully people like the foreign service officer at the American Embassy.

"I will get right on this, consulate general. I will fax you a warrant to inspect the American ship immediately. It is an American ship, correct? It is not flying under another nation's flag, correct?"

"That is right," the consulate general says. "I gave the captain of the ship a brand new flag to replace the tattered stars and stripes on the stern of the ship."

"But you said she did not give you permission to board the ship."

"They snatched the flag from me and still refused to let me board the ship. I saw the crew replace the flag myself."

"Consulate general, I will fax the permit of inquiry to your office immediately. And we will check with the United States Navy regarding a former commander who is currently the captain of a freighter. Was it a huge freighter, sir?"

"No, it was an ancient and rusty one, mid-sized."

"That is curious," the foreign service officer says.

"Yes, it is."

The consulate general plays golf at the Clovelly Country Club the next day.

Then he drives down to Fish Hoek without even having a drink with his fellow players. They won't stop him from boarding this time.

The *S.S. Nomad* has disappeared.

The next day, he gets a call from the foreign service officer in Pretoria, who tells him that no recently retired commanders of the Navy are currently the captains of freighters, large or small.

"So she lied to me, and the *S.S. Nomad* disappeared from the port after the captain refused to let me board it," the consulate general tells the foreign service officer.

"That is curious," the American in Pretoria says. "Let me throw a wider net than just the Navy. It might be an operation run by the CIA or Homeland Security."

"Homeland Security?"

"Their CWMD section."

"What's that?" Like the Ambassador to South Africa, the consulate general is a politician and a businessperson, not a career diplomat.

"That's the Countering Weapons of Mass Destruction section of Homeland Security."

"Why South Africa?"

"As I'm sure you know," the foreign service officer says, "South Africa has successfully manufactured eight atomic bombs at Pelindaba and Pelindaba East, at their Y-Plant, called Valindaba."

The consulate general, a political appointee, did not know this. However, the original briefing documents he never bothered to read after being appointed a consulate general by the American ambassador reveal the information.

"Although the South Africans say they stopped the program while they were building their eighth bomb, melting down the plutonium into ingots, they have never proven to us, or anyone, that the bombs no longer exist. They are considered a serious threat to the security of the world."

"Of course," the consulate general says, and by his rushed, aggressive tone, the foreign service officer understands that the man does not know about the Republic of South Africa's atomic capabilities.

"That's why I originally said that this might involve a threat to the national security of the United States," the consulate general suddenly adds.

Although he does not say it, the Foreign Service Officer thinks: "*Nice recovery.*"

Then he glances at the Grandfather clock in his office, which has never worked, and realizes that even political appointees might be right twice a day.

He realizes that the Consulate General in Cape Town may have stumbled onto something important. To protect America, because that is his job, he decides to throw a broader net.

He hooks something at Homeland Security.

After another bad night with almost no sleep, Roberta Macumber, trapped under guard in her townhome in

Georgetown by government agents, gets a call from the new Director of Homeland Security.

"I'm sending a car over to bring you down here for an important meeting," the new director says.

"I no longer work for Homeland Security," Macumber says, "and I still haven't repaired all the damage your goons did to my townhome."

"I owe you an apology."

"You owe me a lot more than just an apology."

"I believe that's true," the new director says. Macumber says nothing. She knows you get more from silence than from talking, especially when you don't know what's happening.

"Can I please send a car for you, Assistant Director Roberta Macumber?"

"Are you suggesting that I have my old job back?"

"It's my understanding that you merely took a few days off, at full pay, Assistant Director Macumber."

Roberta thinks that this will be very interesting. She also knows she can protect director Mac McKlane better from the inside than she can from her home, playing solitaire games on a new computer with no access to classified Homeland Security material.

She agrees to the ride back to Homeland Security.

The agent who appears is the same one she swore at two days earlier. He dumped the contents of her desk on the floor and slammed her laptop shut, breaking the screen.

"What's your name?" she asks.

"Agent Fuller," he answers.

"What's your first name?"

"Buckminster Eugene Fuller," he answers. "People call me 'Buck.'"

"Did you file what I said to you in your report like you told me you would?" she asks.

"What report is that Assistant Director Macumber?" he asks, apparently suffering from a severe short-term memory loss.

"I told you to 'F off,' Buck."

"And yet here I am, Assistant Macumber, at your service." He holds the rear door open.

"I'll ride in the front with you, Buckminster Fuller."

"As you wish, ma'am," he says, closing the back door and opening the front one.

"What branch of the service were you in," she asks him as they pull away from her townhome.

"I was never in the service, ma'am."

"How did you become an agent at Homeland Security?" she asks.

"I applied for the job straight out of law school," he says."I went to the FBI for some training first. My father was a police detective in New York City. I think that probably helped me get this position."

"I'm sure it did."

Roberta Macumber decides that she will have a difficult time concealing the whereabouts of General George McKlane, Mac's team, and almost 150 Raiders, Rangers, and SEALs from people who should probably not be involved with Homeland Security's CWMD section.

During her trip to the office, she also sets a reminder on her brand new Motorola encrypted cellphone to contact her lawyer to make sure she is not breaking any Federal or local laws. She deletes it before hitting "Save."

She does not know how many people at Homeland Security have access to her new cellphone, despite its ability to encrypt messages.

When she arrives at the headquarters of Homeland Security at the Nebraska Avenue Complex, the agent called Buck takes her to her former office.

She recognizes very few faces outside her door.

The people who do know her make a point of not looking at her.

She turns on the brand new computer on her desk and enters her usual password. It still works. There are no files other than a few folders holding information from the past 48 hours.

None of them contain important information. The messages include Roberta Macumber in the copy or blind copy group of people who receive them.

She uses some agency software on her Motorola cellphone that is only available to senior Homeland Security staff. She's glad that she remains categorized as such. She uses the program to sweep her office for bugs, and she finds half a dozen. She does not remove any of them.

Her phone rings, and a message dings on her screen. It's from the new Acting Director of Homeland Security.

"Please join me immediately in the conference room," the message says. The phone call duplicates the request.

"I'll be right there," she texts on the computer, hanging up the phone without saying anything. Someone has installed one of the six listening devices inside her phone.

Buck stands up in a glass-enclosed cubical near her doorway as she exits her office. He accompanies Macumber to the conference room.

"You are my shadow," Roberta says to Buck.

"I am your protection," he answers.

Roberta thinks this is a fascinating response, a suit of armor wrapped in a possible threat. She is thankful that he has mistakenly warned her about the treacherous journey she has decided to take. *Thank you, Buck*, Roberta thinks.

She reminds herself to sweep her home for bugs after work. Roberta won't disable them but instead direct each one to different versions of her Apple Itune Playlists, all classical or traditional opera.

They will eventually figure it out, but by that time, she will probably be in hiding.

Roberta enters the conference room, and so does Buck, who stands in a corner to cut off any exit towards the conference room door. She sees three people, two of whom she recognizes and has met.

"Good afternoon, Acting Director," Macumber says, without putting any emphasis on the word, "Acting."

"Good afternoon, Secretary," she says to the Secretary of State of the United States.

Macumber turns to the third person. "I apologize. ma'am, but I do not know who you are."

She is an attractive woman, extremely well dressed, and very well made up. She is probably older than she looks.

The unknown woman stands up, walks around the conference room with a young gait, and says, with a slight accent, "We met about a year ago at a seminar, and I have always thought of you as one of Homeland's leaders. I am currently the Ambassador to the Republic of South Africa."

Macumber smiles and shakes her hand, asking: "Ours or theirs, ambassador?" She already knows the answer by this time because she remembers the woman, but playing dumb can be smart.

The ambassador smiles. She was born in South Africa, became an American, and lives in Palm Beach, near Mar-a-Logo. The Senate recently approved her appointment.

She returns to her seat, sits down, and says: "Ours, but you already knew that."

"*Be careful, Macumber,*" Roberta reminds herself.

"Please," the acting director of Homeland Security says, "have a seat."

Roberta takes the fourth seat in the room at one end of the long conference table and rolls it to where the three people have huddled together. Then Macumber sits down.

"Why did you do that?" the Secretary of State asks.

"Because we are all on the same side," Roberta Macumber says.

The South African Ambassador says: "My consulate general in South Africa contacted me last night about a ship docked in Cape Town."

Roberta gives her the blankest look she can muster. When the Ambassador says nothing, Macumber wrinkles her forehead, obviously confused.

"The name of the ship is the *S.S. Nomad,*" the Acting Director finally says.

"I'm sorry, but this doesn't mean anything to me. Does the ship carry the American flag?"

"When my consulate general tried to board the ship, the captain refused. The captain is a woman, and she told him she had been a commander in the United States Navy."

Roberta Macumber considers all this with a wrinkled forehead, still confused.

Then she brightens a little and says, "Can't you force your way aboard with a warrant of inquiry?"

"We could if the ship hadn't sailed away in the middle of the night," the Ambassador says.

"Oh," Macumber says, looking a little disappointed. "But if it's a big ship, you could pick it up with aerial reconnaissance, couldn't you?"

"It's a freighter, a fairly small one," the Ambassador says. "There are hundreds of such ships along the coast of South Africa and around Madagascar. It would be a needle in the haystack sort of exercise."

"Sounds like drugs," Roberta Macumber says. "But you could check retired commanders. Not a lot of women in that group," she says, looking at the Ambassador, who is the only other woman in the room.

"We did, and there are no retired commanders, male or female, running small freighters anywhere in the world."

"*Give to get,*" Roberta thinks. She weighs the dangers of putting them on the right track and then misleading them. It will give her more time to improve her disappearing act. "*Will it hurt Mac's chances of success?*" she wonders. They are all watching her. She makes her decision. "*Give to get.*"

"If she's a Navy commander, maybe she's active, not retired," Roberta says.

"We already check ...."

"No, we haven't," the Acting Director of Homeland Security says. He nods to Buckminster Fuller, standing in the corner, who slips out the door, returning within four minutes.

"Bingo," he says. "Commander Maria Montoya is on special assignment from the Navy, on a small freighter with no name in her official orders. They're under lock and seal by Homeland Security."

"Let's take a look at them."

"We can't," Buck says. "It's more than classified. There's only one person who can do that without breaking the law, which, if it got out, could send anyone reading it to jail for a long time."

The Ambassador, the Acting Director, and the Secretary of State all look at Roberta Macumber.

"It's not her," Buckminster Fuller says. "It's General George McKlane III."

"General McKlane? I thought he was a full colonel," the Acting Director of Homeland Security says.

"The Marines promoted him for this task," Roberta Macumber says. "And there's no way he's going to raise his head in the middle of whatever he's doing in Africa to get it blown off."

"What's he doing?"

"I don't know, except that it's a CWMT directive." The Ambassador looks a little confused. Macumber adds: "Countering Weapons of Mass Destruction."

They all look at one another.

The secretary of state reaches for a sugar-coated donut in the untouched pile of snacks on the conference table and swallows it in three quick bites.

"I think I have an idea," Roberta Macumber says. "I was never privy to the classified documents, but I'm pretty sure copies of everything are either backed up somewhere or maybe even on the computer that Buck took away from me at my townhome."

She looks at Buckminster Fuller and says, "although you did bust it up a little when you took it."

Roberta looks back at the leaders in the room. "Get a Federal judge to let you take a peek in the interest of national security. That will work."

"Thank you for your help, Roberta."

She understands the meeting is over. She stands and shakes each person's hand.

She has successfully sent them down a rabbit hole.

Buckminster Fuller follows her out."

"Thanks for protecting me, Buck." She slips her arm through his, but he immediately raises his arm, removes hers, and shifts away from her, showing open anger and hostility.

"There's nothing on your computer except a bunch of Windows crap. Someone ran it through a file shredder and scrubbed it clean. I tossed the disk yesterday."

"You shouldn't have done that," Roberta tells him. "I never scrubbed that disk. Any qualified hacker could probably recover the information."

"Thanks for dropping me in the shit," he says.

Chapter 12

The monthly meeting of the board of directors at the Diamond Trading Company occurs at 11:30 am at the main office in Gaborone, the capital of Botswana. The usual expensive lunch will follow it outside the boardroom where all the members mix and usually make small talk.

Everyone passes through two security stations to enter the room. These are both handled by Muslim guards, which is unusual. An expected non-Muslim guard called in sick just before the meeting. Later, the police find him shot dead in his home. Fentanyl pills speckle the floor. He may have shot himself as the drug took him to the edge of oblivion. Nobody heard the shot, which came from a silenced Glock 17 dropped from the victim's right hand, with 13 rounds still in its double-stack magazine and one in the chamber.

Oddly, the guard was left-handed, something never mentioned in the coroner's report.

As the board members pass through the security stations, they stop several Muslims to inspect their belongings further.

"Excuse me, sir," they say to each detainee. "Will you please unlock your attaché case?"

"Of course," they say.

Into each opened case, the inspectors place a fully-loaded Glock-17 or 22 with suppressors attached.

"Thank you, sir. Sorry for the inconvenience."

There are twenty times more bullets at the conference table as the board meeting begins than company directors.

The relatively new managing director starts to give a PowerPoint presentation on the sales growth of diamonds and the planned diamond cleaning operation, which will replace the small scientific process currently monopolized by De Beers across the street.

Several directors working for De Beers object to these stimulus plans, and an argument breaks out across the conference table.

The new managing director, who has forgotten to turn off the screen saver on his laptop, sees his family and dog suddenly appear on the screen.

Some directors laugh. Nobody notices one of them standing up and moving to the boardroom entrance holding a Glock 22 with a six-inch suppressor.

The managing director hits a button and says, "Sorry about that."

He turns back to the screen, which suddenly shows a splatter of red across it.

Many of the directors think it's a graphic effect in the presentation. Then they realize that every Muslim member of the board is standing up. Pop-pop-pop. It continues until only the Muslim members are left.

They do not immediately leave the boardroom.

The company secretary, a Muslim woman responsible for the minutes, records a new motion from the remaining directors that transfers the Diamond Trading Company Botswana control to ISIS Ltd. It also erases the 50% share held by De Beers.

"Please make a note that this has been agreed upon by all the members of this board of directors who also sit on the board of the De Beers Diamond Trading Company," one of the Muslim directors says to the secretary who creates a transcript of the meeting.

"You seem a bit rattled," another director says to the young Muslim secretary, who has an MBA in finance.

She lowers her head and meekly says, "I did not know we would discuss a very successful hostile takeover today. But not before I recorded the votes of the De Beers directors before they had heart attacks."

The remaining directors laugh, putting their pistols back in their briefcases and snapping them shut.

"Let's go and enjoy our lunch," their leader says. "I think there's more than enough for us today."

They laugh again, but they are surprised before they enter their private dining room. The Muslim board members come face to face with an emissary of Jalaluddin Shekau, the leader of ISIS in Southern Africa. He is an imposing man who speaks carefully, with a hint of Sheikdom in his modulated voice. He is perhaps a disgruntled prince from Saudi Arabia, although his skin is dark. He congratulates them on their success. He talks briefly about ISIS finally finding a seat at the table with other nuclear powers of the world.

"May our brothers at Pelindaba East, in the Y-Plant, show the same courage that all of you have shown here today in Gaborone."

They are flattered by this dark prince as his sweeping hand suggests they enjoy their lunch. They ask him to join them. He declines and says he has already enjoyed some of their food, although he feels more spices would improve their banquet. He must now return to Pelindaba.

He watches them with a smile on his face as they leave their briefcases on a table just outside the banquet room.

The Muslim directors have made a mistake.

heartbeats

Colin Rafiki and his men reach their Muslim supply store at 01:00. They change their gear.

"Do we have to wear these shoulder-to-toe wraps," one of the Navy SEALs asks. "It's almost impossible to use my assault rifle covered up like this."

"They're called thobes," Colin says. "The gowns are made of the finest silk, combined with a little cotton."

"That's nice," the SEAL says. "I've always wanted to be a fashion model."

Colin pulls out a box cutter and slices the thobe down the front, leaving just a foot of fabric attached at the top.

"How's that?"

"Perfect, I thought you were going to circumcise me," the Navy SEAL says.

They both laugh.

The men just wearing metal-framed turbans have no problem drawing their weapons.

Nor do the men wearing the close-fitting, chain mail Kufis fit snugly down to the top of their ears.

The women wearing Hijabs and Chadors have no problem using their weapons. They all have their guns out and in plain sight.

"Let's go," Colin says.

He leads them all down the silent streets of the capital of Botswana, avoiding the front gates of the Diamond Trading Company Botswana.

Looking down the alleyways, Colin sees the guards are asleep on the job, as usual.

He circles his men and women to a back door into the main complex.

"Well," he says, "this is where we find out if our Muslim friend on the inside is real. Get ready to fight our way in if this doesn't work."

Weapons point at the back door.

Colin taps the metal three times with the butt of his assault rifle.

"He might be sleeping," Colin says.

A man opens the door, and the whites of his eyes enlarge as he sees so much death staring him in the face. Colin says something to him, and his eyes return to normal.

"Okay," Colin says, backing off to whisper to his warriors, who keep their weapons pointed at the doorway.

"I want each of you to take those wads of cash that I gave to you and give them to this guard as you enter the building. If you can, say '*ke a leboga, rra,*' which means ' thank you.' He will appreciate it."

They each hand their cash to the man, who has a hard time stuffing it all in his clothing. He is surprised at how many people speak Setswana, although they all do it quite poorly.

When he closes the door, he does this from the outside, heading home quickly so his wife can hide the hazard pay he has earned.

The man has given Colin a detailed map of the Diamond Trading Company Botswana headquarters. The team heads for an empty room adjacent to the banquet hall. It is an unfinished structure built with double walls of cinderblock. The blueprint indicates it will be a toilet facility. The double walls of cinderblock topped with a thick metal plate roof suggest it might also be a bomb shelter under construction for the company's management.

There's a "closed" sign hung on the door, in English, the business language of Botswana. Colin opens the door, closing it on the inside for safety. It takes two people to close the door. It feels like the inside of a bank vault, although the walls have thick glass slits above vents on all four sides.

"We need to wait here, probably for five or six hours, maybe more," Colin says. "No lights. Use your night vision equipment only."

He pulls up a strip of duct tape on the wall, exposing a recently drilled hole with an almost invisible wide-angle lens he can look through to keep track of the banquet hall and boardroom entrance beyond.

He notices that some men and women get comfortable on the floor immediately, often snuggling.

"Make sure your safeties are all on," he says. "Sleep if you can. But I don't want one of you to shoot me if I pinch your nose when you're snoring or tape your mouths during orgasm."

"You took all our money away from us," one of the Navy SEALs says. "You have left us destitute in a strange, foreign land." Many laugh but then quiet down when their night vision gear shows Colin holding his index finger to his lips. He looks through the peephole and sees a guard slowly making his rounds. He covers the peephole up again with duct tape.

After about 30 seconds, the door to the empty room groans as the night watchman throws his weight against it. Every weapon in the room silently points at it.

Colin holds his breath.

The guard walks away.

He has no key to the door, and Colin is not sure that a key even exists. The door only locks from the inside, with multiple bolts.

For the next hour, nobody sleeps. Gradually, they turn the safeties on their weapons from off to on. Most of them catnap sitting up. Nobody snores. Some of the couples have quiet orgasms.

There are four window slices in the top of the empty room, one on each wall, and Colin sees the outline of the northern window lighten as daybreak creeps across Botswana. It is impossible to hear any noise from the city waking up.

After a while, all three other windows suddenly brighten as someone turns on the banquet hall lights.

Through the drilled hole, Colin watches a handful of people setting up the banquet hall. When they finish, three window slices go dark again.

The inside windows brighten again around 10:00. Several men try to push the door open, groaning in their efforts. Colin realizes they probably use the unfinished room as storage space for utility carts as they prepare lunch for the people in the board meeting. But the door does not open. There is no entry handle or outside lock.

"Sometimes," Colin whispers to his fellow warrior who speaks Arabic, "luck is the most powerful weapon of all." They freeze as a half dozen men try to open the door. They're glad that the empty room is a future toilet or a bomb shelter, or both. The door does not budge.

The room is light enough, from the slit windows near the ceiling to make night vision equipment unnecessary.

Colin looks at the warrior next to him and says, "You look Arabic."

"That because I am Arabic," the Muslim Marine Raider says with a smile.

"I want you in a traditional white thobe and Arab headdress. I want to look like a sheik, a prince. Once the board meeting starts, I want you to stand at the entrance to the banquet hall. You can't have an assault weapon, but here's a Glock 44 LR .22 with a six-inch suppressor that will fit under your robe. You're going to be on your own when the meeting is over. You will also hear them murdering all the board members who are Infidels. They will probably use suppressors, but you'll hear the pops."

He hands him the Glock, which he clears and then resets with the safety "on."

"Who am I?" the Muslim Army Ranger asks.

"You are an emissary of Jalaluddin Shekau, whose brother is the head of Boko Haram in Nigeria. He's the guy who kidnapped a bunch of Nigerian women. It created headlines around the world."

"Jalaluddin Shekau." He says it correctly.

"Jalaluddin Shekau is in the process of trying to turn ISIS into a nuclear power by stealing the atomic bombs built by South Africa at Pelindaba East, in the Y-Plant. General Mac McKlane will hopefully stop him and his men."

"Jalaluddin Shekau, Pelindaba East, Y-Plant, ISIS becomes a nuclear power."

"I'm asking you to do something life-threatening."

"No kidding," he says. "I sort of felt that might be part of the deal."

"If anything goes wrong, we're with you. We'll enter the banquet hall immediately."

"You promise the team members won't shoot me?"

"Have you pissed off any of the women?"

"No, sir. I am in love with one of them."

A Marine Raider next to him says, "That would be me. And nobody's jealous. If they are, I'll kill them."

They laugh.

Colin's men and women have become a tight-knit group.

"Then, you're safe," Colin says. "Can you pull it off?"

"Does a camel shit in the desert?" he replies.

All of the Muslim board members are seated at their tables. Their leader is sorry that the Arab prince they met when coming out of the boardroom has not joined them.

He wants to hear more about ISIS suddenly becoming a nuclear power.

Two-thirds of the banquet hall remains empty. The serving staff does not understand why. Then the heavy door to the new toilet facility slowly opens.

A dozen Arab men and women come out of the room, but they have weapons pointed at the Muslim board members. The staff disappears.

The Muslim secretary of the board meeting, standing on one side of the banquet hall, tries to join the people who flee, but the representative of Jalaluddin Shekau stops her with a surprising punch to her face that knocks her out.

"What is this?" the leader of the Muslim board members shouts as he sees the prince knock the secretary to the ground, out cold.

He thinks Jalaluddin Shekau is mistakenly trying to consolidate his power over ISIS in the region. Surely he knows it is not necessary.

Suddenly, the Arabs who entered the room lose their disguises. They reveal themselves as soldiers, with American Flag patches on their uniforms. Finally, all board members stand and move towards the table and their briefcases, their weapons.

The man they thought was an Arab Prince blocks their way to the table filled with suitcases. The spokesperson for Jalaluddin Shekau points his Glock 44 LR .22 with a six-inch suppressor at them and says, *"'aeidakum bi'anakum sawf tuqabilun Allah aleazim bi'asrae mimaa yumkinuk aitikhadh khatwatayn 'akhriin."*

"I promise you will all meet the great Allah if you take one more step." The board members all freeze.

Colin Rafiki and his troops had expected gunfire, but none of the Muslim men seemed to be armed. They are all standing, most of them looking at the Arab prince pointing his Glock at them.

"Have a seat, gentlemen," Colin Rafiki says. They look at him and continue standing.

"NOW," he says. "Or, if you want, we can shoot every one of you."

They immediately sit down, some of them on the floor instead of in a chair.

Colin walks up to the prince.

"Good job," he says.

Colin opens a briefcase, then another, then a third one. Each one contains a Glock with a suppressor.

"Keep them covered," he says. "If anyone moves, shoot first. We can ask questions later."

Colin Rafiki turns and enters the boardroom, going to each victim and checking for a pulse. They are all dead.

He comes out of the boardroom and calls over a Marine Raider and a Navy SEAL.

"Go through these briefcases and empty every gun magazine. Put the bullets in your pockets, including the chambered rounds. No, wait. Hang on a second. Don't do anything yet."

He goes through swinging doors to what appears to be a deserted service kitchen. He finds a pack of thin gloves used by people serving food. As he's about to return, he sees a security guard run through the kitchen door on the other side.

"Stop," he says, pointing his assault weapon at the man. The security guard has a holstered pistol. Nobody in the complex has heard any shooting yet. The guard is outgunned and halts immediately, holding up his hands.

"Tell your commander and anyone else here to take the rest of the day off," Colin Rafiki says. "I have a commando force with me, and they can't wait to kill people. Do you understand what I am saying?"

The man continues to hold up his hands, which openly tremble. The guard does not answer. He turns and goes back out the swinging kitchen doors with his hands in the air, expecting to die. He ducks quickly out of view, running as fast as possible.

Colin knows he does not have much time left before the Botswana Armed Forces show up.

He returns to the banquet hall and gives the briefcase inspectors the thin rubber gloves and plastic bags.

"Make sure the murderers' fingerprints remain on all the pistols." Then he walks back into the boardroom filled with dead people.

It has only one entry door. Colin knocks on the walls, and they are not hollow, probably cinder block construction.

He returns to the banquet hall, seeing all the briefcases piled back on the table.

Each one contains a cleared weapon with the murderer's fingerprints on it in a sealed plastic bag.

"If it were up to me," he tells the Muslim board members, "I would kill every one of you right now. Maybe I will, even if it's a war crime."

He cocks his pistol and holds it up to the forehead of the nearest board member, who squeezes his eyes tight.

The military team with Colin holds its breath, feeling unease at this act.

They wonder if the CIA operates under the same military code of justice they have sworn to honor and uphold. Colin steps away and lowers his weapon.

"It would be a waste of a good bullet," he says. "Put them all back in the murder room."

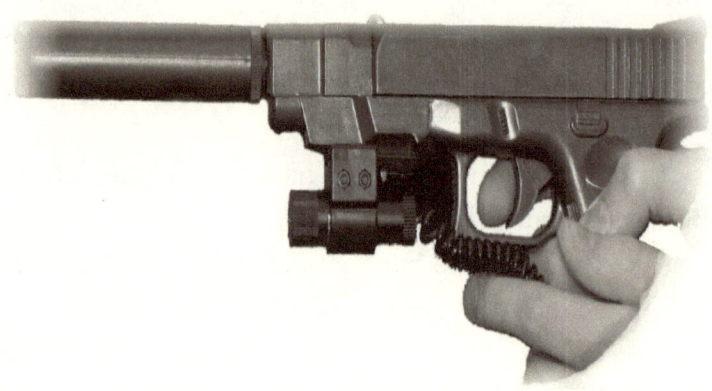

The Muslim board members slowly re-enter the scene of their crime.

"Sit at the board table where you were during the board meeting," Colin says.

They all pick a seat, but Colin knows that they have not chosen their original positions because many of the choices have bullet holes in them.

A Marine Raider shows Colin industrial chain links from the room still under construction outside the boardroom, where they hid for many hours.

"Perfect," Colin says.

He steps into the boardroom.

Colin tells the men, and one woman who has recovered consciousness with a bloody nose and a bruised eye, "The first one of you who tries to escape from this room will die, understood?"

Nobody says anything.

Colin points his Glock 44 LR .22 with a six-inch suppressor at the man who winced earlier when he held his gun to that board member's forehead.

"Understood?" Colin says.

Nobody says anything.

Colin fires a shot, a "pop" through his suppressor, just past the man's head and into the wall behind him.

Suddenly virtually all of the board members say that they understand correctly.

"Now, I want to see all of your cellphones." Colin looks at his own and says, "We know how many you have, whether they are on or off." It's a bluff, but every board member throws their phone into the center of the table. Colin looks at his cellphone again and smiles, raising his Glock slowly. Two spare phones suddenly join the pile on the boardroom table.

A Marine Raider bags all the cellphones, wearing evidence gloves as he does so.

Colin backs out of the boardroom, and they chain the thick wooden doors shut. He looks at his men and women.

"I did not kill anyone," he says, "just a warning shot to get their attention." The Marine Raider, with a bag full of phones, nods in agreement.

"So, let's eat," Colin says. "I recommend the salmon."

He makes sure everyone spreads out, at different banquet tables, with clean lines of fire.

He briefly considers moving everyone back into the toilet built like a bomb shelter, but he decides against it. A hiding place can quickly become a prison.

"Keep your weapons at the ready and visible, " he says. "We will not be the first to fire. Remember that."

Eleven years after the nation achieved independence in 1966, it created the Botswana Defence Force. Initially, a small military police group secured the nation's sovereignty, although the bush wars involving Rhodesia (Zimbabwe), Zambia, Namibia, and South Africa's incursions changed the size of the Defense Force in the mid-1970s.

Botswana is one of the few African countries which have direct and essential ties to the United States. Over 50 Botswana officers receive military training in America every year. It has accumulated to the point where over 80 percent of the Botswana Defense Force officers have direct ties to the United States military. Colin knows many of them, including the Chief of the Defense Staff, Lieutenant-General Gaolato Magoko, a friend and a leader.

He phones the Botswana Defense Force, and after going through four layers of their military hierarchy, he reaches the person to whom he needs to talk.

"General Gaolato Magoko," Colin says, "it's good to hear your voice."

"And yours," the general says. "That's a very formal greeting, Colin. What sort of trouble have you gotten yourself into this time?"

"Well, sir, I have invaded your country with a handful of American Marine Raiders, quite a few Navy SEALs, and some Army Rangers."

"Ah," the general says, followed by silence.

"We are all on your side, General, and we are fighting for the future of Botswana."

"I am older now than the last time we met, Colin. Give me a moment while I put my heart back in my chest and my stomach in my belly."

They both laugh.

Colin says, "We are in Gaborone at the Diamond Trading Company Botswana headquarters, in the banquet room next to the boardroom. I believe that your local forces will probably attack us within the hour. They will try to kill us. We will, of course, defend ourselves."

"Ah," the general says, "I will call you back, Colin."

The entire conversation has been on speakerphone — the information ripples through the room to those who are too far away to hear it first-hand.

"Remember to keep your weapons at the ready and visible," Colin repeats.

Then he adds, again, "We must NOT be the first to fire our weapons."

The warriors have stopped eating, living in a race between a phone call and bullets.

Colin's Motorola rings.

"You have always been a fortunate man, Colin," the general says. "the entire Logistics Command at Sir Seretse Khama Barracks in Gabarone is on an anti-poaching exercise several hundred miles away from your position. There are five conscripts in the barracks, and they are still arguing about which one of them wants to be a hero."

Colin laughs.

"And where are you, general?"

"I am with the Diamond Trading Company Botswana security guards, and we are about to enter the building with holstered weapons. You have already met one of them in the kitchen, I believe."

The general enters the banquet room five minutes later, surrounded by security guards who hold their weapons down, pointing at the ground.

The entire group with Colin stands up and salutes the Botswana general.

He acknowledges this and then walks over, hugging Colin and giving him a double pat on the back.

Then they talk, alone.

Colin explains what happened and where they hid during the boardroom massacre.

"What is that room?" Colin asks. He shows the blueprints of it to the general. "It has a double wall of cinder blocks, a thick metal roof, and a door that takes two people to open and close. It's categorized as a toilet."

"Sounds like a bunch of shit," the general says, and Colin laughs. It is how their relationship has always been over the past two decades, moving through important, often deadly subjects with humor and laughter.

"I think it's a bomb shelter," Colin says.

"No crap," the general says. They laugh again.

The general gets in touch with the Gaborone Police Commander, whose men and women officers will remove the evidence of the briefcases and the murderers currently locked in the boardroom. It takes the commander three minutes to appear in the banquet hall.

"I have heard no shooting," the commander says, staring at the well-armed people surrounding him.

"All the killers' pistols had suppressors," General Gaolato Magoko says.

Colin asks one of the Navy SEALS to hold up a Glock 17 with its suppressor still attached in a clear, plastic evidence bag. The police commander examines it and then puts it back into the briefcase, which will become evidence in a trial.

He also has a bag of cell phones to examine.

The general reads the board meeting minutes on a hand-held, large-screen device containing some blood specks on its edges.

The screen has been wiped clean with tissue paper. The general asks the police commander to join him and Colin and bring the badly bruised woman who acted as the boardroom secretary.

The general looks at her and says: "Who hit you?"

"One of them," she says, sweeping her arms at the Americans. "They were all dressed like Muslims."

An Army Ranger stands up. "I hit her because she was trying to escape with the staff serving food. I did not want to kill her."

"He is a Muslim," Colin says to the woman. "He is an American Muslim, highly decorated, in the Army Rangers."

The general asks the secretary if she has transmitted the minutes written on her hand-held device to anyone.

"I have not had the time," she says.

The general pulls out his pistol and puts it on her forehead. "Are you sure?" Colin and the police commander back away from the table.

"I swear on the grave of Muhammed," she says, showing no fear of death.

The general returns his pistol to its holster. "I have always liked that grave," he says. "It's where he belongs."

For a moment, it looks like the woman might spring at the general for this insult.

There are too many of them.

If she had only worn her explosive vest, but that would have never gotten through security.

The general studies her for a moment, feeling her hatred, and then he slowly passes the hand-held device to the police commander of Gabarone. "Please also show it to my CIA friend, Colin Rafiki."

The woman tries to spit on the table, but she does so poorly because she has a dry mouth filled only with hatred.

After Colin and the police commander both read the minutes, Colin says, "So ISIS is behind all of this. It would have been a very hostile takeover."

They all see the Muslim boardroom secretary smile.

"And Botswana would end up with no percentage of ownership in our diamond mining operations," the police commander says.

He looks over his shoulder at the Army Ranger, who stands up.

"You should have shot her."

The general erases the minutes on the hand-held device and hands it back to the police commander. "There may be a lot of useful information on that computer. Information we do not want to share with the CIA." He smiles at Colin.

"Of course," the police commander says, admiring the patriotic skill of the general. Colin thinks but does not say, *"That is a very clever move."*

"Please," General Gaolato Magoko says to Gabarone's top cop, "continue with your duties. I will deal with the American military and the CIA. Lock up the murderers, including this woman. Gather all the evidence. Your coroner's office will have to take many gruesome pictures in the boardroom, currently chained shut. We have imprisoned all the murderers there. Make sure you have lots of handcuffs."

The general turns to Colin.

"I assume the ISIS terrorists in the boardroom have no weapons of any sort."

"I don't think so. The most dangerous weapon in that room is probably a pen or pencil. But there are quite a few terrorists in there, so you never know. Check and cuff them one at a time and securely."

The police commander tells Colin Rafiki that he knows how to do his job, and the General kicks Colin lightly under the table.

Then the general looks at the police commander and says, "We need to know how their weapons bypassed the security devices at the entry to this complex. We have enemies among us. I admire the police work you did last August when a retired member of the Tanzania Peoples Defense Force coerced his counterpart in our police force, leasing guns to bandits. Your work was as brilliant as your testimony in Tanzania. I have often exemplified your leadership and integrity in the Morogoro trial as a supreme example of patriotism to Botswana and its leadership. Please, continue with your duties."

The police commander leaves, feeling quite pleased with himself, instructing two men to bring the handcuffed woman.

"You're much better at this than I am," Colin says when the police commander leaves.

"Yes, I am," the general says: "How the hell did you get all these people and their weapons in here?"

"Back door."

"Have you ever come through the front door of any place, Colin?"

"Only if I have to," he says.

"How do I get all of you to leave Botswana?"

"Fill up our three Denel Oryx helicopters with Jet-A fuel, and we're gone."

The general leans back. "Ah, so it was you."

"Me?"

"You scared the presidential plane on a 'show the flag' trip to Francistown. He quickly returned to Gaborone two days ago. The president, who does not trust me, has asked for a thorough investigation. I asked him why his accompanying Canadair CF-5 fighter jets did not shoot down the three Denel Oryx helicopters as they invaded Botswana."

"They flew out of the main base near Molepolole with no bullets," Colin says.

"Maparangwane Air Base, to be exact. The President of Botswana does not trust the current Chief of the Defence Staff Air Wing. The president only lets his fighter jets use invisible bullets."

"Who's the current Air Wing Chief he's afraid of?"

"Ah, that would be me."

Colin laughs. "And how's your thorough investigation going so far."

The general holds out his arms, encompassing the entire banquet hall.

"I have captured all of you," he says.

"Well, you have accomplished your president's goal. But please don't try to arrest us."

"Ah," the general says.

After a minute, the general says, "I think this will probably take some stagecraft."

"All it will take is Jet-A fuel for three Oryx helicopters," Colin repeats.

"Yes," he says. "You shall have that."

"Good. When?"

"Where are the helicopters?'"

Colin stares at him.

"Ah," the general says, "the president of Botswana does not trust me, Colin, but you must."

"We have been friends a long time," Colin says, "and I do trust you. I also do not want to help you fulfill your president's worst fears."

"You can not do that because his fears of being overthrown have no basis. He married my second cousin, a witch. She is more than enough punishment from my family."

"I think I knew that," Colin says, shaking his head and laughing. "The Denel Oryx helicopters landed on fumes where you and I met the first time, many years ago, near the Notwane River."

The general puts his Motorola on speakerphone. He calls the garrison adjacent to Sir Seretse Khama International Airport.

One of the five conscripts on duty answers, standing quickly at attention when he realizes the general is on the other end.

"Sir," he says.

"There are still five of you?"

"Yes, sir, all standing at attention, sir."

"At ease, men. One of you get paper and a pencil and write this down. You do this job correctly, and every one of you will receive a meritorious promotion to Corporal with a chance to become an officer cadet."

Five men say, almost in unison, "Yes, sir."

"You will commandeer a troop carrier." Colin holds up two fingers. "Make that two troop carriers. I assume at least two of you have driving licenses."

"Yes, sir. We have four licenses between the five of us, General, sir."

"Now comes the tough part. We need a petrol lorry filled with Jet-A fuel. It must be Jet-A fuel, not diesel or gasoline. Got that, men?"

"Yes, sir," one man says, "Jet-A fuel. My best friend works at the Seretse Khama fueling depot here, sir."

"Good soldier," the general says, "I can tell you're officer material."

"Where are we going, sir?"

"Once everything is in place, I want you to convoy to the main headquarters of the Diamond Trading Company Botswana two blocks off the Airport Road. If you pass the

Mugg and Bean on the Airport Road, you'll know that you've gone too far."

"I know where it is, sir. I applied for a job there before joining the army, sir."

"Well, it looks like they lost a good man, and we gained one. Get moving, men. This maneuver requires speed, but please don't break any speed limits getting here. If you have trouble with anyone, have them call me. You will see my number on your phone in a moment. Share it with no one. That's an order."

Five voices say, "Yes, sir."

The general turns off his speakerphone.

"Thank you, General." Colin Rafiki says, standing up and saluting him, as do all his men and women, with a chorus of three different military chants: "Oorah," "Hooah," and "Hooyah."

Nobody notices one of the security men slip away during the excitement.

The Muslim guard leaves his turban behind a food cart in the banquet hall.

heartbeats

Colin and his men know precisely where the Denel Oryx helicopters landed on fumes.

The ISIS warriors only guess that it is near the old dam on the Notwane River, and the security guard who gave them the information sends them to the wrong side of the dam. They are not within shooting range of the helicopters.

The petrol lorry filled with Jet-A fuel is an obvious target, and as they finish topping up the first Oryx helicopter, Colin hears the bullets cracking through the afternoon heat.

His warriors see the terrorists running along the dam.

"Keep running," Colin says. "You can't shoot very well when your running."

The ISIS terrorists know this, but they need to get close enough to the helicopters and the petrol lorry to ensure they don't need to rely on a lucky shot to destroy their enemy's escape. Colin's men and women move as quickly as possible towards the terrorists.

The Rangers, Raiders, and SEALs are better shots, using superior weapons, all with telescopes.

The conscripts from the Seretse Khama barracks feel as if they are watching a movie, crouching near the petrol lorry, and instructed by their general to defend it to the death.

A random gunshot hits one of the conscripts, who spins around and sits on the ground. A black Marine medic immediately treats him.

"You're going to live; you'll be all right," she says. She packs the arm wound and plunges a sharp needle into the conscript's thigh. All of the pain suddenly disappears.

The Botswana army conscript thinks the Marine Raider may be the most beautiful woman in the world. He wants to ask her name, but his tongue cannot move.

She kisses his forehead, a memory he holds as he falls asleep, and then the Marine Raider grabs her assault weapon and rejoins the fight.

The terrorists cannot get close enough to hit the petrol lorry. The general's conscripts pull it behind the helicopters.

Now the ISIS troops realize they are in danger. They have no missiles they can fire. They are outgunned and vulnerable on the old dam.

There is nowhere to hide as the superior American force bears down on them.

Suddenly they are no longer concerned with the escape of the helicopters and the enemies of ISIS.

The terrorists try to disappear into the brush along the riverbank. Some of them wade into the water, trying to swim. The American forces hear screaming as the ISIS terrorists discover the Notwane River is most famous for large, hungry crocodiles.

Everyone returns to the helicopters, which they finish filling with Jet-A fuel.

Colin walks up to General Gaolato Magoko, whom he salutes. Then they hug like the old friends they are.

"You are the luckiest man I know," the General says.

"And you are one of the best generals I know."

"Bull shit."

"I mean it. Look at what you've done today. You have saved your nation from a hostile takeover, which would have turned Botswana into an ISIS stronghold."

"They're still here."

"Not as many of them as yesterday."

"And not as many of them as there will be tomorrow."

Colin salutes the general again and boards the last Denel Oryx as it starts to lift off. They lost three men and one woman in the battle. They take their bodies with them.

"Where are you going?" the general shouts as the helicopter kicks up a cloud of red dust.

"On vacation," Colin shouts back with a wide smile.

The general says "bull shit" and gets into one of the troop carriers returning to the barracks with the conscripts.

"You are all heroes," he says. "You are going to officer's training school, some of you in America."

In the disappearing helicopters, Colin sets their coordinates for Pelindaba. Over the intercom, relayed to all three helicopters, he tells his team to get some sleep and turn off all of their communications gear.

"We may wake up fighting."

Chapter 13

During the 28-day passage of the *S.S. Nomad* from Brooklyn, New York, to Cape Town, South Africa, General Mac McKlane, Captain Maria Montoya, Major Sookie Ringer, and Chief Warrant Officer Shadrach Ringer have many private conversations. They always occur in the captain's suite, and they focus on the Y-Plant at Pelindaba East.

In the first meeting, Sookie says: "You're asking us to commit suicide."

"Radiation poisoning," Shadrach says.

"That's possible," Mac says. "I have told you I will always speak the truth, so, yes, this could be called a suicide mission for one or both of you."

"But it does not have to be," Captain Montoya says.

"I'd like to discuss that part of the deal in some detail," Shadrach says.

"We will," Mac says, "but first, I want you to understand what happens if ISIS manages to get the bombs before we do."

"If they are bombs," the captain says. "They may have been 'melted down' into radioactive, enriched uranium bars."

General McKlane tightens his lips and glares at Captain Maria Montoya.

"My ship, my rules," Montoya says.

"Her ship, her rules," Shadrach says.

McKlane sits back and invites the captain to speak with an open hand gesture that recognizes her position.

"Shadrach, you and Sookie won this assignment because you both have extraordinary stamina and powerful lungs," the captain says. "Sookie, you were an all-American swimmer in college who almost made it to the Olympics. And Shadrach, you were the first person actually to succeed in the Houdini Room."

"We would like to keep our powerful lungs," Sookie says directly to Mac.

"There's an excellent chance that you will," Captain Montoya says. "You may suit up and enter the area where the South African version of my engineer's 8000 cubic meter Houdini Room exists, but you might never have to go anywhere near the radioactive material."

"How does that work?" Mac asks.

"Operation Jellybean," Captain Maria Montoya says. They talked about it for three weeks.

heartbeats

Jalaluddin Shekau has very few weapons and no missiles as he approaches the Y-Plant at the South African Nuclear Energy Corporation at Pelindaba East.

The ISIS leader's weaponry has been spent or destroyed in the Battle of Soweto outside of Johannesburg.

Several weeks earlier, he spoke to the great leader, Tarad Muhammed al-Jarba, the Muslim leader who replaced Abu Bakr al-Baghdadi as the head of ISIS after the devils from the United States murdered Abu Bakr in Syria.

"You will have more weapons soon," Tarad Muhammed tells him. "They will be bought with diamonds."

Jalaluddin Shekau has never told Tarad Muhammed al-Jarba about his armory at the Orlando East Mosque on Mofutsanyane Street. In ISIS, secrets cement relationships.

The battle of Soweto and its success damaging the South African Defence Force, especially its air wing, has already reached the ears of the leadership of ISIS.

"You have used your weapons well," he tells Jalaluddin, who says nothing in return. The failure of ISIS at the Diamond Trading Company Botswana remains unknown.

"Our men at Palindaba East have more weapons for you," Tarad Muhammed al-Jarba tells his field leader. "When you get near the Y-Plant, turn on your cellphone."

The connection ends, and Jalaluddin Shekau watches the guards change at the massive steel fortress of the Y-Plant. He notices one of the guards wearing traditional Muslim headgear. His pockets seem to bulge, and Jalaluddin Shekau imagines that they are diamonds. Suddenly, four Saab Gripen fighter jets roar overhead towards Botswana, flying low.

Jalaluddin Shekau's men hide in an oversized, six-foot-tall storm drain under the road leading to the Y-plant entrance. After a few minutes, many start eating the junk food they stole from the Bait and Tackle Shop. Some of them fall asleep because of an unexpected spike and sudden drop in their blood sugar counts.

Jalaluddin Shekau must wait for darkness. He posts guards at either end of the oversized storm drain, with orders to shoot anyone who does not respond to an Arabic challenge. Only then does Jalaluddin Shekau open his

Motorola cellphone and turn it on. He does not know from whom the call will come.

heartbeats

For many years after the death of apartheid in South Africa, the United States has tried to reclaim the highly enriched uranium produced by the 20-megawatt nuclear research reactor at Pelindaba. The SAFARI-1 reactor delivered by Allis-Chalmers Corporation in 1965 included Uranium 235, the only nuclide existing in nature that is fissile with thermal neutrons. The enriched uranium is a critical component of both nuclear power generation and military nuclear weapons.

In 1967, South Africa built a SAFARI-2 reactor, also at Pelindaba. They said that they abandoned the project two years later because plutonium production drained too many resources from their goal of becoming a nuclear power.

They did, however, manage to produce some radioactive, fissionable material. South African scientists started to focus on a weapons building program, helped by a nuclear engineer from Pakistan working in the U.K.

The South African Atomic Energy Board built two test sites in the Kalahari Desert in 1976 and 1977. Soviet intelligence detected them and shared their knowledge with several United States Intelligence services. An American Lockheed SR-71 spy plane confirmed their existence.

On August 28, 1977, *The Washington Post* quoted an anonymous United States diplomat saying, "We were 99 percent certain that the construction was preparation for an atomic test."

It never happened. South Africa plugged the test holes once their secret was out. They opened one briefly during the South African Bush Wars against Cuban forces in Angola in the 1980s, but it was a negotiating tool, and they resealed the test site later.

Apartheid finally died in 1994, and then Nelson Mandela became the first president of South Africa's newly-elected and racially mixed parliament.

Scientists had built South Africa's first atomic bomb 12 years earlier. They produced seven of them, with an eighth under construction, and then they ended the program.

The original agreement between America and South Africa in 1957 included a 50-year collaboration under the U.S-sanctioned program called "Atoms for Peace." It ensured that any fissionable, enriched, weapons-grade uranium produced by SAFARI-1 would go back to America.

Not a single ounce ever returned, although South Africa continued to repeat the mantra of being the only nation in the world that voluntarily stopped its atomic program after successfully making a nuclear bomb.

South Africa continued to operate its weapons testing facility near Arniston in the Western Cape. It included launch pads and tracking systems that they maintained and improved by renting the complex to other nations.

Since the rise of ISIS as a political and military entity, a primary focus of both the CIA and the Countering Weapons of Mass Destruction (CWMD) Section of Homeland Security had focused on South Africa's enriched uranium. The weapons-grade U-235 remained the least secure source of atomic power in the world. As the military might of South

Africa drops lower each year, the problem becomes more severe, and ISIS knows this.

So do Homeland Security and the CIA.

The *USS George H.W. Bush* had just started a 28-month docking plan in Norfolk in February 2019. Its incremental availability was interrupted by an unexpected trip around the Cape of Good Hope to the Indian Ocean with a skeleton crew and no visible aircraft on its flight deck. However, an entire Marine Corps Wing of Hornets exists below deck.

The ship waits approximately 50 nautical miles east of Port Louis, Mauritius. The Landing Signals Officer of the Nimitz-class supercarrier guides eight Sikorsky UH-1 Black Hawk helicopters onto his flight deck. They arrive at night.

The USS George H.W. Bush captain orders the Black Hawks to be taken three stories below the flight deck to the main hanger. They disappear into a secure area where only a handful of military operatives worked to disguise them.

They emerge from below decks two nights later, at 04:00. An ensign about to finish his watch on the Flag Bridge catches a glimpse of them.

"When did we start selling Black Hawks to Syria?" he asks the Officer of the Watch, a Navy commander. He knows they are old UH-1 Black Hawks, relics from the Vietnam War era. A gunner is visible in each door as they load the troops. "I thought only Marines flew those garbage cans."

The *USS George H.W. Bush* captain shakes hands with the Syrian soldiers climbing into the Black Hawks down on the flight deck.

On the Flag Deck, the Navy commander looks at the ensign and says, "You never saw what you are looking at."

The ensign, a recent graduate of Officer Candidate School at Naval Station Newport, Rhode Island, says, "That's positively Orwellian, sir."

The ensign graduated near the top of his class. The commander, a Navy SEAL, is in his face immediately.

"Stow it, ensign."

"Yes, sir."

"If you say one word to anybody, ever, I will personally throw your sorry ass in the brig and have you court-martialed. Or, I might just throw you overboard."

"Yes, sir."

"You did not see anything."

"No, sir, I mean, yes, sir. I did not see anything, sir."

"That's an order."

"Yes, sir."

He does not see the Black Hawks lift off the deck, one after the other in perfect formation. He does, however, see their blips on the radar sweep.

"What are you looking at?" the commander asks.

"Nothing, sir. I see nothing.

"Keep it that way."

"Yes, sir."

"Forever."

"Yes, sir."

The Syrian Black Hawks and soldiers cross over Madagascar and land at an abandoned airbase not far from the Indian Ocean shoreline of Mozambique.

Late at night, Colin Rafiki's three Denel Oryx helicopters land in Witkoppen.

He puts them down near the other five helicopters, including a Denel Rooievalk attack helicopter. As he walks past it, he notices that the "Red Falcon" cannot fly. A lot of bullets have clipped its tail.

Their noisy arrival wakes up anyone sleeping. Many of McKlane's troops switch the safeties on their weapons to "on" when they see Colin Rafiki.

"Welcome to my humble air force base," Bootie says.

"Who got their tail feathers trimmed?" Colin says, pointing at the damaged "Red Falcon."

"Who the hell are you?" a South African general asks, stepping into the circle surrounding the CIA agent.

"Colin Rafiki, general."

"You're an American?"

"By choice," Colin says. "I am Kenyan by birth." He holds out his hand, then drops it when the general refuses to shake it.

"So, Bootie, I see you've been making friends while I was away."

Colin spots a woman in the crowd, holding the hand of a baboon. "And I see you're still monkeying around, Commander Nelson. Glad you made it. And your ugly dog."

"Who you calling an ugly dog?" Samuel Nelson asks with a wide smile. Fubar is flat on the ground next to him, sound asleep. He does not sense danger.

"So you're the CIA agent," the general says.

"Yes, sir, and I'm happy to say that the ISIS hostile takeover of the DeBeers operation in Botswana never reached a vote. General Gaolato Magoko sends you warm regards."

Colin knows that Magoko and the South African general are friends.

They fought together in the Congo many years earlier, and they have stayed in touch.

The general holds out his hand, and Colin shakes it.

"Why are you all here?" the general asks.

Nobody answers, although almost everyone knows.

General McKlane finally says: "We want to make sure that ISIS does not become a nuclear power."

"What are you talking about?" the South African says.

"Pelindaba East," McKlane says.

"I seriously doubt if they can break through our security at Valindaba," the general says.

"I hope that's true," Mac says. "Just as I am certain that you did not think ISIS would reduce your airpower by 50 percent when you woke up yesterday."

The South African general's jawline tightens.

Colin Rafiki lowers his voice and says, "ISIS has people working on the inside at Pelindaba East, general. And the men who attacked your forces are probably waiting outside the gates."

"They cannot get to the fissionable material," the South African general says. "It would be a suicide mission."

Shadrach and Sookie shuffle their feet, looking at Mac with eyes that say, "*I told you so.*"

Bootie van Zale says: "Unfortunately, General, suicide missions are something at which ISIS excels."

A Navy SEAL pushes into the crowd and says: "They've gone hot. They've turned on their cellphones. We know where they are."

Colin turns on his cellphone to verify this, and he also receives a message.

"You'll have to excuse me for a moment," Colin says. "Don't do anything until I get back. It will only take a moment. Please, wait."

While he's gone, Bootie tells the general that at least 12 known ISIS terrorists are already working in the Y-Plant, eight of them as nuclear scientists.

"How do you know this, Bootie?" the general asks.

"I've been a member of the National Intelligence Agency for over 25 years, General."

"Why are you only a major?"

"Because I've worked for our intelligence agencies for over 25 years, general, and the higher your rank, the greater your scrutiny from politicians and fellow officers. Sometimes, it's important to be an unnoticed failure, sir. Especially if you're a White Afrikaaner."

Bootie does not know if the general's smile represents satisfaction or recognition.

It does not matter.

"Where do we go from here?" the general asks, turning to Mac McKlane.

"Let's wait for Colin to return, sir. I think he's going to tell us something we don't know right now."

heartbeats

Samuel and Sharonda Nelson decide they must leave Fubar at Bootie Nelson's farm.

"He's saved our lives many times with his head-lowering and '*fluuf-fluuf-fluuf*' warning," Sharonda says.

"He stopped me from setting off a tripwire attached to a Claymore Mine up in Tanzania," an Army Ranger says.

"He needs to retire now," Samuel says. "I wish he could have stayed with Colin's stepfather up in Chimala, but we know how that turned out."

A Navy SEAL says, "I think Fubar deserves The Budweiser." It's the nickname for the SEAL Trident pin.

Another SEAL adds," 'He never rang the bell."

The first man takes off his Navy SEAL Trident and pins it onto the worn leather collar around Fubar's neck. The men standing nearby all salute one of the ugliest dogs they've ever known. Fubar sits up. He barks.

"Jesus," Sharonda says. "That's the first time I ever heard Fubar's voice. He's never barked before."

"That's because he thought he was a Marine," the SEAL who awarded him his Trident pin says." "Marines never volunteer anything. Fubar only just now realized he's a hardened, intelligent Navy SEAL."

Fubar barks again, and everyone laughs.

"He's going to like living here," Bootie says. "But now you have to figure out what to do with Sophia."

"Can't my monkey stay here as well?" Sharonda asks. Fubar lays on the ground as Sophia grooms him.

"I don't think that will work," Bootie says. "She's getting a lot bigger, and baboons go wild at her age. Their hormones start to kick in."

"What do we do with her?" Samuel Nelson asks.

"I think she's a chacma baboon, and I know there's a troop of them about six miles from here. We can release her there and see if they accept her into the troop."

"What if they don't?"

"Then, one of the males will probably kill her."

"Uh, she's like my child," Sharonda says.

"I know. But Sophia can't go with you, and she can't stay here," Bootie says.

It takes a while, but Sharonda finally realizes that she must release Sophia into the wild.

She talks to the Marine Raider, who shot Colin Rafiki's stepfather before the terrorists hanged him behind his home in Chimala, Tanzania.

"I want the same deal for Sophia," Sharonda tells the Ranger, who agrees reluctantly.

The Nelsons, Charlton Tremwallis, Holly, the Marine Raider sniper, Bootie, and Sophia get into one of the Oryx helicopters and fly to a bridge over a dry river bed six miles north.

As they land on the road in the middle of the bridge, they spot the troop of about 40 baboons. Tears roll down Sharonda's face as Samuel takes Sophia from her arms. They tether her to a long rope and lower her over the bridge to the dry river bed.

Sophia, terrified, does not make a sound.

Samuel jerks the rope, and the slip knot comes loose. At the last minute, Sophia jumps up, trying to grab the line, but she misses and falls back to the ground.

Sharonda is weeping openly.

The troop slows moves towards the bridge.

They have lived in this area for generations, and they have no fear of people, cars, or even helicopters.

They view them as sources of food.

Cars have stopped on both sides of the bridge, blocked by the aircraft, watching the spectacle.

"We should go," Samuel says.

Then he sees the Marine Raider sniper, as well as Charlton Tremwallis with their weapons, steadied on the bridge railing, ready to fire.

Samuel reaches for Sharonda, and they both hold one another tighter as the troop approaches Sophia.

"She's so little," Sharonda says. Samuel says nothing.

The troop slowly surrounds Sophia. Suddenly, a 50-pound male stands up and snarls at Sharonda's pet monkey. Tremwallis quietly says, "Don't shoot yet."

The male baboon sticks his nose in the rear of Sophia, shoving her a little. Sophia offers no resistance and makes no noise. The male stands up again, but he does not snarl.

"Don't shoot," Charlton repeats.

The troop begins to move up the dry river bed, away from the bridge. Sophia joins it somewhere in the middle of the hierarchy.

Sharonda still sees Sophia, the smallest monkey in the troop. She hopes she will turn and wave goodbye, but, of course, she does not. She has returned to the wild.

"She's the only American monkey in Africa."

"They have accepted her," Samuel says.

The Ranger sniper and Charlton Tremwallis lower their guns, and they all move back towards the helicopter to return to Bootie's farm.

Sharonda remains tearful, but not with sadness. On the short trip back, Charlton looks at Holly and says, "I never told you this, but you and Sophia have a lot in common. I came very close to shooting you once in Virginia."

Holly smiles at him. "I know," she says. "Mac told me about it at Walter Reed."

"If you hadn't been kissing him ."

"I know, Charlton. I'm glad you held off. Being accepted into a tribe is important."

Holly smiles at Sharonda, who remains sad and happy.

heartbeats

Eight Syrian Black Hawks refuel at an abandoned airfield in southwestern Mozambique. The hardened Syrian fighters relax outside the landing perimeter. Many appear to be veterans of the Kurdish Border Wars.

Excluding the pilots, there are 140 combat veterans, eight of whom are women.

All of the women are door gunners, strapped into their combat positions with old-fashioned monkey harnesses. Each has qualified as a professional sniper. They only use their medium 7.62mm machine guns for ground cover fire.

They have sniper rifles clipped to the helicopter's cabin wall next to them, used initially by Swedish Armed Forces in 1989 but now famous worldwide. The women stay away from all of the male combat veterans.

Only two women speak a Kurdish dialect, one Kurmanji and the other Hewrami.

English is their common language.

"I think I know why the commander made us all door gunners," one woman says.

"Why's that?" another woman asks as she tightens her bulletproof vest.

"The average life expectancy of a door gunner in these old crates, according to legend in the Vietnam War, was around five minutes."

"This is not Vietnam," another woman says.

"Plus, men are almost always wrong."

Their laughter contains more nerves than bravado.

The helicopters reload and stay on the ground. Most of the men and women go to sleep, including the pilots. A small perimeter force remains awake.

The commander of the Syrian forces waits for a one-word message on his Motorola cellphone. It will either say "go" or "no."

At Bootie van Zale's 10-acre farm in Wittkopen, after talking to the person who sent him a message, not from the CIA but the Pentagon, Colin Rafiki types "GO" and hits the send button.

A reply immediately asks, "Are you certain?"

"GO," he shouts again in capital letters, twice. "GO."

Then he walks back out to the group gathered outside.

Colin looks at the General of the Air Force and says, "There are eight Syrian Black Hawks headed to the Y-Plant."

"Syrian Black Hawks?"

"Yes, sir. They will reach Pelindaba East in about two hours, flying in low from a fueling station at an unused airstrip in Mozambique. Before that, they were in Ethiopia. They are old UH-1 Black Hawks but well-armed with missiles and door hammers. The eight choppers probably have between 130 and 145 ISIS terrorists on board."

"What's a door hammer?" the general asks.

"A machine gun, sir."

"Don't forget the terrorists who just went hot on the ground," says the Navy SEAL, who delivered that message. "We know where they are, just outside the Y-Plant, but we don't know how many there are."

Bootie says, "I just told the general that our intelligence says there are another eight ISIS agents inside the Y-Plant, and two of them are senior nuclear physicists."

Mac says, "Let's go talk about this, but I think we need to talk fast."

He leads the general, the squadron leader, Bootie, Colin, Shadrach, Sharonda, and Holly into the dining room."

"Our strategic plan is called Operation Jellybean," Mac says. "Commander Maria Montoya developed it during a 28-day training mission aboard the *S.S. Nomad,* with the help of the Pentagon, the CIA, the FBI, and Homeland Security."

Bootie coughs loudly. Mac looks at him. "The *S.S Nomad* disappeared from Cape Town yesterday," Bootie says

Mac McKlane brushes this off, but he feels it in the pit of his stomach.

A part of the plan has already vanished.

"Did anyone bother talking to my government?" the General of South Africa's Air Force asks.

"No, sir," Mac says.

"Why not?"

"Because you are the enemy," Mac says.

A good deal of oxygen goes out of the room.

"Excuse me? We are the enemy?"

"Yes, sir, but we have no interest in destroying you politically or militarily."

"So, we are a friendly enemy, General McKlane?"

"If necessary, sir, America will wipe out much of what's left of your military. I sincerely hope that it will not come to that."

The South African general looks at Bootie and asks, "Did you know about this?"

"No. he did not," Colin Rafiki says. Mac McKlane repeats what Colin says.

"Bootie?" the South African general asks, staring at him. Colin and Mac both stop breathing.

"No," Bootie says. "I like jellybeans, but I know nothing about a clandestine operation that the Americans call Operation Jellybean."

"We are running out of time," Mac McKlane says.

"To do what?" the South African general asks.

Jalaluddin Shekau's open Motorola cellphone suddenly speaks. It is a woman's voice, and she brings him greetings from his brother, Abubakar Shekau, the head of Boko Haram in Nigeria.

"Northern Nigeria is now an Islamic State," she says. "Even the great Ibrahim Babangida, the richest politician in the country, hides behind the walls of his multibillion-dollar mansion in Niger state. We have killed tens of thousands of infidels and chased almost three million of them from their homes. We now own Nigeria."

"It is not like my brother to boast of such things," Jalaluddin Shekau tells the woman on the phone.

"No, it is not," the woman says. "It is me who brags, not your brother."

"Who are you? You speak our language with more song than power."

"I am from Afghanistan, with the voice of the Nuristani. I beg your forgiveness, Jalaluddin Shekau."

"Let me speak to your leader."

In the Denel Oryx helicopter heading towards the blip identifying Jalaluddin Shekau and his terrorist group, Holly Smolkes McKlane hands the phone to Colin Rafiki, whose

Arabic is rusty and flawed. He gives the phone to the Muslim Marine Raider, who speaks the language fluently. Nobody else says a word, then Holly and Colin start an Arabic background conversation smothered by the sounds of their helicopter.

"We have taken over the diamond mines in Botswana," the Marine Raider lies. "They are far more valuable than the oil fields we lost in Syria."

"Who are you?" Jalaluddin Shekau asks."

In Colin Rafikis's background Arabic conversation with Holly, he suddenly says, "Abu Hamza al-Amriki," The Marine Raider immediately understands. He says, first in Arabic and then in English, that he is the senior commander and recruiter from Syria, an Albanian-American.

"I am Abu Hamza al-Amriki," he says.

Jalaluddin Shekau says nothing, and then he asks again, "Who is the woman?"

In a whisper that barely reaches above the sound of the helicopter, Abu Hamza al-Amriki says: "Malalai."

Malalai is the Joan of Arc of Afghanistan, long dead, who took off her veil and used it as a flag to lead Afghanistan's warriors to victory against the British over a century and a half earlier.

She did this on her wedding day.

Other great female Afghan warriors have been nicknamed Malalai since then, most recently the young girl who shot down a gunship near the end of the Russian occupation of Afghanistan.

She fired a surface-to-air missile supplied by the Americans, destroying a helicopter flown by a Russian pilot who was her father and abused her mother.

She was famous in the Islamic state, but she died in America with her twin brother when they tried to poison the waterways of Virginia.

Jalaluddin Shekau says, "Malalai is dead."

Holly McKlane takes the phone and says, "I did not die with my brother, Ahmed Khan, in America, *rahimah rahatan fi aleadharaa.* (may his spirit rest in the comfort of virgins)." She explains that she has waited for almost three years to exact her revenge. "Now, the time has come."

Jalaluddin Shekau at first is silent, then he says, "Millions will pay for the death of your brother, Malalai."

The Marine Raider pretending to be the 29-year-old senior commander and recruiter in Syria, Abu Hamza al-Amriki, says, "There are eight Syrian Black Hawk helicopters that will soon land near you. They include over 140 freedom fighters to help you make ISIS a nuclear power."

He waits a moment to see if there's a response. He hears none. He then adds, "All of these men will be under your command, Jalaluddin Shekau."

"Finally," Jalaluddin Shekau thinks, *"I will earn even greater recognition than my child-stealing brother receives in Nigeria as the leader of Boko Haram. He kills tens of thousands. He steals schoolgirls. I will kill millions with the atomic bombs we are about to take from the South Africans."*

"You must tell me when the Syrian Black Hawks land," Jalaluddin Shekau says.

He repeats this request twice before he realizes nobody is there.

In the oversized six-foot-tall storm drain under the road leading to the Y-plant, all Motorola cellphones are also suddenly dead, completely useless. Jalaluddin Shekau has never seen this happen before.

The terrorists can hear helicopters landing in the distance behind them. In the darkness, they cannot see them. Jalaluddin's men lack the night vision equipment of the men and women slowly approaching them.

Jalaluddin Shekau posts extra sentries outside either end of the oversized, six-foot-tall storm drain under the road leading to the Y-plant.

"Demand identification from anyone who appears, but no shooting unless you recognize extreme danger," he tells the sentries.

The conversation between Jalaluddin Shekau and Abu Hamza al-Amriki has spread to all the men in the tunnel.

The word "Malalai" moves quickly through the oversized drain pipe.

Ten minutes pass.

"I am Malalai," a woman whispers.

She crouches above the sentries on the embankment of the Pelindaba Y-Plant entry road covering the six-foot-tall storm drain.

Her weapon points at them, although they do not know this. She conceals it in the darkness of night as well as in her black clothing. Her assault rifle has a suppressor on it.

"She is here," a sentry rejoices. "Malalai is here."

A foreign nation has leased South Africa's weapons testing facility near Arniston in the Western Cape.

The empty launch pads and tracking systems await the nation's latest military weapons, a package of three medium-sized ballistic missiles purchased from China. They have a range of between 620 and 1,860 miles, depending on payload and trajectory.

Only 12 ISIS warriors survive the attack on Colin Rafiki's troops near the old dam on the Notwane River. They regroup for a 780-mile trip due south to Arniston, near the southernmost tip of Africa.

Botswana has only one helicopter to make the trip, and it must refuel along the way.

The Eurocopter Super Puma can carry all the survivors of Colin Rafiki's attack, but they must make the jump in two stages because of its 530-mile range. The entire trip takes six hours, with refueling.

The terrorists still alive must first steal the Puma helicopter from the Gaborone Sir Seretse Khama International Airport.

It takes them three hours to reach the transport chopper, but only a few minutes to persuade two pilots, both Muslims, to make their unexpected flight.

The ease of their theft surprises the Muslim survivors.

The Puma is a transport helicopter with no armament, although the sliding doors are locked open. Muslims with assault weapons fill them, ready to fire.

"Keep low," the leader of the terrorists says to the pilot and his co-pilot. "We need to stay off the South African radar screens."

"You must turn off all your cellphones," the co-pilot says to the terrorists.

The ISIS warriors have been in the air for about ten minutes when the co-pilot suggests this.

In Witkoppen, Bootie van Zale shows the blips coming out of Gabarone in Botswana to the general who heads the South African Air Force.

Colin Rafiki is on his encrypted cellphone talking to Botswana's Chief of the Defense Staff, Lieutenant-General Gaolato Magoko, who tells him, "They have stolen our only Puma helicopter. It just returned from the poaching exercises. I wish I had left some of the conscripts there, Colin."

"They would be dead. Do you know the terrorists' flight plans? They probably never filed one, right?"

On Bootie's phone, the blips coming out of Gabarone suddenly disappear.

The general on Colin's phone says, "A member of the ground crew, who hid behind some crates in the hangar, said they were going to Arniston in the Western Cape."

"Crap," Colin says.

"What the hell is in Arniston?" Gaolato Magoko asks.

"Launching pads," Colin says. "I have to go. Thanks, old friend."

"Hang on a second," the general says. "How much danger exists here in Botswana, Colin?"

It is not a rehearsed question, and Colin wonders why the general deviates from their planned discussion. What is he not telling him?

"You know that bomb shelter they called a toilet, where we all hid after we slipped in the back door at the Botswana Diamond Trading Company in Gaborone?"

The general says nothing.

Colin says, "Well, hurry up and finish building it. I think you have about 48 hours, although whatever comes off those launch pads in Arniston probably will be aimed at the capitals of South Africa, not Botswana."

"I see you are enjoying the vacation you told me you were taking," the general says.

Colin smiles. He appreciates his old friend's humor.

After he hangs up, General Magoko wonders why Colin Rafiki wanted him to play dumb about Arniston.

Every military leader in Africa and the middle east knows about Arniston.

Bootie and the head of the South African Air Force listen to Colin's speakerphone conversation.

He looks at both of them and says, "Arniston, that's their destination. Tell me, general, who is renting Arniston right now?"

South Africa's Air Force head makes a phone call to Bloemfontein and then another to Cape Town before he finally says, "Syria."

heartbeats

South Africa scrambles four Saab Gripens out of Air Force Base Makhado near the border of Zimbabwe on a trajectory that will bisect the Eurocopter Super Puma helicopter carrying 12 terrorists and two Muslim pilots.

These swept-wing planes send Jalaluddin Shekau and his men into the oversized storm drain just south of the main entry gate at the Pelindaba Y-Plant.

"We need to put down, now," the Eurocopter co-pilot says, putting a fingerprint on his radar. "The South Africans Saab Gripens will close on us in twenty-five minutes."

"We need to hide," the pilot says.

Ten minutes later, the Puma disappears into the bleakness of the Great Karoo Desert beneath green and brown camouflage, 95 miles northeast of Calvinia in the Northern Cape.

The Saab Gripens track the Orange River into the Northern Cape province, passing 15 miles south of the Super Puma's hiding place.

"Look there; you can see them," the Muslim pilot says.

The Mach 2 passing of the Saab Gripens thunders in the sky a few seconds later, although untrained eyes do not see the jets.

The pilot opens a baggage compartment in the rear of the Puma, revealing six FIM-92 Stinger Surface-to-Air missiles, all made in America.

He points to an outcropping of reddish rocks around a mile away. "You must set up your missile attack there. Otherwise, they will destroy the Puma."

"And you must turn on your transponder to call the infidels home to Hell," the ISIS leader says. He suddenly seems suspicious. "But how did you know we would need these weapons?"

"I did not. The President of Botswana ordered them from the armory when the South Africans attacked Debswana and almost shot down the Presidential jet as it flew over Francistown."

"You must turn on your transponder," the leader says.

"But, I do not have to keep it on."

"They must still know where we are. We must call the South Africans into our arms." He smiles at the cleverness of his request.

"Your cellphones will confuse them. Your signals will draw them like camels to water."

The ISIS leader understands that the cellphones will probably require the death of six of his warriors.

"This will eliminate half of my force," he says.

"They will rest in the arms of peace and beauty."

The leader calls his men together and tells them what they must do to fulfill their destinies.

"Who among you are the best runners?"

They all raise their hands.

"Praise God from whom all blessings flow. You must race to that bush over there and back to me. You must circle the bush. Now, stack your weapons and line up."

The pilot wants all of the weapons in the baggage hold that initially held the SAMs.

Before he can suggest this, the terrorists line up, and their leader shouts, "Go."

The sprint covers 200 yards. It is a dash of death, and they know it, but they all try to win. The five men who fail hang their heads, panting and defeated. The leader comforts them, saying that their time will come.

He hands the unpackaged and armed Stinger Surface-to-Air missiles to the winners as if they were medals. Each SAM weighs almost 35 pounds.

A two-person team normally operates the weapon, but a single warrior can manage it.

The ISIS leader does not want to eradicate his entire force to accomplish this operation. He does not want to be the only freedom fighter to arrive at the launching pads at Arniston in South Africa.

"Turn off all your cellphones. Pace yourselves when you run to that outcropping of rocks over there. When you arrive, get yourselves deep in the crevices. The planes will come from the west."

The pilot points to the western horizon. Then, he whispers something in the leader's ear.

"When you are ready, the last person to arrive at the rocks must turn on his cellphone and call me. Then all of you will turn on your cellphones, but only after I have answered the call of the last man to reach the rocks."

He asks each man to repeat what he has said, embracing them after doing so and then releasing them towards the distant rocks with their FIM-92 Stinger Surface-to-Air missiles.

"Go with Allah. Run with the wind."

The string of six warriors expands and contracts as they sprint and jog towards the rocks. They start at different times, beginning with the slowest man. Several stumble, fall, pick themselves back up, and continue.

As they run, the leader has their assault weapons put into the baggage compartment where the FIM-92 Stingers had been. The pilot whispered this suggestion to him in case the men in the rocks died in victory. They will have to make their move to the refueling area quickly.

The first terrorist arrives at the rocky outcropping after about 15 minutes, and the last reaches the rocks five minutes later. He was the fastest runner.

In the cockpit of the Puma, the pilot turns on his transponder, sending a clear signal to the Saab Gripens searching many miles away. Sitting in the co-pilot's seat, the ISIS leader watches the blips of the swept-winged Gripens slowly turn back towards the Puma helicopter's location.

The leader's phone rings.

"We are here. We are ready."

"Turn on all your cellphones."

As they do this, the pilot of the Super Puma switches off his transponder.

The South African pilots see a slight shift in the target, but it is barely discernable. However, they drop their airspeed to Mach 1 and then below that for their targeted run.

As they fall back through the sound barrier, the flight noise washes again over the swept-wing jets.

The thunder which breaches the speed of sound moves in front of them.

It is a mistake, an unexpected early warning system for the terrorists hiding with their Stingers in the rock formation a mile from the camouflaged Puma helicopter.

"Turn on your transponder for five seconds and then turn it off again," the leader says to the Puma pilot.

Switch on.

The South African pilots suddenly pick up two targets.

"Five and four and three and two and one." the pilot carefully counts.

Switch off

The ISIS leader calls his men in the rocks and tells them to turn off their cell phones. "Do it immediately."

The leader turns off his cellphone, and both helicopter pilots check to ensure they have done the same.

The South African Wing Commander goes from one target to two and then to none.

"Make a pass," he says. "Spread out. See if you can spot the bloody bastards."

Six surface-to-air missiles suddenly rise out of the rocks, reaching for the Gripens, which throw out survival flares as soon as they realize they have become prey rather than hunters.

One of the Saabs almost survives.

Its pilot increases his airspeed and climbs sharply.

He sees a surface-to-air missile streak past him.

A second Stinger slams into the heat of his turbine afterburners as he breaks over Mach 1.

The combination of the explosion mixed with the sound barrier-breaking creates an impressive demonstration of noise and detonation.

No parachutes appear.

Not a single terrorist dies.

Chapter 14

Several more terrorists step out of the storm drain to see Malalai. She has materialized magically, and the men raise their weapons over their heads, rejoicing in her presence.

At the other end of the storm drain, Jalaluddin Shekau and all of his remaining freedom fighters scramble up the embankment to greet the famous sister of Ahmed Khan.

One of his men stumbles over something in the moonless night, and he recognizes it is another warrior in the dimness of the stars.

He welcomes the Syrian fighter to Jalaluddin Shekau's freedom fighters, and then he quickly realizes the warrior is not a friend.

He sees the American flag arm patch on the warrior's jacket. It is the last thing he sees.

The four sentries who celebrate Malalai's arrival notice the flashes from her gun, but only one survives long enough to hear the "pop" of the silenced assault weapon with which she greets them.

Jalaluddin Shekau drops his gun and holds up his hands in surrender, the final terrorist remaining alive in his group. His English is not good enough to understand the words "extreme prejudice."

He rolls off the embankment, dead.

Nobody can be sure who pulled the trigger that ended the terrorist's life.

"Shadrach? Sookie? Are you ready to go?" Mac asks.

"We are," Sookie says. "Let's go, honeybuns."

"The last time you called me that was three years ago in Virginia," Shadrach says.

"I know," she says. "And we both survived, right?"

"We're ready," Shadrach says to Mac, putting his arm around Sookie. "But if I don't make it, I want 'honeybuns' engraved on my tombstone."

All of Mac McKlane's troops stand up on the road leading to the Y-Plant at Pelindaba East.

They say nothing.

They salute Sookie and Shadrach, and so does General Mac McKlane, who says: "We're all behind you."

"Well, I wish you could all get in front of me," Shadrach says. "Besides, I hate jellybeans."

He salutes his commander. So does Sookie.

"You love jellybeans," she says, dropping her salute.

"Yeah, but Operation Jellybean doesn't taste quite as sweet, does it?"

Mac looks to the east. The first shades of dawn begin to lighten the horizon.

"You never know," Mac says. "You might learn to love Operation Jellybean."

A formation of eight helicopters appears as tiny dots in the distance.

"Black Hawks," Mac says.

Standing next to him, Colin Rafiki says: "It's nice when an operation comes together like this."

"Syrian Black Hawks," Mac says.

"Syrian?" Sookie says.

"Loaded with Syrian soldiers," Colin Rafiki says.

"Seriously?" Shadrach says.

"I think there's about 140 of them," Mac says, "not counting the pilots. They're all combat veterans."

"And this is a good thing?" Shadrach says.

"They are going to open the doors for you at the Y-Plant," Mac says. "They're going to help you steal South Africa's fissionable material."

"So, they'll go in the heavy water tank instead of Shadrach and me?" Sookie asks.

"No. That's your job," Mac says.

Sookie looks at Shadrach and repeats, without smiling, "Let's go, honeybuns."

In South Africa's Free State, Bootie van Zale is in Bloemfontein, monitoring the Saab Gripens with the Chief of the Air Force, his Squadron Leader, and the Commander of the South African National Defense Force.

On radar, they watch the Saab Gripens fly over the Great Karoo Desert in the Northern Cape and turn back towards Copperton after sweeping across the coast near Saint Helena Bay, a hundred miles north of Cape Town.

The South African Commander sees the blips of the terrorist target appear, stationery, shifting slightly. Then the objective doubles and blinks out.

"Incoming SAM," the wing commander says over his monitored intercom. "Flaring."

"Where the hell did they get surface-to-air missiles?" the commander asks in Bloemfontein.

The air force chief says, "Botswana has a dozen Mistral MANPADS, but they weigh close to half a ton each. I doubt if they've set them up in the middle of our Great Karoo." Over the intercom, he says, "This is the chief of the Air Force, Wing Commander. Anyone. What sort of SAMs are they using?"

The Saab Gripens begin to blink out.

None of the pilots feel like having a conversation, nor can they.

"Missed me," one pilot says, and then it blinks out as well. The week started with 17 Gripen multi-role fighters in South Africa's air force, four of which were under repair with two more entirely out of commission, used only for spare parts. Terrorists have destroyed most of the Gripens in less than a week. Only a single serviceable Gripen remains.

The only sizeable airborne combat capabilities left are the Denel Rooivalk "Red Falcons," located far from South Africa's nuclear facility west of Pretoria.

"Close down Arniston," the Commander of the South African National Defense Force says. "Cut their electricity, backup generators, phone lines, wireless capability, their launch pads, everything. I want them completely dark."

The commander looks at Bootie. "Do you agree, Major van Zale?"

"Yes, sir, absolutely," Bootie says, surprised at the speed with which the commander connects some dots.

"What the hell is coming out of Mozambique?" the commander asks, pointing at eight dots that cross the border south of the Kruger National Park, aimed at Pelindaba East and the Y-Plant at Hartbeespoort Dam.

"No idea, sir. Their speed suggests helicopters."

"Mozambique has two Russian attack helicopters and three utility helicopters," the commander says

They all stare at the eight dots.

"Bootie?" the commander says.

"Permission to call the American general and the CIA agent, commander."

"Do it, now, on speakerphone, and don't tell them that they are on speakerphone, Bootie."

"Yes, sir."

He dials Colin Rafiki, who answers.

"Rafiki," Bootie says.

He has never addressed him that way in his life, and Colin immediately knows others are listening to their conversation. "I see eight blips on my radar inbound from Mozambique. What and who are they?"

"I see them, too, Bootie, but I have to make a phone call to get an answer. I don't know who they are. I'll call you back within 10 minutes."

Colin Rafiki closes the connection and looks at General Mac McKlane.

"What do we tell them?"

"Same as always, Colin. Tell them the truth. But wait a few minutes to do it."

Colin smiles.

Mac McKlane's army of warriors advances on the Y-Plant, approaching the outer gate. They move off the road, onto the embankment, as the sun breaks through the horizon.

Colin dials Bootie.

"I see eight Black Hawk helicopters landing inside the security perimeter of the Y-Plant, Bootie."

"Americans," the commander says.

The chief of the air force repeats this, adding a curse word in front.

General McKlane takes the phone and says, "Bootie, these are Syrian Black Hawks. And they're filled with Syrian terrorists. You can probably hear the gunfire."

"I do," Bootie says.

In Bloemfontein, they all hear it. The commander takes the phone and asks, "When did America start to sell Black Hawk helicopters to the Syrians, General McKlane?"

"I'm a soldier, commander, not a politician. I'm sure someone in our State Department can answer that question, but I can't. I know what Syrian soldiers look like, and there are over 100 of them inside the Y-Plant right now, maybe more. And every one of those Black Hawks is decorated with the Syrian flag, sir."

"Give me Major van Zale."

Bootie takes his time when he gets the phone.

"Sir," he says.

"How many men does the General command."

"Over 100, sir."

The commander muffles the phone against his chest and looks at the Chief of the Air Force, who says, "I've seen them in action, and they're quite impressive."

"Major van Zale, will the General put his forces under your command?"

Bootie looks at Mac, who takes the phone and says, "That will not happen, commander. These are American Army Rangers, Marine Raiders, and Navy SEALs. They only answer to the United States and me."

"Can you defeat the Syrians, General McKlane?"

"Only if I can get through the gates to kill them," he says to the South African Armed Forces Commander.

"How far are you from the entrance?"

"Maybe a hundred yards, uh, 60 meters."

"The gates will be open when you get there, General McKlane. Good hunting."

The terrorists in the rocky outcropping in the Great Karoo turn their phones back on.

"Should we leave our equipment in the rocks?" the quickest runner says into his phone before heading back to the Puma to continue their trip to Arniston.

He asks this question three more times, receiving no reply, although they hear gunfire.

Their fellow terrorists celebrate their great victory, but apparently, they have all forgotten to turn on their encrypted cellphones.

"Leave the equipment," the fastest sprinter says, and they all head back to the helicopter at a slow trot.

They can see the Puma suddenly appear as its concealment comes off.

The destruction of the Gripens transfixes the leader of the terrorists. The five warriors, who lost the race to the bush and back, celebrate by firing their weapons in the air. The pilot and co-pilot drag off the camouflage from the Puma. Then they lie prone on the ground.

The ISIS terrorists suddenly begin to fall, targets of the pilot and co-pilot.

Some try to reverse the taped cartridge cases, and one of them succeeds, but he dies, firing a stream of bullets into the dirt.

Only the leader remains standing, with five fellow terrorists trotting towards him but still over three-quarters of a mile away.

The pilot climbs into the helicopter's cockpit and then quickly takes the Puma through its start-up procedures.

The terrorist leader lunges at an assault weapon near to him and dies before he can reach it.

As the main rotor comes up to speed, the co-pilot gathers the guns from the dead terrorists and throws them into the open hatch.

He climbs in and gives a thumbs up to the pilot, who changes the blade pitch on the swashplate connected to the flight controls.

The helicopter lifts off with the remaining terrorists a quarter of a mile away, but now they are running as fast as possible.

"We're off the ground," the pilot says into his encrypted cellphone. "Mission accomplished."

The voice of Colin Rafiki says, "Go low, go slow, and stay black."

"The story of my life," the pilot says. He turns his phone off to the laughter of the CIA agent.

His co-pilot is at the hatch, shooting at the remaining terrorists on the ground.

Some of them live, but their cellphones remain on as the Puma heads back to Botswana.

Twenty minutes later, South Africa's remaining delta-wing Saab Gripen fires three missiles at the signals its radar picks up on the ground.

Even with death, redundancy exists.

"Did you destroy the helicopter?" the Chief of South Africa's Air Force asks.

"No sign of it," the Gripen pilot says.

"Search towards Arniston."

Listening in, Colin Rafiki smiles as he and General Mac McKlane walk through the gates of the Y-Plant.

Colin says, for the second time, "You have to love it when a plan comes together like this."

Shadrack and Sookie Ringer have already disappeared into the Y-Plant.

As Colin and Mac approach the entry door, dozens of white-coated scientists scramble through it.

They run as fast as they can down the roadway, away from Pelindaba East.

The eight Black Hawks have landed in the parking lot. None of the scientists feel comfortable claiming their cars.

At St. Elizabeths West Campus in Washington, D.C., Roberta Macumber is at one end of a rectangular mahogany table in a conference room with the Acting Director and the Under Director of Homeland Security.

They are waiting for the Deputy Attorney General, who will be the only person in the room confirmed by the U.S. Senate.

Roberta Macumber has never met him. The Acting Director of Homeland Security has played golf with him and the president at the Doral resort in Miami, Florida.

He arrives and gets right down to business.

"Missus Macumber, we do not believe that …."

"I'm no longer married," Roberta says. "Use my first name or my title, Deputy Attorney General. My husband died many years ago."

"Does she have a title?" he asks without taking his eyes off of Macumber.

After a noticeable stretch of silence, Roberta says, "I believe I am an assistant director of Homeland Security, sir. At least that is what my paygrade suggests."

"In that case, Madam, you are overpaid."

After a short silence, she says, "Madam? I am not running a whorehouse here, Deputy Attorney General."

A snicker from the Under Director of Homeland Security draws a sharp glare from the DAG.

Without moving his eyes off the Under Director of Homeland Security, the Deputy Attorney General says, "Ms. Macumber, where is General McKlane?"

"Which one?" Roberta asks.

The DAG immediately turns his glare on her. He uses his eyes like a weapon. She laughs.

"I am not playing a game, Roberta Macumber."

"Yes, you are Deputy Attorney General, you are playing a dangerous game with the lives of great patriots serving this nation with honor, integrity, morality, and even mortality, their spilled blood.

"These are men and women who might be able to beat the terrorists now that our government has turned them loose with the assassination of the second most powerful person in the sovereign state of Iran."

She watches blood creep up the neck and into the cheeks of the Deputy Attorney General.

"ISIS is defeated," the Under Director of Homeland Security says.

The Deputy Attorney General silences him by saying, "The Islamic State of Iraq and the Levant is not, you moron."

Roberta Macumber says, "See? We have already started to reach agreements." She smiles at the Under Secretary of Homeland Security, then she continues.

"I believe Major General George McKlane is currently working at the Pentagon and about to retire, hopefully with three stars as a lieutenant general, gentlemen. The original George McKlane, a Marine captain in the Korean War, awarded the Medal of Honor, died last year. I had the honor of attending his Florida burial at sea; his grandson, General 'Mac' McKlane, my boss, was recently promoted to brigadier general in the Marine Corps. He is somewhere in southern Africa. I am not sure where."

"We believe you do know where," the Acting Director of Homeland Security says. "The Deputy Attorney General is here to take your sworn testimony."

The DAG smiles at her.

"Please stand and raise your right hand." He looks down at a piece of paper and reads, "Do you solemnly swear to tell the truth, the whole ...."

Blood rushes back into his cheeks. Roberta Macumber remains seated and raises one finger on her left hand.

"I have a law degree from Georgetown, Deputy Attorney General."

She lowers her hand.

"I believe you graduated from the Western Michigan University Thomas Cooley, which has distinguished itself as the worst law school for two years in a row by the American Bar Association, according to their Standard 509 reports."

Both Homeland Security men look at the Deputy Attorney General, a significant contributor to numerous politicians with money he inherited but never earned.

Roberta says, "You have no right, legal or otherwise, to intimidate me like this because I am a woman. I will bring suit if you try to do so without proper authority and warning to allow adequate preparation on my part and, of course, with my lawyer present."

She stares at each man, counting slowly to five in her head as she does so. They are on her turf.

"We could have had a productive meeting here," she says. Silence follows, and she smiles.

"I am going to have you arrested," the Deputy Attorney General says.

"On what charges?"

"Oh, we'll figure something out," he says.

"That's almost a perfect thing for you to say," Roberta Macumber says, pushing her Motorola cellphone out in front of her where they can see its "record" button blinking.

"Get her fucking phone," the DAG orders.

The under director of Homeland Security reaches for it. The men are surprised that Macumber does not attempt to stop them.

"They are wondrous inventions, these Motorolas," she says. "This particular model not only records what we say, but it also transcribes every word on a server beyond your reach."

Macumber stands up.

"You know where to find me," she says. "I'll either be in my office or my townhome. You can arrest me on trumped-up charges in either place. When you do, a full transcription of this meeting and many others will immediately go to the *Washington Post*, the *New York Times*, and major news outlets in America, including Fox News."

"Are you trying to blackmail the Department of Justice, Ms. Macumber?"

"Not at all. I am telling you the truth, the whole truth, and nothing but the truth, so help me God, mister Deputy Attorney General."

She walks out.

"Turn the fucking thing off," the DAG tells the under deputy of Homeland Security, who has no idea how to do it. After a lot of recorded swearing, the acting director of Homeland Security finally shuts it down.

Roberta Macumber returns to her office.

A man and a woman appear at her door within three minutes. She looks up. Only Macumber's slightly raised eyebrows register surprise.

"That was fast," she says.

"You were expecting us?" the man says.

"What's the charge?"

"She was not expecting us," the woman says. "I think we made it just in time."

"What's the charge?"

"No charge," the woman says. "You need to come with us now."

"Why would I do that?"

"Colin Rafiki wants to talk to you."

As the three of them hurry to the elevator, the men coming from the conference room see them.

"Jesus Christ," says the under deputy of Homeland Security. "She already has bodyguards. We need some arrest and search warrants fast and restraining orders."

"No," the Deputy Attorney General says. "I recognize the man accompanying her, but not the woman. He works at the Central Intelligence Agency, high up. I assume his partner does as well. We have a serious problem that I need to discuss with the Attorney General." He heads for the elevators.

Roberta Macumber never gets to her townhome. She is in the front seat of a black, government-issue Chevy Suburban that travels north to a truck stop in Maryland. The CIA woman drives, and the man in the back gives her a rundown on Colin and Mac. He gives her three phones, two burners that she will discard after using, and a replacement of her encrypted Motorola.

"It contains the conversation you just had with the DAG and the Homeland Security, uh, leadership," the man tells her. "You'll enjoy their conversation after you left before they figured out how to turn the Motorola off. More importantly, do not contact Colin until tomorrow, when you get to Vermont."

"You're driving me to Vermont?"

"No, you drive yourself," he says as they enter the vacant part of a truck stop."We're parting company here. Your route is on the GPS." He hands her a paper copy of it.

Another black Chevy Suburban pulls up next to them at the truck stop.

Three people get out and quickly switch the plates on the vehicles as Roberta watches them. One man reaches under the car she was in and examines a small, blinking device. He nods.

"It looks like the DOJ has been tracking us this far," the man says to Roberta Macumber. "Your wheels are clean."

"You people scare the crap out of me," Roberta says.

"Colin told us you would probably say that."

"It's one of the first things I told him, but then I trusted him. Can I trust all of you?"

"Do you have a choice?" the woman who drove them to the Maryland truck stop asks.

"So you're going to drive to Vermont," a different agent says. "The plates will stop any law enforcement from stopping you. The troopers will recognize the government plates. They might tweep you, but keep driving safely. Give the state police a thumbs up. They like that."

"What's a tweep?"

"A tiny squeak from their sirens. But none of them will turn on their flashing red and blue party hats."

"What if they do?"

"Then, they're not for real." He hands her a weapon.

"You're kidding," she says.

"If they try to stop you," he says, "they're probably going to kill you, Ms. Macumber. So that's going to have to be your call."

"You people DO scare the crap out of me."

Everyone shuffles their feet.

Then the apparent lead agent says, "Our team's nickname is the Metamucil Brigade."

They all laugh, even Roberta, a little.

A woman from the SUV that Roberta will be driving pops the rear hatch and shows Macumber a beat-up blue luggage bag.

"Don't use any credit cards and try not to show any ID. Show them this if it's necessary."

She hands her a Vermont driver's license with her picture, but neither her name nor the address she's going to. It looks real.

"I don't have a lot of cash on me," Macumber says.

The woman points to the luggage bag. "You do now, and a lot of it is in small denominations. None of the bills are new. Remember to lock the car if you stop somewhere for a bite, which you will. There's over twenty grand in there. If you don't like the clothes we picked out for you, go on a little shopping spree. But no credit cards."

The man who gave her a weapon says, "If a police car does try to stop you, call the only contact number on either of the burner phones as you're slowing down. Then it's up to you. We'll take care of any cleanup."

Roberta looks at the CIA agent saying this and says: "So you are tracking me?"

"Yes, we are, but no tracking device, helicopters."

"Why do I need two burner phones?"

"Backup. The other side may take more than one, uh, there may be multiple attempts to get to you. Just remember we are your guardian angels."

"I don't see a pair of wings anywhere here. None of you have even shown me your IDs."

They all show her their CIA credentials. They each shake her hand and pile into the Chevy Suburban. One agent snaps the DOJ's tracking device back on their SUV first.

A helicopter appears far above the truck stop.

Alone, Macumber feels she has been through an initiation ceremony to a club she did not ask to join.

She gets in the driver's seat, puts the gun in an open slot of the door, puts the Motorola cellphone in her jacket, and the burners in the front seat divider. The tank is full, and Roberta turns on the GPS.

She gets her first tweep on the New Jersey Turnpike, and the sound of it almost makes her put a dent in the SUV's roof.

She gives a thumbs up to the State Trooper who races past her, but she can't see him at night.

She pulls off the turnpike south of Cape May, New Jersey. She needs to sleep.

"The Metamucil is kicking in," she says out loud as she pulls into a Motel 6.

The only ID she shows is cash.

She hears a helicopter faintly in the distance.

The following morning, she enjoys a few free donuts and hot coffee, then she continues north, watching a helicopter dip itself left and right a quarter of a mile in front of her. "Hello."

It happens on the Palisades Parkway, south of Bear Mountain State Park in New York.

A State Trooper behind her suddenly turns on his flashing lights and pulls out.

He will probably try to cut her off.

It surprises her, but she remains calm despite the taste of combat in her mouth.

She remembers the metallic tang from the amalgam fillings in her teeth. It's a reminder from her days in Vietnam when she was one of America's first female combatants.

Roberta Macumber feels her throat tighten, and she moves the weapon into her lap as she starts to slow down.

She reaches for one of the burner phones.

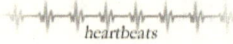

In South Africa, Shadrach and Sookie Ringer turn a corner and walk into the control room at the Y-Plant. The Syrian wing commander greets them.

"Welcome to Pelindaba East," the Syrian commander says. He points his assault weapon at the floor. "Notice the two people wearing white coats against the wall?"

"I see them," says Shadrach, without lowering his weapon an inch.

"They are ISIS scientists. Six more of them are locked in that room over there."

"You speak English very well," Sookie says, pointing her M27 at him.

"That's because I'm a Buckeye, born outside of Columbus, Ohio. And Ohio State should have been ranked Number One in the college football playoffs. They should have played against Oklahoma instead of Clemson. It would have been a much better championship game."

"Uh-huh. So when did you become a Syrian terrorist?"

"Never did that, major. I'm a Navy SEAL like everyone else here. I guess we just grabbed the wrong uniforms when we got up this morning."

"I hope you killed whoever was wearing them," Shadrach says. "Are all of you people Navy?"

"Every one of us, Chief. All SEALs, even the medics."

"Do you have an accurate layout of the plant?"

"Right there on that big screen."

Sookie and Shadrach start to study the large display in the center of many screens in front of them. The rest of the core team join them: Marine General McKlane and First Lieutenant Holly McKlane, Marine Lieutenants Ernestine and Charlton Tremwallis, Navy Commander Sharonda, Marine Captain Samuel Nelson, and as many of their warriors as can crowd into the Y-Plant at Pelindaba East.

None of them shoot the Syrians.

General McKlane has told them that it is a deception.

Outside the Y-Plant, more of Mac's men and women and the combatants dressed in Syrian uniforms set up a circular perimeter.

Half of the Navy SEALs disguised as Syrians switch from live ammunition to blanks and fire at imaginary enemies in the bush, making noise, not war.

"OK," Sookie says, putting her finger on the Y-Plant layout. "Here's the containment tank, and here's the radiation gear we have to wear in the anteroom next to it. Are you ready to go?"

"Honeybuns has your behind," Shadrach says.

"Ha-ha. You go first, Chief." She hands him a portable Geiger Counter.

She hesitates.

She points at the plant diagram and says, "what's this room just off the containment center.?"

"That's a bedroom for people who spend the night here," someone says.

"Before we go in the chamber, Shadrach and I are going into that spare bedroom," she tells McKlane.

She takes Shadrach's hands and says, "Come with me, honeybuns. We have something to discuss."

She looks at McKlane, and he smiles.

Shadrach puts down the Geiger Counter.

McKlane wants to say they're in a hurry, but he says nothing. He understands the love between Sookie and Shadrach goes far beyond the words, "I love you."

"Take off all your clothes, Honeybuns,' Sookie says when they're alone in the overnight room.

As he does this, Sookie herself removes her clothes, but more slowly.

"Even the combat boots?" Shadrach says.

"We'll keep those on, pants down to the ankles."

She shuffles over to him.

"I stopped taking contraceptives four weeks ago," she says, holding his hardness in her hands and rubbing herself at the same time.

"Sookie, I love you," he says. "You need to spread your legs. The pants might be a problem."

"You are going deeper into me than you ever did before," she says, kneeling on the bed with Shadrach behind her. He sees her spread the lips of her vagina, and it is already wet, glistening, waiting for him.

"Slowly," she says as he enters her. "Yes, now deeper." She arches her back, and he holds her breasts. She brings her legs together.

"Oh, my God," Shadrach says. He has never felt this sort of pleasure in his life. Her love surrounds him, squeezes him, and he explodes inside of her.

"I can feel your love pumping into me, Shadrach. I can feel it."

It lasts longer than usual, but he finally slips out of her. He looks for a washcloth or towel, but she says, "No, darling, my love, my life."

Shadrach thinks he understands.

"I want your baby to grow in me."

"I'm a little afraid of that."

"Why," she asks as they start to dress. "You'll make a wonderful father."

"The radiation," he says.

"Oh."

Finally, she laughs.

Shadrach smiles but does not understand.

Sookie is the toughest woman he has ever known, someone he can communicate with as if he were talking to a warrior in a foxhole next to him.

"Well, if the child is born with four arms and six legs," Sookie says, "we'll have to call him 'Spider,' Honeybuns.'

Shadrach shakes his head and forces himself to laugh.

"You're tougher than I am, Sookie."

"I know," she says. "Let's suit up and find the atomic bombs. And I love you, Shadrach, more than I love myself."

"And I love you more than life itself."

"Let's not test that one, Honeybuns."

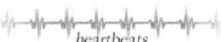

McKlane and his warriors watch the monitors showing the antechamber leading to the 8,000 cubic foot copy of the Houdini Room.

It's similar to their training area aboard the *S.S. Nomad* months earlier, but the silver-colored tank at the Y-Plant does not show what's inside.

Shadrach and Sookie hold each other before they suit up in their radiation gear.

"If this is it," Sookie says to him, "I want you to give me the sloppiest kiss ever, Shadrach."

It lasts a long time, and finally, they hear the voice of Mac McKlane telling them, gently, that it's their turn to save the world. Both Shadrach and Sookie manage to smile. As they finish suiting up, they hear muffled applause from the men and women watching.

"They should applaud after what we just did," Shadrach says. "I'm thinking of marrying you."

"We've already done that, honeybuns."

"Well, we should do it again after this honeymoon is over, Sookie, my love."

"Deal," she says, although she's not sure he sees her smile or her tears through the tinted glass of her nuclear gear.

Shadrach slips the Geiger Counter into a clear, plastic pocket on the front of his radiation suit, face up so he can see it. They move through the doorway leading to the 8,000 cubic foot, silver replica of the Houdini Room.

Shadrach climbs up an outside ladder, crouches at the top of the chamber, and slowly starts turning a wheel that unlocks an entry point.

"You know, Mac, there's no more radiation here than there was in the antechamber."

"That will change when you crack open the Houdini Room," Sookie tells him over the intercom.

Both he and Sookie hear Mac's voice in their earphones say, "Stop," then "Get down the ladder and cover in place." Shadrach slides down the ladder with his feet outside the foot bars, holding onto the outer portion of the ladder with his thick gloves like a fireman. He hits the floor hard, stumbles, and Sookie throws herself on top of him.

An explosion covers them with dust.

Chapter 15

As the State Trooper's car with flashing lights pulls abreast of Roberta Macumber's SUV on the Palisades Parkway, she flips the safety off on her Glock 44.

She's coasting her vehicle.

She's focused, losing some of her peripheral vision.

She puts one of the burner phones on her lap, turns it on, and connects to the number that comes up on its screen.

She hits the button that rolls down her window.

She raises the Glock 44 LR .22 with a six-inch suppressor just out of sight. It's hard to drive with a pistol that feels like a sawed-off rifle.

She feels her heart beating.

The State Trooper appears in the outer lane, at least five car lengths beyond her, increasing the distance between their two vehicles as he chases someone speeding.

"Jesus Christ," Roberta says out loud, "if I were faster on the draw, you'd be dead."

The burner phone shows a text that says, "False Alarm. Well handled." A helicopter dips above her and disappears over the trees to her left.

She hears her heart pounding in her ears. She still tastes what almost happened.

She rolls her window back up and continues north, getting off at the nearest exit to calm down, pulling onto the gravel at the side of the road. She looks at the Glock 44 LR .22 with a six-inch suppressor in her lap and slowly puts the safety back on.

She gets tweeped three more times before she arrives at her destination deep in the woods at the bottom of Lake Champlain in Vermont.

It's late in the afternoon, and as she rolls her banged-up suitcase onto the porch of the small log cabin, she hears a helicopter overhead. It heads into the sunset over the lake, and she sees it dip left and right twice.

She finds the key, as planned, under a massive turtle sculpture at the side of the entry.

The front door looks like wood, but she has to lean all her weight against it, thinking at first that the key does not work, and this is a setup. There's no rust on the door hinges because it opens smoothly, but it feels as if she's entering a bank vault.

The door must weigh a ton. Macumber taps on its glass window panes and realizes that they are three inches thick. The door looks like wood, but it's solid metal.

"This log cabin is a fortress," she says to no one.

On the granite kitchen counter, a folder reveals the fortification layout. Macumber sees a note that has a phone number and says, "Call Colin Tomorrow."

It's starting to get dark. Macumber switches on some lights using a multi-circuit panel on the pantry wall. She claps her hands twice and laughs at herself when no lights turn on. She flips the switches on and off one at a time. The last one, next to an almost invisible button, illuminates the entire outside area. She quickly turns it off.

Macumber flips on the recessed high hats in the kitchen as she studies the blueprint of the cabin. She looks back at the light panel, gets up, and pushes the barely visible button next to the switch that illuminated the grounds around the entire cabin.

The floor just beyond the kitchen drops down almost a foot and slides back under the floorboards. It makes virtually no sound. Roberta's first thought is that someone is down there. She pulls out her Glock and turns off its safety. She crawls carefully towards the brightly lit opening, and then she stands up and walks down into a bunker with a wall of monitors that show every room in the cabin and every possible view outside of it. The outdoor shots all show the cabin as well as the area surrounding their location.

A switch adapts the outside monitors to night vision. In the approaching darkness, she toggles the views back and forth. She sees a fox moving on the forest floor. It disappears and reappears as she engages the scotopic vision.

"You people do scare the crap out of me," she says, and she's not talking to the fox.

Because she sees the cabin in every outdoor view, she understands the concealment of the cameras in the forest. The CIA embedded the high-definition, miniature cameras in trees surrounding their fortress on the edge of Lake Champlain. Someone could look straight at them and probably never see the lens.

Roberta Macumber stifles a yawn, surprised at its loudness in her noise vacuum. She needs to sleep.

She returns upstairs and checks the refrigerator, and opens some of the cabinets. There's plenty of food. The bar could put a party of six people out, stone-cold drunk for a week. She smiles at a small sign that says, "Do Not Smoke unless you're on fire."

She relocks the front door with its multiple deadbolts, turns off the kitchen lights, and goes back down the stairs to the safe room, carrying her battered blue suitcase and the folder with the cabin's layout. The two bedrooms upstairs looked comfortable, but she does not like bunk beds.

There are a shower and a small bedroom off the main bunker area, with a comfortable king-sized bed and a 72-inch, flatscreen television on the wall that can pick up over 1,700 channels in 18 different languages, according to the operation booklet on the bedside table. Macumber does not turn it on.

The main room contains another well-stocked refrigerator and cabinets with food and water but no liquor. A small sign says, "Don't drink and hide."

She hits a button at the bottom of the stairs, and the floor near the kitchen whispers back into place. She pushes "lock" and hears multiple floor bolts shunt slowly into place.

In the bunker, the silence is profound. Roberta hears and feels her pulse from head to toe. She takes a shower and then plays a while with the night vision monitors. The fox is gone, but a sizeable feral cat with no tail, perhaps a bobcat, scratches some trees and then marks them. She sees a deer, a possum with four babies on its back, and two raccoons.

She turns off the high-definition night vision. The bed is comfortable, she closes the door, and she quickly falls into sleep with no dreams.

She does not see armed men positioning themselves around the fortress that protects her. Their red and green laser lights hold steady on the windows and doors of the cabin. They also sparkle on the SUV parked outside.

heartbeats

One of the ISIS scientists at the Y-Plant in South Africa turns and runs towards the main control panel. He hits a button that starts a two-hour countdown in large, red numerals.

Sharonda hits him as hard as she can with the butt of her assault weapon, and the scientist drops to the floor, unconscious. Samuel Nelson grabs the other scientist and drags him over to the panel.

"What is it?" Samuel asks.

The scientist says nothing, and Samuel shoots him in the leg, a flesh wound. "What is it?" he asks.

Mac McKlane tells Shadrach to get off the 8,000 square foot Houdini Room in the containment building and shelter in place. Then Mac pulls out his pistol and points it at the unconscious terrorist whom Sharonda cold-cocked with the metal butt of her assault weapon. Mac looks at the scientist whom Samuel has just shot in the leg.

"What does that countdown mean?" Mac asks, slowly and visibly turning off the safety on his pistol.

The terrorist looks at the countdown and smiles.

In a crisp, Oxford-educated British accent, the ISIS terrorist says: "Welcome to Chernobyl, my dear fellow." He opens his white lab coat and shows them packs of plastique wrapped around his body. They grab his hands before he reaches the detonator. They handcuff him behind his back. They shove him into the room where they detained six other terrorists, dragging the scientist knocked out by Sharonda with him. They close the heavy metal door behind them.

A muffled explosion occurs 68 seconds later, and one minute after that, everything in the plant shuts down. Emergency lights work, but nothing else except for the flashing red warning lights that identify exit doors, a suggestion which many people follow.

Mac turns to the wing commander and says, "Get your Black Hawks at least 20 miles away from here, but be ready to come back and rescue us if I call you."

In Bloemfontein and Cape Town and Pretoria, a dusty red light that nobody has paid attention to for years, although everyone knows what it's for, starts to blink. Above the glowing button, in Afrikaans, it says, "Ineenstorting." Below the blinking light, it says, "Meltdown."

The electric grid shuts off over tens of thousands of square miles of Southern Africa.

Emergency generators and floodlights kick in from Gabarone in Botswana to Mbabane in Swaziland, from Kimberley in the Northern Cape to Ladysmith in the Kwazulu Province of Natal.

Pretoria and Johannesburg go dark in the Gauteng Province. Half of Bloemfontein in the Free State blinks off

Almost all of Maseru, the capital of landlocked Lesotho, does the same.

Satellite images show that someone hit the "off" switch in Africa's southern hemisphere.

The Western Cape and Eastern Cape provinces remain bright as satellites record their nighttime imagery, but a black hole appears north of them.

It does not take long for scientists in Europe, America, Asia, Russia, China, and Australia to speculate that a nuclear meltdown is underway at the SAFARI-1 atomic facility.

In many areas, wireless communication still works, but that too will become spotty once recharging cell batteries becomes impossible.

People in Southern Africa start lining up for gas to fill their petrol canisters. Most of the stations have pumps requiring electricity, and few have backup generators to make the petrol flow.

Solar power rechargers disappear from shelves within minutes through the broken windows of establishments closed for the night.

In Bloemfontein, the Commander of South Africa's Defense Force remains extraordinarily calm.

The head of the Air Force, however, is screaming at his cellphone.

"What is happening? What is going on? Talk to me, General McKlane. Is anything under control?"

At the Y-Plant, General McKlane is holding his cellphone at arm's length. It sounds as if the speakerphone is on, but it's not.

"One of the scientists working here, an ISIS terrorist, hit a button on the main panel, and it has started a doomsday countdown on your nuclear reactor. We are trying to turn it off, but nobody knows how."

"Force the terrorist to turn it off, for God's sake," the chief of the Air Force says. "Break his legs, break his arms."

"He's dead," General McKlane says.

"Why the hell did you kill him?"

"He killed himself. He was wearing an explosive jacket under his white coat. We threw him in a room with all the other scientists who didn't escape. He killed them all."

"Bloody hell."

"Indeed, it was. The ISIS scientist's last words, just for the record, were 'Welcome to Chernobyl, my dear fellow.' That's when everything shut down here at the Y-Plant."

The chief of the Air Force looks at the commander of the South African Defense force.

He does not understand why the Russian-trained commander is smiling.

heartbeats

Roberta Macumber wakes up and turns on the television. She walks out of the bedroom and stops, turning around and staring at the screen.

CNN has a banner scrolling across the bottom that says: "DOOMSDAY IN SOUTH AFRICA."

She steps into the main room and is about to open the trap door when she freezes.

The screens show men above her walking around, although she cannot hear their footsteps. She quickly turns the sound off on the television, hoping that they have not heard it. She sees more men, all with guns, on the screens showing the cabin's landscape.

She sees no women.

She watches one man repeatedly pushing the button that opens the entry to her safe room. He has a tool kit and starts to dismantle the electrical panel.

She picks up her Motorola cellphone and dials Colin Rafiki, but he does not answer. She does this three times without hearing a voice on the other end.

After a few minutes, her cellphone vibrates. She picks it up, and Colin says: "Where are you, Roberta?"

"I'm in the cabin on the lake in Vermont. I am in the safe room beneath it. The sliding door is locked, and there's a bunch of men, all men, trying to get to me. I think they will kill me if they do. Where are you, Colin?"

She tries to keep her voice calm.

"South Africa," he says. "Ask them who they are."

"How do I do that?"

"See the microphone to the left of the screens?"

"Yes, I see it."

"Turn it on. There's a volume dial next to it. Turn it all the way to the right, then flip up the scramble switch. That will make you sound like the voice of God."

"They know I'm here, Colin. And they know I am not God or even the Virgin Mary. One of them has removed the plate on the light control panel in the kitchen, and he's trying to figure out how to open the trap door to get to me."

"He can't. Not as long as you've locked it."

"I have."

"He could put 20 pounds of plastique on top of that sliding door, and all he'd do is blow the roof off the cabin. All you'd hear would be a tiny pop. So ask them who they are, Roberta. Put me on speakerphone. And as soon as you ask the question, switch off the microphone."

She sits down, flicks the microphone button to on, turns up the volume all the way, and throws the scramble switch. The men outdoors point at the roof of the cabin. She sees four huge mega speakers rise through the roof and all point in different directions.

She puts her mouth on the microphone and says, "Who the fuck are you people?"

She turns off the scrambler and the microphone. The mega speakers disappear back into the roof.

She hears Colin laughing, a deep, rich sound, and then he says, "God does not talk like that, Roberta. Well, maybe in the Old Testament He might have."

Both inside the cabin and outside, all of the men are holding their heads on the screens. The man working on the panel has his ears covered. Blood seeps through his fingers.

Roberta says: "Wow. The voice is stronger than the sword. Can I say anything else to them?"

Colin says, "The guys in the cabin probably wouldn't hear you. They'll need vestibular rehabilitation therapy, and some of them probably suffered a concussion. The people outside will feel dizzy, but they remain dangerous. Hang on a while. I'll have some people there within an hour."

"How will I know who the good guys are?"

"They'll be alive. Stay in the safe room until someone holds up a piece of paper with my name on it."

"How's Mac doing? He's with you, right?"

"Yes. Right now, Mac's busy trying to save the world."

And then Colin is gone. She considers calling him back to ask about the CNN doomsday headline but doesn't. She watches men in the cabin, staggering around, holding their heads. The man working on the electrical panel looks dead. Men stumble in from outdoors and drag people out. She watches one of them, a bit unsteady, plant something under her car, probably a bomb.

She goes back into the bedroom and watches CNN's report on the meltdown of the SAFARI-1 nuclear reactor outside of Pretoria.

It's mid-afternoon in South Africa, and the channel shows satellite imagery from the previous night when that nation and its neighbors plunge into darkness. The producers go back and forth on a replay of this event. It's like turning that part of the continent into an on/off switch. The darkness was instantaneous.

Then CNN started to interview a retired director of the Allis-Chalmers Corporation, a Wisconsin company that sold the SAFARI-1 reactor to the white supremacist government of South Africa in 1965.

The sale included some enriched uranium, U-235, to get things started.

"Save the world, Mac," Roberta says to the screen.

heartbeats

The commander of the South African Defense Force sends up a dozen observation drones from Bloemspruit. They hover over Pelindaba, showing soldiers firing into the bush surrounding the Y-Plant.

"What the hell are they shooting at?" he asks. "Drop the dromes down closer."

As the drones carrying small military cameras hover lower, they become targets. One after the other, the small drones crash to the ground.

In Bloemfontein, the air force chief asks the drone pilots to rerun the video he saw as the final drone crashes into the Y-Plant parking lot.

"Did you want us to record the search, sir?" the pilot leader in Pretoria asks.

The chief of the air force frowns and then rolls his eyes slightly. He suggests that the drone pilot leader send up more drones immediately.

"We'll have to source them out of Makhado and Hoedspruit, sir."

"Then do it, and have them maneuver when they get there, instead of acting like clay pigeons in a skeet shoot. Make sure they bloody well record everything."

The air force chief looks at the commander, whom he has never seen act so calm.

Perhaps that is why he holds the top spot in South Africa's military hierarchy.

"How many Atlas Oryx helicopters do we have in reserve?" the commander asks the chief of the air force.

"We have 22 operational, sir."

"I want all of them loaded with our special forces at Limpopo." The room goes quiet.

All the senior officers who hear the commander's request have no idea that four special forces regiments operate out of Phalaborwa in northern Limpopo. The forces supposedly disbanded years earlier.

The air force chief says that the Atlas Oryx helicopters must fly north from the Western Cape.

"Then load them up with the special forces regiments based at Langebaan in the Western Cape. Do it now."

"Yes, sir."

He did not know about special forces at Langebaan.

"They will have to refuel."

The commander stares at him.

"Yes, sir," the chief of the air force says, and he makes calls to the airbase at Bloemspruit to make sure that there are fuel and a means of pumping it available to the Atlas Oryx helicopters flying in.

He hangs up by telling the base commander that "nothing is impossible if you want to keep your job, your rank, and your pension."

"Well done," the commander tells him.

heartbeats

The blast in the Y-Plant at Pelindaba does not injure Shadrach or Sookie.

They stand up, brush themselves off, and check their Geiger counters.

"We have slightly elevated radioactivity," Sookie says over the intercom. "And we're covered with a lot of dust."

"Uh, I think I see stars," Shadrach says.

"Are you dizzy?" Mac asks.

"No. I mean, I see stars. There's a hole in the roof above the silver Houdini room."

The hole is wider than the Houdini Room.

"Can you climb back up the ladder?" Mac asks.

"Sookie's already climbing," Shadrack says. I'll follow when she gets to the top. I'm not sure how structurally sound the ladder is after that explosion."

"The real explosion was outside the Y-Plant," Mac says. "The electrical grid beyond the turbine building took a serious hit. Every transformer blew out, but there's not a big increase in radioactivity there, either."

Sookie reaches the top and starts to turn the wheel to let them look into the Houdini Room. Shadrach joins her, and they open the hatch. The hole in the roof is four times larger than the entry into the Houdini room. They check their Geiger counters, which still register average radioactivity. They both turn on their military-grade tactical flashlights and stare into the containment structure, expecting to see a reactor's control rods, a steam generator, or hot ingots of U-235 in heavy radioactive water.

"Uh, we're looking at eight giant bullets, Mac. They're huge. Other than that, this is an empty room," Sookie says.

"Bullets?" Mac asks

"They look sort of like .45 caliber bullets, but they're about nine feet tall, and if I hugged one of them, I don't think my hands would reach a quarter of the way around them," Sookie says.

"We're climbing down an access ladder to take a closer look," Shadrack says.

Mac looks at Colin Rafiki.

"Eight atomic bombs," the CIA agent says.

"Why blow a hole in the roof?"

"Easy access."

A female Marine Raider with a degree in nuclear engineering comes up to both men and says: "Radioactivity is slowly rising outside the plant, Mac."

Colin Rafiki says, "That would be the Safari II reactor built by South African scientists and supposedly decommissioned several decades ago. It's probably the actual power source from Pelindaba East. It's a plutonium reactor that produces weapons-grade material. That's why the scientist blew himself up. He took his pals to hell with him, and maybe us as well. We probably are facing a Chernobyl-sized disaster."

"Where the hell is the Safari II reactor?" General Mac McKlane asks.

"I think it's probably hidden, located somewhere underground," Colin says.

"We may be standing right on top of it," says the Marine Raider with a degree in nuclear engineering.

Shadrack and Sookie Ringer reach the bottom of the containment structure.

"The big bullets have four metal eyelets near the bottom of each cartridge holding them," Shadrach says. "There's a panel on the wall down here, and one of the buttons on it has a label that says O-o-p D-a-k."

"What does 'Oop Dak' mean, Bootie," Mac asks. Before Mac can say anything, Sookie presses it, and the ceiling slides open very slowly, revealing stars fading into an early morning sky.

"Open roof," Bootie says over the phone.

"Looks like it will be a nice day," Shadrach says.

"Easy access," Colin repeats.

He shuts off this phone and signals Mac to shut off his as well.

Then he says, "Get those helicopters back here, Mac, and let's see if they can lift the oversized atomic bullets with rappel ropes. Those are atomic bombs. With no troops on the helicopters, they should be able to lift a ton and a half."

Mac turns his phone back on and tells Sookie and Shadrach to lift out the bombs by attaching the rappel lines to each one. Then he shuts the phone off again.

In Bloemfontein, the commander asks Bootie what Mac McKlane means.

Bootie looks the commander in the eyes and says he doesn't have a clue.

As the ceiling over the containment area slips out of view, Sookie hits another button.

The entire wall on the left side of the Houdini Room slides to the right.

It reveals what looks like an electrical guidance system at the bottom of a broad, metal-grate staircase. Multiple railings drop down about thirty-five feet.

"Uh, I think we discovered the SAFARI-II reactor," Sookie says.

Emergency lights flicker on and off, showing a control room very similar to the one currently occupied by Mac and Colin and the rest of the team fighting terrorism.

Scientists wearing protection gear work frantically in the new control room, and both Shadrach's and Sookie's Geiger counters register extreme radiation.

The control room has flooded with over half a foot of heavy radioactive water.

Sookie hits the second button again, and the wall slides back into place. She tells Mac what she's seen and what she's done.

"Don't hit the 'Oop Dak' button," Mac says.

"We're out of here," Shadrach says. "You first, Sookie. Don't look back. Move it."

She climbs the ladder and slides down it using Shadrach's fireman's drop, without falling at the bottom as he did. She smiles, feeling a little dizzy, watching the top of the ladder and expecting Shadrach to appear.

Her smile slowly fades.

"Shadrach," she says.

"Honeybuns," she says more loudly.

"Shadrach."

He does not make it to the top of the ladder.

heartbeats

Roberta Macumber sees but does not hear the helicopter sweeping across Lake Champlain towards her fortified log cabin. It hovers over the dock at the bottom of a path leading up to the back porch. She sees a machine gunner vibrating in the doorway of the chopper as he sprays bullets into the woods, but it remains a silent movie. Three men step onto the dock with assault weapons and move towards the cabin as the helicopter settles on pontoons.

Roberta looks for bodies in the woods, but she sees none. Then one of the men from the chopper kicks a log, and it turns into a body rolling down the embankment near the cabin. She notices that all their assault weapons have suppressors on them.

Even the door gunner on the helicopter appears to have a silenced machine gun.

The landing party drags more men from the woods, all dead, and they pack them into the SUV she drove. She thinks about warning them about the probable bomb in the car. She turns the volume from loud to low, and she's about to switch on the microphone when she sees them drag some heavy material over the car.

It takes all three men to accomplish this.

Then they stand back about a hundred feet, and one of the men activates the bomb with a handheld device. The material they pulled over the car balloons outward, then settles back. They wait a few minutes and then remove the cover of the destroyed SUV, which still burns. They drag the cover back to the helicopter and load it into the open hatch.

The silence of the entire operation spellbinds Roberta Macumber, and for a while, she does not see the message held up to the camera in the kitchen area. The hand-written note contains two words: "Colin Rafiki."

Roberta still does not trust anybody or anything, but she knows she must open the entry to her bunker. As the secret floor drops and slides backward, she points her Glock at a large man standing at the top of the stairs.

"Don't shoot the good guys," he says.

"How do I know you're one of the good guys?"

"Because Colin told you the good ones would be the people who are still alive. I'm alive. Don't shoot me."

Roberta climbs the stairs without lowering her gun. The man backs away slightly and carefully puts his ID on the kitchen counter. He's with the CIA.

"We don't have a whole lot of time, Ms. Macumber."

"Call me, Roberta."

"Roberta. We have about twelve or thirteen minutes to disappear. Be careful when you follow me out of the cabin. We're booby-trapping it."

"You believe in the big bang theory," Roberta says, feeling foolish at her attempt at humor.

"You bet we do." The man laughs.

He closes the door behind her as she steps onto the porch. She sees the other men laying invisible fishline across the front steps.

"How long is the SUV going to be burning like that?" she asks.

"It should be fully-cooked in seven more minutes," the CIA agent says, leading her off the back porch. "They won't discover much, although you did leave your passport and a few credit cards in a burn bag on your body."

"My body?"

"That's you in the front seat," he says. "Nothing will be identifiable."

"Teeth?"

"You didn't have any of your own."

"But it's a man's body."

"Not in seven more minutes."

"Jesus, you guys ...."

".... scare the hell out of you. Colin said ...."

".... I would say that."

"Yup. Let's get out of here."

They load up the helicopter and fly low, under the radar, across the bottom of Lake Champlain.

They turn north over the water.

It's a clear day, but they hear thunder in the distance, far behind the direction from which they have come.

"I guess they found you," the CIA man says as his partners push the lead-lined tarp out the hatch. It hits the water and sinks immediately, including the teeth.

The helicopter stays below 100 feet past Burlington, Vermont, and Plattsburgh, New York.

Around noon, they cross into Québec, Canada, and turn northeast, landing at another cabin on the Pike River south of Bedford.

It appears to be a twin of the cabin in which she just spent the night.

They all have dinner together. One of the agents turns out to be an excellent chef.

Roberta tells him, "You know, you could have made a living in a restaurant."

"I often do," he smiles.

"You're going to Africa," the CIA senior agent says.

"I don't have a passport," Roberta says.

"Yes, you do."

He takes out a folder with her passport, some credit cards, and her driver's license.

"These are real," she says.

"Yes, they are."

"Christ, I left the luggage in the cabin. I never even opened it. There was over $20,000 in it."

"Chump change from a Mexican cartel that tunneled under the brand new wall our government is building on the southern border. There's a nice new piece of luggage with your clothes in it, and a lot more than 20 grand. Here it is."

She opens the suitcase.

"These are my clothes."

"Yes, they are, although we added some camo and safari outfits that you might find useful in Africa."

"How do I get to Africa?"

"Well, Colin said you were an outstanding swimmer in high school."

He lets it just hang there.

"I was all-prep in freestyle, but how did Colin know that? Wait a second."

All the men are smiling at her.

"I'm tired. That's not fair."

The lead agent slides the First-Class ticket across the table from Jean Lesage International Airport in Canada to Paris and from there to Antanànarivo, the capital of the island nation of Madagascar.

"We'll fly you to the airport tomorrow morning."

"OK, so when I use this passport or any of my credit cards or my driver's license, they will track me down. They will know that I'm alive."

"They will know that a thief broke into your townhome in Georgetown and stole a lot of your stuff, including this nice new MacBook." He slides her computer across the table to her.

"Madagascar," she says.

"A freighter anchored off the coast of Madagascar."

"The *S.S. Nomad*," Roberta says.

Chapter 16

Sookie Ringer climbs back up the ladder to look into the containment tank. As she does so, she says, "Mac, you better suit up some more people if you want to get these atomic bombs out of here. The radiation levels are high."

"How high?"

"I'm getting over 1,000mSv at the top of the tank, and it looks like Shadrach has gone goofy on me. He doesn't answer, and he's wandering around the bottom of the tank."

Mac says, "The rads kill the transmitters."

Sookie only hears part of this, but she understands. She also realizes that Shadrach is signaling to her. He points to his head. She points to her head. Is he dizzy? She loops her hand around. He gives her an "X" signal. He points to his head again, then his body, then his legs, then his chest.

Sookie holds up one hand and her gloved index finger, the letter "I." He gives her a thumbs up. Then he holds up two fingers, indicating, "The second word." They're playing a deadly game of charades.

He hugs himself.

She holds her hands like a heart. Is Shadrach trying to say, "I love you?" He gives her a thumbs up on love but thumbs down on the word.

Shadrach rolls both his hands simultaneously, and then he tosses something imaginary in the air. He catches it and turns his hand again and again. "*I want some pizza?*" she thinks. "No, I need." She uses an invisible rolling pin, and he gives her a thumbs up. Then he walks over and shakes the ladder on the inside of the containment tank.

He points at the eyelets on the large bullets. Hell, he could have done that at the start, and Sookie would have known what he needed. Sometimes, men are so stupid.

She gives him a thumbs up and slides back down the ladder outside the Houdini Room. She walks into the Containment area and sees over a dozen men suiting up in radiation gear.

"Shadrach needs a ladder," she says after opening her headgear. "He needs a ladder to reach the eyelets on the atomic bombs."

Fifteen minutes later, helicopters hover over the opening at the top of Pelindaba's Y-Plant. One by one, they lift eight atomic bombs out of the containment tank. The final one has Shadrack attached to it, but he does not remember his lift to safety. His radiation suit fills with sickness and nausea, but he's alive.

Eight helicopters head back across the border into Mozambique. Mac's team and troops remain behind with the Navy SEALS masquerading as Syrians. They prepare for battle northeast of the Y-Plant. Radiation levels creep higher.

The cooling towers no longer expel steam.

"The SAFARI-II reactor will gradually approach a point of no return if the cooling towers don't work," a Navy SEAL who has nuclear training says.

McKlane is on the phone. "This is General George McKlane III. Can you hear me, commander?"

"Yes," the Commander of South Africa's Defence Force says in Bloemfontein.

"We are an armed force of approximately 300 men and women southeast of the Pelindaba Y-Plant, commander. We demand safe passage out of your country."

"You are *northeast* of the Y-Plant, McKlane. We can see you and your troops. Do you know what a 'Red Falcon' is, General McKlane?"

Mac looks at Colin Rafiki, who scribbles on a piece of paper quickly.

"Yes," McKlane says. "The Denel Rooivalk attack helicopter. I believe we disabled one on Bootie van Zale's farm in Wittkoppen, where your Chief of the Air Force is currently located, together with his wing commander."

"We still have a dozen of them on their way to surround you, along with 20 Atlas Oryx helicopters, each carrying 20 of our Special Forces troops. They should reach you within 65 minutes."

"Commander, we are not your problem. Your SAFARI-II reactor will make this part of South Africa a wasteland, just like Chernobyl in Russia. I suggest that you dump the troops and use your Atlas Oryx helicopters to transport cement to seal off the SAFARI-II reactor as quickly as possible."

The commander says nothing.

"America can help you, commander."

The commander says nothing.

An hour passes without any communication as Mac's army moves northeast towards Mozambique.

Mac McKlane sees a line of helicopters approaching in the distance.

He can not tell if they are Atlas Oryx helicopters or the disguised Black Hawks returning to pick up as many of his warriors as possible. Even if they double up in the choppers, many will be left behind if they are the Black Hawks.

"The Syrian Navy SEALs go first," Mac says, receiving a signal that the helicopters are friendly.

Then he adds: "The rest of us move towards Mozambique. Be ready to fight for your lives."

heartbeats

The acting deputy attorney general says "good" and hangs up the phone. He looks at the acting Homeland Security director and his assistant.

"We'll have no more problems with Roberta Macumber," he says. "Now we have to figure out what we do with our rogue general and his army marauding through Sub-Saharan Africa. I want you to go back to your headquarters and get someone there to tell us where he is and what the hell he's doing."

There's a fourth person in the room to whom nobody has paid any attention.

She is the only person there who has received Senate approval for her position.

"I think I might know what the General is up to," she says. "Or at least I know how he got to South Africa."

"What do you know?" the acting deputy attorney general asks the woman.

The ambassador to South Africa says, "What do you know, *ambassador?* That is how you will address me, acting deputy attorney general."

The DAG stares at her a moment too long.

"But before I tell you what I know, *acting* deputy AG, please explain to me why Roberta Macumber, someone I know and respect, is no longer a problem."

Again, the DAG stares at her, but she thinks he looks like a deer in the headlights this time.

Finally, he mumbles, "That would be classified."

"That would be classified, *ambassador,*" she says.

"Yes, of course, that would be classified, madam ambassador, uh, sir."

She sighs and stands up. "You're not very good working with women deputy attorney general, are you?"

Before he can fumble an answer, she walks out of the room. All three men stare at the open door as she disappears towards the elevators.

The assistant to the acting Homeland Security director decides to memorialize this meeting in a recorded and written memo as soon as he gets back to his office. He knows danger when he sees it.

For now, he remains silent.

"I think we should send a senior female lawyer in the AG office to talk to the ambassador," the acting Homeland Security director says.

"You run your department, and I'll run mine," the acting DAG says, scooping up a folder and walking out of the conference room.

The ambassador to South Africa, a naturalized citizen of America, born in South Africa, calls her neighbor in Palm Beach, the President of the United States. The ambassador wants to talk to him about something private and possibly significant.

He immediately agrees to an afternoon meeting in the White House.

heartbeats

After the Black Hawks evacuated the men and women that initially flew to the Y-Plant at Pelindaba East, General Mac McKlane and his remaining forces move as quickly as possible away from the area.

Many men in his unit are experts at hotwiring cars, and all the vehicles left in the Y-Plant parking lot by fleeing workers join a ragtag caravan escaping towards Mozambique.

"What kind of car is this?" Mac asks his Army Ranger driver. "Doesn't look like the Y-Plant scientists suffer from fat paychecks."

A voice in the back, where six men cramp into space for three, says: "It's a Zhiguli VAZ, general."

"Mac. Call me 'Mac.'"

"It's sort of like an Italian Lada 124, without the trimmings. When Italy shut down the Lada plant in Milan, they sold it to the Russians, and they ended up giving it to the South Africans when their version of the carmaker went bankrupt in 2006. They shipped the entire plant down here, for free, with lots of strings attached, Mac."

"There are always strings attached to Russian gifts," someone else says.

"A half a million of these things are still on the road in Russia," the original speaker says. "I have no idea how many still operate down here. They supposedly built the last one in 2001, but this one looks new."

"New?" asks Mac.

"Yes, sir. It's automatic, and it has a radio."

"That makes it new?"

"Yup. I've been in some of these tanks in Russia. They never die, and they always remain uncomfortable, and they all had stick shifts and no radio."

"And bad shock absorbers," Mac says.

The convoy is less than 320 miles from Mozambique. In Bloemfontein, the South Africans see it snaking east towards the border, and they finally send the "Red Falcons" after them.

At the same time, their Denel Oryx troop carriers head towards the Y-Plant to control the SAFARI-II reactor. South Africa's senior nuclear experts are aboard. The mechanized South African forces that initially were going to attack the American troops at Bootie van Zale's farm head towards Pelindaba East with truckloads of transformers.

Mac's caravan of hotwired cars is about forty miles northeast of the Y-Plant when a "RUN FOR COVER" text message squawks on every Motorola cellphone in the group. Men and women spill out of the convoy and sprint as far as possible away from the cars. In the distance, they see a line of a dozen attack helicopters approaching from the southeast, Denel Rooivalk "Red Falcons." Each aircraft has a pilot and a weapons system operator who controls a 700-round cannon and 16 anti-tank guided missiles, and a machine gun.

The helicopters have left air-to-air missiles and aerial rockets at the 16th Squadron air force base in Blooemspruit near Bloemfontein, loading the "Reds Falcons" with air-to-ground weapons useless in air combat. It's a suggestion from Bootie van Zale to the Commander of South Africa's Defense Force.

"We need to maximize our strike on General Mac McKlane's retreating caravan," Bootie says.

The commander agrees. It's a severe mistake, at least Bootie hopes so.

As the Red Falcons approach the caravan stopped on the highway leading into Mozambique, the weapons system operators release their guided missiles, well over 100 of them.

The destruction is total. A few of Mac's men and women hiding a mile away in the bush and rocks, who were veterans of the Persian Gulf War, watch and remember the obliteration of Iraq's Republican Guard by Scout and Apache helicopters during the Battle of 73 Easting.

After their first pass over their smoldering objective, the Red Falcons form up to empty their 700-round cannons into the American troops hiding in the area. The weapons operator of the first Red Falcon helicopter gets ready to pull the trigger.

Suddenly, his Denel Rooivalk turns into a massive fireball. The 11 helicopters following the first one pull up. They release decoy flares to counter the infrared air-to-air missiles fired by eight Black Hawks with Syrian markings approaching them.

One of the Red Falcons almost escapes by climbing and then shutting off its engine.

It fires all its magnesium flares and freewheels back toward the earth for a hard landing.

The pilot tries to restart the helicopter before it crashes, but either he fails, or an air-to-air missile discovers its infrared signature at the moment of impact.

In Bloemfontein, the commander watches his attack helicopters blink out on the screen in front of him. He looks around for Bootie and discovers he is gone. Before he can give the order to find him, the voice of the wing commander of the Denel Oryx troop carriers at the Y-Plant comes over the intercom.

"We're touching down in the Pelindaba parking lot, commander, but we're showing serious radiation levels."

"You have six nuclear engineers aboard your ships. Get them to shut down the Safari II reactor."

"Yes, sir."

The wing commander gathers together all the nuclear engineers. He gives them their orders, and they suit up in radiation gear.

They enter the Y-Plant.

As the mechanized division from Witkoppen arrives, they repair the burnt-out transformers in the electrical grid beyond the Y-Plant. Many of them start to feel nauseous.

The conversation inside Pelindaba East is monitored in Bloemfontein as well as onsite.

"All the systems are down," a nuclear scientist says.

"Entering Safari-I's containment tank," says another.

"What do you see?" the commander in Bloemfontein asks. "Tell me exactly what you see and how many of them."

"Uh, I see one, sir."

"One?"

"Yes, sir. A silver ball, sir. One silver ball."

The South African Defense Force Commander slams his baton on the desk, making the men around him step back. They watch a monitor fall off the counter, and nobody tries to catch it. No one moves.

"You don't see anything else?" the commander says.

"Well, there's the entry control panel into the SAFARI-II plant, sir, and the silver ball, which has a clip on the side that probably opens it."

"Open it."

"It might be a bomb, sir."

"Open it."

The commander in Bloemfontein hears a popping sound but no explosion.

"What was that?"

'Well, sir, it looks like, uh, the silver ball cracked open and spilled out a bunch of oversized jellybeans."

"Jellybeans?"

"Yes, sir. But with the radiation level I see on my Geiger counter, I don't think anyone should eat them."

"Shut down the Safari II reactor."

"Opening the entryway."

After about a minute, the same voice says, "Closing the entryway. SAFARI-II shutdown initiated. There may be some heavy water on the control room floor, sir, which means we might have a partial meltdown. The good news is that there are no open-air fires. However, the cooling towers showed no steam when we landed."

"What does that mean?" the commander in Bloemfontein asks.

Several voices answer at once. "Decommission."

Another nuclear engineer says, "Commander, we must decommission the SAFARI-II reactor before it's too late."

"And how long will that take?" the commander asks.

Nobody answers.

"How long?"

Finally, someone says, "30 to 40 years."

Another nuclear engineer says, "Maybe longer."

"You will not decommission the SAFARI-II reactor," the commander says. "Make it work. I don't care if it kills you. Make it bloody well work."

Nobody says anything.

The men around the scientists receive an order that the nuclear experts do not hear. The South African Special Forces step back and level their weapons at the atomic engineers.

"If I were you, mates," the Special Forces leader says with a heavy Afrikaans accent, "I'd take a chance on fixing the SAFARI-II reactor."

"*As u ons doodmaak, sterf u almal.* (If you kill us, you all die,)" says an Akrikaans scientist.

"We are all born to die," the Special Forces leader says in English. He does not lower his weapon.

"Then, let's work together."

The Special Forces receive another order from the commander in Bloemfontein.

They all lower their assault rifles. Everyone will try to save the SAFARI-II reactor.

The American Ambassador to South Africa is greeted warmly by the President of the United States.

"I hope you're enjoying your vacation," he says, without standing up as she enters the Oval Office.

"I am, Mr. President, but I think we have a problem."

"I don't like problems."

"A naval ship called the *S.S. Nomad,* a freighter actually, has suddenly disappeared off the coast of Cape Town in South Africa."

"Why is that a problem?"

"I believe General George McKlane III used it to disembark a large force of American soldiers into sub-Saharan Africa to fight ISIS forces pushing into that area from the north."

The President stares at her, showing nothing.

"I believe it has something to do with Homeland Security's Countering Weapons of Mass Destruction section. I have an acquaintance I met once named Roberta Macumber high up in the CWMD, the assistant of General McKlane, and she has also recently disappeared. I don't know her that well."

"Why would she do that?"

"I have no idea, but I had a meeting with the Acting Deputy Attorney General and the Acting Head of Homeland Security a few hours ago, and, frankly, I am worried about Roberta Macumber. I have the feeling that something is going on in our South African portfolio that I do not know about or understand."

The President looks at her.

He pulls out a cellphone

He asks, "What can you tell me about Roberta Macumber at Homeland Security?"

The South African Ambassador realizes that he has not pushed any buttons on his cellphone.

She sees in a reflection in the window behind him that the cellphone screen remains dark.

The President puts down the phone.

He looks at her and says, "Macumber is re-assigned, working in another division."

"I see."

"Don't worry your pretty little head about this. Homeland is doing a great job over there. Now, I have an urgent meeting. Thanks for stopping by."

As the ambassador leaves, another door to the Oval Office opens.

"She's dead," the man says.

"Hang on. I can't start killing ambassadors. I can recall them, destroy their careers, shovel dirt on them, but I can't bury them in it."

The man looks at the President and says, "Assistant Director of the CWMD, Roberta Macumber, is dead."

"Oh, well, so I was right when I told the ambassador she was re-assigned."

The man smiles and slips back through the door he entered, saying, "Indeed, she has been."

Six hours later, Roberta Macumber steps off a plane on the island nation of Madagascar. A helicopter takes her thirty-five miles over the Indian Ocean and lands on the deck of the *S.S. Nomad,* where she meets Captain Maria Montoya and four uniformed Navy SEALs. After the helicopter takes off to Madagascar, Captain Montoya shows her a detailed government printout announcing her death in a Vermont cabin on Lake Champlain.

Roberta reads it and says, "Well, this just proves that there is life after death."

Maria Montoya laughs in surprise and knows she is going to like Roberta Macumber.

"Your stateroom is ready. Get some shuteye, and we'll talk later over dinner."

"How's Mac?"

"Still alive."

"How's Colin?"

"Still alive. Get some sleep. Mac's whole team is still together, and every one of them should be aboard the *S.S. Nomad* before nightfall."

Roberta awakens five hours later to the sounds of helicopters and people shouting. She looks out the porthole in her suite. Roberta sees a line of Syrian helicopters spread out, slowly moving over the ship's stern, depositing things that look like giant bullets on the deck. She doesn't know what they're doing because of the sealed porthole. Still, she sees the helicopters flying back towards Africa in the approaching sunset, unburdened by the oversized bullets they dropped off on the *S.S. Nomad.*

Macumber hears a tap on her cabin door. She opens it with her pistol pointed at whoever she meets.

"Don't shoot me, Roberta."

"Mac," she says. "Mac, Mac, Mac."

She's never hugged him in her life, but now she does.

"I thought you were a Syrian soldier from the helicopters attacking the ship."

"No, those are American helicopters violating the rules of war by dressing up with Syrian insignia."

"What are the big bullets hanging below them?"

"The South African atomic bombs that they said they melted down to weapons-grade uranium a few decades ago, only they never did."

"What do we do with them?"

"Not sure, but they're nice bargaining chips for wherever we go from here."

"They tried to kill me, Mac."

"Who's 'they.'"

"I can't be certain, but it sure looks like it was the acting deputy attorney general in cohorts with the acting homeland security director. I have a hard time saying that."

"It goes higher than that, Roberta, at least according to Colin Rafiki."

As Mac McKlane says Colin's name, the CIA agent appears at her cabin door.

Roberta immediately grabs him and throws her arms around him.

He's huge, she realizes.

She blushes. She can't remember the last time she felt blood rush into her cheeks, and she takes a few steps backward and says, "Oh, my goodness."

It is a phrase she had not used since her early teenage years when she first liked boys.

"You saved my life, Colin Rafiki."

It takes a while for Roberta Macumber's voice and pulse to return to normal.

Mac says, "Not all the men and women have returned yet. Within an hour, the team should be aboard. Then we have to figure out what we do next."

Colin says, "We have to figure out how to survive."

Later that night, Roberta Macumber hears a knock on her cabin door. She has just taken a shower and wears a thick, terrycloth bathrobe. She opens the door. It's Colin Rafiki

Roberta feels her heartbeat. "Oh, my goodness," she says again.

"I saved your life," Colin says with a smile, and once again, she blushes. "You owe me nothing, but I would like to know why I saved your life. I think you are a stunning, powerful woman. I want to know you better."

"Oh, my goodness," she says. She has never been shy, and yet she feels that way now.

"Would you like me to leave?"

"No," she says.

He enters her suite and sits in a chair next to the portal. The chair seems very small for him, and he stares at the floor. She thinks he is a very handsome man, but very uncomfortable. She walks over and sits on the bed, feeling uncomfortable herself. Colin talks to the floor without looking at her.

"My wife died eight years ago, and I have been celibate ever since then. She was my soulmate. I never thought I would want to make love to another woman again."

"What was her name?" Roberta asks. Her voice is almost a whisper, and Colin looks at her.

"I called her Zipper," he says. "Zipper Khamisi Rafiki."

"Zipper?" says Roberta. "That's a strange name for someone from Kenya."

"Tanzania," Colin says, "the daughter of Kibwe Khamisi." And then he laughs, a deep laugh that fills the room, showing tears on his cheek.

Roberta is quiet. Then she asks, "Why Zipper?"

Colin laughs again, a bit embarrassed, saying: "In private, she often rubbed her hand against the zipper of my pants." He looks at Roberta and sees her blush deeply.

"I'm sorry," he says.

After some silence, Roberta says: "My husband died ten years ago, and I also have been celibate ever since. He also was my soulmate." She turns her wedding ring around her finger. "So, I guess we both feel a bit like virgins. I don't know where to go from here. I'm not afraid. I don't know our next move from this moment."

"Virtual strip poker?" Colin says.

"How do we play that?"

"We each take off an article of clothing, no losing hands. I'll start.'"

"He lifts off his shirt, and all Roberta sees is muscle."

"Oh, my goodness," she says, standing up from the bed and removing her terrycloth robe. She is naked.

"My God, you are a beautiful woman."

"Thank you. Colin. Your zipper seems to be having a problem. I say that with respect for your soulmate."

He drops his pants and underwear.

"Oh, my goodness," she says as he lifts her, seemingly with no effort, and slowly slides inside her.

"Tell me if I go too deep."

She wraps her legs around him and pulls their bodies tight together.

They fall on the bed, moving slowly, then faster, and climaxing together, trying not to release the shout they both feel deep in their stomachs, an exclamation of love that neither of them has felt for years.

Then they talk like old friends, about their jobs and their lives and their beliefs.

She talks about her dead husband.

He talks about his dead wife

They shed mutual tears over their passings, an extraordinary and genuine bond of sadness.

It seems as if they have always known one another. Neither has talked this way to another person since their spouses died, peeling back the layers of their personalities until only the truth remains.

When she wakes up, Colin Rafiki is still there, smiling at her. "I never thought I would fall in love again," he says.

"I forgot to brush my teeth before I fell asleep," she says, feeling foolish, running her tongue over her teeth. "Do you mean what you just said?"

Colin smiles at her and says, "I guess we'll have to start brushing our teeth together. I forgot to brush mine as well."

He pulls her closer to him, and once again, she says, "Oh, my goodness," but without blushing or shyness.

He smiles and says, "I think we're going to be together for a long time, Roberta Macumber."

"I hope so," she says, then, "I love you, too."

After the death of her first husband, she also never thought she would fall in love again. She feels Colin deep inside of her, in every way.

In Washington, at Homeland Security's headquarters, the acting director is standing in front of a large portrait of Roberta Macumber with a black ribbon slashed across one corner. Birth and death dates appear on its pedestal.

"You all knew this extraordinary member of our team far better than I did, and we are working hard to determine the circumstances of her death," the acting director says.

The memorial room is crowded, with many people forced to stand.

More rumors exist than facts. Someone in the back, lowering their head, shouts: "How did she die?"

"Who asked that question?" the acting director asks.

Nobody responds.

"It was a woman's voice," the under director of Homeland Security says. "Please, identify yourself."

From another area of the room, another person shouts: "How did she die?"

The under director sends some of his people into the crowd to identify the questioners. As they do so, a chant starts, growing in volume.

"How did she die?"

"How did she die?"

"How did she die?"

The acting director holds up his hand, and the chant starts to fade.

Silence creeps into the room.

"Roberta was found in a cabin in Vermont on Lake Champlain. It was not a Homeland safe house. We are trying to determine who owned the land. Roberta died in a car explosion, which also destroyed most of the cabin. It also killed several national security people who were protecting her. If anyone knows anything that can help the FBI or National Security, please contact the under director or me. It is a tragic event, and it is a classified matter. I expect each of you to treat it as such. Roberta Macumber had no children and no living family, but she had many friends."

He places a white lily on the golden frame base that holds her picture.

He briefly wonders whether or not the photo of her was photoshopped.

She is a beautiful woman.

He looks at the crowded room and says, "Our friends judge us in death, and this meeting shows how exceptional Roberta Macumber was. I wish I had known her better."

"Meeting adjourned," the under director says, drawing a sharp look from many of those present, including the acting director. Someone says, "What an asshole."

The acting director, under director, and half a dozen of their hand-picked associates leave the room.

"That was a stupid thing to say," the acting director says to the under director.

"They need to know who's running this ship."

"It most certainly is not you," the acting director says.

The acting deputy attorney general of the DOJ waits in the office of the acting director of Homeland Security. The acting director asks the under-director to leave them alone.

"And close the door."

The acting DAG waits, then he says, "Roberta Macumber is still alive."

"We recovered her body," the acting director says.

"We recovered an unidentifiable body. We assumed that it was Roberta Macumber, although the absence of any teeth and the lack of a pelvic area sent clear warning signals. We recovered other bodies as well. But I'm convinced she's still alive."

"What makes you think that?"

"Someone broke into her townhome two nights ago, after she left the office, and they were extremely selective in what they stole."

He explains that the robbers made no mess during the event. They emptied no drawers on the floor, threw nothing around, and her computer was missing.

"So it looks like a setup. Macumber, or someone using her ID, flew out of Jean Lesage International Airport in Quebec on a flight to Paris yesterday morning. From there, the person, or as I suspect, Roberta Macumber herself, flew to Antanànarivo, the capital of Madagascar, an island off the east coast of Africa. We have people investigating, and they should be in Madagascar within eight hours."

"Jesus."

"I don't think he's going to help us," the acting deputy attorney general says. "We've traced the ownership of the cabin in Vermont, but someone has thoroughly scrubbed all of the title work. The supposed buyer four years ago seems to have been a young sergeant in the American Civil War over 150 years ago, and the previous owner is the state motto, 'Freedom and Unity.' Nobody has ever paid real estate taxes. It's a property ghost."

"What does that mean?"

"The cabin probably belonged to the Central Intelligence Agency. I remember the last time I saw Macumber in these offices. She was escorted to the elevators by at least one CIA agent, possibly two. You thought they were bodyguards."

"Why would the CIA protect her?"

"We're trying to figure that out, but the CIA doesn't cooperate with the DOJ, Homeland, or even the White House. They operate under a different set of rules, based mostly on the plausible deniability of covert operations."

"What the hell does that mean?".

"They're professional liars."

He stares at the acting director, counting to eight in his head to emphasize his following words.

"And they kill people."

Chapter 17

Ultimately, well-experienced experts fix the problems at the Y-Plant in Pelindaba. They all come from the special forces regiments based at Langebaan in South Africa's western cape. They have two things in common.

They have seen and studied nuclear meltdowns.

They are all Russians who witnessed the aftermath of Chernobyl in their nation.

They operate under the command of a black lieutenant general who answers directly to the Commander of South Africa's defense force. The commander is a communist.

Within 72 hours of going dark, the water towers at Pelindaba East begin to show steam. It takes another 24 hours to replace transformers and stabilize the electronic grid.

After four nights of sporadic lights viewed from satellites focussed on South Africa, the black hole in that continent dissolves into a maze of lights strung throughout the republic and its adjoining nations.

heartbeats

None of the eight helicopters with Syrian insignia are lost as they return to the *S.S. Nomad*. One by one, they drop off the Atomic Bombs and the survivors of General Mac McKlane's team. They originally numbered 145 men and women. Over 10 percent of them have died. They lower the dead to the deck and then wrap them in white for burial at sea. They leave no men or women behind.

Seven of the Black Hawks return to Mozambique. One Black Hawk remains aboard the *S.S. Nomad.*, tethered to its stern deck. There are over a dozen qualified Black Hawk pilots in General Mac McKlane's group. The original pilots go with the seven UH-1s returning to Africa.

The Navy SEALs, who wore Syrian uniforms, pile into the seven helicopters in Mozambique. They all return to the *USS George H.W. Bush*, still floating in the Indian Ocean. Their commander carries a letter from General Mac McKlane addressed to the Acting Director of Homeland Security.

Aboard the *S.S. Nomad,* Commander Maria Montoya presides over a group that includes three troop commanders representing the Army Rangers, Navy SEALs, and Marine Raiders. Mac McKlane's team consists of Roberta Macumber, Colin Rafiki, HollyMcKlane, Ernestine and Charlton Tremwallis, Sookie Ringer, Sharonda, and Samuel Nelson.

Shadrach is in sickbay, with severe radiation poisoning, and he may not survive.

"I have Shadrach's proxy vote, if there is any voting," Sookie says.

"There will be," Mac says.

"About what?" Sharonda asks.

"Let's just talk for a while," Mac says.

"I think I have to put something on the table first," Commander Montoya says. "I have been ordered to return to base immediately."

"Where's 'base?'" Holly asks

"Brooklyn, New York, after checking in first at Cape Town, South Africa, where Navy SEALs currently stationed on the *USS George H.W. Bush* will swarm up the gangplank. 'Swarm' is the bullying and threatening word used in my orders from the head of the Joint Chiefs of Staff. I have already answered this order with a statement of my own."

"What did you reply?" Roberta Macumber asks. General McKlane looks at the commander, waiting.

"I told the Secretary of the Navy that if we entered South African territorial waters, that country could and probably would demand that we return their eight atomic bombs that are currently in our hold. I would have to comply with such a demand unless we were in a state of war with South Africa or if some treaty between our sovereign nations allowed me to refuse to return the atomic bombs."

"And his reply was?" Mac asks.

"That would be classified," Montoya says.

"I think that frames our discussion well," Mac says, "regardless of what the response might have been."

"Explain the framework to me," Samuel says."

Mac says, "Tell us what happened to you, Roberta Macumber. I understand that they first escorted you out of Homeland Security, and then they asked you to return later, at which point they said they would arrest you. Have I got that right?"

She tells the story, ending with, "They tried to kill me, and Colin saved me."

"What the hell is going on?" Holly asks.

"Homeland Security is being hollowed out and turned into a political weapon at its highest levels," Mac says.

"By whom?"

"By the executive branch, perhaps directly or through suggestions from the Commander in Chief, the President of the United States of America."

"That's crazy," Sookie says. "I voted for him."

"Many of us did," Mac says.

"Who's running Homeland Security?"

Colin says, "The Senate has confirmed neither the Acting Director of Homeland Security nor the Deputy Secretary. None of you know them. They both appear to be political appointees with little or no knowledge of what Homeland does. However, they are fiercely loyal to the Commander in Chief. If they step out of line, they're gone."

"What the hell is going on?" Holly asks again.

"It sounds like the inmates have taken over the asylum," Samuel says. "And our lives are at stake."

Colin says, "They are hollowing out every cabinet-level department as they appoint political loyalists to head them. They are letting the hardcore workers with experience leave through attrition. The White House is even preparing a political hit list of bureaucrats they do not think they can trust. It's similar to the McCarthy era. America is a flawed democracy run by someone who would rather be a king."

"He might make a good one," Charlton says.

"Democracies don't have kings," Ernestine says.

"How do you explain the United Kingdom or the Kingdom of Sweden?" Charlton says to his wife.

"None of that matters," Commander Montoya says. "The chain of command takes precedence, whether we like or dislike the people in their positions."

"Unless they try to kill you," Roberta Macumber says. "That puts a bullet hole in the rules, doesn't it?"

Nobody says anything for a while, then Mac says, "I'm going to tell you a story."

"Oh, goodie," Holly says, crossing her arms and staring hard at Charlton Tremwallis.

"A few years ago, well, two thousand years ago, Emperor Claudius supposedly took one of the legions of Rome, the Ninth, and he sent them to Africa. They were one of four legions that, much earlier, propelled Emperor Julius Caesar to power when he conquered Brittania."

"How big was a legion?" Sharonda asks.

"Ten cohorts, about 3,600 heavy infantry supported by enough cavalry and light infantry to bring the strength of the legions up to around 6,000 men," a commander in the Navy SEALs says. Mac nods.

"Why did Claudius send them to Africa?" Samuel asks.

"Nobody knows, and a lot of top-notch archeologists say it never happened, although Roman ruins in Rhodesia, now called Zimbabwe, suggest that they were there," Mac tells his patriots.

"What happened to them?" Holly asks.

"The Ninth Roman Legion disappeared, vanished, supposedly within two generations. Nobody knows why, and no one knows how. And that's the end of my story."

Everybody stares at Mac and then at each other to see if someone understands the purpose of his story.

"You're suggesting that we are the Ninth Roman Legion?" a colonel in the Marine Raiders finally says.

"I'm suggesting that it might be the worst-case scenario that we face," Mac says.

"Uh, by my count, there are not 6,000 warriors in this gathering, Mac," Samuel says.

"And no cavalry, either," Holly says.

Everyone is quiet, most looking at Mac, until Sharonda finally says, "We disappear within two generations?"

"Not necessarily," Mac says. "We have some powerful negotiating chips, including eight atomic bombs and some highly-qualified personnel."

"You've got to be kidding," a commander in the Marine Raiders says. "Sir."

"He's not kidding," Commander Maria Montoya says. "My ship, my rules."

She looks at the military leaders in her suite. "I'm going to say something to you that I am not allowed to say to you. I do this because everyone in this room and anyone aboard this ship is a true American Patriot. You have spilled blood, proving it. You deserve to hear the truth."

Colin Rafiki looks at Montoya and shakes his head.

"Don't do it, commander," he says.

On the northeast grounds of the U.S. Naval Observatory in Washington D.C., the vice president sits with five of the six members of the Joint Chiefs of Staff: the Chairman, the Vice-Chairman, the Chief of Staff of the Army, the Chief of Naval

Operations, the Chief of Staff of the Air Force, and the Commandant of the Marine Corps.

The Chief of the National Guard Bureau is the only military leader not present.

"I want, first, to thank all of you for coming here on the weekend," the vice-president says. They are in his home, not his White House office.

None of the military leaders acknowledge this common pleasantry. They have orders to appear at Number One Observatory Circle, where the vice-president lives in a house built in 1893, initially for the superintendent of the U.S. Naval Observatory. Three of them had to cancel their weekend golf matches to attend the meeting.

"Gentlemen," the vice president says, " I speak for your Commander in Chief."

"Is there some reason he could not be here?" the Commandant of the Marine Corps asks.

"I do not control the President's agenda," the VP says.

All the generals and the admiral know that the president is probably playing golf in Florida.

He's been at Mar-a-Lago for three days, taking another long weekend.

The VP says: "We have a rogue army of American soldiers wandering around Africa. A recently promoted one-star general leads them. This renegade's name is George McKlane III, and it appears he has between 100 and 200 men with him. His force consists of renegade Army Rangers, Navy SEALs, and Marine Raiders. We have reason to believe that this group is responsible for turning the lights out in the Republic of South Africa and a near nuclear meltdown."

The Commandant of the Marine Corps says, "Mr. Vice President, I know Brigadier General George McKlane, and his father, Major General George McKlane, and his grandfather, Captain George McKlane, whose funeral I attended off the coast of Florida. Captain McKlane won the Medal of Honor in Korea."

"Well, that's certainly a lot of Georges," the Vice President says, "and we all know that Congress makes a lot of mistakes, don't we?"

"I don't understand what mistakes you're referring to," the Chief of Naval Operations says.

The vice president says, "Sometimes they award the Congressional Medal of Honor to the wrong people."

The Joints Chief of Staff Chairman turns red in the face and says, "There is no such thing as a Congressional Medal of Honor, Mr. Vice President."

They all know that Pence never served.

The Joint Chief continues: "Your father won the Bronze Star in Korea, awarded in 1953. I've seen it promoted on your office wall in the White House, sir, along with its commendation letter, almost as if you had won it yourself. I am certain your father would tell you that Captain George McKlane's award is known simply as the Medal of Honor. Congress has nothing to do with it. And Captain George McKlane deserved it because of extraordinary bravery in Korea, an act of courage that saved many of our men."

All the military men agree with this.

The Chief of Staff of the Army says, "What intelligence do you have that says General Mac McKlane, whom I also know personally, has become a renegade?"

The vice president stands up. "This meeting is over. The president is clearly correct when he says he knows more than all the generals."

Nobody moves.

The vice president storms out of the room in his home and talks to Marlon Bundo, his pet rabbit. It has an accessible Instagram account. Both of his cats died within six months of one another, so he can't stroke them for comfort.

"We'll call the president," he tells the rabbit.

America's top military advisors slowly shake their heads and leave the white 19th Century house at Number One Observatory Circle.

They each know that they will soon have a call from the President of the United States and that what just happened might shorten their careers into early retirement.

The Commandant of the Marine Corps and the Chief of Naval Operations get together and send an encrypted coded message to Commander Maria Montoya aboard the *S.S. Nomad* near Madagascar

heartbeats

The President of the United States calls in the American Ambassador of South Africa.

He thanks her for her previous meeting with him and talks to her about the *S.S. Nomad.*

"Your analysis was correct," he tells her.

"Thank you, sir."

She has no idea what analysis she has given him in their previous meeting. It had been brief, and the president dismissed her as if she were a schoolgirl after mentioning a freighter that had disappeared from Cape Town.

"I do not trust our military leaders nor our intelligence sources. However, I do trust you."

The ambassador has a hard time not feeling flattered by this statement.

"You have many contacts in South Africa," the president says. "And you speak Afrikaans."

"Yes, sir," she says.

The president pulls a large satellite map out of a cardboard tube and puts it on the table, which he has to pin down with paperweights on all four corners so it won't roll up again. He points to a small ship off the coast of Madagascar.

"This is the *S.S. Nomad*," he says. "I want you to send this immediately to the General of the South African Defense Force. He is an Afrikaaner. I want you to call him first and tell him that you are sending this intelligence to him. Speak to him as a friend in his language."

"I always have," she says, although she detests the man. He is a communist, trained in Russia, and he has no love of America.

"Am I to give him instructions or suggestions, sir? What should he do with this intelligence?"

"Tell him to put the *S.S. Nomad* on the bottom of the Indian Ocean."

The commander of the *S.S. Nomad* says: "I received an encrypted message from the Commandant of the Marine

Corps and the Chief of Naval Operations last night, and that information is classified."

She looks at Colin Rafiki and smiles. "It will remain classified. Both men expect to be reassigned or retired by the White House. Also, this has nothing to do with Chimala or Tanzania. The Joint Chiefs of Staff refuse to accept the false belief supported by the administration that General George McKlane III and his military men and women are a rogue army murdering innocent people in Africa."

Everyone in the room starts talking at once, except for Montoya, Rafiki, and McKlane. The commander of the *S.S. Nomad* waits for everyone to calm down. They finally acknowledge her hand held up, palm out, asking for silence.

The commander says, "I will, however, share with you a message my radio operator just received from the commander of the *USS George H.W. Bush*. They did not encrypt the message, and the commander of the aircraft carrier did not classify it. I believe that was a personal decision of the commander of that aircraft carrier, a friendly warning."

Colin Rafiki knows nothing about this, and he shows it by leaning forward in his seat.

"The *USS George H.W. Bush* is currently moving towards our location and will arrive in approximately four and a half hours. The flattop's commander says he can go slower if we need more time."

"More time for what?" Holly asks.

"To escape," Commander Maria Montoya says.

Pandemonium again runs into the freighter captain's raised hand. Silence slowly returns.

"Discipline, people," General McKlane orders.

"They intend to arrest and court-martial all of us," the commander of the *S.S. Nomad* says, "myself included."

An uproar does not follow Captain Maria Montoya's statement.

People are stunned, silent, and angry.

The commander of the Navy SEALs says: "I'm willing to stand trial for killing terrorists."

A lot of "Me as well"s lift the room's volume back up to the silencing hand of the commander.

Armed men and women are irritated by an unexpected enemy they have spent their careers protecting, the United States of America's politicians.

Colin Rafiki stands up.

"Your unity will ultimately defeat the sheer stupidity of all of this," he says.

Mac adds: "However, your careers will carry the asterisk of a court-martial, even after you are proven innocent. You need to realize that."

Colin looks at a number of the top leaders in the group. "Every one of your careers will suffer damage, perhaps beyond repair. Being right, patriotic, or truthful means nothing. This political process will destroy all of you."

"The Ninth Roman Legion," Sharonda says.

"In two generations, nobody will even remember us," her husband, Samuel, says.

"Here's what I would like to do," General McKlane says. "It may or may not work, but it's better than marching to the slaughterhouse."

heartbeats

The *USS George H.W. Bush* develops turbine problems in the Indian Ocean as it turns towards Madagascar.

The Nimitz class nuclear-powered aircraft carrier commander goes on record in a phone call from the bridge to the Chief of Naval Operations in Washington. He asks for the contents to have an official government record.

"This would have never occurred if we had not left Norfolk before completing our drydock repairs."

"Understood and so noted," the Chief of Naval Operations says.

The USS George H.W. Bush commander says that he will immediately send several Black Hawk helicopters on his flight deck, still emblazoned with Syrian insignia, towards the *S.S. Nomad* to keep an eye on the renegades aboard that ship.

"Understood and so noted," the Chief of Naval Operations says.

Nobody mentions the Syrian markings emblazoned on the Black Hawks.

As each helicopter lands on the freighter's stern, a team of Marine Raiders removes the pilots at gunpoint. Pilots under Mac's control replace them and take off.

Two Black Hawks tether three atomic bombs beneath them. They are lighter than expected.

The helicopters carry no passengers other than the pilot, co-pilot, and a machine gunner in the open hatch.

They fly to Mozambique, where they refuel at the abandoned airbase.

Then they forklift six of the eight atomic bombs sideways into the passenger compartments of the two Black Hawks and head east over the Indian Ocean, flying low.

Radar does not see them. They open the passenger doors and tip the helicopters slightly as they drop towards the water; the machine gunners and co-pilots roll the atomic bombs out the hatch one at a time.

They drop less than fifty feet to six-foot waves below, splashing into the ocean at points where the water is over 24,000 feet deep.

Then the helicopters return to the *S.S. Nomad,* under radio silence and invisible to radar.

The Black Hawks used, and the others have enough fuel for the original pilots to make it back to the *USS George H.W. Bush* aircraft carrier.

"What did you see?" the flattop's commander asks the returning pilots.

"They took the atomic bombs out of the hold and flew them to Mozambique," the pilots report. "They held us at gunpoint, mostly Marine Raiders, sir."

"Did you see anything else?"

"Yes, sir. Many American soldiers were in the hold, cuffed, including Commander Maria Montoya, who repeatedly shouted to us for help. Some of them were in a hospital structure that looked like it was part of a city. Others were under watch in an oversized boxing ring. It was all bizarre, sir. They even let us videotape it, sir."

"Anything else?"

"There was a Marine General who led the renegades, sir, a General McKlane There weren't that many people on his side, I'd guess less than two dozen. You wouldn't think they could get the drop on a few hundred of our best warriors, would you, sir?"

"That would depend on who was in charge of the armory," says the commander of the Nimitz class nuclear-powered aircraft carrier. "We're going to fix that as soon as we get underway."

They videotape the debriefing of the pilots and co-pilots briefly held under guard on the *S.S. Nomad.* The USS George H.W. Bush commander smiles when he hears one of the helicopter co-pilots mention control of the armory as the reason for the General's treasonous success.

An encrypted copy of the debriefing goes to the Marine Corps Commandant at the request of the Chief of Naval Operations, with a note that ends with the initials ATP. The commander says that it means "As Transmitted Promptly." It stands for "According To Plan."

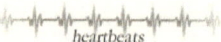
heartbeats

Once the USS George H.W. Bush aircraft carrier pilots take off in their UH-1 Black Hawks, Captain Maria Montoya is released and taken topside for a meeting in her captain's suite with General McKlane.

"Let's assume they buy it," Mac says. "You heard the discussion we all had before we handcuffed everyone. I'm not sure everyone's imprisonment can guarantee their freedom. Some of them may still face court-martials."

"There were a lot of warriors that disagreed with what you're doing," Commander Montoya says.

"I know. I have the feeling that some of the SEALs would put a bullet in my head if they could."

"I don't think that's a bad thing."

Mac's eyes widen.

Montoya laughs.

"Don't get me wrong, Mac. I mean, it's good that they consider your move unpatriotic and anti-American. It will underscore the genuine nature of your decision."

"Do you think I'm making a mistake?"

"No."

She says this quickly, turning it into the truth.

"And the two bombs we have left?"

"They are part of your decision, and you will probably need them as bargaining chips. If they remain on my ship, it could lead to an explosive situation, pun intended. I don't want them on the *S.S. Nomad*. That would be a serious mistake, and they would demand to know the location of the other six atomic bombs."

"They are not in Mozambique, Maria. That much I can tell you. I swear it's the truth."

Holly walks into their meeting and looks at her husband and the captain of the *S.S. Nomad*.

Well," she says, "I can tell from the looks of you two that the honeymoon is now officially over."

Mac laughs.

"That's why I married her," he tells Commander Maria Montoya. His wife adds, "And the sex." They all smile without laughing.

"I hope we can meet again someday."

"You must testify against me," Mac says.

"I know," Maria Montoya says. "And I will because it will protect you, Mac, not me."

Mac looks at her, and he sees her eyes water slightly.

Mac stands up and hugs Maria Montoya. "You will make a wonderful admiral," he says.

"The helicopter's waiting, Mac," Holly says. She also hugs the captain of the *S.S. Nomad*.

As they leave the captain's suite, Mac says, "Don't release any of the men and women in the hold until we're well clear of the area. I have the feeling that some of the Navy SEALs would like to shoot down our helicopter. I admire their patriotism, even though our politicians abuse it."

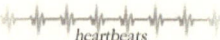
heartbeats

It is nighttime before the aircraft carrier starts to move towards the *S.S.Nomad.*

Early in the final watch, just after 23:00, the commander's attention focuses on a series of radar blips coming out of South Africa, heading to where the *S.S. Nomad* remains anchored.

"What the hell is that," he asks nobody because he already knows what they represent.

South Africa is about to attack the *S.S.Nomad.*

"Launch stations. I want a dozen fully-armed Hornets flying under Wing Commander Robertson in the air in ten minutes."

Alarms go off throughout the ship. Crews swarm onto the flight deck as well as pilots.

The commander contacts the *S.S. Nomad.*

"You've got a dozen bogies coming at you from South Africa, Commander Montoya. Moving at helicopter speed, and that tells me that they are, uh, let's see – " he studies the South African armaments section of his military encyclopedia.

"My guess is that they are attack helicopters, not troop carriers, so I'm guessing Denle Rooivalk 'Red Falcons.' They carry air-to-ground or air-to-air missiles and a four-hundred round canon, plus a swivel machine gun under the co-pilot's cockpit," Captain Montoya.

The commander's chief engineer says, "They're nasty, and they will reach you in about twenty minutes."

"Thanks for the warning," Maria says.

"Go dark, commander, and lower every single one of your lifeboats immediately."

Over the intercom, the flattop's commander says to his wing commander, "Blow every one of those South African bastards out of the sky."

The first mate gives the wing commander the exact coordinates. It takes time to launch all the Hornets.

As the final one clears the deck, everyone on the bridge sees explosions on the nighttime horizon.

It is the battle of the *S.S. Nomad.*

All the commander can say is, "Jesus Christ."

Maria Montoya is on the deck of the *S.S. Nomad,* which only has four lifeboats.

It's a freighter, not a passenger ship.

She hears the helicopters before she sees them, and they come in low, perhaps thinking most people sleep on the darkened ship.

As the "Red Falcons" fly across the stern and the bow, dozens of assault weapons greet them, first on the port side and then echoed on the starboard side. Four South African helicopters plunge into the Indian Ocean, but there are too many of them.

The "Red Falcons" regroup out of range. They launch their air-to-ground missiles, all of them. The *S.S. Nomad* lights up the sky as the South Africans creep forward, cautious cats playing with dying mice.

The entire ship is on fire and sinking.

The "Red Falcons" unload their 400-round cannons into the *S.S. Nomad*.

They can see people aboard who remain alive.

Suddenly assault weapons fire leaps up the helicopters from four lifeboats they did not see.

And then the skies are filled with Marine Hornets that quickly send the remaining "Red Falcons" into the ocean.

Within thirty minutes, all of the blips that originated out of the Makhado airbase disappear.

None of the "Red Falcons" survive.

South Africa has turned into a nation with virtually no functioning air force.

After two hours, the *USS George H.W. Bush* finds the survivors of the *S.S Nomad*. Commander Maria Montoya was blown off the bridge in the attack, and she survives with some broken bones.

So too does Sookie Ringer, probably the best swimmer on the ship. Shadrach apparently does not make it, which is better than radiation poisoning. Sookie tells people that he is still alive, "I know it. I feel it." She gathers sympathy but not belief. Almost four dozen Navy Seals make it, along with a few dozen Marine Raiders and half a dozen Army Rangers.

They also receive orders from the Secretary of the Navy to anchor in place because of COVID-19, a novel coronavirus for which no vaccine exists.

It gives them plenty of time to play taps as they bury over 200 people at sea.

Several sailors aboard the *USS George H.W. Bush* are already in sickbay with hacking, dry coughs, and respiratory problems that require ventilators. One of them dies from Covid-19 within 48 hours. The disease spreads quickly throughout the ship, although most of the sailors will live.

At the unused airfield in Mozambique, Colin Rafiki sits on one of two secured atomic bombs in the Black Hawk that they flew off the stern of the *S.S. Nomad* three and a half hours before the expected arrival of the *USS George H.W. Bush*. General Mac McKlane sits on the other nuclear device.

The passengers in the cargo compartment include Holly McKlane, Roberta Macumber, the Nelsons, the Tremwallises, and Bootie van Zale, who showed up at the deserted base in Mozambique in a Denle Rooivalk "Red Falcon" helicopter.

"I flew it alone out of Bloemfontein," Bootie says. "I refueled at Makhado, and now we need to blow it up."

There are other warriors with them. The pilot and co-pilot of the Black Hawk they took from the *S.S. Nomad* are both Marine Raiders.

In the passenger cabin, sixteen other men and women, Marines and some Army Rangers, share space with the two atomic bombs and the Homeland Security team.

They are mostly asleep.

Not a single Navy SEAL has joined the renegades.

The pilot of the Black Hawk is a lieutenant commander in the Marine Raiders, and his female co-pilot is a warrant officer who is also a demolition expert.

She looks at Bootie and says, "We have over 200 pounds of C-4 plastique in the Black Hawk's arsenal."

She rigs up the Red Falcon in fifteen minutes.

The explosion registers on South African radar.

"Maybe they'll think your dead, Bootie," Mac McKlane tells him as their small army escapes in the Black Hawk unnoticed.

They skim over the landscape heading into Zimbabwe and then Botswana.

None of them realize what has happened to the *S.S.Nomad* off the coast of Madagascar.

They will learn all of this later.

"I'm sorry that Sookie and Shadrach Ringer could not join us," Mac McKlane says.

"I'm not sure Shadrach will survive his radiation poisoning," Sharonda Nelson says. "As a nurse practitioner, I think it's important to get him into the sickbay on the aircraft carrier. And I know Sookie will not leave his side."

Colin makes an encrypted call to his old friend in Botswana, General Gaolato Magoko, who comes on the line almost immediately.

"How's your vacation going, Colin?"

"Wonderful, and I've got some gifts for you."

The Chief of Botswana's Defense Staff, Lieutenant-General Gaolato Magoko, is silent. Then he asks, "Will they cost me my life?"

Colin laughs.

"Do you remember when you told me you never wanted to become the leader of Botswana?" Colin asks.

"Yes, I do, and it's the truth, Colin. I told you the president is married to my second cousin, which is sufficient punishment for his miserable life. I have no intention of overthrowing him."

"Then perhaps you would like to give him the gifts I have brought for you, Gaoloto."

Colin is one of the few people who can use the Botswana general's first name.

"Tell me about these gifts, Colin."

"I am bringing you two atomic bombs. The great nation of Botswana is about to become the only nuclear power in Africa."

General Magoko says nothing.

"Do you have a problem with this, sir?" Colin asks.

"You are painting a target on the back of my nation, Colin Rafiki."

"Your nation has always been a great ally of America," Colin says. "Botswana is perhaps our only faithful ally in Africa. You are a graduate of West Point, as are many in your officer corps. We need you on our side, Gaoloto."

"Where did these atomic bombs come from?"

"South Africa," Colin answers.

"They will probably want them back."

"America will not let that happen, and we, as well as ISIS, have destroyed much of their military power. If America is not at war with The Republic of South Africa, it will be quite soon. You might want to choose sides before that happens, Gaoloto. Please understand that this is not a threat. I speak as your friend." The phone goes silent again.

Mac holds out his hand, and Colin gives the Motorola device to him.

"General Magoko, this is General Mac McKlane. I am a director of Homeland Security as well as a Marine Raider."

"I have met your father at the Pentagon," General Magoko says, "as well as at West Point."

"I did not know that."

"And now you do." The line goes silent, and then General Magoko asks General McKlane, "Will America erase the target on my nation's back?"

"We will protect your interests, general."

"That is not an answer."

"We will protect your interests with our own lives, General Magoko. I include my own in that solemn oath."

In the silence that follows, Mac hands the phone back to Colin. General Magoko tells them to land at the Gaborone Sir Seretse Khama International Airport.

It is a quiet ride towards the future, despite the noise of the helicopter blades. None of them know that the United States has destroyed South Africa's air force.

But all of them know that The Ninth Roman Legion has been born again.

Temple Emmet Williams: His first book, published at the age of 70, was an award-winning memoir called **Warrior Patient:** *How to Beat Deadly Diseases With Laughter, Good Doctors, Love, and Guts.* It received a **B.R.A.G. Medallion** from the Book Reader's Appreciation Group and a **2015 Gold Medal at the Reader's Favorite Book Award**s in Miami, Florida. It won an **International Red Ribbon** in The Wishing Shelf. It has been a best-seller on Amazon.

Temple grew up in Ohio. He went to Hotchkiss and Yale University. In 1964, he was nominated two times for the Pulitzer Prize as a reporter for the *World-Telegram & Sun* in New York City for a seven-day, front-page series called "I Was A Subway Cop." He worked as an Editor at *The Reader's Digest* and was the managing editor of an anti-apartheid international news magazine in Africa, *News/Check.*

He was a copywriter and creative director at leading advertising agencies worldwide, including Leo Burnett and Ogilvy Mather.

He lived in Africa for six years and in Europe for almost as long. He and his wife, Kerstin, who is also his content editor, currently live in Boca Raton, Florida.

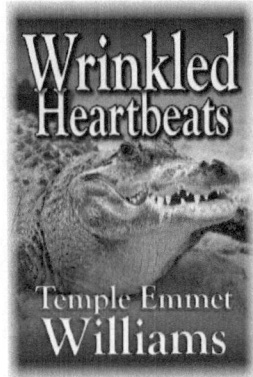

Wrinkled Heartbeats is the author's first "Heartbeats" novel, which the 2016 **Next Generation Indie Book Awards** chose as one of six finalists in the category of **"Best First Novels under 80,000 words."** It won the coveted Awesome Indies Approval Badge. It also won a **Silver Medal** in the crowded **Action Fiction category** at the **Reader's Favorite Book Awards** in Miami, Florida.

Poison Heartbeats is the second novel in the "Heartbeats" series, and it won the **top prize in the Action Fiction category at the Next Generation Indie Book Awards** in 2017 at the Harvard Club in NYC. It earned the coveted Awesome Indies Approval Badge and a BRAG (Book Readers Appreciation Group) medallion. The **Midwest Book Review** called it "a deftly crafted and extraordinary novel, very highly recommended." In Miami, Florida, it also won a Bronze Medal in the Action Fiction category at the Reader's Favorite Book Awards.

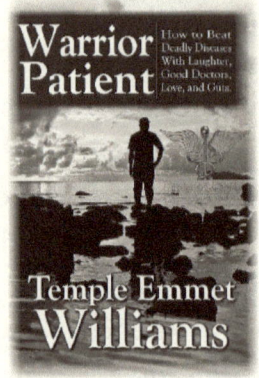

Warrior Patient is a best-selling, true story that will change how you approach the miracles of modern medicine. Read the stunning and surprisingly funny *autobiography of Temple Emmet Williams*, who recovers entirely from a relentless series of medical problems, many resulting from the system designed to prevent them. Enjoy the *wryly amusing story* of someone who recovers from cancer, kidney failure, dialysis, deadly infections, partial blindness, shingles, large open wounds, a hernia, and a little bit of amputation. It's a funny story.

The journey takes almost three years to accomplish, but today the patient survives and continues to laugh. Almost miraculously, he recaptures "normal," even in the Age of the Covid-19 Varients.

Learn how to beat deadly diseases with laughter, good doctors, love, and guts. **Warrior Patient** has *won many awards*, but none so meaningful as the letters from readers who say: "I think this book may have saved my life."

www.ingramcontent.com/pod-product-compliance
Lightning Source LLC
Chambersburg PA
CBHW051537250626
47157CB00001B/85